COLD WHITE FURY

SILENT SCREAM

When the light revealed Tanner's face, Jennifer's relief was quickly forgotten. As she took in the blank hollows of her son's eyes and the slack lie of his features, panic rose again, bubbling up in her throat like a caustic liquid. The dog stood beside the chair, whining and nudging Tanner's hand with her nose, her rising pitch matching the growing sense of urgency Jennifer felt herself. Jennifer squatted, grabbed the boy's arms, and shook him gently.

"Tanner?"

No response. Jennifer shook him a little harder; her voice rose in pitch.

"Tanner? Tanner, please! Snap out of it!"

Tanner mumbled something that Jennifer couldn't quite make out.

"What?" she asked hopefully. "What is it, honey?"

Tanner's next words came out frighteningly clear.

"Stop the killing."

Cold White Fury

Beth Amos

HarperPaperbacks
A Division of HarperCollins*Publishers*

HarperPaperbacks
A Division of HarperCollins*Publishers*
10 East 53rd Street, New York, N.Y. 10022-5299

ISBN 0-06-101005-7

HarperCollins®, ®, and HarperPaperbacks™
are trademarks of HarperCollins*Publishers* Inc.

Cover illustration by Danilo Ducak

First printing: September 1996

Printed in the United States of America

Visit HarperPaperbacks on the World Wide Web at
http://www.harpercollins.com/paperbacks

❖ 10 9 8 7 6 5 4 3 2 1

To Kookasa,
for sparking my imagination in so many untold ways.

ACKNOWLEDGMENTS

Though there are a number of staff people and physicians at Johnston-Willis Hospital who helped to make this book possible by providing support, technical assistance, and encouragement, I want to give special thanks to Dr. George Johnson for sharing some of his vast neurological wisdom, and to MRI technician, Kelly Gursky, for taking the time to walk me through the various functions and hazards of that miraculous machine.

A huge debt of thanks goes to my agent, Linda Hayes, of Columbia Literary Associates, Inc. Mere words seem inadequate—suffice it to say I think she is a remarkable woman and a superb agent. Of course, no thanks would be complete without a nod to my editor, Jessica Lichtenstein, whose insight, wisdom, and kindness made me believe once again that editors really are human beings, just like the rest of us. And a special note of thanks to Wesley Gibson—for his superb teaching, his tireless faith in my ability, and his willingness to nurture me along.

Finally, a warmhearted thanks to my family. To my parents, Frank and Laura, for instilling in me that painful work ethic; to my sisters, Cathy, Laurie, and Amy, whose own outstanding accomplishments have always pushed me toward greater competitive heights; and to Scott and Ryan, who, though they didn't always understand, never complained.

Richmond, Virginia
June 1995

COLD WHITE FURY

PROLOGUE

Had Tim Bolton known that the remainder of his life was measurable in mere minutes, it's doubtful it would have made him any more tense. The strain he was feeling was evident in the white-knuckled grip he held on the steering wheel, the scowling V his brows made above his nose, the thin-lipped line of his mouth, and the ramrod set of his shoulders. But his tension generated from another cause altogether—a cause that, if asked, Tim Bolton might have said was more frightening, more foreign to him than mere death.

A vacation.

A vacation fit Tim Bolton's lifestyle like a too-small suit that bound and chafed at the tender areas of his skin—a fact his wife, Jennifer, knew all too well. She sat beside him in frustrated silence, having given up on her attempts to engage him in conversation some forty or so miles ago.

She supposed she should have expected this. Tim was a uniquely driven man, with a seemingly innate inability to endure more than a few hours away from his research. Unlike most marriages, in which wives worried about competition from other women, Tim's mistress had always been his work. Though Jennifer had to admit that the progeny of this relationship had been undeniably fruitful: a doctorate in bioengineering, a job with Bioceutics, and status as one of the leading geneticists in the country. All by the age of twenty-nine.

Still, when she'd heard that Tim's boss, Peter McClary, had not only insisted Tim take some time off, but had also offered his mountain cabin in West Virginia as a scenic and isolated retreat, Jennifer had been unable to contain her excitement. Surely Tim could set aside his work for one short week. But after three hours on the road, Tim's obvious preoccupation was dampening her hope as much as the constant rain outside dampened the day. Now, an awkward and pervasive silence filled the car, broken only by the pattering of drops on the Volvo's roof, the rhythmic slap of the windshield wipers, and the occasional gurgling coo from their six-month-old son, Tanner, who was quietly entertaining himself in his infant seat behind them.

As they wound their way over the curving, mountainous road near the border of Virginia and West Virginia, Jennifer gazed out at the view surrounding them. Behind them were the lower, rolling foothills of the Blue Ridge, the hovering haze and the deep green of spring combining to tint them the gray-blue color that gave the mountains their name. Along the road's edge, bright sparks of color burst everywhere: the vibrant yellows of daffodils and forsythia, the delicate lavender of redbuds, and the pink and white flowers of the dogwoods and pears—all of it blanketed in the tender, yet vibrant green of new leaves, still curled around themselves like a newborn baby's fist.

Ahead, the slopes grew steeper and more jagged. The wooded terrain had given way so that the road was edged on Jennifer's side by craggy striations of rock. Here and there a scraggly conifer jutted out of the stone wall, clinging tenaciously to the vertical climb. Pregnant clouds scudded across the sky, birthing a steady drizzle of cold rain. The sun occasionally managed to peer through, casting a subdued and silvery light on the ground below so that individual spots were highlighted, making them seem somehow magical as the vibrant colors manifested themselves against the dreary, gray light of day.

On the other side, out Tim's window, the road dropped away over a mist-covered valley of velvet green. Tiny rents in the mist revealed peeks at the life below: scattered farmhouses, teetering barns, a field of young calves huddled beside their mothers. Behind and below them, Jennifer caught an occasional glimpse of a red Volkswagen Beetle wending its way along the serpentine curves like a ladybug, making a childhood chant run through her mind: *Ladybug, Ladybug, fly away home. Your house is on fire, and your children will burn.*

The sound of a whimper drew Jennifer's attention away from the scenery and toward the backseat. She twisted around and saw that Tanner had fallen asleep, his puckered lips sucking frantically on one finger. Jennifer smiled as she watched him, drinking in the sight. She could stare at him for hours, never tiring of the miracle of his existence. It gave her the same pleasant sinking sensation in the pit of her stomach—like cresting the first big hill on a roller coaster—that she'd felt when she first saw Tim. And small wonder. Tanner favored his father strongly—the same long, narrow nose, heavy-lidded, brown eyes, and thick black hair. Not so much as a trace of her own fair complexion and blond hair.

She wondered if Tanner's personality would be like his father's as well. So far he seemed to be as quiet and introspective as Tim, almost brooding in the way his eyelids stayed at half-mast, as if he were contemplating some weighty thought that so totally consumed him he needed to block out the outside world.

At that thought, Jennifer shifted her gaze back to her husband, noting the furrowed look on his brow, and sensing the frustration boiling up inside him. She winced as she watched his grip on the steering wheel tighten even more, so that his fingernails carved tiny half-moons in the palms of his hands. She sighed heavily.

Hearing her, Tim looked over, and a weary smile softened the grim set of his mouth. Jennifer watched his eyes rove over the faint freckles on her face and then follow them downward, where they led like a connect-the-dots game to her chest. She smiled back at him, her hope renewed by the spark in his eye as he reached across the breach between them to give her thigh a reassuring squeeze.

It was this one moment of inattention—the last tender moment they would ever share—that probably saved Jennifer's life.

There was an odd popping sound and Jennifer saw the steering wheel jerk violently beneath Tim's left hand. The front end of the Volvo lurched into the oncoming lane and Tim made a frantic grab for the wheel with both hands, yanking it back. Jennifer knew he had overcorrected even before the car began its sickening sideways slide, the back wheels skidding over the solid yellow line.

The slide picked up speed as the Volvo crested a hill and started down the other side. Jennifer watched in horror as Tim's foot slammed on the brake pedal, only to have it give way, sinking to the floor. In the next instant, her eyes registered the oil tanker that was lumbering up the hill toward them, coming around the curve dangerously close to the center line.

Jennifer saw Tim's arm muscles strain as he tried to gain control of the car. She heard the tanker's horn bellow an ear-shattering blast. The car's front tires hit the gravel shoulder, spewing up a tiny storm of dust and stone. And with a sickening sensation deep in the pit of her stomach, Jennifer watched as the Volvo slid inexorably toward the looming grille of the truck, like iron drawn to a magnet. A shrill screeching noise cut through the air and some distant part of Jennifer's mind recognized it as her own scream blending with the piercing shriek of metal on metal. It was a soul-shattering sound that seemed to go on forever—bouncing around inside her head, echoing off the rock wall beside them, and infiltrating the valley below.

Jennifer's first conscious thought was that the rain had somehow caught fire. She felt spots of cold wetness strike her face, but it burned where it touched her skin. She struggled to open her eyes, succeeding with only one as the other was glued shut with blood. With one hand she reached up and gingerly explored her face, grimacing when her fingers found a mushy lump above her left brow. She dropped her hand and turned toward Tim.

He was moaning, his head lolling from side to side, the Volvo's steering wheel pinned up tight against his chest, the car door pushed in so far it caused him to lean at an odd angle. He was covered with blood—on his shirt, his face, his hands, his lap. Jennifer had never seen so much blood.

She looked through the fractured front window and saw the twisted remains of the fuel truck, its image kaleidoscoped in the cracked glass. A large gash split the tanker's side and liquid fuel spewed out like Old Faithful, raining down on the Volvo and through a large hole on Jennifer's side of the windshield. The acrid sting of gasoline assailed her nose, and with a sudden, horrifying clarity, Jennifer understood what the fiery rain was. Her heart leaped as she thought of Tanner.

She tried to twist around but froze halfway, grimacing as a piercing pain shot up her back. When the spasm passed, she tried again, more slowly, only to be thwarted by the restraint of her seat belt. She fumbled with the release and finally managed to turn herself around.

Tanner sat in his infant seat, awake but quiet, his brown eyes like the frozen stare of a deer caught in headlights.

Jennifer heard Tim mumble, "Tanner," and the sound of his whispered anguish nudged her into action. She yanked up on her door handle and pushed, but the damned thing didn't budge. Sucking in a deep breath, she tried again, pushing harder, the movement causing an agony of pain to rip through her back. Still it resisted. With a moan of frustration, she slumped back against the seat.

"Get Tanner," Tim groaned.

Jennifer turned her head to look at her husband. His face was covered with rivulets of blood, his hair plastered to one side of his forehead in a crimson paste. His breaths were short and labored. At first his eyes were closed, but then he opened them, and Jennifer uttered a strangled mewling sound as she registered the awful fear and pain she saw reflected there.

With a final, desperate surge of will she attacked the door one last time, heaving herself against it so hard she thought she would break. She screamed in pain and frustration, her face red and bulging from her efforts. As the last of her energy and will drained away, the door finally gave way with a mighty groan, opening a mere foot before the twisted metal of the front fender stopped it.

That small measure of success gave her a new burst of energy, and she closed her mind to the numerous pains that tore through her body as she squeezed out through the opening. Once outside, she stood leaning over the hood a moment, letting the icy rain snake down the back of her neck until she was convinced her shaking legs would hold her. Then she stumbled to the back door, muttering a prayer of thanks when it opened without difficulty. She reached in, released the restraint around Tanner's infant seat, and pulled him out.

Frightened by his terrible stillness, she gave him a cursory check, relieved to find no obvious injuries. She held him close to her shoulder and hurried around the back end of the car to Tim's door, stopping short when she saw that the mangled cab of the oil tanker was embedded in the side of the Volvo. Ethereal, gray smoke oozed from beneath the truck's hood, and she saw the driver slumped over the wheel, apparently either unconscious or dead. A large chunk of smoldering rubber from one of the truck's tires lay curled in the road, its edges torn and ragged so that the thing looked like the dead carapace of some giant beetle.

Ladybug, ladybug, fly away home. Your house is on fire . . .

A loud *pop* from somewhere inside the mangled metal shook her out of her reverie, and she retraced her steps back to the other side of the car. Shifting Tanner to her hip, she stuck her head and one shoulder through the back door.

Tim's breathing was now little more than a whistling moan, his bloodied face frozen in a grimace, deathly pale in the few spots where his skin showed through. At the corner of his mouth, a small bubble of bloody spittle grew and shrank with each breath.

"Tim!" she yelled, her voice shrill. When he didn't respond, panic rose in her throat like bitter bile, making her next words come out in a stertorous sob. "Ti-im! Ple-please! Oh, God! Tim!"

Tim's moans stopped, and he rolled his head to the side, his eyes straining to see her. "Take . . . Tanner," he whispered. A long string of bloody drool rolled from his mouth and fell onto the seat beside him.

"I *have* Tanner," she said with anguished impatience.

"I need you now, Tim. Please!" She reached her free hand in and touched his shoulder. Even through the thick flannel of his shirt, he felt frighteningly cold. Fear clamped over her heart like an icy fist.

"Take . . . Tanner," he said again. His eyes closed tight, as if the effort of speaking took every ounce of concentration he had left.

Jennifer shook her head wildly. "No! Not until I help you out. Please, Tim! Try! You have to get out! You have to!" she wailed.

Tim took a deep, shuddering breath, his face wrinkling in agony. His eyes opened so wide they bulged. "Take . . . Tanner. Run! NOW! Going . . . to blow!" With that, his eyes rolled back and his head fell forward, a long string of bloody spittle hanging from his lip. A slow, wheezing leak of air escaped from his mouth with a sound of terrifying finality, and his body suddenly went slack, as if he had been a marionette whose puppeteer had just dropped all the strings.

Jennifer stared at him in utter disbelief. Then both her mind and her eyes slammed shut. She reared back out of the car and threw her head back. Her mouth opened in a quivering, anguished O, and a keening wail echoed through the cold, damp air.

"No-o-o-o-o!"

Tanner started to cry, and the sound snatched Jennifer back from the precipice. She held her son close, nuzzling her nose in his hair, taking in the gentle, baby smell of him and cooing soft words in his ear. For a moment she allowed herself to be lost, her only awareness the soft warmth of her son's body against her chest.

Slowly, reality crept its way back in.

Tanner's sweet smell was overwhelmed by the stench of gasoline. Jennifer opened her eyes, and everything snapped into sharp focus. Gas spewing everywhere.

Sparks and smoke coming from the truck. Her clothes and her son's reeking of gasoline.

Instinct kicked in, and Jennifer started to run.

The road was as slick as ice where the cold rain and the gasoline had mixed. Jennifer held Tanner tight to her chest, one hand wrapped protectively around his head, the other beneath his buttocks. Her legs struggled against the steep incline, while her back screamed with pain as her grip on Tanner made her body sway awkwardly from side to side. With single-minded purpose, she kept her eyes focused on the crest of the hill, feeling that getting around that curve was her only hope.

Her goal was mere yards away when the whole world exploded. The percussion from the blast lifted her off the ground, spun her in the air like some crazy top, then flung her toward the ditch near the road's edge. Her arms tightened instinctively as she struggled to hold Tanner to her chest against the terrible force that pushed her. Seconds before she hit the ground, her mind went blank, and the world disappeared behind a veil of velvet blackness, leaving her mercifully unaware of the fact that she landed on her back with a resounding blow, fracturing two of the vertebrae. She never knew it when one of her legs snapped like a dry twig, a jagged edge of bone tearing through her calf. She had no way of knowing that her body cushioned the blow for Tanner, or that she still held him in a death grip. Nor was she aware of the gravel and rock and bits of metal that rained down around them, one of them a tiny, red-hot sliver of metal, as fine as a needle, that was propelled by the blast through Tanner's scalp, through the soft spot on the back of his head. It drove its way through his brain, the heat searing and cauterizing its way through his cerebellum, until it finally came to rest near the rear portion of his midbrain. Though conscious, Tanner felt nothing, his senses dulled by the force of the blast, and the brain tissue itself lacking any nerve endings for pain.

Moments after the blast, a red Volkswagen Beetle rounded the curve and came to a halt. A lone man, dressed in a faded, red flannel shirt and blue jeans so worn the knees and seat were almost white, climbed out and stared at the conflagration. Despite his casual dress, there was an air of sophistication about him: the poised set of his shoulders, the neat trim of his carefully coiffed blond hair, the manicured cut of his fingernails. He strode over to the ditch where Jennifer's crumpled and unconscious body lay with Tanner still held tight against her chest.

Tanner's eyes focused on the man briefly. Then his tiny fists balled up, his scratched and bleeding face scrunched into a frightened grimace, and he began to squall, his cries echoing off the rock wall beside the road.

The man bent down and felt along Jennifer's neck with two fingers. After a moment he stood, walked back to the Volkswagen, and reached in to grab a car phone. He dialed a number and stood waiting a moment, staring at the cloud of oily, black smoke boiling up from the mangled heap of metal that was the remains of the Volvo and the fuel tanker. He spoke into the phone, nodded, and pushed the button that disconnected his call. Then he dialed again, his fingers punching the digits 9-1-1.

The next thing that Jennifer's mind registered was the feel of warm hands and cool sheets. Gradually she became aware of voices, seemingly dozens of voices, coming at her from all directions. She struggled to open her eyes, only to clamp them shut again when they were assaulted by blinding white light. Then her mind registered the pain—a white-hot knife slicing through her back and legs. She tried to cry out, but all she heard was a weakened and pitiful moan. The pain was excruciating, like a living thing, an alien with tendrils that snaked through her body, obliterating everything else so that she never felt the needle that was thrust into her arm.

Slowly, the tendrils began to withdraw, retracting into the alien body, leaving behind a wonderfully numbing sensation. Jennifer felt herself floating, drifting away, carried by the soft comfort of that sweet cloud, leaving the awful pain behind.

And then she was with Tim, back on that first day they had met in the college library. She stood patiently at the copy machine as he flipped through page after page of a thick book, dropping in one coin after another, while she watched the light from the copier dance across his face. When he turned to look at her, his face wearing an apologetic grin, she was instantly smitten by his crooked smile, the incredibly dark depths of his eyes, and the shock of dark hair that kept falling stubbornly onto his forehead despite his attempts to push it back.

"I'm almost done," he said, and his voice caressed her ears.

She smiled back at him, wanting to tell him she would gladly stand there waiting forever if she could just keep watching him. Aware of the intensity of her stare, his nervous fingers missed the coin slot and a dime rolled across the floor toward her feet. She watched him bend over to pick it up, saw his eyes fix on her long legs and follow their slender, tanned length all the way up to the bottom of her shorts. Her smile widened.

Realizing he'd been caught, Tim straightened and flashed her an uneasy smile, the corners of his mouth twitching. Their eyes locked for an eternal moment before he turned back to the copier and continued. After another five pages, with his eyes still focused on what he was doing, he said, "Would you have dinner with me tonight?"

"I'd love to."

He looked at her then, his hand frozen over the coin slot, ready to drop another dime in.

"How about now?" he said.

"Okay."

Tim held his hand out to her.

She reached with her own, but just as she was about to touch him he began to fade away, his body growing transparent, his face frozen in astonishment. She tried desperately to reach him, but there was no substance to him anymore, just a filmy apparition that eventually faded into nothingness. Her mind screamed in agony as reality crashed down on her. She cried out for Tim, then for Tanner, her arms flailing about in empty space.

"It's okay, miss," a soothing, female voice said near her right shoulder. "Your little boy is okay."

Jennifer turned and tried to bring the face that went with the voice into focus. It was blond, pretty, and surrounded by white light. An angel then.

"Where is Tanner?" Jennifer asked, her throat feeling as if it were lined with sandpaper.

"In the room right next to you," the angel answered. "Would you like to see him?"

Jennifer nodded, not wanting to try and use her throat again. The angel disappeared, and Jennifer closed her eyes, feeling the soothing cloud try to envelop her. Then she remembered Tanner and forced her eyes open, trying to resist the temptation of that wonderful cloud. The nurse returned, carrying Tanner in her arms, and Jennifer struggled to lift her head, running her eyes over him anxiously. She saw some small scrapes and scratches, but he looked otherwise unharmed.

"Just a few scrapes and scratches," the angel said, echoing Jennifer's thoughts. "You will both be fine."

Jennifer dropped her head with relief. The angel smiled, Tanner cooed, and Jennifer—with one last aching thought for Tim—closed her eyes and let the cloud carry her away.

1

EIGHT YEARS LATER. . . .

Though it was far too hot and sticky for most people to even consider baking, Jennifer was up to her wrists in a large bowl of cookie dough, while the oven ticked its way up to four hundred degrees, sending shimmering waves of heat into the room. Even though it was only mid-June, the temperature hovered in the mid-nineties; not all that unusual for central Virginia, but boding a summer on the hot side of normal. With the air-conditioning off and the oven on, the temperature in the kitchen hovered well above the one hundred mark. Trickles of sweat wove their way down Jennifer's side, and she gave an occasional shrug in a futile attempt to loosen the clinging dampness of her blouse. Her fingers plunged in and out of the sticky batter like some mindless machine, until cramps forced her to rest. She paused a moment, holding up her dough-covered hands like a just-scrubbed surgeon, and stared out the kitchen window.

Even Mother Nature was suffering from the heat. Like an army of sentinels, the trees that surrounded the house on all four sides stood still and listless, without so much as a whisper of breeze to rustle their limbs. The grass, which last week was vibrantly green and delicate after the spring rains, already bore patches of the yellow-brown color that marked its dormant summer stage. A blue jay hopped lazily across the yard, cocking a desperate eye at the hard clay earth, searching for the worms that had been so abundant just a few days before.

A rivulet of sweat trickled down Jennifer's nose, and when she reached up to swipe at it with her arm, a small chunk of cookie dough fell from her fingers onto the floor.

"Damn!" she muttered. She turned her face over her shoulder and hollered: "Butterscotch!"

At her summons, a large golden retriever hurtled into the kitchen, nails clicking on the tile floor as she skirted around the butcher block table and chairs in the middle of the room. She slid to a halt at Jennifer's feet and promptly plopped her butt down, her bushy tail sweeping tiny dust bunnies across the floor. Brown eyes rimmed with red lashes looked up eagerly, while a pink tongue panted almost lasciviously.

"There's a snack for you," Jennifer said, pointing toward the mess on the floor.

The dog lowered her head, sniffed, and found the treat. Seconds later, the only sign of the spilled dough was a rapidly evaporating wet mark on the tile. Pleading eyes were once again fixed on their master's face.

"I should have named you Hoover," Jennifer laughed.

Butterscotch whined in response, wiggling her butt with excited anticipation.

Jennifer shrugged. "Sorry, Scotch, no more."

The dog ignored her, continuing to stare and creating a small puddle of drool on the floor at her feet. When Jennifer turned away the dog whined one last time, made a final sniffing exploration of the floor around her, and then padded out of the room.

Jennifer looked at the bowl of dough, saw a clump of unmixed flour, and attacked it again. The cookies were cream cheese spritz—Tanner's favorite—so she sweltered without complaint, singing along with a Michael Jackson tune on the radio. She squeezed the dough in rhythm to the music, her hips swaying with the beat. Though her hands ached, she enjoyed the feel of the stuff as it squished between her fingers and probably could have stood there happily kneading for quite a while if it hadn't been for the phone's sudden and insistent ring. Rolling her eyes, Jennifer cursed under her breath and yanked a dish towel off the refrigerator door handle, using it to pick up the phone.

"Hello?" she said with irritation.

"Jen? It's Carny. Catch you at a bad time?"

"Sort of," Jennifer answered, her voice and demeanor both softening considerably in response to her friend's sultry, Southern tones. "No big deal. What's up?"

"Tanner's had a little accident."

The effect of the words—haunting words that had tiptoed through her dreams, words she had anticipated with a resigned sense of fate for eight years—was immediate and devastating, like a hard punch to her gut. Jennifer felt a little tingle of fear start at the base of her spine and crawl up toward her neck. She held the phone in a white-knuckled grip, afraid to speak, afraid to breathe.

"He's okay," Carny added quickly. "Don't panic! He took a spill on his bicycle is all. Missed the turn onto the path at the bottom of the hill here in my backyard."

Jennifer's breath eased out by degrees, like a slow leak from a balloon. "Where is he?" she asked.

"Here, lying on my couch, complaining because I won't let him up. Actually, I think he's more embarrassed that I saw him than anything else."

That calmed Jennifer some. It sounded like the same old rough-and-tumble Tanner. Still, she couldn't shake off the horrible sense of dread that had settled over her so quickly.

"I'll be right over." She replaced the phone and half

ran out the door, pushed on by a sense of urgency, as if Tanner's well-being depended solely on her ability to get there as quickly as possible.

Carny's house was within two minutes' walking distance along a path through the woods, though a thick grove of trees hid it from view. To drive there—down Jennifer's long driveway, onto the highway for a quarter mile, and then down Carny's twisting road—took almost five minutes. Jennifer opted for the shorter route, running across the yard and onto the shaded trail, dodging an occasional low-hanging branch and the ruts left by Tanner's bicycle. Though the temperature in the shade was several degrees cooler, Jennifer was wringing wet with perspiration when she emerged on the other side.

Carny's house was much like her own and a few others spaced out along Highway 6 where it meandered through rural Fluvanna County: a two-story, redbrick home dating back to the early part of the century. Rumor had it that most of the land out here had at one time been part of a large plantation that had succumbed to the economic ravages of the Civil War. It had been parceled out and sold in four-acre chunks, though the main house still stood some six miles down the road, its once-white pillars now turned a crumbling brown, what was left of the structure held together by thick vines that had consumed the walls like a rapidly spreading cancer. Carny's house, like Jennifer's, had been built in a hollowed-out section of woods so that it was bordered on all sides by a mixture of statuesque old trees—mostly oaks, maples, elms, and pines. A few dogwoods and redbuds struggled for their share of space, the blossoms that had been flourishing just weeks ago now withered into brown remnants that clung stubbornly to the branches.

As Jennifer approached Carny's front porch, she spared a look of grudging admiration to the azaleas that rimmed the house and which, not long ago, had been a spectrum of horticultural mastery in shades of white, red, lavender, and pink. Carny had a knack for growing things. Sometimes Jennifer thought it was Carny's nasal drawl that coaxed the plants along, as she had a habit of talking to them, even going so far as to give each one a name. In fact, Carny had so many plants in and around the house, she had gone out and bought one of those name books for babies. How she kept them all straight in her mind was beyond Jennifer. It was all she could do to remember her own name some days. And forget about anything resembling a green thumb. Last year she had tried to plant some azaleas, nurturing them along, watering and fertilizing and even talking to the stupid things when they started to yellow. Yet despite her well-intentioned efforts, they were dead within a few months. Though she was willing to admit that a green thumb was not one of her stronger attributes, she suspected Scotch had contributed to the azaleas' demise, as the dog had considered the area where they were planted as her own personal potty.

Carny had left the inside door open, and as Jennifer reached to open the screen door she realized her hands were still coated with greasy cookie dough. She peered through the screen into the darkened house and hollered. "Carny?"

"Come on in!"

"I can't." She held her hands up in front of her.

Carny's curious face emerged from the darkness. Though her fair skin had always looked abnormally pale beneath her shoulder-length, straight black hair, seen through the gray mesh of the screen she looked positively ghostlike. "What in the world?" She grinned crookedly, one eyebrow cocked.

"It's cookie dough," Jennifer explained, as Carny held the door open for her.

"Spritz?" came a hopeful voice from the next room.

Both women laughed, and Jennifer felt her tension begin to ease away.

She found Tanner sprawled out on Carny's white couch, a Baggie full of ice held to his forehead. His dark hair was pushed back, creating a spiked fringe around his face. Jennifer winced when she saw the dust covering his clothes and the rust-colored mud caked on the bottom of his shoes. In contrast to the dated appearance on the outside, the inside of Carny's house was done over in a modern, contemporary style—lots of white, chrome, and glass. Hardly a house made for kids or dirt, but then Carny didn't have any of either.

"Yes, they are spritz," Jennifer said, smiling as she approached her son. "They were *supposed* to be a surprise." She stood next to him, hands on her hips, looking him over. Other than his head, she could see no obvious injuries.

Tanner gazed up at her, grinning widely. "You're making a mess of your pants," he said with mock disgust.

Belatedly, Jennifer realized what she had done and looked down, frowning at the buttery smears and clumps of dough clinging to her shorts. Carny sniggered behind her, and Jennifer turned, shooting her a dirty look.

"How about being the friend you profess to be and getting me something to clean this stuff off." Jennifer smiled wickedly and held her hands poised above one of the white chairs. "Before I put them on your newly upholstered furniture."

"Gotcha," said Carny. She gave Jennifer a snappy salute and turned toward the kitchen, trying unsuccessfully to keep a straight face.

Jennifer knelt beside Tanner and gently pushed the ice aside so she could examine his head. A tiny chunk of cookie dough fell from her hand and onto his hair, resting there like a dandruff flake big enough for the Guinness record book. Along the top of his eyebrow there was a knot the size of a jawbreaker.

"Ooh, looks nasty!" she said, her voice gently teasing. "What did you hit?"

"A tree."

Jennifer bit her lip and gave her son a stern look. "I hope you didn't hurt the tree. Carny will kill you."

"Thanks a lot, Mom!" Tanner said, rolling his eyes and grinning. "Besides, Carny knows. She saw the whole thing."

"How do you feel?"

"I have a headache."

"I'll bet you do." Jennifer reached up to ruffle his hair and stopped when she remembered the mess on her hands.

Carny returned with a wet towel and Jennifer started working on the cookie dough. The stuff was terribly thick and greasy; no matter how hard she wiped all she managed to do was spread it around.

Tanner stared up at her and giggled.

"What's so funny?" Jennifer asked, smiling.

"There's two of you," Tanner answered. Then his eyes shifted toward Carny. "And two of you!" He pointed a finger, and his hand hung in the air, wavering.

Jennifer's smile faded, and her hands froze. "You see two of me?"

Tanner nodded.

Carny stepped up and held three fingers in front of Tanner's face. "How many fingers am I holding up?"

Tanner's face screwed into a frown as he studied her hand. Then he said, "Four? No, wait. Five! No, four." He giggled. "Hold 'em still!"

Jennifer shot a worried look at Carny.

"Better take him to the ER," Carny said. Then, with a pointed look at Jennifer's still-greasy hands, she added, "I'll drive."

* * *

Tanner remained almost annoyingly cheerful during the half hour drive to the hospital. The emergency room was relatively quiet for a Sunday afternoon, and Jennifer uttered a silent prayer of thanks when they were summoned from the waiting area within minutes of their arrival. Normally, hospitals made her edgy. There were too many unpleasant memories associated with them. But she was so concerned about Tanner's welfare that for the moment she forgot her surroundings. She and Tanner followed a nurse back to the examination area while Carny stayed in the waiting room.

Tanner climbed up onto a stretcher and sat with his legs dangling over the side. He stared wide-eyed at the wall panel at the head of the stretcher, where an assortment of tubes, nozzles, gauges, and machinery stood ready and waiting. Another nurse, a little older than Jennifer and wearing heavy makeup and an overprocessed blond frizz, came over and introduced herself.

"Hi! I'm Carolyn." She tugged at a curtain that hung from a track in the ceiling and pulled it around the perimeter of the small cubicle, enclosing them together in their own little world. Then she handed Tanner a hospital gown and told him to undress.

Jennifer thought about asking the nurse to leave the tiny cubicle. Tanner was at that age where his nakedness, or anything close to it, embarrassed him. But when she saw that the nurse had discreetly turned her back, seeming to be deeply interested in whatever information was contained on the clipboard she had carried in with her, Jennifer decided to let it go. She helped Tanner slip off his shirt and shorts, taking care to keep herself positioned between him and the nurse, just in case.

"What seems to be the problem?" the nurse asked, turning back toward the stretcher and focusing on Tanner mere seconds after his gown was in place. Jennifer suspected the woman's attention had not been too thoroughly diverted by the clipboard; her timing was a little too coincidental.

Jennifer summarized the events surrounding Tanner's injury as she knew them. When she mentioned his double vision, the nurse said, "Really?" and turned to scribble something on the clipboard. Jennifer tried to see what it was, but the scrawl was indecipherable.

The nurse set down her pen and grabbed the blood pressure cuff that was mounted on the wall. Jennifer saw Tanner go rigid and instantly forgot her curiosity about the clipboard. She stepped behind him and gave his shoulder a reassuring squeeze as the nurse pumped the cuff.

"There now. That didn't hurt a bit, did it?" the nurse asked as she ripped the blood pressure cuff from his arm. The sound of the Velcro coming apart seemed preternaturally loud within the tiny curtained space.

Tanner shook his head nervously.

"Now let me check your pulse," the nurse said, gripping Tanner's wrist between her thumb and two fingers.

Jennifer had always thought a pulse was counted for thirty seconds, maybe a full minute. But as the silence stretched around them, she thought this one must be taking at least five minutes. "Is it okay?" she asked when the nurse finally let go of Tanner's wrist and once more scribbled on her clipboard.

"It's fine," she said with a quick, plastic smile. "But we still need to let Doc Webber take a look at him."

She turned and disappeared through the curtain, only to be replaced a moment later by a white-haired man wearing a lab coat and sporting a stethoscope around his neck. The name, "Dr. Michael Webber," was stitched across his breast pocket. He, too, carried a clipboard—probably the same one, Jennifer realized. She wondered if the speed of his arrival was due to the slow pace of things in the ER, or because Tanner's injury was more serious than she had originally thought.

"Hi, Tanner," the doctor said, holding out his hand. "I'm Dr. Webber."

Tanner took the man's hand and shook it.

"I hear you took a tumble on your head."

Tanner nodded. "It's just a bump," he said, touching the knot on his head. His eyes slid almost imperceptibly to the wall panel at the head of the stretcher. "It doesn't even hurt that much," he added quickly.

"Well, that's good," Dr. Webber said. He pulled a penlight from his breast pocket and flashed it in Tanner's eyes. "Pupils equal and reactive."

"Is that good?" Jennifer asked, chewing on the side of her thumb. She could taste the faint remnants of cookie dough.

"Very good," the doctor answered. He held both of his hands out to Tanner, palms down. "Squeeze my hands as hard as you can," he instructed.

Tanner reached up and squeezed.

"Is that the best you can do?" Webber teased. "What a wimp!"

Tanner's face screwed up and he squeezed again, his knuckles turning white.

"Okay! Okay! I give up!" Dr. Webber shook his hands after Tanner let them go. "You got some power in those paws!"

Tanner smiled.

"Can you tell me what day it is?" Webber asked.

"Sunday."

"What month?"

"June."

"What year?"

"1995." Tanner's smile grew bigger. He was enjoying this little quiz.

"And who is the president of the United States?"

"Billy-boy Clinton."

Jennifer's eyes grew wide, and she hid her smile behind her hand.

"Billy-boy?" Dr. Webber said slowly, giving Jennifer a sidelong glance.

Tanner shrugged. "That's what Mom calls him."

Webber chuckled. "Okay. How many fingers am I holding up?" he asked, wagging two fingers in front of Tanner's face.

Tanner's expression grew serious as he squinted. "Three. Or maybe four," he said uncertainly.

"Hmm." Webber scratched his chin. "Diplopia."

Jennifer's hand dropped away from her mouth, and she moved a step closer to the stretcher. "What's diplo . . . diplopia?" she asked, her voice breaking slightly as she tripped over the syllables.

Dr. Webber waved a dismissing hand. "Just a fancy medical term for double vision."

"Is it a problem?" Jennifer struggled to keep her voice level. She didn't want Tanner to suspect how worried she was.

"Could be. Or it could just be an aftereffect from his bump on the noggin. I want to do some skull films to rule out a fracture, and I think a CT scan would be in order as well, just to be on the safe side."

A disembodied voice came from over the curtain. "The CT scanner is still down." Jennifer recognized the voice as the nurse's.

Dr. Webber rolled his eyes. "All right then. We'll do an MRI instead," he said loudly. He looked at Jennifer. "An MRI is more detailed anyway," he added with a shrug.

"What's an MRI?" Tanner asked, his eyes wide as quarters.

Dr. Webber hiked one hip up onto the stretcher next to Tanner, folding his arms over his chest. "Well, do you know what an atom is?"

"Of course!" Tanner said, sounding insulted. "Those are the little particles that make up all mass," he said with a definitive nod.

Webber's eyebrows arched. "Pretty impressive!" he said. "Well, an MRI is a giant magnet contained inside a machine. If we send some sound waves into your body and then turn the magnet on, it makes all the atoms inside your body start to vibrate, like they're doing a dance. Each kind of atom only knows how to do one kind of dance, and we can turn the vibrations into pictures so we can see if your insides are dancing like they're supposed to. That way we can tell if you really have a brain in there!" Webber tapped a finger against Tanner's forehead.

"Of course I have a brain!" Tanner giggled.

"Well, we'll see."

"Will you let me look at the pictures?" Tanner asked.

"Sure." Dr. Webber smiled.

"Cool!"

Webber turned to Jennifer. "Has he had any other health problems? Any surgeries?"

Jennifer shook her head.

"No pacemakers or artificial joints?"

"No."

"Good." Seeing the worried look on her face, Dr. Webber gave her arm a little squeeze. "Don't worry. I don't think there's a thing wrong with him. I just want to make sure we check everything out thoroughly."

Jennifer nodded, unable to speak past the growing lump in her throat.

Dr. Webber disappeared through the curtain, and

Carolyn's blond frizz poked through an instant later, making Jennifer feel like a spectator in some chintzy magic show. She was relieved when Carolyn withdrew her head and flung the curtain aside.

"Okay, Tanner. Time to go for a ride. Mom, if you'll have a seat in the waiting room, we'll come and get you just as soon as Tanner is finished." Carolyn released the stretcher brake with her foot and slid the side rails up, giving each one a jerk to be sure they were locked into position.

Jennifer nodded hesitantly, biting her lip so she wouldn't cry. She bent down and kissed Tanner's cheek. "You behave yourself," she whispered. Now she was seeing double as two Tanners fuzzed together through her tear-filled eyes.

Seeing that his mother was about to cry, Tanner straightened his shoulders. "I'll be fine, Mom," he said with casual nonchalance. Actually he wasn't feeling all *that* brave, but he hated it when his mother cried.

Jennifer gave him a weak smile and ran a hand over his head. "I know you will," she said. "See you soon."

Tanner was tall for his age—at eight, almost nine, he was nearly to his mother's shoulders already—but as Jennifer watched the nurse wheel the stretcher away, she thought he looked pathetically tiny and vulnerable. She watched until he disappeared through a set of double doors. As the doors closed with an audible hiss of air she was suddenly assailed with memories—awful memories— memories of lights and voices and incredible pain, both physical and emotional. She glanced around frantically, but all of the staff people seemed preoccupied, hustling and bustling about even though there were only two other patients she could see.

Hugging herself, Jennifer hurried back out to the waiting room, dropping into a seat next to Carny. She knew she couldn't talk and was therefore grateful that

Carny didn't ask any questions. But what Carny did do was reach out and grasp Jennifer's hand. That was all it took. Jennifer burst into tears and buried her face in Carny's shoulder.

Once his mother was out of sight, Tanner's bravado evaporated as quickly as the wet spot on the kitchen floor had when Scotch licked up the cookie dough. Carolyn steered him down a cold, brightly lit hallway, stopping before a pair of heavy wooden doors. She punched a large metal button on the wall and the doors opened with a whoosh, as if by magic. Though he was scared stiff, Tanner had to admit the doors were pretty cool. Like on *Star Trek*. Carolyn parked his stretcher and handed a sheaf of papers to a huge bear of a man with a full beard.

"Skull series and then an MRI," she said. Then she was gone.

The man studied the papers and then looked down at Tanner. "Scared?"

Tanner nodded.

"Don't be. This is no big deal. Absolutely painless. All we're going to do is take your picture a bunch of times." He tossed the papers onto a desk and pushed Tanner's stretcher into a nearby room.

Tanner stared at the huge X-ray machine that hung from the ceiling and bit his lip, trying to fight back tears. He wished his mother was here.

The bearded man positioned the stretcher next to a metal table and leaned toward Tanner, his elbows resting on the railing. "I promise you, this is easy. It's just a big, fancy camera. Nothing will hurt you."

Tanner stared back, tears welling in his eyes. His hands began to shake, and he shoved them beneath his back.

"Look," the man said. He leaned down close to Tanner's ear and whispered, "If anything I do hurts you even a teeny tiny little bit, you can kick my butt! Okay?"

Despite his fear, Tanner grinned. "Okay," he said.

It turned out that the bear-man was right. Except for the fact that the table was cold and hard, the skull X-ray was pretty easy. When it was over, the bear-man had Tanner scoot back onto the stretcher and wheeled him off to another room.

Feeling calmer now that he had experienced the first test virtually unscathed, Tanner's fear surged back when his stretcher halted outside the next room. It was much colder here, and the machine in the middle of this room was a lot bigger. It looked like a gigantic metal doughnut with a bed in the middle of it and a lot of lights and buttons on the outside. Tanner had seen something like it on *Deep Space Nine* once. A time portal, or something like that.

Bear-man took off Tanner's watch, then examined his hands and neck. "Got to make sure you're not wearing any metal," he explained. Satisfied that all was in order, he wheeled the stretcher into the room and positioned it alongside the machine's bed.

"Okay, buddy. Scoot over."

Tanner did as he was told, but he did it reluctantly. A shiver shook him as he lay back. He watched wide-eyed as bear-man turned to leave the room, pushing the stretcher ahead of him. Tanner started to ask him to stay—he didn't want to be left alone in here—but then a pretty girl with red hair and freckles came into the room.

She walked over to Tanner and smiled. "Hi. I'm Kelly. You're Tanner, right?"

Tanner nodded. The girl looked friendly enough, but he still wished bear-man was there. For all he knew, this girl might be some type of alien or something, like the pod people. Maybe she was going to put him in that machine and transport him to some other planet, where they would probably eat him for dinner.

"There is no reason to be afraid, Tanner," Kelly said. "This is really no different than the X-rays you just had. But it is *extra* important that you don't move while we do this, so we need to put your head inside this special frame here." She pointed to a plastic cylinder-shaped thing that looked kind of like a birdcage.

Tanner's eyes rolled wildly as he tried to watch Kelly position his head inside the contraption.

"Now, I'm going to go to the control panel over there," Kelly said, pointing to a glass window. "When I get there I'm going to push a button that will make your stretcher here slide up inside this machine. Sometimes people feel funny when they get in there because it's such a small space. So I'm going to put this washcloth over your eyes so that you can relax better. Okay?"

Tanner was so scared, his nod came out as more of a spasm. Being in a small place didn't bother him. He had a fort out in the woods that he'd built from scraps of wood he'd found, and he kind of liked the way it was small and cozy inside. And sometimes, when he wanted to have a fort in the house, he closed himself inside his bedroom closet. As long as the light was on, it didn't bother him at all. But this machine was something different. He still wasn't convinced it wasn't some weird alien transporter or something.

"The machine will make some really loud clicking and humming noises, but you won't feel anything," Kelly explained. "And there's a microphone in there, so I can hear anything you say. But I would rather you not talk because then you might move your head. So if you get too scared or anything, you just hold up one finger like this," Kelly said, demonstrating. "If that finger comes up, we'll stop everything. I promise." She drew a little X over her chest with her finger. "Cross my heart and hope to die."

That made Tanner feel a little better. Cross your heart *and* hope to die was serious stuff. Maybe it wouldn't be so bad. After all, he did have some control over this thing. Kelly had said so . . . *sworn* so. But when the table beneath him started to slide into the hole of the doughnut, he had to fight to keep his finger down.

Jennifer sat in the waiting room, her eyes red and puffy from crying, her hands busily shredding a tissue into microscopic pieces. The sights, sounds, and smells of the hospital had brought back the memories with a vengeance.

"I'm sure he'll be fine," Carny drawled, reaching over and rubbing her back.

Jennifer flashed her a quick smile of gratitude, then cast a mournful glance around the waiting room area. She shuddered and shifted her eyes to her lap. "I can't help it, Carny. This place reminds me so much of the accident. And Tim."

"I know," Carny said softly. "I'm sorry you have to go through this. But that was then, and this is now. Just because something awful happened once, doesn't mean it will happen again. In fact, according to the law of averages, it's less likely to happen."

"Spoken like the math teacher you are," Jennifer said with a halfhearted grin. Then her face turned grim, and she shook her head. "It's just that life changes so quickly! If you had asked me nine years ago if I thought it would be possible for Tim to be gone, I would have laughed in your face." She snorted with disgust. "What a fool." She stared at her feet for a moment, then turned to Carny. "Sometimes I feel as if I have this sword of Damocles hanging over me all the time. Like the troubles aren't over with yet. You know?"

Carny frowned. "Don't you think you're overreacting a little?"

Jennifer sighed, leaned forward in her chair, propped her elbows on her knees, her chin in her palms, and stared at the floor. "I don't know. Maybe I am. I *hope* I am. Because I'm telling you, Carny, if anything happens to Tanner, I don't think I could survive that." She looked up again, this time with tears in her eyes. "Not again," she said, her voice hitching.

Carny's frown deepened. "I'm sure he'll be okay. I saw him hit that tree, and though he did take a good bump on the head, he wasn't knocked out or anything. Kids get hurt like this all the time. I'm sure the X-rays are more of a precaution than anything."

Jennifer nodded, dabbing at her eyes with a miniscule piece of tissue.

Carny reached over and patted her hand. "Try to relax. He'll be back before you know it."

Jennifer leaned back in her seat and closed her eyes. She forced herself to take some slow, deep breaths and tried to relax. But something, a niggling fear, kept pushing into her mind. When it had gnawed at her long enough, she sat up, slapping the arms of the chair with her palms. "I can't stand this! What's taking them so long?" She stood up and marched over to the reception desk. "Excuse me."

The woman behind the desk looked up at her. "Yes?"

"I'm Jennifer Bolton. My son, Tanner, is having some X-rays back there, but he's been gone an awful long time. Can you please check on him?"

"Certainly, Mrs. Bolton."

The woman got up and disappeared through a doorway, while Jennifer stood waiting, maintaining a staccato rhythm with her fingers on the countertop. When the woman returned a few minutes later wearing the same plastic smile Carolyn, the nurse, had worn earlier, Jennifer couldn't help but wonder if they were taught that smile as part of their job training.

"Everything is fine, Mrs. Bolton. They're getting ready to do the MRI now. It will be just a little longer."

"Is Tanner okay?"

"He's fine," she answered with practiced tolerance. Then she effectively dismissed Jennifer by shifting her attention to a stack of papers on the desk.

"Well?" Carny asked when Jennifer came back to her seat.

"They're still doing the X-rays," Jennifer said irritably, chewing the side of her thumbnail and studying the stains in the carpet at her feet.

"So, why the long face?"

Jennifer shrugged. "I don't know. I just feel like something isn't right."

Dr. Webber was standing in front of a wall-mounted light box as the bear-man pushed the first of Tanner's skull films into a metal clip at the top. Webber scanned each one slowly, rubbing a finger across his chin. "That's odd," he muttered. He took down the films and pushed three new ones into place. His eyes widened, and he moved closer to the film.

"Shit!" He turned to the bear-man. "Call into MRI *stat* and tell them to stop!" Then he flew from the room.

About the same time Dr. Webber was studying the second set of films, Kelly was moving Tanner into the tunnel at the center of the MRI machine. Even before the stretcher began to move, the pull of the superconducting magnet was working on Tanner's body. The atoms inside his head began to resonate, each in a characteristic pattern. The tiny metal sliver that had been inside Tanner's brain for the past eight years began to vibrate faintly, moving a fraction of a centimeter until it was resting up against his pineal gland. The atoms inside the gland began to resonate wildly, stimulated by the battering of radio waves and the magnetic pull of the now-ionized metal sliver.

As Kelly settled in front of her console she saw the first image appear on the screen—varying shapes and shades of gray representing the structures of the head. An odd black line appeared at the center of the image and Kelly felt her blood run cold. At the same instant she saw the line, a voice boomed over the intercom.

"Stop the MRI stat!"

Kelly stood up so abruptly, she tipped over the stool she had been sitting on. The loud clatter of it hitting the floor combined with Dr. Webber's bursting through the door made her nearly jump out of her skin.

"The kid has a metal object in his head," Webber said breathlessly. "Get him out of there!"

Kelly's face blanched, making her freckles stand out vividly. She ran into the room and pushed the switch that moved the motorized stretcher out from the machine. Then she snatched the washcloth off Tanner's face.

Tanner blinked a few times and then looked up at Dr. Webber. The man's eyes looked wild, frightened, and his hair was standing almost straight up on end where he had run his hand through it. He was smacking his lips nervously, and Tanner thought he looked like the Tasmanian devil.

"Tanner?" Dr. Webber eased him out of the head frame. "Can you sit up?"

Tanner obliged, rubbing his eyes to clear them.

"How do you feel?"

Tanner shrugged, relieved it was all over. "Okay, I guess." He looked at Dr. Webber, then at Kelly, then back at Dr. Webber. They both looked like they had just seen a ghost.

"Can I see the pictures now?" Tanner asked.

Jennifer breathed a sigh of relief and fairly flew back into the examination area of the ER when the nurse came to get her. But when she saw the worried expression on Dr. Webber's face, her relief quickly vanished.

"Mrs. Bolton." Dr. Webber took her elbow and steered her toward a chair next to Tanner's stretcher. "Have a seat. We need to talk."

There was a tone of solemnity to the doctor's voice that made Jennifer's heart leap. That, and the fact that he wanted her to sit down, didn't augur well. Ignoring his instructions, she reached over and brushed Tanner's hair back from his forehead, scanning him from head to toe. "You okay?" she asked him.

"Fine, Mom. It was really nothing," Tanner said with a wave of his hand, his bravado firmly back in place.

Jennifer chewed her lip and frowned. He certainly looked okay. She turned a puzzled face toward Dr. Webber.

"Mrs. Bolton, has your son ever had any other head trauma? Been involved in any accidents or explosions?"

Jennifer shot a quick glance at Tanner. She had never really discussed the details of Tim's death with him. All he knew was that his father had died in a car accident. She had never seen any point in telling him more than that, afraid that it might give him nightmares or something.

"Well, yes," she said hesitantly. "When Tanner was about six months old. We were involved in a car accident . . . with a fuel tanker. Both the tanker and our car blew up. Tanner and I escaped, but my husband died in the explosion." She watched Tanner from the corner of her eye as she spoke, saw his head pivot sharply toward her, saw his mouth open in shock.

"I'm sorry about your husband," Dr. Webber said.

"Thank you. It was a long time ago." She looked full at Tanner, and he dropped his eyes and began idly picking at a cuticle. She knew she was going to have some explaining to do. "Why do you ask?" she said, turning her attention back to Dr. Webber. She was puzzled as to what that long-ago nightmare could possibly have to do with Tanner's current problem.

"Was Tanner examined after the accident?" Webber asked, ignoring her question.

Jennifer's mind flashed back, saw the nurse she'd thought was an angel, saw her holding Tanner. All the hurt and anguish of that day flooded into her mind with such suddenness it took her breath away. She squeezed her eyes shut and swallowed hard, making a conscious effort to push the memory back down.

"Yes," she answered. "Except for a few cuts and scrapes, he was fine." She was starting to get annoyed with the doctor's evasive questioning. "What does this have to do with anything?"

Dr. Webber still ignored her, staring off into space, his face screwed into a contemplative expression, his hands jingling change in the pocket of his lab coat. Jennifer bit her lip so hard she tasted blood. She wanted to shake the man! Just when she'd decided she would, he answered her.

"Your son has a piece of metal embedded in his head. A tiny, needlelike sliver. At first I thought it was some sort of weird artifact on the X rays, but in the posterior views it's pretty apparent."

Jennifer fell into the chair as if someone had just kicked her feet out from under her. "Metal in his head? How can that be?" Now that he had finally told her, she almost wished he hadn't. Her face flushed hot; her hands turned icy cold. She felt her throat tighten and took in a large gulp of air, just to assure herself that she could still breathe.

"Oh, it's quite possible, and not all that uncommon, really," Webber explained. "People live perfectly normal lives with pieces of shrapnel, even bullets, in their heads."

"Then it's not a problem?" she asked hopefully. The thudding of her heart in her ears subsided a smidgen.

"Well, it wouldn't have been. But, unfortunately, we didn't see the metal object until the MRI was started. The magnetic field created by the scanner can move metal objects inside someone, damaging the surrounding tissue."

"Meaning?"

Webber hesitated, running a hand through his already-mussed hair. "Well, it can cause hemorrhage, brain damage, that sort of thing."

Jennifer's hands felt like blocks of ice. She wedged them between her knees. "Was Tanner's moved?" she asked slowly, feeling as if she had to concentrate on shaping each syllable with her lips.

Webber took in a breath and exhaled slowly. "I'm not sure. I don't think so," he added quickly. "We did a second set of X rays, and if it was moved at all, it wasn't much. The problem is, even a small amount of movement can cause damage."

Jennifer wanted to scream. She wanted to stand up, grab the good doctor by his lapels, and tear him apart bit by bit. What had they done to her son? A mini matinee of flickering horror show images surged through her mind: Tanner drooling and demented; Tanner hooked up to some machine that breathed for him; Tanner staring off empty-eyed into space. A million questions came to mind, scary questions she wasn't sure she wanted to ask. Or Tanner to hear.

Webber continued, apparently oblivious to her near hysteria. "So far, Tanner seems unaffected. But I think we need to keep him here overnight. To keep a close eye on him in case there is a problem."

That did it for Tanner. Even if his mother had to see it, he was scared. He never thought he'd have to *stay* in this place.

"I don't want to stay here," he whined. His eyes appealed to his mother: huge, frightened, pleading. "I want to go home."

Jennifer fought an urge to gather him up in her arms and run away with him as fast as she could. Instead she stood up and grabbed both his shoulders, giving them a firm squeeze.

Dr. Webber said, "The hospital isn't all that bad, Tanner. Your mom can stay here with you." He folded his arms over his chest and assumed a stern expression. "And they have a Nintendo on Pediatrics that you *have* to play with. Doctor's orders!"

Tanner considered this last bit of information. Nintendo was good. He'd always wanted one, but his mother kept saying it would ruin his mind. She said kids got addicted to it and played it all the time instead of doing more important things like reading a book, or doing their homework, or playing outside in the fresh air. But if the doctor said he *had* to play with it here, then surely she wouldn't say no to that. Right?

Dr. Webber asked Jennifer, "Who is your family doctor?"

"Dr. Singleton."

"Good man," Webber said with an approving nod. "I'll give him a call and let him know what's going on. He'll probably come by and see Tanner in the morning."

He reached over and clapped a hand on Tanner's shoulder. "So, what do you say, Tanner? Think you can handle one night here at the Nintendo Hotel?"

Tanner chewed his lip, looking back and forth from his mother to the doctor. Then he shrugged.

"Okay," he said. "If I gotta."

2

Jennifer briefly filled Carny in on the X-ray findings and the need to spend the night at the hospital.

"Would you mind going back to my place and sticking that cookie dough in the fridge?" Jennifer asked.

"No problem. Be happy to. And I'll take Scotch over to my place for the night so she doesn't get too lonely."

Jennifer looked back at her with grateful affection. "Thanks, Carny. I don't know what I'd do without you." She sandwiched Carny's hands between her own, giving them a gentle squeeze.

Carny smiled at her. "Hey, what's a best friend for? Don't worry about a thing except Tanner. If you need anything, call me. Okay?"

Jennifer nodded.

"I'm sure Tanner will be fine."

Jennifer said nothing, not wanting to contradict her friend, but just as fearful of tempting the fates by agreeing with her.

Carny sighed deeply. "Are you going to be okay?"

"I'll be fine," Jennifer said unconvincingly.

Carny studied her a moment, her head cocked to one side. "Want me to come back later?" she offered.

Jennifer shook her head. "No, thanks anyway. I'll call you if I need anything."

Carny paused, seeming to weigh Jennifer's conviction. "All right then," she said, turning Jennifer in the direction of the exam area. "Get back in there before Tanner gets too spooked and decides to go AWOL." She gave Jennifer a little shove on the butt. "If he gets discharged in the morning, call me and I'll come to pick you up." With that, Carny left.

Half an hour later, Jennifer and Tanner were holed up in a pleasant but antiseptic room on the pediatric floor. Despite the casual air created by the colorful cartoon wall murals and a playroom loaded with every conceivable toy known to man, Jennifer couldn't help but be reminded of her own stay in the hospital eight years earlier. The multitude of white coats, the slightly acrid smell of the iodine solution that seemed to be used everywhere, and the gentle squeak of crepe-soled shoes all carried with them memories she had tried so hard to suppress—memories of pain and suffering and abject misery. Time had done much to heal the physical damage, but it had done little with the emotional consequences. Those wounds, it seemed, were still fresh enough to manifest themselves in showers of fright and depression now that she was inside a hospital again. Though she knew hospitals were meant to be places of good medicine and healing, the only association she could summon up was one of incredible physical pain. If she had to go through those two months of agony today, she doubted she would have the strength to survive it. She almost hadn't survived it then.

As bad as the pain had been (and at times, it had been excruciating), it wasn't the only source of her suffering. With time, the physical pain had become bearable. But rather than providing an interval of relief, all it did was free up space in her mind for the mental agonies to move in. Tim's death was a reality she hadn't wanted to face. Gone was the future she had so carefully planned. Gone was the father of her child. Gone was the rest of her life. Or so it had seemed at the time. She had come to look forward to those injections of mind-numbing pain medications that allowed her to slip off into an artificial sleep and dream of Tim alive and whole again, his crooked smile gazing back at her, his gentle hands holding her. When the effects of the medication inevitably wore off, reality would come crashing down on her, its weight more than she thought she could bear. She became so dependent on the state of listless apathy induced by the drugs that she experienced an almost-violent anger when they were stopped. It was many months later before she was able to look back on that time with enough objectivity to realize that she was addicted—both mentally and physically—to the narcotic effects. Had it not been for her love for her son and Carny's unfailing support, she doubted if she would have ever returned from that period of separation from the world.

Now, as she settled into a chair next to Tanner's hospital bed, Jennifer wondered how she could have ever welcomed death. The thought of being separated from Tanner left her with such an intense sense of loss, it was an almost-physical pain. As she watched him sitting cross-legged on the bed, wearing yellow pajamas decorated with *Scooby Doo* characters, and laughing as the nurse let him listen to his heart with her stethoscope, she felt a near-desperate love for him. She was consumed by a need to protect him, to shelter him from the painful realities of life.

Her eyes studied him: that shock of dark hair hanging down on his forehead, long, sooty lashes most women would kill to have, the fine layer of down that covered his ruddy cheeks, his bare feet sticking out from the bottoms of pajama pants that were a size too big for him. Oddly, it was the sight of his feet that triggered yet another memory of that long-ago time.

It was during the period when she had been struggling with her desire to let go, to seek the peace of mind and body that it seemed only death could bring. Carny had sneaked Tanner onto the floor, for they didn't normally allow babies to visit. She had settled him in Jennifer's lap, taking care to avoid her injured leg and the traction that was rigged up over half the bed. Tanner, his cherubic face smiling at her from her lap, had wriggled and cooed, flailing his tiny arms and legs with the joy of seeing her face. In the process, he kicked off one of his booties. She remembered staring at his tiny foot, studying the creases in his sole, being fascinated by the delicate perfection of his toenails. His feet had looked so fragile, so soft and vulnerable and perfect. A surge of maternal protectiveness had coursed through her—a feral, almost primeval feeling. Almost as if she was a creature of the wild, struggling to survive and protect her young. Love for her son had welled up inside her, consuming her, an emotion as old and eternal as time itself.

It had been a turning point for her, giving her the motivation to live, the drive to heal. Watching him now, she felt that same surge of ferocious, almost-painful love and was stricken with a fear that she would lose him—and with him, herself. *Please, God*, she thought. *Let him be okay.*

The evening passed quickly enough as she and Tanner played video games together (now was no time to be concerned with the possible ill effects of Nintendo) and shared a dinner of macaroni and cheese, corn, and cherry cobbler. It was after ten when Tanner's eyes started to take on a familiar, heavy-lidded appearance. He fought his sleepiness for a while, aided by his excitement over the strangeness of his surroundings. But eventually he succumbed, curling up on his side like a roly-poly bug, his head tucked half under the covers. Jennifer settled herself in the chair, gazing out the window at the lit parking lot below, watching the employees for the new shift arrive, and listening to the gentle sound of her son's breathing.

Though she was exhausted, sleep eluded her. She shifted and squirmed in the chair, trying to find a comfortable position. Each time she thought she had it, a nurse entered the room and ran Tanner through the same barrage of tests they had been performing all evening. Every hour they woke him, shined a flashlight into his eyes, asked him questions to check his orientation, and made him perform a number of little hand and eye coordination tasks. Jennifer watched from the chair, smiling despite herself as Tanner's answers became more irritable with each entreaty. She envied his ability to drop back into sleep, while she only managed to snatch a few minutes of light dozing. Consequently, neither of them was in the best of moods when a breakfast tray arrived a little after seven.

Jennifer gratefully accepted a cup of coffee from one of the nurses and sipped it as she watched Tanner pick at a plate of anemic-looking scrambled eggs and bacon.

"Aren't you hungry?" she asked him.

Tanner frowned, stabbed at a piece of bacon, and held it aloft on the end of his fork. The ends of the bacon strip drooped like the ears on a basset hound. "This is gross," he said. "It's floppy. I hate floppy bacon!" He flung the meat back down at the plate, but it flew off the fork prematurely and landed on the blanket.

"Tanner!"

He scowled back at her, dropped his fork on the plate with a clatter, and threw himself back against the pillow. He crossed his arms tightly over his chest, his lower lip stuck out defiantly.

Jennifer sighed, glanced at her watch, and hoped someone would come in soon and tell them they could go home. She shifted in the chair, felt her cramped muscles complain, and stretched in an effort to relieve them. Just then, a man wearing one of the ubiquitous white lab coats breezed into the room.

"Good morning!" he said with a cheerfulness that neither of the other two people in the room shared. He was very tall—well over six feet—and had the lean, hard body of a runner. His movements were fluid and graceful as he reached out a hand to Jennifer. She took it, a little surprised at how warm it was. As best as she could recall, it seemed that everyone who worked in a hospital had cold hands. His grip was firm and confident, and she briefly studied the long fingers. As her eyes roved upward, they met a very squared jaw and a wide mouth that smiled amiably. A deep dimple graced one cheek, and deep-set, green eyes gazed back at her through wire-rimmed glasses that sat above a nose that appeared to have been broken once or twice, but was otherwise rather patrician. His hair was dark blond with a few wisps of white, parted on one side. Though it was obvious he had tried to tame it straight back from his high forehead, it fell forward over his right eye. Despite an aura that seemed to exude a certain confidence and self-assurance, when he released her hand he combed his fingers through the errant lock of hair on his forehead in a self-conscious gesture.

"I'm Dr. Singleton," he said, smiling down at her.

Jennifer frowned. "No, you're not," she said, feeling a little disconcerted. She was so tired her mind felt fuzzy, but she was alert enough to know that this man was not Dr. Singleton. Though she and Tanner had been blessed with generally good health over the years, they had still had occasion to visit the doctor's office for minor injuries, flus, physicals, and such. Dr. Singleton was a somewhat portly, elderly gentleman in his fifties or sixties, with warm brown eyes, white hair, and a white beard that gave him an uncanny resemblance to Colonel Sanders. Jennifer stared at the impostor, her suspicions roused and her maternal hackles up, waiting for an explanation.

The stranger opened his mouth, presumably to explain himself, but Tanner spoke up first. "You're Dr. Singleton's son," he said from the bed.

The man turned toward Tanner with a puzzled smile. "That's right," he said. His brows drew together until they almost met over the bridge of his nose. "Have we met?"

Jennifer, looking as puzzled as the doctor, stared at Tanner and said, "No. How do you know this man, Tanner?"

Tanner shrugged. "I don't know." His hands picked at the ribs in his blanket. "I just . . . know," he said with a half smile.

Jennifer shifted her attention back to the doctor. She was sure she had never seen him before. In fact, she wasn't even aware Dr. Singleton had a son. And had she known, she never would have guessed that the man standing before her was in any way related to the short and rotund Dr. Singleton they knew.

"He's adopted, Mom," Tanner said.

Jennifer's jaw dropped as she whipped her head around to stare at her son.

"You seem to have me at a disadvantage here," Dr. Singleton said, shifting his feet uneasily. "How did you know that?"

Again Tanner shrugged. "You said so," he answered, but his voice lacked conviction. He was staring down at the blanket where he had succeeded in working loose a long thread. "I heard you."

"He didn't say any such thing, Tanner," Jennifer said, shooting a worried glance at the doctor.

"But I *heard* him," Tanner insisted. He looked over at his mother with a wide-eyed plea.

There was a long, awkward moment of silence, during which Jennifer and Tanner gaped at one another, and the doctor gaped at them both. Then Dr. Singleton cleared his throat with a little "ahem" and approached the bed. He pulled a penlight from his pocket and said, "Let me take a look at those pupils." He shined the light into first one eye, then the other. He then ran Tanner through the same series of tests and questions that the nurses had been requiring all night. Jennifer watched anxiously, feeling confused, stunned, and a little frightened.

"Well, he seems fine," Dr. Singleton said when he was done. He stuck his hands in his pockets and stared at Tanner a moment, his expression concerned. "I don't see why he can't go home. But I'd like to see him again in the office in a few days."

Jennifer nodded, still staring at Tanner. She had a thousand questions she wanted to ask but was too dumbstruck by Tanner's little performance to voice them.

"Be sure and specify Eric Singleton when you make the appointment," the doctor said. "Though he's planning on retiring soon, my father is still at the office, and it gets a little confusing at times."

Finally Jennifer shifted her gaze to the doctor. "Are you sure he's okay?" she asked.

"Everything checks out. All of his vital and neuro signs are normal. He's a lucky boy. If anything untoward happens, call me. But I think he'll be fine."

Jennifer nodded.

"See you in the office then," he said. He turned and, with his white coat flapping behind him, left the room.

Jennifer watched him go, fighting an urge to run after him and drag him back, to make him check one more time, just to be sure. After a moment, she turned to Tanner. "How did you know all those things about Dr. Singleton?" she asked him.

"He *said* them," Tanner snapped.

"He did not, Tanner. And please don't use that tone of voice with me." Jennifer took a deep breath and tried to calm herself. It had been a long, sleepless night for both of them. "Tanner, honey, I was sitting right here, and I never heard him say anything about being adopted."

"Well, I did!" Tanner's face turned a dark shade of red and he resumed his posture of defiance: arms crossed, lip pouting, face scowling.

Jennifer chewed the inside of her cheek and debated whether or not to push the issue. She didn't want to upset him; the past twenty-four hours had been trying enough. And surely there was some simple explanation for what had happened. Maybe Tanner had overheard something one of the nurses said.

"What do you say we get you dressed and go home?" she said finally, deciding to let the matter drop. "I'll bet Scotch is wondering where in the heck you are."

At the mention of his dog, Tanner's face brightened. "Okay," he said, throwing back the covers and bounding out of the bed. "If I gotta."

Later that afternoon, Jennifer was sitting on her couch, her hands wrapped around a steaming mug of coffee, while Carny was curled up in the chair next to her, holding her own mug, her feet tucked up beneath her. A plate of cookies sat on the coffee table between them. Scotch and Tanner rolled around on the floor playing a game of tug-of-war with one of Tanner's socks. It was an activity Jennifer generally discouraged, as Scotch had developed a habit of chewing holes in all of Tanner's socks. But the sound of Tanner's laughter and the semblance of normalcy it lent the day left her not only tolerant, but grateful.

The day had been comfortably warm and the air

smelled clean and sun-baked. Jennifer had left the front door propped open to let the early evening breeze in through the screen door. The sun had taken on a fiery glow, and as it moved toward the tops of the trees in the bordering woods, its rose-colored light streamed in through the doorway and the windows, highlighting every speck of dust in the room. Jennifer sighed.

"What's wrong?" Carny asked.

"Oh, nothing really. I was just realizing how long it's been since I last dusted." She ran the back of her hand across her forehead and fluttered her eyes. "A woman's work is never done," she said with great melodrama.

Carny laughed. "You got that right!"

Jennifer smiled back at her and then reached forward to grab a couple of cookies off the plate. "It was really sweet of you to bake up these cookies for me," she said.

"Hey? What's a best friend for?" Carny dropped her voice to a conspiratorial whisper and winked. "Besides, they're my favorite, too."

Jennifer marveled, not for the first time, at the incredible friend she had in Carny. Actually, "friend" was inadequate; in the eight years she had known her, Carny had become the sister she'd never had.

They had met on Jennifer's first day as a teacher at Hillenberg Elementary—in fact, her first day as a teacher *anywhere*. After graduating from college, she had been unable to find any immediate openings. Then she became pregnant with Tanner and decided to spend her pregnancy playing housewife. It had bored her almost to tears, so that she was looking forward to the baby's birth with an almost-obsessive anticipation. Though Tanner kept her plenty busy those first few months, when a job opened up at one of the local elementary schools, Jennifer decided to take it. The decision was made with great inner turmoil, as it meant finding day care for Tanner, something she was not particularly thrilled over. But the need to do something with her education and training was overpowering, and the memory of all those months of stifling boredom was still fresh in her mind.

Her anxiety level that first day on the job was off the scale, both because of the newness of it and the discomfort she felt over relegating Tanner's care to strangers. Her fears were hardly alleviated when one of the students in her class spent the better part of the morning blowing spitballs at her whenever her back was turned. By the time lunch rolled around, she had retreated to the teacher's lounge, feeling frustrated and angry.

Not knowing any of the other teachers in the room, she had taken a seat near the window and opened her lunch sack, intending to enjoy a few minutes of quiet solitude. And maybe by eavesdropping on the conversations of the others, she could pick up some hints. She had taken one bite out of her sandwich when the door to the lounge opened and a slender, attractive woman with long, dark hair came in and dropped into the seat beside her.

"What have I done?" the woman drawled, shaking her head and letting out a heavy sigh.

Jennifer studied the woman a moment before she said, "Bad day?"

The woman tittered and rolled her eyes. "Now that's the understatement of the year!" She shook her head in frustration. "What ever made me think I wanted a career as a teacher?"

"I know what you mean," Jennifer agreed. "Today is my first day, and I spent most of the morning trying to figure out who was spewing spitballs at me."

"Your first day?"

Jennifer nodded.

"Mine, too." She smiled warmly and extended a hand. "Carny Calahan."

Jennifer returned the smile and shook the proffered hand. "Jennifer Bolton. Nice to meet you."

"Spitballs are nothing," Carny said with a dismissive wave of her hand. "I found a live frog in one of my desk drawers and someone Super-Glued the chalk to the tray."

"You're kidding!" Jennifer laughed so hard, she almost choked on a bite of her sandwich.

"Wish I was."

They talked all through lunch that day—and the next and the next—until it became a ritual. They commiserated over the trials and tribulations of trying to teach what Carny referred to as "the little monsters." They shared details of their personal lives: Carny's frustrations over her nonexistent dating life and the dearth of available single men, Jennifer's frustrations over having a man who was never home. Their friendship eventually extended to the hours beyond school, and when Carny's elderly neighbors announced that they were putting their family home up for sale in preparation for a move to warmer climes, Jennifer jumped on it.

She had fallen in love with the place immediately. It was constructed of sturdy brick, built back when houses were made to last. The rooms were large and airy, with huge windows that admitted plenty of light. Granted, some of the doors had a tendency to stick, the plumbing clanged and groaned when the water was on, and the floor in the kitchen was a bit crooked, but the location—nestled in the woods where there was plenty of room for Tanner to play without fear of traffic and other city dangers—was ideal. The fact that Carny lived in the next house over eliminated any final doubts.

They had been in the house only two months when Tim died.

It was Carny who held things together, caring for Tanner while Jennifer recuperated. Their bond grew even stronger, its growth magnified by the horrors that life had wrought. It was during this time that Jennifer told Carny about her mother, the fact that she was willing to share this darker side of her life offering testament to the value Jennifer placed on their friendship. Aside from Tim, Carny was the only person who knew the horrible truth that had led to an estrangement so complete, Jennifer told everyone she met that her mother was deceased.

Over the years, Jennifer was, at times, perplexed by the closeness of her relationship with Carny, for they couldn't have been more different. Where Carny was dark, petite, and willowy, Jennifer was tall, well rounded, and fair. While Carny worked full-time and had to count every penny, Jennifer only worked part-time now as a substitute. Tim's life insurance policies and a settlement from the gas truck company had left her with close to three-quarters of a million dollars. She had paid off the house, bought a new car, tucked away a nest egg for Tanner's college education, and banked the rest, living off the interest on her savings and investments. She really didn't have to work at all. Still, she enjoyed teaching, enjoyed the children, enjoyed her coworkers. And once Tanner was old enough to attend school, her schedule meshed well with his, eliminating the need for baby-sitters or day care.

She and Carny were even different with regard to their social lives. While Carny had carried on a string of short-term, rather emotionally charged relationships with a variety of men, Jennifer had been content for the most part to devote herself to raising Tanner and keeping Tim's memory alive. It was only recently that she had allowed herself to bury Tim once and for all and venture into the world of dating.

Tanner derailed Jennifer's train of thought. "Can I go outside and play with Scotch, Mom?"

Jennifer hesitated. She wanted to keep a close eye on him, despite the doctor's assurances that he was okay and the fact that he seemed to have no residual effects from all that had happened. But she didn't want to turn him into a housebound hypochondriac either.

"Okay," she said reluctantly. "But just in the yard. Stay out of the woods."

Tanner propelled himself off the floor and out the door. Scotch, ears flapping and tongue lolling, was close on his heels. Both women cringed as the screen door slammed shut with a loud bang.

"Ahh," Jennifer said with a grin. "Life has returned to normal."

Carny smiled briefly, then cautiously broached the subject that neither of them had wanted to discuss in Tanner's presence. "That's pretty weird about the metal in Tanner's head," she said

Jennifer nodded her agreement. "I know. Thank goodness it hasn't hurt him any." She watched through the screen as Tanner tossed a ball around the yard, and Scotch fetched it back. "Still, I can't help but worry about it." She shifted her gaze back to Carny. "There's something about the idea of a chunk of metal sitting in my son's brain that doesn't exactly fill me with a sense of calm."

"It *is* a bit scary," Carny agreed. "Has Tanner said anything about it?"

"No. In fact he has avoided the whole subject. I think he's still upset over Tim," she added, flicking her thumbnail against her finger and frowning.

Carny cocked her head in puzzlement. "Upset over his death you mean?"

"Not exactly. More over the circumstances of his death. He never knew before about the explosion, or that he and I were also involved, until he heard me explaining it to the doctor last night."

"You mean you never told him?"

Jennifer cast her friend a guilty look. "I didn't see any point in giving him the gory details," she said defensively. "I thought it might give him nightmares or something."

Carny shrugged and took a sip of her coffee. "You're probably right. Although I doubt hearing the details now has bothered him that much. It all happened so long ago, and it isn't like Tanner remembers Tim or anything. I'll bet he's already forgotten about it."

"Maybe," Jennifer said unconvincingly, recalling the shocked look on Tanner's face in the ER. She was saved from further self-flagellation by the sound of a car pulling up outside and Tanner's voice hollering from the yard.

"Mom! Evan's here."

Carny set down her coffee cup and unfolded herself from the chair. "That's my cue. I'm outta here," she said. "Catch you later."

Jennifer walked Carny to the door, and they both watched through the screen as Evan Reeves climbed out of his silver Porsche and brushed irritably at the dust settling on his shirt. Country living was not in Evan's blood, and the endless dust was one of his pet peeves. He was a compulsively neat person, and his endless parade of suits were always impeccably pressed and clean. His house—a modern, sprawling rancher in one of the more eclectic suburbs—more closely matched Carny's tastes. It was done over in the latest contemporary style, with little clutter and lots of wide-open spaces. Whenever Jennifer and Tanner visited there, Jennifer felt as if she was fighting a never-ending battle to keep her dirt magnet of a son from leaving smudges and fingerprints on everything he came in contact with. Still, despite their differences, she liked Evan.

She had met him last fall at a cocktail party put on by the school district in an effort to rally support for a school bond issue that was on the upcoming ballot. It was the first social event Jennifer had gone to since Tim's death, and then only under duress after weeks of badgering from Carny. Later, she had to admit she had thoroughly enjoyed herself, though she suspected her enjoyment was due, in part, to being more than a little starstruck by all the celebrities that were there: politicians, philanthropists, a well-known author, some local news anchors, and even the actress, Sissy Spacek, who lived on a farm outside of Charlottesville. Watching Carny make the rounds, eliciting all the latest gossip and exercising her well-honed flirting skills on every man in the room, had only added to the fun.

Surrounded by all the glamour and feeling attractive and feminine for the first time in years, Jennifer was primed for Evan's good looks, warm smile, and flirtatious banter. He weaseled a phone number out of her, then pushed his luck even further by coaxing her into a dinner date later in the week. Over the months that had ensued, he had wooed her slowly and carefully, using all of his charm (and he had loads of it), to convince her to give him a chance.

She had succumbed eventually, though the battle was not particularly painful. At forty, Evan cut a fine picture. Though his hair had lost most of its original black color, it had been replaced by a silvery shade that set well against his tanned skin and cornflower blue eyes. He was tall and trim, though well muscled, with broad shoulders left over from his college swim team days. And he had a keen mind, which combined with his effusive charm, made him one of the most sought-after lawyers in the state.

His relationship with Jennifer suited her just fine. He was there without being intrusive. He had never pushed her and had, in fact, shown incredible patience while she struggled to let go of her image of herself as Tim's wife.

The relationship had existed on a level somewhere between friendship and true love for several months now, and neither of them seemed to be in a hurry to change things. The bow on all these wrappings was his rapport with Tanner.

As Jennifer and Carny watched Evan through the door, the afternoon light reflecting off the strands of silver gave his hair a warm reddish glow. He looked toward the door, saw the two women watching him, and waved. Then he went around to the trunk of his car, opened it, and pulled out a large, square, gift-wrapped box. He called Tanner over and stood smiling as the boy wasted no time turning the gift wrap into shreds, while Butterscotch hopped all around him, barking and wagging her tail excitedly.

"Cool!" Tanner yelled. From the box he removed a shiny, fluorescent blue bicycle helmet. He held it aloft for his mother to see, then promptly placed it on his head.

"Damn, Jennifer," Carny said wistfully. "Handsome as hell and great with your kid, too. Some women have all the luck."

Jennifer smiled. She did feel lucky. "Your day will come, Carny. You just haven't met the right guy yet. But he's out there."

"I suppose." She turned and planted a quick kiss on Jennifer's cheek. "Gotta run. See you later." She bounded out the door and toward the path in the woods, exchanging a quick greeting with Evan as she passed. Still wearing his helmet, Tanner ran off with Scotch, and Evan closed the trunk of the car and headed toward the house.

When he was inside, he placed a light butterfly kiss on Jennifer's forehead. "Tanner seems to be doing okay," he observed.

"Thank goodness. I don't think I've ever been so scared in all my life."

"You look tired," he said, holding her shoulders at arm's length and studying her face.

"I am. I don't think Tanner or I slept more than a half hour total last night. Though he seems to have a lot bigger second wind than I do."

Evan chuckled. "I've got ten bucks that says he'll be out like a light by eight."

"No takers here."

"How about if I take you two out for dinner tonight? You don't look like someone who wants to cook."

"That would be nice. Let me get freshened up a bit first." Jennifer went to the door and yelled. "Tanner? Time for you and Scotch to come in and get cleaned up. Evan is taking us out for dinner."

"Okay, Mom. Be right there." Tanner tossed a grungy tennis ball across the yard and laughed as he watched Butterscotch bound after it. Then he took off after her, while Jennifer smiled at the fluorescent blue of his head as he disappeared around the corner of the house.

"Rough day in court?" Jennifer asked as she started up her Maxima. They were taking her car since Tanner couldn't fit comfortably into the back of the Porsche. Evan sat beside her, one hand resting on her thigh.

"Not too bad," Evan said with a sardonic chuckle. "The attorney for the plaintiff only had ten tricks up his sleeve today."

"How's the case going?"

"Well, I think. Though you never know with these malpractice suits. Sympathy plays a big part in the jury's decision. And with the woman's loss of childbearing abilities, it could go either way."

"You're going to lose," Tanner said from the backseat.

"Tanner!" Jennifer frowned at her son in the rearview mirror.

"Well, he is," Tanner said matter-of-factly.

"There is no way for anyone to know what's going to happen yet, Tanner. And it's very impolite of you to be so pessimistic."

"What's pessimistic?"

"It's being too negative," Jennifer explained.

"That's okay," Evan said. "He may be right."

"That's not the point. Tanner, I want you to apologize to Evan."

"Why?"

"Because you've been rude."

"I'm just saying what I know."

"You don't know. You *can't* know." Jennifer took a deep breath and flexed her fingers on the steering wheel. "I don't understand what has gotten into you, Tanner Bolton. You've been acting awfully strange since your fall. All that jabber this morning about Dr. Singleton . . ."

"I *heard* him, Mom!"

"No, you did not!" Jennifer fought back an urge to cry. She was so tired, and Tanner's strange behavior was starting to wear on her nerves. "Why are you lying about this?"

"All right, you guys," Evan interrupted, holding up both hands. "Let's call a truce here, shall we? You're both tired and a little cranky. Let's not let the evening be spoiled."

Jennifer took in a deep breath and blew it out between pursed lips. "I'm sorry, Evan," she said. "You're right."

She drove the rest of the way to the restaurant in silence, occasionally glancing at Tanner's sullen, pouting face in the mirror. She hated to see him so glum, but his strange behavior frightened her. Maybe, she thought, it was the knowledge of the circumstances surrounding

Tim's death that had him acting so weird. She made a mental note to discuss it with him after they had both had some sleep.

Dinner was good, but there was an aura of tension that hung in the air. Even Jennifer's favorite linguini with clam sauce couldn't take away from the tremendous exhaustion that had claimed her ever since the argument in the car. Consequently, she was glad when Evan offered to drive home.

Sensing that she was in no mood for company, Evan brushed his lips against hers as they stood in the doorway. "Tomorrow will be a better day," he said. "With a little sleep under your belt, you'll feel like a new woman."

"I hope so," she said without enthusiasm. The strain of the last day or so had left her feeling as though she would never be right again.

"It will. Trust me." He kissed her again, a little harder this time, said, "I'll call you tomorrow," and then was gone.

Jennifer found Tanner in the kitchen downing a glass of Kool-Aid. "Run upstairs and get into your pj's, Tanner," she told him. "And remember to brush your teeth. I'll be up in a minute." Though it was only a little after eight, Jennifer could tell from the half-mast cast of Tanner's eyelids that he was tired. Her own body fairly screamed for some rest, and she couldn't wait to get into bed herself.

She let Butterscotch out while she freshened up the dog's food and water and rinsed out Tanner's glass. When she was let back in, Butterscotch bounded up the stairs toward Tanner's room. Jennifer knew she'd find the dog in Tanner's bed, but she had long ago given up on trying to break the habit. After checking to make sure all the doors were locked, she started up the stairs.

She was about halfway up when she heard the sound.

At first, she thought it was the wind soughing through the eaves, but then the sound became more guttural. She froze, feeling the hair on the back of her neck rise. The sound came again—a soulful, keening whine, followed by a whimper—and it was coming from the direction of Tanner's bedroom.

She took the rest of the stairs two at a time and hurried down the hall to find both Scotch and Tanner standing in the middle of Tanner's room. Scotch was whining and tugging at Tanner's shirtsleeve, as if she was trying to pull him down. At first Jennifer thought the two were playing, but when she saw the look on Tanner's face, she felt her blood run cold. He was standing dead still, his eyes glazed over, staring off into space.

"Tanner?"

He made no motion to indicate that he had heard her. Scotch whined louder and yanked at his sleeve with her teeth.

"Tanner!"

Still no response. Jennifer reached out and touched his arm. It felt cold as ice. Scotch was fairly frantic now in her attempts to pull the boy down.

"Stop it, Scotch!"

Scotch let go of the sleeve and stepped back, though she continued to stare at Tanner and whine pitifully. Jennifer grabbed Tanner's shoulders and shook him.

"Tanner? Look at me! Tanner?"

Suddenly the boy's eyes shifted. Jennifer saw him focus in on her face.

"Tanner? Are you all right?"

He said nothing at first; he simply stared at her with a slightly puzzled expression. Then an odd smile crawled across his face—a smile that made Jennifer think of a lunatic character she had seen on an episode of *Tales from the Crypt*. She shivered.

"It was Dad," Tanner said. His voice had a ghostly, almost-ethereal quality to it.

Jennifer's arms pimpled with gooseflesh. "What?" she hissed.

"It was Dad," he repeated. Though he appeared to be looking at her, his eyes had a dreamy, faraway look. "I was talking to Dad."

At first Jennifer was stunned. Then she breathed a miniscule sigh of relief. She had feared there was something terribly wrong with Tanner physically, some leftover vestige from that chunk of steel in his head. Instead it was psychological. Most likely a combination of his exhaustion from the night before and the emotional upheaval he had experienced when he learned the truth about his father's death. Psychological problems weren't great, but they weren't life-threatening. They could be fixed. A little talking, a lot of love, maybe even some counseling. Whatever it took, they could beat it.

She opened her mouth to tell Tanner it was okay, opened her arms to pull him into her, but before she could utter a single word his head jerked, his eyes rolled back, his teeth clenched together, and his whole body began to tremble.

Scotch barked—a loud, piercing bark that made Jennifer jump—and grabbed at Tanner's sleeve with her teeth again, this time succeeding in pulling the boy down. Tanner began to twitch all over, his hands clenched into fists, his head thrown back, his eyes rolled up in their sockets. The twitches grew in strength until his whole body was in spasm.

"Oh, God! Tanner!"

Jennifer tried to hold him still, but his thrashing was too strong. She gave up on his flailing arms and legs and tried instead to keep a firm grip on his head, holding it in her lap to keep it from banging against the floor. His body twitched violently, and tiny curds of white foam formed at the corners of his mouth. Jennifer watched helplessly, wanting to run and call for help but afraid to leave his wracked and tortured body long enough to do so. Tears streamed down her face, and she began to mumble.

"Oh, God! What's happening? Tanner, please stop. Tanner, *please* stop!"

Scotch lay beside them, her eyes fixed on the convulsing boy.

"Tanner, please stop. Tanner, please stop. Please, please, please stop."

She continued her chant, her voice growing more desperate with each repetition, until she saw that Tanner was turning blue. Then her chant gave way to choking, gasping sobs.

She shifted her position and tried to cradle his head in her hands so she could give him mouth-to-mouth, but he was thrashing about so much, she couldn't get her lips on his. So she continued to hold his head, rocking back and forth on her knees, fearing he was dying, yet refusing to let her mind even consider the gut-wrenching possibility, knowing instinctively that if her son died, she would, too.

"Please, God, no-o-o-o-o!"

Almost as suddenly as it had started, the twitching stopped. Jennifer lowered her head and stared at Tanner's face, her hands shaking, her chest heaving with sobs, afraid of what her son would look like dead.

His body lay still and flaccid, as limp and lifeless as a rag doll. Jennifer felt the first crack in the mirror that was her mind. In a moment, she knew, the whole thing would shatter into tiny pieces.

Tanner's chest moved.

Jennifer swiped a hand across her eyes to clear them and fixed her gaze on his chest, part of her disbelieving, part of her willing it to move again. She waited. His chest rose and descended . . . rose and descended. The white foam on his lips formed a small bubble and popped.

Jennifer raised her eyes to the ceiling and whispered, "Thank you, God!"

As the frightening purple hue of Tanner's skin gradually faded back to its normal pink, Jennifer gently lowered his head to the floor. Then she stood up on trembling legs and made her way to her room, where she dialed 9-1-1.

3

About the time Tanner Bolton was convulsing on his bedroom floor, Barry "Butch" Hanover was heading out the door of the Redeye Bar and Grill, his home away from home of late. He stumbled across the threshold, grinning stupidly, accompanied by the hollers of the coworkers he was leaving behind still snugged up to the bar.

"Go home and get some for me, Butch!"

"Shame you got that ball and chain around your neck!"

As the door closed behind him, Butch heard John Mueller order another round of shots for the bar. He stood there on the front stoop, his eyes glazed, his body wavering like a reed in the wind, and for one long, teetering moment, debated turning around and going back inside. Then, as if a hypnotist had snapped his fingers, he came to life, spit on the ground, and stepped off the stoop to meander his way toward his pickup.

He was feeling pretty good some twenty minutes later when he pulled onto the rutted mud track that served as his driveway. A half dozen or so shots of whiskey with beer chasers *always* left him feeling pretty good. The pickup bounced along the road like a bingo ball and Butch remembered, as he did every night, that the truck needed a new set of shocks. Just another item on the list of "things needin' doin'" as Eliza always called it. But there never seemed to be enough time or enough money to work on that shitty little list. There was always something more important, like unwinding down at the Redeye with the boys or shooting a few racks of pool. He knew Eliza would start harping about it the minute she had half a chance and prayed that she'd be in bed when he got home. Butch hated to waste a good high by having to try and act sober while she slammed into him for the hundredth time about his drinking.

The woman simply couldn't understand that a man had certain needs. He worked his ass off in that god-damned packing plant—had been for five years now—and if he wanted a little peace and quiet and time to unwind with the boys before going home to a houseful of scream-ing brats, then by God he'd earned it! If that dumb bitch, Eliza, was too thick to understand that, then maybe he'd have to try again to knock some damned sense into her! After all, he was a man! Not some pussy-whipped young boy still wet behind the ears!

You'd think that after eight years of marriage, the woman would have him figured out, understand his needs. But, no! The dumb bitch just kept harping on him, night after night after night after night. Always the same old shit about his health suffering, and how the alcohol was killing him.

As he rolled up in front of the house, he belched loudly and grimaced—not from the belch, but because he could hear Eliza's damn whining voice inside his head, lecturing at him the way she always did. Hell, she'd actually gotten him worried enough that he even went to see the doc for a checkup a few months ago. Okay, so there were a few things wrong—some enzymes that shouldn't have been up, were, or some horseshit like that. But the doc had given him some vitamin injections, and now he was feeling better than ever.

He climbed out of the truck, swaying slightly, and stood a moment staring at the house, trying to get his balance in check. Even at night, with the forgiveness of the dark hiding the run-down shithole he called home, he was filled with disgust when he looked at the place. They'd been living here going on four years now, and he laughed to himself as he remembered how excited he and Eliza had been when they first happened onto the dump. It was a "real house," Eliza had squealed. Not some sleazy, flea-bitten apartment like they'd had before. What a joke! Hell, the place was nothing more than an oversize rathole, stuck out in the middle of nowhere, planted square in the middle of bumfuck Egypt. The old geezer who owned the place had been happy as a pig in shit when he found someone stupid enough to rent the heap. The old fart got so excited he started wheezing like a leaky accordion, then coughing so hard his face turned blue. Butch thought the old man was gonna up and kick the bucket right there, keel over right in front of him and Eliza and the kids, just cause he finally found Mr. and Mrs. Gullible.

Butch spit on the ground. Yep, that was him. Mr. Gullible! Maybe he should write a book. Call it *Gullible's Travels*.

He laughed at his own joke, pushed himself off the truck, and wove a path toward the front porch. The house leaned at an angle, and Butch almost fell over when he tried to counterbalance himself as he climbed the steps. He crossed the porch, sidestepping the hole where the wood had rotted away (another item on the goddamned "things needin' doin'" list) and muttering to himself. He didn't bother even trying his key; Eliza never locked the door. Who'd want to take anything they had, anyway? Any dumbshit burglar desperate enough to want their junk was welcome to it.

The living room, like all the other rooms, was small

and dark and smelled of mildew. Eliza had tried to brighten up the place a bit when they'd first moved in, hanging cheap drapes and buying some furniture she rummaged up at yard sales. But it had been a hopeless cause. Like trying to dress up a toothless, sagging old woman in a cheap prom dress.

As Butch pushed the door closed behind him, he saw the thin line of white light that shone through the space under the bedroom door. He cursed under his breath, started to spit, then remembered he was in the house. Then he thought, what the hell, and hocked one out anyway.

He knew Eliza was up and waiting for him behind that door, and with the thought his head began to throb. He rubbed his temples and paced back and forth. Damn! The bitch was really starting to get on his nerves! He was in no mood for one of her screaming arguments. He'd worked hard to get his buzz on, to numb the realities of his pathetically dull life, and he'd be damned if he'd let the shrew ruin it for him! Not again! He hiked his pants up and took a deep breath. No, dammit! He wasn't gonna take any shit off her tonight!

He threw open the bedroom door, making it bang against the wall and giving him the satisfaction of seeing Eliza jump. She was in bed, the covers up to her waist, her back against the headboard, one of them trashy romance novels from the library propped open on her knees. He grinned menacingly, and she glared back at him, her mouth pulling into a fine line, her beady dark eyes piercing him.

The longer Butch stared at Eliza, the more hideous she looked. Her expression of contempt and disgust was a challenge to him, an affront. How dare she look at him like he was something that just crawled out of the earth! Hell, she came from poor white trash with a waste of a father and a drunk of a mother. She oughta be grateful he'd saved her from that shithole by getting her preggers when she was eighteen and marrying her sorry ass.

Eliza's eyes bored into him.

Butch's nerves started to jangle, and he clenched his fists as he felt his buzz start to fade away beneath a building fire of red-hot anger.

"Have a good time?" Eliza sneered at him. "How much of this week's grocery money is left? Any? Or did you suck it all down again with that bunch of idiots you call friends?"

Eliza's shrill voice scraped along Butch's spine, eliciting shudders of agony. Her flapping gums looked like an ever-widening hole that spewed forth the sewage she threw at him. Butch felt the fire inside him grow, the flames turning white-hot, licking at his brain. His nerves felt raw and exposed.

"You just never learn, do you?" Eliza taunted. She closed the book on her lap and slammed it down on the floor next to the bed. "You piss our money away like it was nothing! Look at this place!" She made a sweep with her arm. "It's a goddamned pigsty! Is this what you want out of life? Is this as good as it gets for you? Huh, Barry?"

She glared at him, leaning forward in the bed, her sagging tits lying like half-empty sacks of flour beneath the faded, cheap cotton gowns she always wore to bed. Watching her, Butch found it hard to believe he had ever found the bitch attractive. Not that it mattered now. After the sixth kid in as many years, he had finally figured out that their screaming bunch of rug rats was gonna keep on growing if he didn't stay away from her. Christ, she seemed to get pregnant if he so much as looked at her! Of course she blamed the fact that he hadn't touched her in almost two years on his drinking, too. *Everything* was blamed on his drinking. The woman couldn't understand that a man had certain needs, dammit!

"You're a pig, Eliza," he managed to mutter.

"*I'm* a pig? Me? You lazy, good-for-nothing jerk!" She hissed at him. "Look at yourself! Go ahead, take a good look in the mirror! You're nothing but a worn-out, drunken piece of shit! You're not a man! You're nothing but shit! You can't even perform like a man. That thing dangling between your legs ain't good for nothing but catching fish!" She leaned forward and grinned cruelly. "No, not even a fish would bite on that worm!" she sneered.

That did it! His buzz was totally gone, ruined again by the bitch. He drew his eyes down to a steely glint and spun on his heel from the room. He strode out to the pickup, his footing sure and steady now, sobered by anger. He yanked open the truck door, reached behind the seat, and pulled out his shotgun. Cracking the gun open to be sure both barrels were loaded, he opened the glove box and shoved another half dozen shells into his pocket. Then he went back inside.

He had the satisfaction of seeing Eliza's foul mouth form a surprised O as he leveled the gun at her.

Then he had the even greater satisfaction of blowing her brains all over the headboard before she could utter one more word of trash.

He stood there a long time, staring at what was left of Eliza, feeling his anger grow rather than ebb.

Now look what the slut had made him do! She'd made him commit murder, for Christ's sake! He'd fry for sure! And it was all her goddamned fault!

He heard a noise behind him and turned to find his eight-year-old son, Jimmy, staring at him from the doorway, his eyes wide and accusing. Damn kids! Now he had witnesses.

His anger escalated another notch and, without a moment's thought, operating on nothing more than blind fury, he leveled the gun at his son and pulled the trigger.

The blast lifted the child off the floor and threw him into the hallway wall, leaving a grotesque red smear where he slid down into a heap.

The rational part of Butch's mind was totally gone now, a passionate anger all he had left. Anger for what his life had become. Anger for what the bitch had made him do.

He jammed a hand into his pocket, reloaded the gun, and stormed into one of the other bedrooms. The other two boys were sitting in their beds, cowering and whimpering. Little faggots! Eliza had babied them too much. They'd never be real men.

One at a time, he aimed the gun and pulled the trigger.

He reloaded.

Next bedroom. The three girls. He repeated the process on the two older ones, then hesitated when he came to the baby, just one and a half. She stared up at him, eyes wide, body trembling. At first he thought he would spare this one, but then her mouth opened and a keening wail erupted, the same ear-piercing, mind-shattering cry that had kept him awake on too many nights.

Butch shoved two more shells into place, aimed, and fired.

His fury was intolerable now, consuming his mind and soul. Fury at everyone and everything. He looked at the carnage around him, smelled the acrid scent of blood and death, and knew that life had dealt him one final blow. Like things weren't hard enough for him in this world!

He punched his fist through the wall and yelled. "Son of a bitch!"

He reeled out of the room and stomped into the living room, where he started to pace, feeling the adrenaline surge through his body, feeling the heat of his frustration course through his veins. He swung his fist at a lamp, sending it crashing over, the sound of breaking glass sounding an awful lot like Eliza's shrill recriminations.

Suddenly, he stopped, and his face split into a self-satisfied grin. Dropping into a chair, he placed the barrel of the shotgun in his mouth and reached for the trigger. His arms came up a few inches short, incensing him even more.

Even the fucking gun was out to ruin him! His inadequacies fueled the flames of his anger even higher, until his entire brain felt as if it had been consumed, taken over by some alien intelligence. Butch was no longer in control.

He stormed into the kitchen and yanked open a drawer, pulling it completely out, furious as the contents spilled across the floor. He kicked at the mess with his feet, screaming a string of profanity, a strand of spittle flying from his lips to hang off his chin. His foot sent spools of thread, a tube of glue, nails, washers, and every other fucking whatnot that didn't belong someplace else shooting out across the room.

"Goddamned fucking son of a BITCH!"

He snatched up a spool of heavy-duty thread and unwound a length of it. He tied one end to the shotgun's trigger, still rattling off a stream of profanity as his fingers fumbled the knot time and again. By the time he finally had it tied, there was foaming spittle running down his chin, and his face had turned so red it looked like he might explode. He tied the other end of the thread around one of the kitchen table's legs and stepped back until the string was just shy of taut. Thrusting a leg out to the side, he snared one of the chairs with his foot and dragged it into place behind him. With a grin of grim satisfaction, he sat down and again placed the barrel in his mouth.

His feet pushed against the floor, sending the chair sliding backward. The thread tightened on the trigger, pulling it back. And Barry "Butch" Hanover was furious no more.

4

A young, female ambulance attendant pushed the foot end of Tanner's stretcher into the ambulance and explained once again why Jennifer could not ride with her son.

"It's already pretty tight back here." The attendant swept her hand through the air just inside the door. "You can see for yourself. There isn't much room. If something happens, we need to be able to move around quickly. You would be in the way."

Jennifer listened, but her eyes were focused on Tanner, or what she could see of him beneath the white sheet that covered him up to his chin. The female attendant's male counterpart locked the stretcher into place, repositioned Tanner's oxygen mask, and then busied himself laying out a variety of other gear: blood pressure cuff, stethoscope, ophthalmoscope, bottles of liquids, bags of fluids, syringes. He lined them up along the edge of the stretcher, creating a moat of medical paraphernalia around Tanner. The scene seemed to emphasize the female attendant's words, "If something happens . . ."

Even though Tanner had been moving some in the house by the time the ambulance arrived, he was now perfectly still. Jennifer knew he was scared to death, frightened by what had happened, frightened by all the unfamiliar faces and gadgetry, frightened because his mommy wasn't in there with him. Once more she considered arguing with the female attendant. But she realized the girl was too young to understand her depth of emotion, that protective bond between a mother and her child, so she remained quiet and acquiescent, realizing that all she was likely to accomplish was a delay in getting Tanner to the hospital.

Still, when the female attendant climbed into the back of the ambulance and started to close the door, Jennifer grabbed the door's edge, holding it a moment while she called to Tanner.

"Tanner? Honey? I'll be right behind you. Don't worry. I'm here."

The female attendant smiled tolerantly and tugged on the door. Reluctantly, Jennifer let it go and scurried over to her Maxima to follow.

The ambulance used its emergency lights, but not the siren, as it wound its way down Highway 6, the red light casting an ethereal glow on the trees and fields that bordered the road. Jennifer kept pace, following as close behind as she dared, watching the goings-on in the back of the ambulance through the two small windows. So far, everything seemed calm in there. Maybe too calm. *Why are they going so slow?* She fought down a compulsion to drive up to the back bumper of the ambulance and nudge it into moving faster.

Jennifer was relieved when she saw that Dr. Webber was again on duty, but no sooner had Tanner been transferred from the ambulance to one of the ER stretchers than the younger Dr. Singleton appeared.

"Hi," he said, with a fleeting smile at Jennifer. "I was here seeing another patient when the ambulance called in, so I waited around." He turned his attention to Tanner, who, though sleepy-eyed, seemed otherwise normal.

"Hi, Dr. Singleton," Tanner said, his voice a little slurred.

"Hi, Tanner. I didn't realize you liked the hospital so much that you wanted to come back."

Tanner grimaced, then looked at his mother. "Why are we here?"

"Don't you remember anything?" Jennifer asked.

Tanner shook his head.

"Uh-oh," Dr. Singleton said, making a face of exaggerated concern. "Another case of empty skullamous. Otherwise known as the no-brains syndrome." He stroked his chin and looked down at Tanner. "Yep," he said, "the only answer is to amputate." He made a slicing motion with his finger across his neck. "Off with his head."

Tanner smiled. "You're a pretty goofy guy for a doctor," he said.

"So *that's* why they call me Dr. Goofy behind my back."

Tanner giggled, and even Jennifer had to smile.

"Okay," Dr. Singleton said in a more serious tone. "Let's get down to business here."

Jennifer stood beside the stretcher and watched Dr. Singleton perform his examination. It was the usual stuff: lights in the eyes, questions for the head, a hammer to the knees. She watched the doctor's face closely in hopes that his facial expression might give away some of his thoughts, but all she saw were a few laugh wrinkles when he tickled Tanner's ribs. That got her to wondering how old he was. Even if he was fresh out of residency she guessed he had to be at least in his thirties. Probably closer to thirty-five. She hoped he was old enough to know what he was doing.

"Well, I don't find anything abnormal," Dr. Singleton said when he was done with the examination.

Jennifer stared at him in stunned silence a moment.

"How can that be?" she asked finally. "For God's sake, he had a seizure! He's never had one before. Something must be wrong!"

Dr. Singleton reached across the stretcher and placed a placating hand on her arm. In her frustration, her first impulse was to shake it off. But it felt warm and steady and reassuring. So she let it stay.

"I know this is frustrating for you," Dr. Singleton said. "There are some studies we can do. A CT scan to get a better look inside his head and . . . "

Jennifer shook her head vehemently. "No! No more tests! That's how he got into this mess in the first place!"

Dr. Singleton came around the stretcher, took her by the shoulders, and turned her so she was facing him. She kept her arms folded tightly across her chest and looked him in the eye, prepared to do battle if necessary. "That was different," he said. "An MRI operates by using a giant magnet and radio waves. A CT scan has no magnetic properties. It's perfectly safe. I promise you."

His voice was full of concern and compassion. Jennifer studied his face, suddenly fascinated by the tiny flecks of blue and brown in the otherwise green eyes. There was something about him that made her want to trust in him, want to believe in him. But this was her son's life they were messing with. She should probably get another opinion at the very least.

As if he had anticipated her thought, Dr. Singleton said, "I would like to get a neurologist to see him. And if it will make you feel any better, I'll arrange it so you can be with Tanner while they do the CT scan."

She chewed the inside of her cheek, debating. She had never felt so helpless and ignorant. But she knew she was out of her realm when it came to making medical decisions. She was going to have to trust this man, whether she was ready to or not.

"Okay," she said grudgingly, and then, seeing the almost-wounded look on his face, she added, "And thank you. I *would* feel better if I could stay with him."

She was rewarded for her efforts by a warm smile and a gentle squeeze on her shoulders.

"Atta girl," Dr. Singleton said.

Jennifer smiled back at him.

Tanner was much more relaxed with his CT scan than he had been with the first tests. He knew now that even though the machinery looked scary, and he didn't much like having his head pinned down with foam and tape, nothing was going to hurt, and he wasn't going to be zapped into some time warp. Plus, he felt better because his mother was here this time. He couldn't see her with his head taped in position as it was, but he knew she was on the other side of the glass wall. He could feel her presence.

He heard the clicks and whirs of the machinery as it moved around him, though eventually it became nothing more than background noise to the voices in his head. This morning he was hearing only one or two voices at a time, making it easy for him to understand what they were saying. But as the day wore on, the number of voices grew until sometimes it sounded like that day at the playground area at McDonald's when some kid was having a birthday party. Here at the hospital the voices seemed fewer and slower, but there were a lot of big words he didn't understand—words like "carcinoma" and "angiography" and "metatarsal." With nothing to do but stare at the inside of the huge doughnut hole his head was in, the voices took over easily.

He had learned pretty quickly that he needed to keep his mind busy and focused in order to keep the voices out.

Then this afternoon with Evan, he had discovered he could focus on a single person and filter out all the other voices. He had practiced on his mother during dinner and heard how tired she was, and how worried she was about him, and something about hoping Evan would go home for the night.

Then the best voice of all came.

At first Tanner didn't believe the voice because it said it was his father and Tanner knew his father was dead and dead people didn't talk. But then the voice said, yes, I am dead, but I can still communicate with you. That got him really scared. If what the voice said was true, he was talking to a ghost! In his fright he focused as hard as he could on making the voice go away, but it didn't work. Then he tried letting all the other voices in to drown out the ghost voice, but that didn't work either. So finally, defeated, he listened. And the voice told him about how much it loved him and loved his mother, and how it missed them, and how it was there to help them. It was a nice voice really, and one time Tanner even thought it sounded familiar, as if he remembered it. But he didn't remember his father at all. The voice told him that was okay—it would help him to remember and to know.

Tanner focused on the voice now, trying to bring it back, but all he could hear was the others. The machine clicked and whirred, words danced around in his head, and eventually the incessant murmur of voices inside his mind lulled him to sleep.

When he awoke, the voices were gone, and they were taking away the foam and tape from around his head. His mother stood behind the glass window, smiling and waving at him. He smiled back at her as he hopped down off the table into a wheelchair.

Tanner, Jennifer, and Dr. Singleton all squeezed into a dimly lit viewing room. Dr. Singleton took a piece of film and slid it into the top of a horizontal row of light boxes that ran along one wall. The light box flashed on, went dark, then came on again, emitting a glaring white light that revealed a dozen or more little pictures on the piece of film.

Dr. Singleton pointed to one of the pictures with a pen he pulled out of his pocket. "This is the metal object they saw on the skull films."

Jennifer studied the spot he pointed out, at first seeing nothing more than a bunch of different shapes in varying shades of gray. Then she noticed a fine white line where he was pointing. It looked miniscule. Hardly bad enough to have caused all this excitement.

Dr. Singleton glanced down at Tanner, who was sitting in a wheelchair positioned behind and between him and Jennifer. "Can you see it?" he asked him.

Tanner nodded, wide-eyed. "Is that my brain?"

Dr. Singleton smiled. "Yes, it is. And a darned fine one, too. One of the best I've ever seen."

Tanner eyed him suspiciously "Really?" he asked, unsure if he was being teased.

"Would I lie?"

Tanner didn't answer largely because he really didn't know. But he didn't think Dr. Singleton would lie to him. The doc just felt . . . well . . . *right*. So he turned away and once again stared at the pictures.

"What part of his brain is this?" Jennifer asked, pointing to the general location of the metal object.

Dr. Singleton traced the pen around a light gray area near the center of one of the pictures. "The foreign body is resting in the midbrain area, just behind and below the corpus callosum." He set the pen down and put the backs of his hands together, lacing his fingers. Then he bent his hands at the knuckles until his palms faced inward. It reminded Jennifer of a game she played as a child and the ditty that went with it ran through her mind:

This is the church,
And this is the steeple,
Open the doors
And see all the people.

Dr. Singleton said, "The corpus callosum is a network of nerve fibers that joins the two halves of the brain together like this." He held his hands up to demonstrate. Then he picked up the pen again and traced around another smaller spot. "The radiologist thinks the metal object is up against the pineal gland. That's this little dark spot here."

Jennifer asked, "Did the metal sliver cause his seizure?"

"More than likely. There's no obvious damage anywhere, but it's possible that the metal might have triggered some unusual nerve impulses if it was moved."

Dr. Singleton pushed his glasses up on his nose with one finger and studied the film in silence a moment. Jennifer watched him and waited, afraid to interrupt his concentration with more questions. When he did finally look at her again, his expression was apologetic. "I can't tell you if the seizure is likely to occur again. We need to do an EEG. Get a readout of his brain waves, to get a better idea."

Great, Jennifer thought. *More tests.*

Dr. Singleton sat down at a nearby desk and gestured to another chair for Jennifer. "Describe the seizure for me again," he said.

Jennifer went over the evening's events: starting with their return from dinner, Tanner's glass of Kool-Aid, and then finding him in his room with that vacant look on his face—something Dr. Singleton called a fugue state. When she mentioned Scotch's odd behavior, Dr. Singleton stopped her.

"Wait, wait," he said, holding up one hand. "You say

the dog was trying to pull him down?" His voice had an excited edge to it.

Jennifer shrugged. "I guess. That's what it looked like. She kept pulling on his shirtsleeve like this." She grabbed her own sleeve to demonstrate.

"Fascinating!" Dr. Singleton said. "I've heard of that before, but I've never seen it."

"Seen what?"

"Your dog, what is his name?"

"It's Scotch. Short for Butterscotch. And it's a her."

"Her. Sorry." He made an impatient wave with his hand. "I think your dog knew Tanner was going to have a seizure. Some dogs have the ability. There have been some studies done trying to figure out how they do it, but no one has come up with anything conclusive. Some of the theories postulate that the dog can smell something different; others embrace the idea that there is some sort of unusual vibration or noise that only a dog can detect. Something to do with the aura that many people experience before they have a seizure: odd smells, ringing sounds, that sort of thing. Nobody knows for sure how a dog can tell when a seizure is coming on, but they can. In fact, they now have training programs for dogs who serve as companions to people with severe epilepsy."

"You mean like a Seeing Eye dog?" Jennifer asked.

"Basically, yes."

Tanner said, "You mean Scotch knew I was going to be sick?"

"That's right," Dr. Singleton said. "And that may play in our favor." He looked over at Jennifer. "It would be interesting to know whether or not the dog started to react before Tanner got into the fugue state in which you found him."

Jennifer thought back, trying to remember the exact

sequence of events. "I . . . I don't know," she said, shaking her head. "I heard the dog when I was still on the stairs. It took me a minute to get up the stairs and into Tanner's room. How long does this fugue state last?"

"It varies. Usually only for a few seconds, maybe a minute or two."

Jennifer looked back up at the series of pictures on the light box, her head spinning with information and questions. It was just too much to digest. She forced herself to take a calming breath and focus on one piece at a time. She studied the gray blob beside the metal sliver. "What about this gland in his brain?" she asked. "The one the metal is up against. What does that do?"

"The pineal gland," Dr. Singleton explained, "is sometimes referred to as the third eye in frogs and lizards. It's associated with the production of certain hormones that regulate our biological clocks. Things like puberty in humans, hibernation in animals, that sort of thing."

Jennifer digested that a moment before she asked, "So what, if any, effect might this metal thing have on Tanner?"

Dr. Singleton chewed one corner of his lip. "I don't know for sure."

Jennifer threw her hands up in frustration. "Great! What *do* you know?" Dr. Singleton's face colored, and she instantly regretted the harshness of her words.

"You have to understand that the human brain is still very poorly understood," Dr. Singleton said defensively. "We only use about one-quarter of its capacity, and even that part is still a mystery in many respects. I'm doing the best I can."

Jennifer reached out and touched his arm. "I know. I'm sorry. It's just that this is all a little overwhelming. I'm just worried. And tired."

Dr. Singleton stood up and walked over to her chair.

He took both of her hands and sandwiched them between his own. He was so tall, it strained Jennifer's neck to look up at him. "I promise you we will get to the bottom of all this," he said softly. His hands felt warm and reassuring around hers, his voice calming. He smiled down at her, making the dimple in his cheek deepen and causing Jennifer to think that he really did have a very pleasant smile. After giving her hands a little squeeze, he released them, and Jennifer shoved them down between her knees.

Dr. Singleton turned to Tanner. "So, Mr. Bolton. What should we do with you next?"

Tanner grinned. "Throw me out with the trash."

"Really?" Dr. Singleton slid a sidelong glance at Jennifer. "Is that what your mother does with you when you misbehave?"

"She said she might one time. When I fell off the ladder outside trying to get my ball off the roof. But she was just joking. She worries about me all the time."

"I'll bet she does. So should we keep you here in the hospital again tonight, where we can make sure you stay out of trouble, or do you think you can behave long enough for me to let you go home?"

Tanner's eyes grew wide, and his feet pushed his wheelchair back a few inches. "I'll behave," he said quickly. "I promise! Please don't make me eat those yucky eggs and bacon again."

Both Jennifer and Dr. Singleton laughed. Dr. Singleton reached down and ruffled Tanner's hair. "Okay. Home it is. But I want to see you in my office first thing tomorrow for that EEG. Nine o'clock, okay?"

Tanner looked at his mother with his eyebrows raised.

"Okay," Jennifer said resignedly. "We'll be there."

"Okay," Tanner echoed with a shrug. "If I gotta."

* * *

Back at the house, Jennifer tucked Tanner into bed and kissed him on the forehead. "Sleep tight, Tan," she whispered.

"Where's Scotch?" Tanner asked, propping himself up on one elbow. His eyes were heavy-lidded, his voice slurred. Dr. Singleton had given him some medication that he said would make him groggy.

"Downstairs eating, I think," Jennifer said, "I'll get her." She went out to the top of the stairs and called to Scotch. Within seconds the dog came bounding up the stairs, shooting past her into Tanner's room, where she hopped up on the bed. After two quick turns, she settled down with her body along the length of Tanner's, her head resting on the pillow next to the boy's. Jennifer smiled and patted the dog on the head.

Tanner turned on his side facing Scotch and threw one arm over the furry neck. The thumb of his other hand found its way into his mouth. The gesture nearly broke Jennifer's heart. Tanner had given up thumbsucking two years ago.

"Good night, Tanner," she whispered. "I love you."

"Love you, too, Mom," Tanner said with a voice thick as syrup.

Jennifer smoothed his hair back from his forehead and tucked the blanket in around his shoulders.

"Good night, Dad," Tanner added.

Jennifer froze. She stood a long time, petrified to move so much as a muscle, resisting an urge to glance around the dimly lit room. She listened to the even rhythm of Tanner's breathing, stared at the soft down that lined his cheeks, inhaled the faint scent of little boy sweat. Gradually, her muscles began to unwind, and her stance became more relaxed.

God, how I love him! It was times such as these when she ached for Tim, wishing he could be alive to see their son the way she saw him now—asleep, with the youthful mark of innocence stamped on his tender face. Though she felt sure Tanner couldn't possibly have any memories of Tim, she thought he must miss his father terribly. Why else would he be carrying on these imaginary conversations? She suspected he often felt lost, lonely, and abandoned. And she, of all people, could understand that. The death of her own father had been devastating.

It had happened during her second year at the University of Virginia. One night she got a call from a woman who identified herself as a nurse in an emergency room in Portland, Maine. "We're sorry to inform you . . . blah, blah, blah. A sudden and massive coronary . . . blah, blah, blah. Your mother asked us to call . . . blah, blah, blah." It had all seemed so cold and impersonal.

His death had hit her hard. He had always been her hero, her confidant, her guiding wisdom, her pillar of strength. She worshiped the man and loved him with everything she had. There was no one in the world she felt closer to. Their bond had grown especially strong in the year or so preceding his death—when he was on his own—even though they were separated by miles. She had even toyed briefly with the idea of postponing college so she could move back to Portland to be with him. But he had assured her he was fine, and that her education was more important. How foolish she'd been to believe him.

Though the doctors had thrown about a bunch of technical terms—coronary occlusion and myocardial infarction—Jennifer knew what had really killed her father. A broken heart.

The shocking news of her mother's affair had stunned Jennifer, eliciting an anger that surprised her with its ferocity. It had simply devastated her father. Though her mother had begged for understanding and forgiveness for what she admitted was a profound error in judgment, Jennifer's father could not bring himself to give it. Nor could Jennifer. In her mind, there was no forgiveness. Her father's death only served to harden her heart even further. As far as Jennifer was concerned, her mother had killed her father. Killed him just as surely as if she'd held a gun to his chest and pulled the trigger.

During the year after her father's death, Jennifer struggled to understand and forgive what her mother had done, frightened at the prospect of losing the only real family she had left. But she never could—whether from stubborn pride or a sense of justice she neither knew nor cared. Finally, tired of battling her own inner turmoil, she made the decision simply to cut the woman out of her life. She severed all communications, never telling her mother about her marriage to Tim, or about Tanner. She hung up whenever the woman called (eventually getting her phone number changed to an unlisted one) and returned all her letters unopened. If anyone asked, Jennifer told them both of her parents were dead.

Though it took a while, her mother finally gave up all attempts to contact her. It had been almost seven years since Jennifer had last heard anything. Her primary feeling was one of relief, though at times the loneliness had been almost overwhelming, particularly after Tim's death.

She sighed and gave her son one last look. Tanner was her family now. And she would do whatever it took to keep him safe. She would never disappoint him, or betray him, or let him down the way her own mother had. Not as long as she had an ounce of fight and breath left in her. Quietly, she padded down the hall to her own room, grabbed a blanket and pillow from the bed, and returned to Tanner's bedroom, where she spent a fitful night trying to get comfortable in the rocking chair beside the window.

* * *

The morning dawned gray and thick, the humidity competing with the temperature to see which one could hit one hundred first. Tanner woke up complaining of a headache, scaring Jennifer at first, until she remembered Dr. Singleton's warning her that he might have a bit of a hangover from the medication. Other than the headache, Tanner seemed to be his usual self, chattering his way through breakfast and polishing off a large bowl of Lucky Charms. Jennifer watched him, taking comfort from the fact that he had his usual rosy-cheeked glow and appeared to be suffering no residual effects from the previous night's events.

The only unusual thing Jennifer noticed was that Scotch, who was normally under her feet anytime she was in the kitchen, was glued to Tanner's side. She lay beneath his chair while he ate, followed him to the sink when he washed out his cereal bowl, and followed him upstairs when he was done.

Jennifer was tempted to follow, too—to help Tanner dress—but she thought better of it. Her son's developing sense of privacy extended to her as well. So she busied herself cleaning up the breakfast mess instead, keeping one ear tuned for Scotch, in case she heard that strange guttural whining again.

When Tanner returned downstairs ten minutes later, Jennifer had to suppress a smile. He had totally ignored the clothes she set out for him, opting instead for his favorite pair of worn, torn cutoffs and his Wile E. Coyote T-shirt. A fierce struggle for independence was yet another character her son had developed recently, and though at times it tugged at Jennifer's heartstrings to realize how quickly he was growing up, she also relished each bit of evidence about who Tanner was going to be. His personality was an entertaining, though at times frustrating, mix of Tim's patience and perseverance and her own streak of independence and stubbornness.

Carny called, and Jennifer gave her a brief synopsis of the past evening's events, promising to call after they were through at the doctor's office. It was just after eight-thirty when they headed out the door. A westerly wind had carried in heavy, black clouds, and Jennifer thought she could both feel and smell the thunderstorm that was brewing.

Dr. Singleton's office was one of twenty or so located in a building adjacent to the hospital. The office was much as she remembered: women scurrying about behind the glass-enclosed reception area, piped-in music playing softly overhead, stacks of out-of-date, well-worn magazines piled on the waiting room seats and tables, a faint antiseptic smell that lingered in the air. There were three other people already seated in the waiting area: two women and a man, their faces buried in magazines as they struggled to maintain their anonymity. Jennifer led Tanner toward two vacant seats along the far wall, and they had barely settled down when a door opened, and someone called Tanner's name. As they rose and headed for the examination area, Jennifer saw one of the women in the waiting room shoot them a look of annoyance as they passed.

"Good morning, Mrs. Bolton!" The person who greeted them was a young, gamine-eyed girl with very short, dark hair and a waist about as big around as a pencil. She didn't look much older than twenty—if that. "You must be Tanner," she said, bowing down to his eye level, which, considering the girl's small size, wasn't very far. Tanner stared back and said nothing.

The girl straightened up and directed her eyes at Jennifer. "I'm Lori, young Dr. Singleton's nurse. That's how we're distinguishing between the two—young doctor and old doctor. Though I'm not sure the senior Dr. Singleton likes it much." She was very animated, waving her hands about as she talked and bobbing her head from side to side. She flashed a smile at Jennifer, giggled stupidly, and then abruptly turned down the hallway. "Right in here," she said, holding open the door to one of the examination rooms. "Dr. Singleton will be right in."

Jennifer took a seat in the only chair in the room, while Tanner climbed up onto the examination table and sat sideways, with his feet hanging over the edge. He eyed the walls, which were covered with framed educational degrees and a smattering of child's drawings, as his legs swung back and forth, his feet banging loudly against the side of the table with each descent.

"Tanner, please!" Jennifer said when she could tolerate the noise no longer.

"Sorry." He dropped his head and smiled sheepishly, peering up at her through that stubborn shock of hair. It was an expression that never failed to soften her heart, and she suspected that Tanner knew it.

The door to the examination room opened and the younger Dr. Singleton walked in. He was minus the lab coat this morning, dressed in a colorful Hawaiian print shirt and a pair of khaki slacks. His hair had been combed straight back from his face, but a small Alfalfa-like cowlick stood up near his crown, causing Jennifer to bite her cheek to keep from smiling. He looked totally different this morning: more human, more vulnerable, less authoritative. Jennifer found herself comparing him to Evan's always-immaculate and well-tailored look.

"Well, hello there, Mr. Bolton," Dr. Singleton said cheerfully. "I take it you had a restful night after you got home?"

Tanner nodded, then shot a questioning glance at his mother.

"And Mrs. Bolton?" Dr. Singleton asked, looking pointedly at Jennifer.

Jennifer shrugged.

"Let me guess," Dr. Singleton said, hiking one hip up on the examination table next to Tanner. "You slept sitting up in a chair in Tanner's room all night. Am I right?"

Jennifer's surprised and guilty expression gave him all the answer he needed. He turned his attention back to Tanner.

"We need to figure out a way to get your mother here some rest. She's too pretty to have those dark circles under her eyes, don't you think?"

Tanner looked at his mother as if the thought of her needing rest like other human beings had never crossed his mind. "I guess," he said.

Jennifer felt herself blushing until the tops of her ears felt so hot she feared they might burst into flames.

"Well, we'll get back to that later," Dr. Singleton said, climbing off the examination table and opening a drawer in the cabinet beneath the sink. "Let's take a look at you first."

Jennifer watched as Dr. Singleton went through the usual litany of tests: flashlights in Tanner's eyes, orientation questions, test of his grip strength. After checking all of Tanner's reflexes with a tiny hammer, Dr. Singleton let him hop down and took his place. He handed the hammer to Tanner. "Here, you check mine," he said. Jennifer smiled as she watched her son try to find the right spots to hit and the right amount of force to hit them with. By the time they were done, everyone in the room was laughing.

"Okay, calm down," Dr. Singleton whispered. "If we have too much fun in here, it will make all my other patients think this is a fun place to be. Then I'll never get any time off!"

As if on cue, the door to the examination room opened. Jennifer looked up and saw the elder Dr. Singleton poke his head in. "May I come in?" he asked.

"Of course," the younger doctor said. Jennifer noted curiously that his facial expression had rapidly changed to one of formal sobriety. "Come on in. I was just about to come looking for you anyway. I wanted to run this case by you."

Even his voice had changed. If Jennifer hadn't been sitting there watching the interchange, she would have sworn there was a third person in the room. It was almost amusing to see the towering and lanky son nervously kowtowing to his shorter, rather chubby father.

The elder Dr. Singleton stepped into the already-crowded room and closed the door behind him. He acknowledged Jennifer with a nod of his head. "Mrs. Bolton. How have you been?"

"I've been fine," Jennifer answered, "but Tanner's had a few problems."

"So I understand."

"You already know?" Eric asked, looking perplexed. "How?"

"Simple enough, really. Dr. Webber and I played a game of golf together yesterday morning and he filled me in on Tanner's visit to the ER. So when I saw Tanner's name on the schedule book, I figured I'd pop in and see how he was doing."

Though the words were relatively innocuous, Jennifer thought she detected a slight tone of condescension in the elder doctor's voice. She found her feelings shifting from amusement to sympathy for Eric as she observed the father-son interchange.

"Well," Eric said, clearing his throat, "his pupils are

equal and reactive, he's alert and oriented times three, has normal muscle tone, good reflexes, negative Babinski. A CT scan done yesterday was normal except for the metal foreign body. He had a grand mal–type seizure last night of relatively short duration with no post-ictal effects other than a little lethargy by the time I saw him in the ER."

Jennifer watched Eric Singleton closely as he rattled the information off to his father. The rote tone of his voice made it sound as if he were reciting facts for a medical school test. Even his manner was different; his posture was stiffer and straighter, and the casual ambience she had come to associate with him was gone.

"What about an EEG?" the elder Dr. Singleton asked.

"Set it up for this morning. In fact, Nick offered to come over here to see the boy since his office doesn't open up until one o'clock today." He turned and looked at Jennifer. "I'm sorry. Nick is Dr. Calutto, a neurologist with an office just a few doors down. I've asked him to take a look at Tanner."

Jennifer nodded slowly. The odd undercurrent in the room left her feeling uneasy.

"Did you witness Tanner's seizure, Mrs. Bolton?" the elder Dr. Singleton asked.

"I did." She described the events for him.

"Anything else unusual? Any behavioral changes?"

Jennifer looked over at Tanner and was startled to see that he was staring at the elder Dr. Singleton with a dark scowl on his face.

"Well, there has been some unusual behavior," she said slowly, watching Tanner's face. His gaze remained fixed on the older man, his eyes so narrowed it made a tiny chill run down Jennifer's spine. She debated mentioning Tanner's fixation on his father. Maybe now, with two medical professionals in the room, was a safe time to broach the subject.

"Tanner says he has been talking to his dead father," she said carefully, trying to keep her voice even and nonaccusatory.

The elder Dr. Singleton's eyebrows shot up. "Really?" He looked over at Tanner, and Jennifer thought he was a little taken aback by the dark intensity of the boy's stare. He quickly shifted his gaze back to Jennifer. "Perhaps I might speak with you outside a moment, Mrs. Bolton? When they are ready to do Tanner's EEG."

With that, a knock came on the door and Lori poked her head in. "Dr. Calutto is here," she announced, stepping aside and holding the door.

Dr. Calutto was younger than Jennifer expected, with a round, almost baby face, gentle brown eyes, and a short pudgy build. With the addition of yet another person in the small examination room, it became stiflingly close. After a brief introduction, Jennifer followed the elder Dr. Singleton out into the hallway, leaving Tanner in the room with Eric and Dr. Calutto.

"Come into my office, Mrs. Bolton," Dr. Singleton said, leading her. "Have a seat."

Jennifer sat in the maroon-colored, leather wing chair the doctor had indicated, while he settled into its mate behind a massive mahogany desk. A tower of charts on either corner of the desk framed his face as he leaned forward, hands folded together, his thumbs twirling around each other.

"I'm not sure what my son has suggested to you regarding this incident with Tanner," he began, "but I am concerned about these personality changes you have seen. You say Tanner claims to have spoken to his dead father?"

"Well, yes," Jennifer answered, trying to keep the edge of panic out of her voice. "When he had this seizure last night, right before he started the twitching, he looked at me and said he had been talking to his dad. It was kind of creepy, actually." She shifted nervously in the chair.

Dr. Singleton nodded, pushing his lower lip in and out. Then he sat back in his chair, crossing his hands over his rotund stomach. "Has he ever made a statement like that before?"

Jennifer shook her head. "No. But I can't help but wonder if it might not have been triggered by the mention of the facts surrounding Tim's death. It came out in the ER the other night—about the crash and the explosion and all. That was the first time Tanner had ever heard the whole story. I could tell from the look on his face that it bothered him."

"I see," Dr. Singleton said. "You could well be right." He sat up, opened a drawer in his desk, and took out a notepad and pen. "I would like you to take Tanner to see a friend of mine, Dr. Andersen." He ripped a page off the notepad and handed it to Jennifer. The name, Dr. Andersen, an address, and a phone number were written on it. "Andersen is one of the best child psychologists in the state. Maybe in the country."

Jennifer frowned. "A psychologist? Do you really think that's necessary?"

"I do. At least for an initial workup. Tanner may have some trouble dealing with this thing about his father's death. Head injuries can also cause some personality changes, and I think Dr. Andersen will be able to give us a better idea of which problems are psychological and which are pathological."

Jennifer nodded, too numb to say anything. Dr. Singleton stood up and came around the desk, holding his hand out. "Tanner will be all right," he said. "Don't worry."

Everyone kept telling her that, but so far she had seen things only get worse. Jennifer took the man's hand, felt him give hers a gentle squeeze, then stood up. Dr. Singleton draped an arm over her shoulders, her greater height making the gesture awkward, and led her back toward the examination room.

"Have a seat here," he said, gesturing to a row of chairs along the hallway. "We don't want to interrupt the EEG."

Jennifer did as she was told. She sat and fidgeted and watched as other patients came and went, the examination room doors opening and closing—all of them, that is, except Tanner's. She checked her watch a hundred times, sure that an hour had passed, startled to see it was only five minutes later than the last time she had looked.

The elder Dr. Singleton came out of an examination room and nearly ran into Lori, the gamine-eyed nurse, in the hallway.

"Isn't it just awful what happened at the Hanovers'?" Jennifer heard Lori whisper loudly. The girl's voice sounded more fascinated than appalled. "I can't believe he killed his whole family!"

"It certainly is a tragedy," Dr. Singleton said, shaking his head. "I feel partially responsible, since Barry was my patient. I should have picked up on the severity of his depression."

Lori touched the man's arm. "It's not your fault," she said. "Sometimes people just crack all of a sudden. It seems you read about senseless violence like that every day in the paper."

"True," the doctor said thoughtfully. "But I still feel somehow responsible. Now, would you do me a favor and send Mrs. Sanders to the lab for a CBC?"

"Certainly," Lori said, taking a chart from a holder beside one of the examination room doors. She knocked briefly, opened the door, and disappeared inside. Dr. Singleton headed back to his office.

Jennifer sat, waiting anxiously and wondering about the conversation she had just overheard. But before she could ponder it much, Tanner's examination room door opened and Dr. Calutto and Eric stepped out into the hall.

Jennifer stood up and nearly ran over to them. "How did it go?"

"It went fine, Mrs. Bolton," Dr. Calutto said. "Everything was normal except for one area of unusual activity about twenty minutes into the test. It wasn't characteristic of anything pathological, so I'm not sure what caused it. I need to take the strips back and look them over more carefully. But there was no sign of epilepsy or any permanent damage."

Jennifer breathed a sigh of relief. "Thank goodness. Can I go back in with Tanner?"

"Certainly," Dr. Calutto said.

The examination room was dark when Jennifer went in, lit only by a small gooseneck lamp in the corner. Tanner was lying on his side on the examination table, curled into a fetal position. A machine with a zillion multicolored wires snaking out of it sat on a cart near the sink. As her eyes adjusted to the dimmer light, Jennifer noticed that Tanner had three small red weals on his forehead along his hairline.

"Tanner?" she said softly.

"I'm awake," he answered.

"Are you okay?"

"I'm fine. Now. But I don't want to do one of those again. It hurt. They screwed a bunch of needles into my head." Jennifer saw a tear slide down his cheek, and she bent down and gathered him into her arms.

"I'm sorry, sport," she said. She rocked him back and forth for a minute until he pushed himself away.

"I'm okay, Mom," he said, sitting up. "Dad was with me for part of the time. He made it okay."

Jennifer stared at her son, saw the obvious belief in his eyes, and sighed heavily. "Oh, Tanner," she said. "Your father is dead. He can't be with you anymore, or talk to you anymore. I know you must have been upset when you heard about the way he died, but it happened a long time ago. I didn't tell you about it before because I didn't want to upset you."

"I'm not upset," Tanner said with frightening calm. "I'm just mad."

"Of course you are," Jennifer said taking his hand. "It's not fair that your father died before you ever got to know him. It's okay to feel angry about it. I did. For a while I was even angry with your father for leaving me. How's that for silly?"

"I'm not mad at *Dad*," Tanner said with exasperation. "I don't know who to be mad at yet. Dad hasn't told me."

Jennifer dropped his hand and stepped back, wrapping her arms around herself. "What do you mean, Tanner?" she asked, her voice both confused and wary.

"I mean, Dad hasn't told me who killed him yet."

A thundering silence permeated the room.

"Nobody killed your father, Tanner," Jennifer said, her words short and tense.

"Sure they did," Tanner said with conviction. "Dad told me so. That accident wasn't an accident."

"Oh my God," Jennifer muttered.

The door to the examination room opened and Eric came in. He stopped, the light from the hallway silhouetting him in the doorway so that Jennifer couldn't see his face. Her face, however, was well lit as the light from the hallway fell on it. Her eyes were wide with fear, her hand was clamped over her mouth. Eric's brow furrowed with worry as he looked at her. "Is everything okay in here?"

Jennifer just stared at him.

He looked over at Tanner. "Tanner? Are you okay?"

"I'm fine," he said nonchalantly.

Eric closed the door behind him and walked over to Jennifer, placing an arm around her shoulders. "Jennifer? What's wrong?"

"Tanner," she said, her voice cracking. "He needs help." A cascade of tears filled, then overflowed her eyes, running down her cheeks.

"He's okay," Eric said, pulling her toward him.

At first she tensed, fearful that any gesture of kindness, no matter how small, would erode the barely maintained control she had on her emotions. But he overpowered her resistance, and the dam broke. Jennifer buried her face in Eric's chest and sobbed all over his shirt, taking in the faint and pleasant smell of him with each gasp.

Eric held her, rubbing her back gently. He saw Tanner watching him over Jennifer's shoulder and winked.

Tanner smiled.

Eric rolled his eyes.

Tanner's smile grew bigger.

Eric stuck out his tongue.

Tanner laughed.

Jennifer, sensing that the mood in the room had shifted, got her sobs under control and stepped back from Eric. There was a large wet spot on the front of his shirt.

"Feel better now?" Eric said, holding out a box of tissues.

Jennifer yanked three tissues out and nodded. She blew her nose and then looked up at him apologetically. "I'm sorry," she said.

"No need to apologize," Eric said, smiling. "You can snot on my shirt anytime you want."

Tanner giggled, and even Jennifer cracked a smile.

"I know you're worried about Tanner, but so far everything checks out fine. The EEG was normal except for that one spot. And it's probably nothing. In fact, Dr. Calutto thought it was just some type of unusual sleep pattern. Tanner was mumbling in his sleep at that point, so it may have been nothing more than a very strong dream image."

"I wasn't dreaming," Tanner said. "I wasn't even asleep."

"Oh, you weren't?" Eric said, teasingly skeptical.

"No," Tanner said. "I heard everything you and that other doctor said. You said something about somna . . . something, and the other guy was talking about R-E-M. I couldn't figure out what a singing group had to do with anything."

Eric frowned. "R-E-M isn't a group, Tanner," he said slowly. "At least not in this case. We were referring to a level of sleep."

Jennifer caught the cautious tone in Eric's voice, and her heart started to thump wildly.

"And I was talking about somnambulism," Eric added.

"Yeah! That was the word!" Tanner said. "What is that?"

"It's a term for sleepwalking," Eric said, clearly puzzled. "You heard all that, Tanner?" His face was a picture of bewilderment and concern.

Tanner nodded. "Well, most of it anyway. I knew you were seeing something funny on the machine but I was talking to my dad, and he said not to worry about it. So I heard most of what you said, except for when I was listening to my dad."

Eric gaped at Tanner.

Jennifer felt all the blood in her body sink to her feet.

The room began to swim, the walls appearing to waver. Then the walls turned to darkness and marched inward. With a little whimper, Jennifer half sat, half fell into the chair behind her.

5

Jennifer suffered the ignominy of having Eric shove her head down between her knees. Feeling both stupid and a little panicked, she struggled to sit up, her hands pushing hard against the arms of her chair.

Eric's warm hand kept a firm pressure on the back of her neck, refusing to yield.

"Give yourself a minute," he told her. "Let the blood get back into your head before you try to get up."

She gave in and let herself go limp. After a moment, the pressure of Eric's hand let up a little. His thumb gently massaged the hollow at the base of her skull.

"Feel better?" he asked after a minute or so.

That was putting it mildly. His fingers on the nape of her neck felt so wonderfully relaxing and soothing, she wasn't sure she ever wanted to move. No sooner had she thought this when the fingers disappeared, taking their warmth with them and leaving the back of her neck feeling as if a cold draft had just caressed it. Wrapping her own hand over the spot, Jennifer sat up, pushed her hair back off her face, and blinked hard in an effort to chase away the dozens of tiny lights that circled her head like a swarm of gnats. One by one, the lights blinked out.

"I'm okay."

"You're sure?" Eric eyed her warily, hands on hips,

head cocked slightly to one side like a robin that's just spied a worm in the earth.

"I'm sure." She stood up. Slowly. She wasn't *that* sure.

Eric cupped her elbow in his hand and led her from the room, signaling for Tanner to follow. Outside in the hallway he stopped, turned her toward him, and scanned her face closely, his hands gripping her shoulders.

"Are you sure you're okay?"

Jennifer nodded.

"Okay then." He let his hands drop and turned to look down at Tanner. "Take care of your mother for me, okay?"

Tanner straightened his shoulders and took on an expression of such solemn responsibility that Jennifer was both saddened and amused.

"I will," Tanner said with great seriousness. Jennifer half expected him to whip off a snappy salute.

Eric looked back at Jennifer. His lips formed a smile, but his eyes showed only concern. "I'll let you know the final results of his EEG as soon as Dr. Calutto gets back to me. In the meantime, if you need me, just call."

"Thank you, Eric."

His eyebrows shot up, and the smile spread.

"What?" Jennifer asked self-consciously. "Did I say something funny?"

"That's the first time you've called me Eric," he said. "I kind of like it."

Jennifer felt a blush surge up from her shoulders to her cheeks and gave a quick glance around to see if anyone had overheard. Convinced no one was paying her any attention, she looked back at Eric, feeling the warmth slowly recede into a glowing little ball somewhere in the middle of her chest.

"I have to get to my other patients," Eric said. He

gave her shoulder one last squeeze and turned to leave. "Remember," he said over his shoulder. "Call me if you need anything." With that he disappeared into a nearby room, leaving Jennifer with an oddly hollow feeling in the pit of her stomach.

She turned away and steered Tanner ahead of her toward the lobby. As they passed another examination room, the door opened, and the elder Dr. Singleton stood in the doorway, his back toward the hall.

"See you next month, Brian," he said to someone in the room. "I'm sure those vitamin shots will have you feeling much better by then. Call me if things get worse. And promise me you'll continue with Dr. Andersen." He turned, pulling the door closed behind him and smiling broadly when he saw Jennifer.

"Everything come out okay?" he asked.

"So far," Jennifer told him. She looked down at Tanner and gasped. He was glaring at Dr. Singleton, his face screwed into a grimace of disgust, as if he had just swallowed a mouthful of Brussels sprouts—the vegetable he hated most.

"Tanner?" she said hesitantly. As if someone had thrown a switch, Tanner's face relaxed and he turned to look at this mother.

"What?" he said, all innocence.

"Is there something wrong?"

Tanner looked up at Dr. Singleton, his face now devoid of expression. "You were lying," he said simply.

Dr. Singleton laughed. "Was I now?" he said.

Tanner nodded. "You didn't give that guy any vitamins," he said.

"Well, now, that's true to an extent. What I gave him was some special medicine to treat his depression. But he doesn't need to know the specifics. In fact, it might be more harmful to his psyche if he did." As the doctor said this, the amused expression he had worn when he first came out of the room evaporated, to be replaced by one of concern and annoyance. "It is certainly nothing for you to be concerned about, Tanner," he said dismissively. Then he turned to Jennifer, shaking his head slightly. "Please," he said, "take him to see Dr. Andersen. As soon as possible." With that, he turned away and headed back down the hall.

Tanner watched his retreating back and said, "He doesn't like me."

Jennifer was stunned. And more than a little embarrassed. She opened her mouth to chastise Tanner for his rude behavior, but he spoke up before she got a word out.

"I'm hungry," he said, shifting his gaze to her as if nothing unusual had happened. "What's for lunch?" He turned and walked back toward the reception area, leaving his bewildered mother to follow.

By the time they got into the car, the threatened thunderstorm had become a reality. The rain came down in sheets, sluicing down the windshield and flooding the roads as it ran off the dry, hard-packed clay. Menacing clouds, heavy with their armament of rain, darkened the sky. The wind howled and tore at everything in its path. This was the type of storm that occasionally gave birth to tornadoes, and Jennifer gripped the steering wheel as if her life depended upon it, her body hunched forward, trying to see through the onslaught of rain as the wipers made a feeble attempt to clear the glass. An occasional burst of lightning coursed through the sky, but rather than making visibility any better, it only complicated matters by temporarily blinding Jennifer.

Tanner, on the other hand, was quite unbothered by this example of Mother Nature's fury. He kept his face glued to the side window, uttering an astonished "Cool!" or "Awesome!" at the pyrotechnic display.

Despite the fact that it was only eleven-thirty in the morning, the leaden light of the day made it feel like late evening. It took close to an hour to make the trip home, a jaunt that normally required just under thirty minutes. When Jennifer finally pulled up in front of the house she breathed a sigh of relief and stretched her arms and neck to relieve some of the tension in her aching muscles.

"I think we're going to have to make a run for it," she said to Tanner, staring out the windshield at the downpour. "I'll race you."

It was a common challenge, one that never failed to get a rise out of Tanner. But instead of plunging out of the car and dashing headlong for the porch as he usually did, he merely opened the car door, climbed out, and ambled slowly toward the house, getting drenched in the process. He didn't even bother to close the car door.

Jennifer called after him, but a loud boom of thunder drowned her out. Cursing, she reached across the seat and pulled the passenger door shut, then bolted out her own. By the time she caught up with Tanner, he was standing on the front porch thoroughly soaked, his hair plastered down around his face, his sneakers making little squishy bubbles as he danced in place.

"What is wrong with you?" she asked him as she fumbled with her house key.

"You better hurry." This, uttered in an odd monotone, was in sharp contrast to his restless shifting. "The phone is going to ring."

Jennifer stared at him, wondering what in the hell was going through his mind now, when she heard the shrill ring of the phone through the door. Her eyes grew wide as she watched her son's face crack a smile.

"I told you," Tanner said.

Jennifer threw the lock, ran inside, and grabbed the phone.

"Hello?" She watched Tanner close the front door. Scotch was there to greet him, her tail wagging.

"Jen? Is everything okay?"

"Oh, Evan." Jennifer swiped at the rainwater that was running down her face from her hair. She tossed her keys and pocketbook onto the couch.

"I've been trying to call you all morning," Evan said, his voice surly. "Where the hell have you been?"

His curt tone made her want to snap back at him, but she was simply too tired. "At the doctor's, Evan. Tanner had a seizure last night after you left."

"A seizure! For God's sake, Jennifer! Why didn't you call me?"

"Geez, Evan. I'm sorry I didn't take time out from calling the ambulance to check in with you first," she snapped, managing to summon up a small amount of irritation after all.

"Sorry." Evan's voice lightened up immediately. "I was just worried about you."

Jennifer took a deep breath and ran a hand through her hair, causing rivulets of cold water to snake down her back. "I'm sorry, too. It's been a rough morning."

"Is Tanner all right?"

"I don't know, Evan." She looked over at Tanner, saw he had turned on the TV and was watching cartoons stretched out on the floor on his stomach, his chin propped up on his palms. Scotch was stretched out alongside him. It was a posture she had seen many times before, and the very normalcy of it relaxed her a little. "I can't go into it right now," she said, not wanting to discuss Tanner while he was within hearing distance.

"Well, look. I've got to get back in court. How about if I stop by later?"

Jennifer hesitated. On the one hand it would be nice to have someone else around, someone she could talk things over with. But right now she felt she needed to focus all of her attention on Tanner. And Evan had a way at times of demanding his own fair share of her time and attention. "Call me first, Evan," she said.

There was a long silence on the other end, and Jennifer suspected Evan was either angry or feeling sorry for himself. Finally he said, "Fine. I'll call you when I'm done for the day."

There was a click and Jennifer realized he had hung up. So, he had opted for anger. On any other day it would have bothered her enough that she would have been back on the phone, trying to make amends. But today she had neither the time nor the energy to worry about it. She replaced the phone on the table and, with one last look at Tanner, headed out to the kitchen to fix them both some lunch.

Carny called around one, and Jennifer filled her in on the latest: Tanner's seizure, the trip to the hospital, and the morning's trip to the doctor's office. She left out the part about Tanner's strange behavior, skirting around the issue by saying only that Tanner was acting a little odd. She wasn't sure why she was holding back, though she supposed it might be because she needed more time to digest it all herself before anyone else started analyzing the situation, and, with it, Tanner.

"Want some company?" Carny offered.

"Actually, no," Jennifer said. "Tanner is looking sleepy, and I'm hoping we can both lie down for a nap soon. Besides, it's not fit for man or beast outside. How about if I call you later?"

"No problem," Carny said. "I'm here if you need me. It takes more than a little ole thunder-boomer to keep me down."

"Thanks, Carny."

"Hey? What's a best friend for?"

Jennifer curled up on the couch and watched Tanner watching cartoons from the floor. Just as she had hoped, his eyes eventually grew heavy. They closed for a few seconds, then abruptly opened. They closed again, a little longer this time, then opened. On the third time, Tanner's head bobbed down, lay on its side, and he was out.

Jennifer got up and stood over him a moment, watching his chest rise and fall, barely able to hear the light whisper of his breathing. She thought about waking him so he could go up to his bed, but she was reluctant to disturb him. In the end she decided to leave him where he was and grabbed an afghan off the couch and threw it over him, partially covering Scotch as well. Then she unplugged the phone so it would not disturb them, and stretched out luxuriously on the couch. Within minutes, she, too, was sound asleep.

She awoke feeling fuzzy-headed and disoriented. The room was pitch-dark, and she rubbed her eyes and sat up, trying to get her bearings.

Something was wrong. She could feel it.

She leaned over, flipped on the lamp, and looked toward Tanner. He was gone. She stood quickly, felt her legs tremble and the room spin, and sat back down. After a few deep breaths, she tried again, more slowly this time.

"Tanner?"

She waited, closing her eyes to better concentrate on her hearing. Aside from the monotonous thrumming of the downpour outside, she heard nothing. She began a methodical search of the ground floor, room by room, flipping on lights as she went, and periodically calling out for Tanner. Satisfied that he was not on the first floor, she hurried toward the stairs, pushing down a rising sense of panic. Her hand was on the rail, one foot poised above the first step, when a noise came, faint and far away. Unable to determine its source she froze, listening, eyes closed, waiting to hear it again. For an eternity she could hear nothing but the incessant tympani of the rain. And then the noise came again.

This time, she recognized it at once. It was the same eerie whining sound she had heard the night before, and the knowledge set her heart to racing. Though muffled, she thought the sound had come from somewhere behind her, not upstairs. She whirled toward the center of the living room, rubbing her arms where goose bumps had pimpled her flesh.

Again she waited, and when the sound finally came, she looked momentarily bewildered, for it seemed to be coming from beneath her. And then she figured it out. She ran to the kitchen and yanked open the door to the cellar. She hesitated, peering into the darkened maw and brushing her hand along the wall for the light switch.

The single bulb came on with seeming reluctance, reflecting dully off the large freezer chest that fronted the wall at the base of the stairs and casting a feeble light into the main body of the cellar. The room below formed a backward L shape off to the left, so that much of it was obscured from Jennifer's view at the top of the stairs. She descended about halfway and bent down to peer through the rail. The main, larger part of the cellar spread out the length of the house, ending in a small, dirt-smeared window high up at the other end. The floor was concrete, the walls gray cinder block embellished with strings of cobwebs. Though the basement was relatively dry, a strong musty smell permeated the air.

Jennifer shivered violently. The cellar had never been her favorite place. There were too many scurrying creatures hiding in the shadows and crevices: hairy spiders the size of half-dollars, centipedes that moved with lightning speed, shiny black water bugs with long, waving antennae, and the worst—cave crickets—humpbacked, spidery-looking things with the heart-stopping habit of leaping incredible heights *backwards*.

Jennifer climbed down another few steps and glanced over at the washer and dryer, which sat along the wall about ten feet from the freezer. They were flanked by a set of white aluminum shelves that jutted out perpendicular to the wall. The shelves were covered with various items: laundry detergents, liquid bleach, dry bleach, water softeners, fabric softeners, stain removers, a collection of household cleaning agents, some miscellaneous articles of clothing, some towels that had been designated as rags, and a box of unmatched socks. The clutter effectively blocked out that portion of the room that extended beyond the shelves.

On the opposite wall was a doorway that led to a smaller room that housed the furnace, water heater, and emergency generator. Much of the main room was cluttered with boxes, old furniture, lawn equipment, and more shelving that held an assortment of tools, hardware, lightbulbs, and other miscellany. There was no sign of Tanner.

Jennifer called out from the stairs. "Tanner?"

Scotch barked in response, and Jennifer realized the sound was coming from the furnace room. She flew down the stairs and into the small room, breathing a sigh of relief when she saw Tanner sitting on an old lawn chair in the middle of the room, facing the furnace. The light from the main room barely penetrated this one, and Jennifer grabbed at the string that hung from a bare bulb in the ceiling overhead.

When the light revealed Tanner's face, Jennifer's relief was quickly forgotten. As she took in the blank hollows of his eyes and the slack lie of his features, panic rose again, bubbling up in her throat like a caustic liquid and settling into her legs like molten lead. She circled him once, slowly, like an animal marking its prey, trying to decide what to do. Scotch stood beside the chair, whining and nudging Tanner's hand with her nose, her rising pitch matching the growing sense of urgency Jennifer felt herself. When Jennifer had completed her circle and was once again facing Tanner, she squatted, grabbed his arms, and shook him gently.

"Tanner?"

No response. Jennifer shook him a little harder; her voice rose in pitch.

"Tanner? Tanner, please! Snap out of it!"

Tanner mumbled something that Jennifer couldn't quite make out.

"What?" she asked hopefully. "What is it, honey?"

Tanner's next words came out frighteningly clear. "Stop the killing."

The words chilled Jennifer, and she shook him again. She was rewarded by a blink. She studied her son's face. Did his eyes look more focused? Or was that mere wishful thinking on her part?

"Tanner?"

He looked at her then, his eyes coming into focus so suddenly it made Jennifer draw back. Then he blinked again—a slow, hard blink—and looked around the room, his expression one of confusion.

"Tanner? Can you hear me?" Jennifer watched him closely, petrified that he might have another seizure.

"It's in the water," Tanner said slowly, still gazing around the room with that bewildered expression.

Jennifer thought he must be babbling. She reached out and sandwiched his face in her palms. "Tanner! Can you hear me? Look at me!"

He grimaced as if in pain.

"Tanner, honey. Can you hear me?"

Tanner looked her straight in the eye, and his face visibly relaxed. "I can hear you."

Jennifer squeezed her eyes shut with relief. "What are you doing down here?" she asked him.

He looked around the room again. "I don't know," he said. "I guess Dad led me down here."

Jennifer swallowed hard. This fixation he had with Tim was obviously getting worse. She recalled the name of the psychologist that Dr. Singleton had suggested and made a mental note to call him as soon as possible.

"Tanner, your dad is dead," she said gently.

"I know that," he said irritably. "Bioceutics had him killed."

Jennifer let out a weary sigh. "Your father died in a car accident, Tanner," she said slowly. "It was an unfortunate accident. A tire blew out on the car. But it was just an accident. Nobody killed . . . "

Jennifer felt something slip inside her mind, sliding away just as she tried to grasp it. Her mind whirled, taking chase. There was something wrong, terribly wrong with what Tanner had just said. What was it? Something that bothered her. She struggled after it, knowing instinctively that she had to bring it back.

Then suddenly it hit her, and she dropped from her haunches and sat hard on the floor, staring slack-jawed at Tanner. She racked her brain frantically, trying to remember all the times she had talked with Tanner about Tim.

Her next words came out whispered and cautious. "Tanner, how did you know the name of the company your dad worked for?"

"He told me."

Jennifer felt an icy-cold hand of fear grip the back of her neck. She stared at the floor, her face carrying a blank stare not unlike the one Tanner had worn a few moments before.

"Mom?"

Jennifer looked up at her son, but didn't answer right

away. She was too terrified—terrified of what would come out of Tanner's mouth next. "Yes?"

"I'm hungry."

His answer was so absurdly normal, her sudden relief so extreme, she laughed. But it was a humorless sound. Without a word, she rose off the floor, took Tanner by the hand, and went back upstairs to the kitchen, with Scotch following close behind.

She sat Tanner down at the kitchen table and went over to the cupboard. She took down a can of ravioli, opened it, and dumped it into a bowl, focusing intently on each movement required, trying to block all other thoughts from her mind. Then she put the bowl in the microwave and set the timer for two minutes, counting down the numbers in her mind as she watched the digital display. When it was done, she set the bowl in front of Tanner, gave him a fork and a glass of milk.

"Be careful," she warned him. "It's hot."

Tanner picked up the fork and dug in.

Jennifer leaned against the counter and watched him, the barrier in her mind crumbling. Unable to block out the thoughts any longer, they flooded in, filling her with a mindless terror—a fear that was darkly ominous, yet frustratingly vague. She had no idea what to do next, where to turn. Then she thought of Eric Singleton, of his kind smile, his warm and capable hands, his calming voice.

She went into the living room and picked up the phone to call his office. She was halfway through punching in the number when she realized the line was dead. A flash of lightning flickered through the window, followed by a roll of thunder that made the panes rattle. Panic wrapped around her again, and she caught herself looking over her shoulder anxiously. This was stupid! She felt as if she were trapped inside some low-budget horror flick. Then she remembered. She had unplugged the phone!

With a nervous titter of relief, she found the cord, plugged it back in, and dialed the office number.

The phone rang about ten times before Jennifer looked at her watch. It was a few minutes after six. The office was probably closed. She was about to hang up when a woman's voice answered.

"Dr. Singleton's office. Can I help you?"

"Yes, this is Jennifer Bolton. Is Eric Singleton still there?"

"I think he's already left, Mrs. Bolton. The office is closed. I was just about to switch the phones over to the answering service."

"Please," Jennifer pleaded. "I need to talk with him. It's an emergency!" She felt a small stab of guilt at this stretching of the truth. Though she knew her situation was not a true medical emergency, it felt that way to her.

The woman on the other end hesitated, then gave an exasperated sigh and said, "Hold on a minute."

Jennifer listened to a radio DJ offering free concert tickets to the ninth caller. Then a male voice came on the phone.

"Jennifer?"

"Oh, Eric! I'm so glad I caught you." The relief she felt at just hearing his voice was so profound she burst into tears.

"What's wrong?" Eric asked, his voice tinged with anxiety. "Is it Tanner?"

Jennifer nodded, unable to speak. When she realized what she was doing, she swallowed hard, trying to regain some control. "Yes," she managed to choke out. "Oh, Eric! I'm so scared for him! I don't know what to do!" She lost her barely maintained control and started to sob again.

"Tell me what happened," Eric said, keeping his voice calm and soothing.

Jennifer tried, but the sobs had total control at that point, and all she managed was a few blubbering noises.

"Never mind. Jennifer? Listen. I'm leaving the office now. I'll come over to your house. Okay?"

Jennifer tried to answer again, but her throat felt as if it were closing off.

"Jennifer? Can you hear me? Are you there?"

She managed to mutter an "I'm here."

"I have your address here on your file. Are you off of Highway 6?"

"Two miles . . . past . . . old mill house . . . third right." Her answer came out in hiccoughs; it was all she could manage. Apparently it was enough.

"I'll be right over," he said.

Jennifer heard a click and then, after a few seconds, a dial tone. She hung up the phone and went to the bathroom to try and get herself back in order.

Twenty minutes after she had hung up, Jennifer heard the peal of the front doorbell. She was surprised Eric had arrived so quickly and figured he must have broken all speed and safety limits getting there. Realizing what he had risked, she felt another twinge of guilt. She left Tanner in the kitchen, where he had finished off his ravioli and was now working on a rather large bowl of chocolate ice cream with hot fudge sauce.

Jennifer opened the front door and a soggy, dripping Eric stepped inside. He shrugged out of his raincoat and Jennifer took it from him, hanging it on a hook inside the living room closet.

"Where's Tanner?" he asked, standing in the foyer, holding one of those little black medical bags and dripping water into a small puddle at his feet.

"He's in the kitchen eating," Jennifer said.

Eric looked around, saw the entrance to the kitchen, and headed in that direction.

Jennifer grabbed his arm. "Wait," she said just above a whisper. "He's okay right now. I need to talk with you."

"Okay." His face was grave as he gave her a quick once-over. "I hope you won't take this the wrong way, but you look like hell," he added.

Jennifer flashed him a weak smile. "Thanks," she said running a self-conscious hand through her hair. She gestured toward the couch. "Please, sit down."

Eric did as he was told, and Jennifer settled down next to him. She filled him in on the events that had prompted her call. "The really strange part of all this is that Tanner said Bioceutics killed Tim." She stared into Eric's eyes. "Eric, I've never mentioned Bioceutics to him before."

"Maybe you did, and you just don't remember it," Eric suggested.

Jennifer shook her head vehemently. "No! I know I never mentioned it. I hated that damn place! Tim spent so much time there that it was a wonder we ever managed to have Tanner. I think he was at his happiest when he was ensconced inside that windowless, airtight laboratory of his. I can't tell you how many nights I sat at home, dinner growing cold, waiting for a husband who never showed."

"I'm sorry you went through that," Eric said.

"Oh, don't get me wrong. I knew what I was getting into long before I married Tim. Even our first dates, back when we were both in school, were marathon study sessions. And he had been at Bioceutics for three years when we got married, so it wasn't like I didn't know I was going to have to share him with his job. I just didn't realize how much I would come to resent it."

Jennifer paused, picking at her thumbnail. "You know," she said, "in one respect, I do believe that Bioceutics killed Tim. They sucked him dry, taking everything he had and then some. When Tim died, I shut

Bioceutics and everything associated with it out of my mind. I know I never mentioned the place to Tanner."

"Maybe he heard it from someone else," Eric said.

"Who? The only person he associates with who knew where Tim worked is my friend Carny. And she knows how I feel about the place. She would never mention it."

Eric pondered the situation a few moments. "So, what are you saying, Jennifer? Do you think Tanner is actually talking to his father?"

Jennifer heard the skepticism in his voice. "I know, it sounds incredible, Eric. But it's not just that. There's all this other weird stuff. How did Tanner know who you were? And that you were adopted?"

"That was kind of strange," Eric admitted thoughtfully. "But I just assumed he had overheard some gossip somewhere. You know, talk among the nurses at the hospital or something."

"That's what I thought, too," Jennifer said. "But today when we got home, he said the phone was going to ring, and then it did. I'm telling you, Eric. Something strange is going on."

Eric rubbed his chin and stared off into space, deep in thought. "I don't know what to suggest," he said at last. "Why don't I go take a look at Tanner just to make sure he's okay?"

Jennifer nodded and stood. Another wave of dizziness hit her and she reached out and grabbed Eric's arm to steady herself.

"And right after I'm done with Tanner I'm going to take a look at you," Eric said. "You really do look like shit."

Jennifer laughed in spite of herself. "Gee, thanks a lot!"

Eric crooked his arm and placed her hand on his elbow. "Come on. Let's go check out the young Kreskin."

Tanner's face lit up when he saw Eric. "Hi, Doc! Want some ice cream?"

Eric smiled a grimace. "No. Thanks anyway. Sweets aren't my thing. I'm more of a meat and potatoes kind of person." He patted his stomach. Tanner shrugged and shoveled in another spoonful while Eric took the chair next to him. "So how are you feeling since your test this morning?"

Tanner rubbed at the weals along his hairline. "My head is still kinda sore. But that's all."

"Your mom tells me you were talking with your father again earlier."

Tanner nodded, mouthing a huge spoonful of ice cream. A tiny string of fudge sauce draped itself over his lip and down his chin.

"Do you see your father when he talks to you?"

Tanner swallowed. "Nope. He just talks." He tapped the side of his head. "Up here. In my head."

"I see," Eric said, pulling at his chin.

Tanner shoveled the last of the ice cream into his mouth, then set the spoon aside and proceeded to pick up the bowl and lick the inside of it.

"Obviously all this hasn't affected your appetite any," Eric said with a smile.

Tanner gave him a messy-mouthed grin, then turned to his mother. "Can I be excused?"

Jennifer looked questioningly at Eric.

"Sure," Eric said. "Just promise me you won't eat anything else for a while. I'm afraid you'll explode!"

Tanner giggled and hopped out of his chair. Scotch immediately got up and stood next to him. "I promise," Tanner said. He skipped out of the kitchen with Scotch close on his heels.

"Make sure you wash your hands," Jennifer shouted after him. There was no response, and she looked at Eric with a shrug and a smile.

"That dog is certainly devoted to him, isn't he?" Eric observed.

"Yes. And he's a she."

"Oh, right. Sorry. I forgot." He smiled sheepishly.

"Well?" Jennifer asked, taking the seat Tanner had just vacated.

Eric shrugged. "He looks fine."

"Your father gave me the name of a psychologist and suggested I take Tanner as soon as possible."

"Maybe that will help," Eric said rather distractedly, tugging on his chin again and staring at a point just over Jennifer's shoulder. "In the meantime, there's something I want to check on. Something that's nagging at me."

"About what?"

He looked at her, saw the pale color of her face, the dark circles beneath her eyes, and the frightened way she chewed on one corner of her lip. "Oh, just something from medical school. I can't remember precisely. Don't worry about that now." He dismissed the subject with a wave of his hand, smiled, and said, "You don't look so good." The smile was teasing but his voice was serious. He opened his bag, took out a small white envelope, and slid it across the table toward her. "Here, these are mild sleeping pills. I want you to take one tonight, so you can get some rest."

Jennifer shook her head. "No, I can't. What if Tanner has another seizure?"

He had expected that. "How about if I offer to stay up and watch him for you?"

"Stay up? Here?"

"Sure. Why not? I don't have office hours tomorrow, so it won't hurt me. And I can use the time to catch up on my medical journals."

"Oh, Eric. I don't know if I can ask you to do that."

"You didn't ask. I offered. In fact, as your doctor I am ordering you to accept."

Jennifer considered the offer, surprised at how much the idea appealed to her. It made her feel as if a heavy load had been lifted off her shoulders.

"Okay," she said with a half smile. Then, as the idea grew on her, "Yes, okay. And thank you." Her relief was so complete, she felt overwhelmed with gratitude and affection. She stood up, went over to Eric, and bent down to kiss his cheek. But just as her lips found their mark the front door banged open and a booming voice yelled out her name, making her jump.

"Jennifer? Jennifer!"

She took a step back from Eric as Evan came crashing into the kitchen, his hair plastered to his skull, his normally immaculate suit wrinkled and soaked. "What in the hell is going on here? Jennifer?"

Jennifer had to stifle a giggle. Evan looked so comical with his usually kempt appearance now resembling that of a drowned rat, his face furiously red.

Evan's scowl deepened. "Where the hell have you been?" he asked. "I've been trying to call all afternoon, but no one answered the phone." His voice was a tightly controlled mix of concern and anger. His blue eyes blazed. Then they shifted and he seemed to notice Eric's presence for the first time. "Who the hell are you?" he asked gruffly.

"I'm sorry, Evan," Jennifer said, crossing the room toward him. She gestured toward Eric. "This is Er . . . Dr. Singleton." Then she swept her hand toward Evan, "And this is Evan Reeves."

The two men eyed each other closely for a second before Evan crossed the room with his hand extended. "Nice to meet you, Doctor," he said with a tone of voice that made the statement doubtful.

Eric rose, shook hands with him, then sat back down. "I hope you can help Tanner with this problem he's having," Evan said. He backed up and threw a possessive, and decidedly damp arm across Jennifer's shoulders. "The boy means all the world to us."

The two men stared, no *glared,* at one another. Jennifer realized they were sizing one another up, like potential enemies preparing to meet in combat. It struck her as mildly amusing at first, but as the contest continued she began to feel irritated. She moved out from beneath Evan's arm and walked over to the counter.

"Take off your coat," she told Evan. "You're soaked. I'll fix some coffee."

Her tactic worked as the two men broke eye contact, and Evan shrugged out of his coat. "Thanks," he muttered. "Coffee sounds good." He folded his coat carefully and laid it neatly over the back of one of the chairs.

"I'm sorry you were worried," Jennifer continued, trying to lighten the tension. "I unplugged the phone earlier this afternoon so Tanner and I could get some rest."

"Where is Tanner?" Evan asked, his voice sounding suspicious, as if he thought maybe they had hog-tied the child and stashed him in the basement.

"He's upstairs," Jennifer said, pouring water into the coffeemaker. "In fact, I should go and check on him."

"I should get going," Eric said, getting up from the table.

Jennifer felt her stomach drop. "Won't you stay for a cup of coffee?" she asked, biting off the pleading "please" she had almost tagged on the end. She was torn. Part of her thought it would be better if he did leave, as it would relieve the obvious tension that existed between him and Evan. But another part of her wanted desperately for him to stay.

"Thanks, but I think I'll pass." He picked up his medical bag and headed toward the living room.

Jennifer escorted him to the door, took his coat off

the hook in the closet, and handed it to him. "Do you have to go?" she asked him.

Eric frowned, started to say something, then bit it off. After a moment he said, "It looks like you're in good hands here. I'm sure Evan won't mind filling in as Tanner's night watchman."

Jennifer wasn't sure, but she thought she detected a note of sarcasm in Eric's tone.

"I'll call you in the morning," Eric said. Then, abruptly, he left.

When Jennifer turned around she found Evan framed in the kitchen doorway, watching. He walked over to her with his arms outstretched. "Are you okay?" he asked, pulling her into his chest and stroking her hair. "You look exhausted."

"I am," Jennifer admitted. "I've been afraid to sleep, wondering if Tanner will have another one of his spells during the night."

"I'm sure he'll be all right," Evan said into her hair. "I'd offer to stay with you tonight and keep an eye on him, but I have to be in court early in the morning."

Jennifer felt like crying. She swallowed hard instead. "How's the case going?" she asked.

"Not well, actually," Evan said, releasing her and leading her to the couch to sit down.

"I'm sorry."

"Well, these things happen," he said with a shrug. "You can't win every case. The thing I hate most is that I'll probably lose this one on emotion. The plaintiff is nothing but poor white trash with five kids she can't support, yet she's making this big deal about the loss of her childbearing abilities. The medical testimony has been mixed with one expert simply contradicting the other." He draped an arm over her back and started drawing lazy circles on her shoulder with his finger.

"Actually, I think my client *did* botch the surgery, but I'm not sure it wasn't the best thing for this woman. She doesn't need another mouth to feed, and Lord knows the world doesn't need another half-witted kid."

"Evan!" Jennifer sat up abruptly, letting his arm fall down behind her. She turned to stare at him. "How can you talk like that? That woman may not have much, but that doesn't mean she doesn't love her children. And birth control would be just as effective without her losing the ability to have children altogether."

Evan had the good grace to look embarrassed. "I know, I know. I'm sorry. You know how I get a little crazy at this point in a trial. Especially when I'm losing."

Jennifer felt his hand settle onto her shoulder again, and she stood up abruptly. "I really should go and check on Tanner."

Evan grabbed her hand and tried to pull her back down onto the couch. "Tanner's fine," he said. "But Evan could use a little attention." He wiggled his eyebrows at her.

"Evan, I can't." She pulled her hand away. "I'm just too tired."

He stood up and tilted her chin up toward his face. "Okay, but only if you promise me a rain check."

Jennifer smiled weakly.

Evan brushed his lips against her cheek, then kissed two of his fingers and placed them against her lips. "I love you, Jennifer," he said softly, his eyes smoldering.

It was the first time he had uttered the expression. Jennifer held her breath, waiting for the words to sink in, anticipating her reaction. She had thought about it often, imagining the moment, always responding with delight and excitement. Yet now that it had finally happened, all she felt was an overwhelming exhaustion. She had no energy left for any emotion, even love.

Evan gazed down into her eyes, and she knew he was waiting for her to respond in kind. But the words wouldn't come. She stood on her toes to kiss him, and said, "Good night, Evan." Then she made her way upstairs to fix up the makeshift bed she had set up in the rocking chair next to Tanner's window, leaving Evan to find his own way out.

6

Not quite twenty miles from the Bolton house, the members of a group that called themselves the MAGI were gathering at a sprawling brick mansion that sat atop Castle Hill overlooking Charlottesville. Though the metal fence that surrounded the house was artfully crafted, it was as deadly as the cottonmouths that were occasionally found fried into crispy commas at its base. At the gate stood a guardhouse, its interior dark and empty on this particular night. Instead, as each man arrived, he was required to utter an assigned password into a small speaker box before the gate. All of them thought the password alone allowed their admittance; none was aware that the box was part of a sophisticated computer system that checked their voice patterns to further assure their identity. Once they were on the estate land, cleverly concealed video cameras spaced along the long, circular drive provided additional monitoring.

Though the lawn was elaborately arrayed with well-trimmed shrubs, magnificent old oak trees, and a lit fountain at the center of the circular drive, the house itself was rather unpretentious. Though large and sprawling, it was constructed of plain brick and bore little in the way of decorative enhancements. Looking equally incongruous—particularly among the arriving cars, which included a Mercedes, a Rolls-Royce, two Jaguars, and a Cadillac—

was the older model, red, Volkswagen Beetle that was parked in the carport at one end.

The eleventh and last member of the group to arrive joined the others in a room that was called, appropriately, the library. They huddled loosely together at one end of a massive, mahogany table that dominated the center of the room, its surface gleaming. Twelve chairs surrounded the table, each one a rich burgundy-colored leather with tufted seat and back, the arms and legs made of the same rich mahogany. The walls behind and opposite the men were lined with shelves that reached from floor to ceiling, every space neatly occupied with hardcover books: some of them classic first editions in mint condition, some less expensive perhaps, though no less valuable for their literary merit, and others that were weighty tomes of information on every conceivable topic from archaeology to zoology. A third wall opened onto a lushly furnished greenhouse that contained a jungle of award-winning flora.

The fourth wall of the room held a fully stocked wet bar backed by a massive antique mirror whose glass rippled in the soft light. Unbeknownst to the men in the room, the mirror was a well-constructed counterfeit that served as a portal for the video equipment set up behind it in a tiny, hidden room. It was from this room that the twelfth member of the group—both the host and the group's leader— watched his guests as he prepared to make his entrance.

The group's leader made one final check of the cameras. Though his fear of someone else monitoring the room's activities bordered on the paranoid, he had no compunction whatsoever about documenting the activities for his own use. The monitors served a dual purpose; they provided insurance by committing the other members, albeit unknowingly, to a celluloid policy, and they also helped the leader to evaluate the meetings, and each participant, once they were adjourned. By reviewing the tapes, he was able to assess the body language and facial expressions of each person present, something he simply couldn't do during the course of the actual meeting. His meeting "minutes," as he called them, gave him all the input he needed to gauge and anticipate each member's particular leanings.

Satisfied that everything was working properly, the leader exited the tiny room and strode into the library with an air of preeminence, suppressing a smile as the other eleven men fell into an abrupt and awkward silence. He scanned the room with a practiced eye before moving to his designated seat at the head of the table.

The leader looked as out of place in this room with these men as a mongrel dog would look in the midst of the Westminster Kennel Club show. While the other men were dressed in expensive suits, tailored shirts, and Gucci leather shoes, he was clothed in a pair of worn blue jeans, a faded blue polo shirt, and ratty-looking sneakers with grass stains along their sides. Most who knew him thought that this habitual uniform, along with his tenacious devotion to the twenty-year-old Volkswagen parked outside, were mere aberrancies—short circuits in an otherwise well-wired individual. No one suspected that the image these eccentricities portrayed was one that was carefully manipulated and honed by the leader. His belief in his own superiority over the average man was so strong, so ingrained, that the accoutrements of his life were a conscious message to others: it was definitely *not* the clothes or the car that made the man. It was intelligence, class, and of course, money.

At thirty-five, the leader was also younger than the other men in the room by at least a decade, a difference that was accentuated by the youthful looks afforded to him by his blond hair, cherubic face, and round blue eyes. Yet the acerbic sting of his tongue, combined with an intimidating manner and a short-fused temper, left little doubt who was in charge.

As the leader took his seat, the other men in the room shuffled quietly to theirs, some eyeing the leader expectantly, others keeping their gaze lowered. When they were all settled, the leader leaned forward with hands folded and arms resting on the table. One by one, he fixed his gaze on each man at the table, finding great satisfaction in the response. As each person met that flinty glare, most for only a brief moment, some tiny quirk revealed their discomfiture: eyes quickly averted, a twitch of a cheek, a fidgeting hand, a subtle clearing of the throat. When he had finished his intimidating survey, the leader smiled, though the smile never quite reached his eyes.

"Gentlemen, welcome," the leader said. "This meeting of the MAGI is hereby called to order."

The acronym, MAGI, stood for the Mid-Atlantic Group Initiative. Its inherent association with the Wise Men of biblical fame made it, in the leader's mind, an inherently appropriate acronym. The appeal it held for him had nothing to do with any religious connotation; rather he felt it offered a definitive description of this elite and visionary assembly.

During his lighter moments (which were not all that common), the leader's fondness for acronyms led him to call their counterpart group to the north, NAG, and those to the south, SAG. The habit generated enough chuckles among the other members of the group that it caught on quickly, so that before long they were referring to the "naggers" and the "saggers" with regularity. If the leader's worst fears were recognized and someone managed to listen in on the group, the eavesdropper would get the impression that the members of MAGI knew their counterparts well, when in fact only one—the leader—had any real knowledge of who was in the other groups, where they met, or even if there really *were* other groups. Secrecy and absolute protection of all identities was the first tenet learned by each member, a rule so ingrained that they even referred to one another during the meetings with code names.

"The first item on the agenda is a report on our initial experiment," said the leader, or Zeus as he was known within the confines of these walls. "I am pleased to say that it was an unparalleled success. The subject killed his entire family and, as an extra bonus, did himself in as well. Eight inferiors eliminated. A fine night's work." The leader nodded toward one of the men at the table. "And we can thank our doctor friend, Hippocrates, for our success."

The other men nodded their approval.

The leader then focused his attention on the man directly to his left. "Item two. It is time, gentlemen, to move on to our Stage Two experiment. Pythias, why don't you explain."

The man known as Pythias shifted nervously, making the leather beneath him squeak faintly. He cleared his throat and ran a finger around the inside of his collar as if it chafed him. When he spoke, he looked at each man in turn, starting to his left and working his way around the table until he ended with the leader.

"I am working on a protocol that combines our special therapy with varying degrees of behavior modification. The biological effects incurred in the Stage One subjects seem to be all we had hoped for. With more behavioral study, we are hoping to achieve greater control over the outcome.

"Our first Stage Two subject is progressing quite nicely. If all goes according to plan, we should have the first soldier in our army of assassins ready in another day or so. The intended target's schedule is known, and we have the opportunity." Pythias smiled then, the resultant expression on his face offering an unsettling mix of pride and malevolence. "Our first bleeding heart liberal should be eliminated by the end of the week," he said cheerfully.

The leader's eyes drew down to a steely glint, impaling

Pythias like a butterfly on a pin and wiping the grin off the man's face like a hand swiping across a steamy mirror.

"I certainly hope you can keep that time line, Pythias. The man's momentum must be stopped. And stopped soon. Senator Tranley is a direct threat to everything we are working toward."

"Yes," was Pythias's only response. His hands fell resolutely into his lap, and, buckling under that fierce glare, he lowered his eyes.

The leader leaned back and folded his arms over his chest. "As some of you are aware, a small snag has developed in our plans. However, I have been assured that the situation is well under control." His eyes shifted pointedly toward two of the members, the one known as Hippocrates, and another, who used the name Socrates.

The two men nodded.

"See to it. I don't like screwups, gentlemen. We must move ahead with our plans. The time is imminently ripe. Every day the papers and newscasts are filled with reports of senseless and increasingly violent crimes. We are well on the way to the very levels of chaos and revolt we seek. We *must* seize the moment and use it to our advantage." He punctuated this last statement by slapping his open hand on the table's surface. A few of the men flinched.

"We are the pioneers of the new world order, gentlemen. The founding fathers, so to speak. Our cause, *The Cause*," he said with great reverence, "is the only answer to mankind's continued survival. The fact that the majority of society is too dim-witted and narrow-minded to see that only proves our point.

"Though none of you had the opportunity to meet the man who made The Cause possible, you are all familiar with Tim Bolton's work. It was his brilliance, his pioneering drive, that laid the groundwork for us. Though his unfortunate death delayed our plans, through hard work and patience we are now at the threshold of success. We must exercise extreme caution and perseverance, gentlemen. Nothing, and I mean *nothing*," he said, glaring at Hippocrates and Socrates, "must get in our way."

For a long moment, no one at the table moved; every one of them had his eyes fixed rigidly on the leader. So perfect was their stillness that, to an outside observer, the men assembled around the table looked like a diorama in a wax museum. Then the melting ice in the bar bucket shifted, and the men all jumped and issued a collective sigh of nervous relief.

The leader grinned, clearly amused by the reaction.

"So gentlemen," he said, "let me share with you the successes our counterpart groups have had with their Stage One experiments." He picked up the top newspaper from a pile on the table beside him and read the headline.

"Crazed Man Involved In Unemployment Office Shooting Spree." He slid the paper toward the man on his right and removed the next one from the pile.

"Community Shocked By Murder Rampage." Again he slid the paper and grabbed another.

"Riots Feared In LA Project."

He continued to read until he had worked his way through the pile. The men at the table scanned each article in turn, nodding their heads with tacit approval. When the newspapers had completed their rounds and were restacked on the corner, the leader leaned forward and again addressed the group.

"So, as you can see, our plans are moving forward. But we must be cautious. Now is not the time for sloppy mistakes. For the sake of review, I would like each of you to go over your current assignment. We'll start with you, Titus."

The leader glanced toward the man on his right, then leaned back and listened as the various phases of the plan unfolded.

7

Everyone in the Bolton household had a peaceful night's sleep, though only Tanner did it in his usual place. Scotch, for some reason, decided to sleep on the floor rather than the bed. And Jennifer, aided by sheer exhaustion—both emotional and physical—managed to ignore the discomfort of the rocking chair. They all woke feeling refreshed and energetic, despite the heavy blanket of humid heat that had been left behind by yesterday's storm.

Jennifer's sense of renewed hope was encouraged by two things: Tanner's usual, cheery morning chatter (an in-depth discussion of yesterday's *He-Man* episode) and the fact that he made no mention of any further conversations with his dead father.

Jennifer fixed scrambled eggs and crispy bacon for breakfast, one of Scotch's favorites as well as Tanner's. Knowing from past experience that the mouthwatering aroma of cooking bacon generally meant a special treat, Scotch even left her self-imposed guardpost at Tanner's feet and hovered instead at Jennifer's. Though having the dog underfoot was a bit of a nuisance, Jennifer was so grateful for this display of normal behavior, the way it had been *before*, that she was loath to so much as think about asking Scotch to move.

After they were finished eating, Jennifer sent Tanner upstairs to shower and dress while she placed a call to the psychologist whose number Dr. Singleton had given her. She was surprised when the doctor himself answered the phone, and even more surprised when he said he could see Tanner that morning.

"Dr. Singleton took the liberty of discussing Tanner's case with me yesterday," he explained. "I was hoping you would call this morning, as I am very anxious to meet the boy and it just so happens I have no appointments until eleven."

"Great," Jennifer said with more enthusiasm than she felt. She glanced at her watch. It was a few minutes before nine. "We can be there by ten o'clock. Would that do?"

"Ten would be fine, Mrs. Bolton. I'll see you then."

While she was waiting on Tanner, Jennifer carried her coffee into the living room and flipped on the TV. She thought a few minutes of repartee between Regis and Kathie Lee was just what she needed to maintain her spiritual uplift. Unfortunately, the picture that came into focus was not Kathie Lee's perky little face but one of those top-of-the-hour news briefs. A woman reporter wearing a somber expression stood beside a blood-smeared wall.

"*This is the scene of the terrible tragedy which took place at the home of Barry Hanover two nights ago. Mr. Hanover, apparently in a drunken rage, shot and killed his entire family before turning the gun on himself.*"

Sickened by what she saw on the screen, Jennifer aimed the remote to turn the set off. But something made her pause. Then it hit her. That name, Hanover, was the one she overheard Dr. Singleton's nurse mention in the office yesterday. As Jennifer stared at the gruesome scene, her coffee, which had smelled wonderful just moments before, became overpowering, like a too-strong perfume. She set the cup on the coffee table and pushed it to the far edge. When she looked back at the TV, the scene had switched from the blood-smeared pans of the Hanovers' walls to six portraits that filled the screen: the faces of the Hanovers' children, smiling and innocent.

"Dead are the Hanovers' six children, ranging in age from eighteen months to eight years."

As Jennifer stared desolately at those six fresh faces, their eyes large, round, and shining, the coffee in her stomach suddenly felt like an oily sludge. For a brief moment, she thought she was going to be sick. Her stomach churned violently while her heart ached with sadness. She forced her eyes away from the set and breathed heavily until the feeling subsided. Then, keeping her eyes averted, she aimed the remote in the general direction of the TV and hit the off button.

By the time Tanner came downstairs, Jennifer was feeling better physically, but she couldn't shake the pall of melancholy that hung over her. Nor could she erase the image of those six tiny faces from her mind.

Whether it was because he sensed the change in his mother's mood, or simply that he was not too thrilled at the idea of seeing a psychologist, Tanner also became sullen and morose. Consequently, the drive into town was tensely silent.

Dr. Andersen's office was one of many in a newly built, four-story glass building two blocks from the hospital. The hallways were large and plush, the carpet spongy, the wallpaper new, the paint still fresh. The waiting room was small—only four chairs—but it made up for its lack of size with large comfortable seats, a bookcase full of coloring books, crayons, puzzles, and games, and a mixed variety of current magazines. A receptionist, with rouged cheeks, silver hair, and Ben Franklin glasses secured by a chain that ran around her neck handed Jennifer a clipboard with the usual requisite forms to fill out. Jennifer had barely written Tanner's name on the first sheet when a door opened and a balding man of medium height wearing oxfords, khakis, and a slightly wrinkled cotton shirt entered the room.

"Mrs. Bolton? I'm Dr. Andersen." He extended a hand, and Jennifer shook it, assessing it as she did. Warm, firm, reassuring. So far so good.

"It's a pleasure to meet you," Jennifer said.

Dr. Andersen turned to Tanner, bent at the waist using his hands on his knees for support, and smiled broadly. "So! You are Tanner Bolton. I've heard a lot about you young man." He extended one hand, and, after a moment's hesitation, Tanner shook it.

Dr. Andersen straightened and looked at Jennifer. "What I would like to do, Mrs. Bolton, is take Tanner back by himself for a little while so that I can talk with him alone first. I would estimate about half an hour. Then I'll have you join us for the second half hour. Is that acceptable?"

Jennifer looked at Tanner. "Is that okay with you, honey?" she asked.

Tanner shrugged. "If I gotta."

"Well, then, shall we go?" Dr. Andersen said, looking at Tanner.

Tanner hopped off his chair and headed through the same door from which Dr. Andersen had appeared. As Jennifer watched her son shuffle away, a lump rose in her throat, and she felt an odd crawling sensation along her spine, like a dog whose hackles just rose. She bit her lip in an effort to quell the sudden impulse she had to run after him and yank him back.

As if he sensed her discomfort, Dr. Andersen placed a gently restraining hand on her shoulder. "He'll be fine. Don't worry." Then he, too, disappeared through the door, closing it behind him.

Jennifer busied herself filling out the forms and trying not to think about what was going on behind that closed door. More than once she caught the silver-haired receptionist watching her over the tops of her glasses. The woman quickly averted her gaze each time she was caught, acting as if she were fully engrossed in something on her desk.

At first Jennifer found the woman's behavior amusing. But after the third round of this cat-and-mouse game it became both irritating and a little unnerving. When she had finished filling out the forms, Jennifer quietly rose from her chair, carried the clipboard back to the window, and slapped it on the desk. She derived some small amount of satisfaction from seeing Miss Silver-hair jump, and with a smug grin she returned to her seat and tried to read the latest issue of *People* magazine.

She managed to succeed in distracting herself when she found an article profiling Senator Edward Tranley, Virginia's most popular politician and a strong candidate for the next presidential election. Though he had won his seat in the Senate on the Republican ticket, it was predicted that his presidential bid would be as an Independent.

His rise on the political ladder had been nothing short of meteoric. Birthed from the slums, he was a self-made man who had risen to his current position through hard work and perseverance. There were no dark and dirty secrets dredged up by the opposition or the reporters. His platform for the senatorial race focused on government reorganization and specialized programs designed to educate and employ the poor, the homeless, and certain minorities. His charm and angular good looks, combined with the loss of his beautiful wife to cancer a few years ago, gave him the air of a tragic hero, solidly locking in the female vote.

It had proven to be an irresistible combination. Fed up with wealthy, conniving bureaucrats who spent more time and money on their own interests than those of the public, the people of Virginia thought Tranley's no-nonsense attitude and history of self-achievement was just the salve needed to soothe society's wounds. He had won by an embarrassing margin. And apparently the rest of America was as enthralled with the man as were Virginians.

Jennifer read the article with great interest. She, like most others in the state, had been singularly impressed with the senator's ideals and charisma. Then, when she met the man at a party with Evan a few months ago, she had an opportunity to experience that charisma firsthand. Charm, intelligence, and grace fairly oozed from his pores. There was an incredible appeal about him, a certain presence that was much more than just his looks or beliefs. Something frustratingly and delightfully intangible. Jennifer had succumbed totally and willingly. There was no doubt in her mind which lever she would pull in the next election.

When she finished the article in *People*, Jennifer looked up and caught Miss Silver-hair peering at her again. Her anger softened by her memories of the senator, Jennifer merely smiled at the woman and picked up another magazine.

Tanner didn't think he liked Dr. Andersen much. The man's smile was pretty fakey, and when Tanner had touched his hand, there was a feeling of something not right. Tanner tried to shut out the background of voices playing inside his head and focus in on Dr. Andersen's voice instead. At first he wasn't able to pick up anything at all, but then he started getting little snatches. Something about "conversion reaction" and then "psychosomatic." It made no sense to him. Then, as he followed Dr. Andersen into the office, Tanner picked up on something else. It wasn't a word or words exactly. More of a sensation. Excitement. And fear. The doctor was afraid of him for some reason. The knowledge made Tanner feel a little better.

In the office, Tanner took a seat on a large couch positioned at one end of the room. Dr. Andersen took one of two chairs across from him, smiled his counterfeit smile, and said, "So, Tanner. Tell me about these talks you have with your father."

Tanner felt it again—that strange sensation of fear and excitement coming from the doctor. "What do you want to know?" Tanner asked him.

"Well—" Dr. Andersen cleared his throat and ran a finger around the inside of his shirt collar. He fixed a steady gaze on Tanner. "Tell me what your father sounds like when he talks to you."

Tanner thought about that a moment. He shrugged. "I don't know. He sounds like a guy."

"Is his voice loud or soft?"

"Soft."

"Is it a deep voice, like a grown man's, or a little voice, like a child's?"

"Deep." Tanner swung his feet up and down in front of him, letting them bounce against the couch's edge until he saw Dr. Andersen's eyes narrow almost imperceptibly. His feet bounced a final time, and he forced himself to sit still.

Dr. Andersen studied him a moment. "Does your father talk to you whenever you want him to?"

Tanner shook his head. "No. Whenever *he* wants to."

"What does he say?"

Tanner shrugged again. "Stuff. Like about how he

loves me. And how he misses me and Mom. And stuff about his work."

Dr. Andersen's eyebrows shot up.

Tanner could feel excitement radiating from the man.

"What does your father say about his work?" Dr. Andersen asked slowly.

"Stuff about some project he was working on. And how the people at work had him killed because of it."

Tanner saw Dr. Andersen's hands grip the arms of the chair. He watched the man's eyes grow large and round, saw his lips disappear into a thin line. Again he got that sensation of fear tinged with an underlying excitement, and he tried to focus in on Dr. Andersen's voice—the one inside his head. Nothing. Some people were easy, like his mother and Eric. But it was almost as if Dr. Andersen's mind was locked up in a box or something, protected from the outside. The same way lead blocked out Superman's X-ray vision. Tanner decided he definitely didn't like this doctor. He wasn't cool, like Eric.

"Now, Tanner," Dr. Andersen said, "I want you to think real hard about the times when you hear your father. Does he tell you anything specific about his work? Like what his project was, or the people he worked with?"

"Not really," Tanner said with a frown. "I don't really hear whole sentences. It's more like just pieces of sentences. Words and things."

"Can you remember any of the words?"

Tanner thought back, trying to remember. His eyes stared across the room; his feet started to swing again. Then he caught himself and held his legs still. He chewed on the side of his thumb instead, his face screwed up with concentration. A lot of the stuff his father said to him was confusing—big words and things he didn't understand.

"Well, there was something about hormones, I think," he said finally. "Does that make sense?"

Dr. Andersen blanched. "Yes, it does. Did you hear your father say something specific about hormones?"

"No." Tanner sensed that the doctor was uneasy. He tried again to tap into the doctor's head voice, but suddenly his father's voice exploded into his mind. *Tanner! Stop! Don't say any more!*

Tanner's mouth fell open, and he stared at the doctor. He had never before heard his father's voice so loudly or clearly.

"Tanner?"

"Yes?"

"Do you believe that your father's voice is real?"

"Yes."

"Do you think it's possible that you just think you hear him?"

Tanner started to shake his head, but Dr. Andersen went on.

"I'll bet you miss not having a father. I remember when I was a little boy, I had an imaginary friend I talked to whenever I felt lonely. I think it would be nice to have an imaginary father around, to talk to you about things that you don't want to talk to your mother about."

"My father is real," Tanner insisted. "I know he's dead. I know he isn't here. But he's somewhere. Somewhere where he can talk to me."

"You mean like a ghost?" Dr. Andersen's voice was skeptical.

"I guess," Tanner said defensively, scowling. His lower lip jutted out, and he folded his arms over his chest.

"Do you talk back to your father?"

"Mom says it's impolite to talk back to someone."

Dr. Andersen smiled. "I didn't mean it that way, Tanner. I meant do you talk *with* your father. You know, carry on a conversation with him."

"Sometimes," Tanner answered sullenly. "Mostly I just listen."

"I see."

Tanner heard his father's voice again. *Tell him I'm not real.*

Dr. Andersen cleared his throat again and did the finger inside the collar thing. The longer Tanner sat here, the more sure he was that he really, really didn't like this doctor.

"Maybe I did make him up," Tanner said, glancing away toward the window.

"What?"

"My dad. I guess he isn't really real. Just make-believe real."

"Oh? Why do you think you want him to be real?" Dr. Andersen spoke slowly, as if he was weighing each word.

Tell him you don't like your mother's boyfriend.

"It's because I don't like Evan," Tanner said. "He's the guy dating my mother."

Dr. Andersen studied the boy closely. *The kid is lying. I'm sure of it. Has his guard up for some reason. Probably ought to change the subject, get him to relax for a while.* "So, Tanner," he said, "tell me what you do for fun."

It was closer to forty-five minutes rather than the promised half hour before Miss Silver-hair told Jennifer she could go on back. She went through the same door Tanner had gone through and found herself in a small alcove. To the left was the receptionist's area, to the right Dr. Andersen's office.

The office was large, but cozy. A plush gray couch lined the wall at one end of the room with two burgundy armchairs across from it, creating a small conversation area structured around an oak coffee table and a beautiful burgundy-and-cream Oriental rug. At the other end of the room, there was a small play area in one corner filled with a variety of toys, coloring books, crayons, construction paper, puzzles, games, and books. A chalkboard hung on one wall, a magnetic letter board on the other. The opposite corner was occupied by a large mahogany desk and a well-used, black leather chair. Like the desk in Dr. Singleton's office, this one was also covered with stacks of charts. The floors were highly polished hardwood, and a window ran from floor to ceiling on each side of the couch, making the room appear bright and warm. A handful of plants—ivies, philodendrons, and ferns—hung over the seating area.

Tanner was sitting on the couch, his feet curled up beneath him, leaning on one of the arms. Dr. Andersen was in one of the chairs, his shoulders slightly hunched over, his legs crossed so that his pant leg rode up exposing an expanse of very white leg above argyle socks. He gestured toward the other chair for Jennifer, and she took it, studying Tanner's face as she sat, looking for clues as to what had gone on.

"Tanner and I have had quite a nice conversation," Dr. Andersen told her. "It seems we have a few things in common."

"Oh?" Jennifer shifted her eyes from Tanner to Dr. Andersen.

"Yes." Dr. Andersen smiled. Jennifer thought it was a plastic and well-practiced smile—plenty of white teeth, the mouth assuming the proper shape, yet the rest of his face looked as if it belonged to someone else. "We both have a great love of Road Runner cartoons and the Super Mario Brothers."

Jennifer smiled and waited, her own face feeling as plastic and posed as Dr. Andersen's looked.

"I think Tanner is fine, Mrs. Bolton."

Jennifer closed her eyes and breathed a sigh of relief.

"I see no evidence of any pathological problems here, and though there is a slight psychological one, it is nothing to be overly concerned with."

Jennifer's eyes opened again and she focused in on what Dr. Andersen was saying.

"Tanner is at an age where he is beginning to develop into a young man. Prepuberty. It is not uncommon for children to experience very heightened emotions at this age. It is also an age where a young boy starts to look for role models for his maleness. A father figure, if you will."

Jennifer nodded. So far she understood everything, and none of it sounded too horrible. Why did she feel that he was holding back on the punch line?

"Because Tanner has never had a father, at least not one that he can remember, he has conjured one up in his imagination."

Jennifer glanced at Tanner and was shocked to see an expression of disgust and contempt on his face as he stared at Dr. Andersen. Quickly she averted her eyes and looked back at the doctor, hoping to keep his attention focused on her so he wouldn't see the way Tanner was looking at him.

"Tanner and I have talked about these discussions he has with his father and Tanner has admitted that he conjures these talks up in his mind. Right, Tanner?"

Jennifer's eyes grew wide as she watched the doctor turn to look at Tanner, and she held her breath in anticipation of his reaction. But nothing happened. She looked over at Tanner herself. He had resumed his placid, smiling expression.

"Right, Dr. Andersen," Tanner said sweetly.

Jennifer watched Dr. Andersen closely. Though the man didn't seem aware of it, Jennifer knew every inflection of Tanner's voice well enough to know that his answer had been patronizing. It was subtle, but it was there.

"So," Andersen went on, clearing his throat and rimming the inside of his collar with one finger, "I don't think there is any cause for alarm here. Tanner would like to get to know his father better, and perhaps you can help him with this, Mrs. Bolton. Show him some pictures and talk with him from time to time about what his father was like."

"We have done that," Jennifer said.

"Good. Very good," Andersen said, nodding his head. It was then that Jennifer decided the good doctor was a pompous ass, one even her eight-year-old son could see through.

Andersen continued, apparently oblivious to his audience's opinions. "I have suggested that Tanner try writing to his father rather than talking with him. There is no harm in that, and he might find it therapeutic. And in the meantime, if there is a male member of your family that might be available to spend some time with Tanner, I think it would be helpful for him to have a male role model."

"There isn't anyone," Jennifer said. "Just Evan. He's my boyfriend."

Dr. Andersen cleared his throat with a little "ahem" and glanced over at Tanner. "I'm not sure Tanner relates all that well to Evan, Mrs. Bolton. How much time does Evan spend with Tanner?"

Jennifer blushed. "Not a lot," she admitted, feeling a pang of guilt. She had purposely kept Evan and Tanner at a bit of a distance from one another, worried that Tanner might get too attached to the man before Jennifer had a chance to sort out her own feelings and decide if Evan was someone she wanted to be a part of their future. She didn't want Tanner to have to go through the anxiety of losing someone he had come to depend on. She had thought she was doing it to protect him. Now she wondered. "Evan's awfully busy," she said, trying not to sound defensive.

Dr. Andersen dismissed her concerns with a wave of his hand. "No problem at all. There are plenty of other alternatives. Big Brother programs, the Boy Scouts, things like that. You must understand that Tanner is on a threshold. He is still very much a child, but the lack of a dominant male figure in your lives has made him feel as if he needs to fill that role, forcing him to mature a little faster than he is ready for."

Jennifer sneaked a quick glance at Tanner and caught him rolling his eyes. She bit her cheek to keep from laughing. Dr. Andersen went on, apparently oblivious.

"I think this feeling that he had to take on the role of the man of the house, so to speak, became so overwhelming for him that he decided to resurrect his father to take over. Acknowledging that his father isn't real is a great first step, but there is more to be done. I would like to continue to see Tanner once a week here in the office."

"What for?" Jennifer asked.

"To monitor his progress. And to make sure things don't deteriorate."

The last part made Jennifer swallow hard. "Deteriorate? How?"

"Well, Tanner is at a vulnerable age, Mrs. Bolton. The years before and during puberty can be a very volatile time for a young man."

"I see," Jennifer said, though she wasn't sure she did at all.

"Well then," Dr. Andersen said, clapping his hands and standing. "That will be all for today." He extended a hand to first Jennifer, then Tanner. "Schedule another appointment for next week with Sylvia."

Jennifer thanked him, took Tanner by the hand, and steered him toward the alcove.

Dr. Andersen saw them to the waiting room door, said, "See you next week," and then went back into his office, closing the door firmly behind him. He sat at his desk, picked up the phone, and dialed. After a moment he leaned back in the chair, his head cocked to one side to hold the phone in place against his shoulder. He cleared his throat when he heard someone pick up on the other end.

"This is Pythias," he said. "I think we have a problem."

Tanner gazed out the side window of the car at the passing scenery. He was glad to be going home, glad to be out of that creepy doctor's office.

"So what did you think of Dr. Andersen?" his mother asked him.

"He's stupid," Tanner said.

"That's not very nice," Jennifer admonished.

"But it's true! He wouldn't believe anything I told him about hearing Dad. And Dad said I shouldn't trust him."

Jennifer's hands tightened on the wheel until her knuckles turned white. "I thought Dr. Andersen said you agreed your dad was in your imagination, Tanner," she said tightly.

Tanner shook his head. "I told him that because that's what Dad told me to say. Dad *is* real, Mom. I swear he is."

Jennifer looked over at him and saw frustration and pain etched in his face. He looked as if he was ready to cry, and she realized things were starting to get to him as much as they were getting to her. They were both walking an emotional tightrope. Maybe it would be better if she just dropped the whole matter. So what if he thought he could really hear Tim? Dr. Andersen seemed to think that it was nothing more than the overactive imagination of a lonely and desperate boy. There was no sign of any brain damage or mental illness. So let it go.

She reached over to pat Tanner's leg. "Okay, honey. If you say he's real, I believe you."

She could feel Tanner's eyes on her, studying her face, trying to decide if she meant what she was saying or if she was merely attempting to placate him.

"I don't want to go back to Dr. Andersen," Tanner said quietly.

Jennifer knew he was challenging her. Right now, she wasn't sure she wanted him to go back to Dr. Andersen either. That wasn't to say he might not need to see another psychologist along the way.

"Okay. No more Dr. Andersen," Jennifer agreed. "Happy?"

Tanner smiled. "Yeah," he said. "He was weird anyway."

"Yeah, he was a bit strange." She reached over and ruffled Tanner's hair, smiling when he ducked away from her hand.

"I hate it when you do that," he said.

"I know. That's why I do it."

When they got home, Jennifer saw the light on the answering machine blinking and went to check the messages. The first one was from Evan.

"Hi, Jen. Got a few minutes for lunch and thought I'd check on my two favorite people. Sorry I missed you. I'll give you a call later. Love you."

The second call was from Eric. "Jennifer, call me as soon as you can. I've found something interesting that might explain what's going on with Tanner. I'm at home. 555–2867."

Evan could wait. She didn't feel like talking to him

right now anyway. And she didn't want to talk with Eric while Tanner was within hearing distance, so she jotted down his phone number and set it aside. Whatever information he had could wait as well. She felt a desperate need for some "normal" time, doing the things she and Tanner usually did on any given day. While Tanner settled down in front of the TV, she headed out to the kitchen and fixed them sandwiches for lunch. They ate in the living room, having an indoor picnic on a blanket on the floor, watching television.

They passed the first part of the afternoon in companionable silence, enjoying the antics of He-Man and Skeletor in a special, doubleheader feature. At two o'clock, when *He-Man* was over, Tanner yawned widely, announced he was going to go lie down for a while, and headed up to his room with Scotch close on his heels, the dog's tail wagging happily now that her master was back at home safe and sound.

Upstairs in his room, Tanner went over to his dresser and opened the top drawer to get out his *Spiderman* comic book. His hand froze in midair, poised above the drawer. The book was gone. He frowned as he stared at the jumble of underwear and socks, then glanced around, puzzled, until he spied the comic book on top of his dresser, one corner of it lying haphazardly over the top of his hairbrush. That was strange. He never left his comic books out, ever since the time Scotch had gotten ahold of one and chewed it into a pulpy mass. He thought back to this morning, remembered using the brush on his hair. But he had not had the comic book out.

He stared at the book intently, positive he had left it in the drawer, knowing that was where it belonged, confused as to how it could have gotten to where it was. As he stared at the book, puzzling over the mystery, it moved. At first he thought he must be imagining it, but then he saw that the one corner no longer rested atop the brush. He stared at it again, waiting for it to move, then *willing* it to move. It did, sliding across the top of the dresser and dropping into the drawer, as if some invisible hand had pushed it there.

Tanner's eyes grew wide with amazement. He knew that somehow, some way that he didn't understand, he had made that comic book move. He cast his eyes around for another object, settling on a Matchbox car that sat on one corner of the small stand beside his bed. Focusing all of his attention on the tiny car, he tried to push it onto the floor. His eyebrows drew down with concentration. He chewed on one corner of his mouth, trying to extend his mind across the room. Suddenly, so suddenly that it made Tanner jump, the car rolled off the stand onto the floor. A slow smile crept over Tanner's face.

He turned to run downstairs and tell his mother about his newly learned trick but stopped when he saw the door to his closet. It was tightly closed, the space at the bottom a darkened crack. The light in his closet was never turned off. Though he sometimes enjoyed using the tiny space as a fort of sorts during the daytime, at night he imagined too many horrors that might be lurking within its depths. His mother had long ago developed the habit of leaving the light on and the door ajar, to assure him that there were no bogeymen hiding in there. In a flash, Tanner understood why his comic book was out of the drawer and why the light in the closet was out and its door shut. Someone had been in his room.

When Tanner disappeared upstairs, Jennifer took advantage of his absence to call Eric. She picked up the piece of paper where she had scribbled down his number and was about to punch it in when Tanner hollered from upstairs. "Mom?"

Jennifer froze, phone in hand. Tanner's voice sounded scared, on edge. Slowly, with an odd feeling of foreboding, she set the phone down.

"What is it?" she yelled back.

"I think you better come up here," he said.

Jennifer took the steps two at a time. She found Tanner standing in front of his dresser petting Scotch's head. "What's wrong?" she asked breathlessly.

"Someone's been in my room," Tanner said, his voice quavering.

"What do you mean?"

"Someone looked through my drawers and stuff," Tanner said. "I know, because my comic book was out and the closet door is closed and the light is off."

Jennifer looked around the room. "Tanner, are you sure? Maybe you just thought you left the closet door open and closed it without even realizing it. Or maybe the lightbulb is blown." She walked over to the closet, opened the door, and tugged at the string that hung down overhead. The light came on.

"See," Tanner said.

"Maybe you turned it off and just don't remember it," Jennifer argued. She headed for the dresser, scanning the open drawer as well as the contents spread out on top. Nothing looked out of place to her.

"I think you're mistaken, Tanner," she said.

"I'm not, Mom!" Tanner insisted, the frustration in his voice clear. "Go look at your stuff. Maybe they messed with your stuff, too." His voice was pleading, and he sounded as if he was about to burst into tears.

Regardless of what had really happened, it was clear to Jennifer that Tanner believed his interpretation of the situation. She stared at her son and shivered. "Tanner, please. You're scaring me! I think you're letting your imagination get a little carried away here. Why would anyone look through your stuff?"

"Mom, please!"

Jennifer felt a surge of emotional energy course through her. She wasn't sure if it was anger or fright or both. But she did know that she'd had just about enough of this insanity!

"Tanner Bolton! You stop this craziness right now or you *will* go back to Dr. Andersen!" She heard the shrill sound of fear and panic in her voice and forced herself to swallow it back down, taking a deep breath.

"Mom, I'm sorry," Tanner said with maddening calm. "Please. Just go look around."

Jennifer studied her son's face a long time. He looked back at her patiently, his huge brown eyes beseeching. Even Scotch's eyes, almost identical to Tanner's, seemed to be pleading with her.

"Okay," she said finally. "Just to prove to you that you're only imagining things."

She turned abruptly and went down the hall to her bedroom. She stood in the middle of the room, arms folded across her chest, one foot tapping impatiently. These insistent imaginings of Tanner's were beginning to grate on her nerves. The more she thought about it, the madder she got. She almost welcomed the anger. It was easier to live with than the fear. She scanned the bedroom quickly, saw nothing out of place, and turned to go back to Tanner's room.

It was then that she saw the box.

It was an ordinary shoe box, filled with pictures and other memorabilia she had of Tim. She had always meant to put them into an album but had never gotten around to it. They had been in the box beneath her bed for years, dragged out on occasion when she wanted to take a trip down memory lane. It had been months, maybe more than a year, since she had last looked in that box. And yet one corner of it poked out from beneath the bed. She bent down and pulled it the rest of the way out. A fine layer of dust coated the lid—all of it, that is, except for a clean area near one end.

Someone had been in the box.

Fear returned with a vengeance, and a vicious shiver shook Jennifer's body. Her mouth felt incredibly dry all of a sudden, and tiny hairs on the back of her neck crawled. She wandered around the room in a daze, examining everything closely, opening drawers, looking in the closet. Tanner was right. Things had been moved. They were subtle differences, things she might not have noticed had she not been looking for them, but they were there.

From the bedroom she flew downstairs and scanned the living room. The glass doors to the fireplace—one of them was slightly ajar. Specks of dust lined the shelves of the bookcase where books had been pulled out and then put back. In the kitchen she found more evidence: cans in the cupboard were out of place, the silverware drawer was partway open, even stuff in the refrigerator had been moved. She stood in the middle of the kitchen, her pulse racing, her mind reeling. *Why would anyone search our house? What could they possibly be looking for? And how did they get in?*

"See?"

She hadn't heard Tanner come downstairs, and the sound of his voice behind her made her nearly jump out of her skin. She whirled toward him, clapping a hand over her pounding heart. "Tanner! You scared the life out of me!"

His face was a tightly drawn mask of fear: pale, wide-eyed, lips trembling slightly. She realized she was going to have to set her own fear aside and be strong for him.

She went over and knelt in front of him, grabbing him by both shoulders.

"It's okay, Tanner," she said. "There's nothing to be afraid of. It was probably just a burglar."

"But nothing was stolen," he said shakily. His eyes searched hers, tears brimming. She pulled him to her, holding him in a savage embrace.

"We'll call the police," she said. "They'll find out who did this."

Tanner held her, the ferocity of his own grip making Jennifer painfully aware of just how frightened he really was. She was overwhelmed by an acute sense of frustration. Frustration and anger. Anger at whoever and whatever had violated the calm of their existence, disrupting the peaceful life she had struggled to build for the two of them. Over Tanner's shoulder, she could see Scotch sitting in the kitchen doorway, head hung low, eyes doleful, tail wagging tentatively. Christ! Even the dog was affected by all that had happened.

She pried Tanner's arms from around her neck and held him at arm's length. She started to try and reassure him, to convince him that everything would be okay. That she'd find some way to work it all out. Except she wasn't very convinced of that herself.

The phone rang, shattering the silence, and they both jumped. Jennifer planted a quick kiss on Tanner's forehead and ran into the living room to grab it.

"Hello?" Her voice came out as little more than a squeak.

"Jennifer? It's Eric." There followed a long, silent pause. "Is everything okay?"

"No." Her throat tightened with threatened tears, and she struggled to get the words out. What was it about Eric that turned her into a blithering idiot every time she heard his voice?

"Jennifer?"

Once again, the sound of his voice, concerned and caring, breached the dam that held her tears in check. "Please come," she sobbed.

"Be there as quick as I can."

Jennifer heard the static silence of the open line, followed by a dial tone. Bless the man! He seemed always to understand what she needed. She hung up the phone, leaning her head against the wall a moment to try and pull herself together. Then she turned to Tanner.

"Eric's coming," she said simply.

Tanner nodded, and Jennifer thought she saw relief sweep over his face. It seemed she wasn't the only one who took comfort in Eric's confident and reassuring presence. She took Tanner by the hand and led him into the living room. They settled on the couch, wrapped together, each taking comfort from the warm presence of the other, waiting for Eric.

Scotch padded into the room behind them and settled herself at their feet. Jennifer was grateful for the dog's presence. Though she wasn't sure of Scotch's ability to defend them, she thought the dog's heightened senses would at least warn them if anything untoward was coming.

They waited, the three of them, in a silence so complete, Jennifer could hear the second hand on her watch as it ticked its way around the numbers.

8

Eric arrived at Jennifer's house in another record-setting time. Clad in a pair of frayed jeans, mud-streaked sneakers, and a denim work shirt, Jennifer thought he looked more like a construction worker than a doctor.

"What's going on?" he asked as Jennifer let him in. His face was deeply flushed and he had a wide-eyed, almost-startled look about him. He stole a quick glance at Tanner. "You sounded awful on the phone."

"Someone has been in the house," Jennifer said, her tone hushed as if she thought someone might be listening. "Everything has been gone through, as if someone was searching for something."

Eric scanned the room, then returned his gaze to Jennifer. "Are you sure? You've been under a lot of stress lately and perhaps . . ."

"I'm sure." Jennifer's interjection left no room for debate.

Eric's brows drew down into a V, and he started pulling at his chin, a gesture Jennifer was coming to know well. "Why would anybody go through your house?" he asked, clearly still not convinced. "What could they have been after?"

Jennifer gave him a quick, irritated shrug. "I have no idea."

"I do," Tanner said quietly from the couch. Jennifer and Eric both turned to stare at him. "Dad said they are after some papers of his. Notes and stuff that he hid about the project he was working on when he was killed."

Jennifer squeezed her eyes shut and ran both hands along the sides of her head, her fingers combing the long strands of her hair. "Oh, Tanner," she moaned. "This is getting too crazy! Wanting to talk with your dead father is one thing but . . ."

"Wait a minute," Eric said, placing a stalling hand on her arm. "I have some things to tell you before you go off on Tanner again. Things you may find interesting."

Jennifer turned toward Eric, studying his face, trying to read whatever thoughts or emotions were hiding behind those green eyes. But he gave away nothing.

"Sit down," Eric suggested, pointing toward the couch.

There was that awful command again. She did as she was told, settling on the couch next to Tanner, feeling her heart do little flip-flops inside her chest. What the hell was she going to hear now? Had Eric discovered something new related to Tanner's problem? Was her son sicker than she thought?

Eric sat in a chair across from them, his face solemn. "I did some research last night into Tanner's case," he began. "There was something that kept nagging at me yesterday, something I remembered from medical school about the pineal gland. It took me a while to find it because I was looking through all of my regular medical school texts and papers. But what I was looking for wasn't in those."

Eric was obviously excited. His hands were animated, his speech rapid, his eyes sparkling.

"What I needed was in a textbook and some notes from an elective class I took. One on parapsychology." He emphasized the last word, pronouncing it slowly. Then he waited, palms up, his eyebrows raised in question, clearly looking for a reaction.

"Parapsychology," Jennifer repeated, looking confused. "You mean like ESP and such?"

Eric nodded. "That and psychokinesis, telepathy, clairvoyance—there are many kinds of paranormal experiences." He fell silent, waiting for Jennifer to absorb where he was heading. It didn't take her long.

"Are you saying you think Tanner is having these paranormal experiences?"

"Yes, I do," Eric said carefully. "The pineal gland has long been associated with some role in ESP. Nothing definitive from a scientifically provable standpoint, but some strong theory and supposition. There are case histories involving damage of some sort to the pineal gland which later resulted in heightened paranormal abilities."

He shifted in his chair and leaned closer. "Not only that," he continued, "but cases regarding poltergeists—you know, things flying off of shelves and such—have been associated with prepubescent children. There's research to suggest that the heightened emotional state of a child that age provides the perfect foundation for this type of paranormal experience."

Jennifer was leaning forward, too, elbows on her knees, her attention riveted on Eric, trying to digest everything he was saying. At least he hadn't told her Tanner had some terrible incurable disease. What he was telling her didn't seem too awful. Did it? There was so much to try and comprehend! She focused on the part about the pineal gland first. "So you think this needle thing in Tanner's brain has stimulated his pineal gland?"

"Precisely! Think about it. The MRI he had not only moved that metal sliver, but it most probably magnetized it as well. Sending all of that magnetic energy into the gland along with the resonance created by the radio waves would have stimulated it like crazy!"

Jennifer turned to look at Tanner, who was watching and listening to Eric intently.

"That would explain how Tanner knew all those things about me that first morning I met him," Eric continued. "He was reading my mind. And that's how he knew the phone was going to ring and all the other things he's been predicting."

"Reading your *mind*?" Jennifer said, her voice rife with skepticism. "That's crazy!" Her mouth twitched into a half smile as though she thought maybe Eric was just making a joke—a bad joke. "Next you'll be telling me he's reading palms! And are you suggesting that Tanner is actually talking to Tim? To his ghost or something?"

Eric took a deep breath and gave the room a wary once-over. "It's possible, Jen. Who knows? There is so much we don't know about life after death. Like this ESP stuff, there is virtually nothing in the way of scientific evidence to support the existence of ghosts or spirits or whatever you want to call them. But there is plenty of material out there to strongly suggest it."

Jennifer shook her head vigorously. "Oh, I don't know, Eric. This all sounds a little too crazy."

"I know it does. But crazier things than this have been proved."

Jennifer thought she felt a draft of air around her head and shivered. She ran a hand through her hair, then nervously tucked a strand behind one ear while she looked around the room. Is Tim's spirit lurking about somewhere? Was Tanner really able to hear him? Was Tim watching and listening to them that very moment?

Eric continued. "Much of the history surrounding ghosts and such suggests that some unresolved life issue leads to the spirit's remaining on earth. Perhaps Tim has been here all along, just waiting for a way to communicate. Then his son suddenly develops these extraordinary powers and bingo!" Eric clapped his hands together, making both Jennifer and Tanner jump.

Jennifer stood up and started pacing the living room. "So are you telling me you think Tanner's suggestion that Tim's death was no accident might be valid? That someone had him killed?" Her voice was tightly controlled. All this time her greatest fear had been that Tanner was brain damaged or crazy. The thought that what he was saying might actually be true opened up a whole new bag of fears. An icy frisson of fear snaked down her spine.

"I'm saying it's possible," Eric said carefully. "I'm not ruling it out at least."

Jennifer paced and chewed at a cuticle.

Tanner asked, "Is that why I keep hearing all these voices in my head?"

Jennifer froze where she was behind the couch. She stared down at the top of her son's head, as if she thought maybe she could see inside there.

"What voices?" Eric asked.

Tanner shrugged. "I don't know. Just a lot of voices. Sometimes I know who it is, sometimes I don't. Sometimes I hear words and sometimes I just get pieces, like feelings or something. Like with Dr. Andersen."

"What did you pick up from Dr. Andersen?" Jennifer asked, leaning over the back of the couch.

"He was afraid of something," Tanner said. "It was like he was afraid of me, except he wasn't. It's hard to explain."

"Maybe something you said frightened him," Eric suggested.

"Maybe."

"Can you remember what you were talking about when you got the feeling he was afraid?"

Tanner screwed his face up a moment, trying to remember. "It was about Dad," he said. "I was telling Dr. Andersen some of the things Dad had told me about work and stuff."

Eric got up and moved over to sit on the couch next to Tanner. "Can you remember any of the specific things your dad has told you?" he asked gently.

Tanner shifted his position and his face puckered even more. He closed his eyes for a moment while Jennifer and Eric waited. Then he let out an exasperated breath. "It was stuff I didn't understand. He talked about how they had him killed, but then it was a bunch of big words and stuff. I can't remember," he whined. He looked precariously close to tears.

"Do you think you could ask your Dad to tell you again?" Eric asked.

"No!" Jennifer shouted, shooting an angry look at Eric. She came around to the front of the couch and knelt in front of Tanner, resting her hands on his knees. "I don't want him to do that." She looked up at Eric. "This is all too weird. We don't know if this is even true. And if it is, we don't know what it might be doing to Tanner."

"I don't think it will hurt him any," Eric said defensively.

"You don't *think* so. But you don't know, do you?" Jennifer snapped.

"I like it when Dad talks to me," Tanner said. "He's nice."

Jennifer rolled her eyes and threw up her hands. "This is crazy!" she said, standing up and resuming her pacing. She fixed her eyes on the back of Eric's head. "What about the seizure he had? Are you telling me *that* was nothing to worry about?" she asked shrilly.

"It's not to be taken lightly, of course," Eric said. "But there was no residual damage, and I think it was a one-time thing."

"You think!" Jennifer accused. "You think, but you don't know! You are not going to use Tanner for some weird medical experiment, Eric!"

Eric held up his hands in defeat. "Okay, okay. But will you at least hear me out on this? Will you think about it? If my theory is right, you and Tanner could be in a great deal of danger. Remember, both you and Tanner were in that car when it crashed as well as Tim."

That made Jennifer pause. She shivered again, and wondered how the room could be so damned cold when it was ninety-five degrees outside. *Are we in danger? Was that accident meant to kill all of us? If so, why have Tanner and I been allowed to live?*

As if Eric read her thoughts, he said, "Perhaps Tim knew something he shouldn't have. Maybe Bioceutics thought you knew it as well. Then, when you survived the accident, they decided to just keep an eye on you. Not to do anything unless you asked the wrong questions. Two accidents so close together would have looked pretty suspicious."

Jennifer backed away from Eric, shaking her head. "This is scary, Eric. I don't want to discuss this anymore." She turned abruptly and headed for the kitchen.

Eric went after her. "Jen, wait!" He grabbed her shoulder just as she was about to go through the kitchen door. When he turned her toward him, he saw the liquid sheen of tears in her eyes. "Jennifer, look, I'm sorry if all this frightens you. But we've got to figure out a way to deal with it."

"I don't want to deal with it," she said petulantly. She looked away, afraid to meet those eyes.

"We have to. You're not alone in this. I'll help you in any way I can." He lifted her chin so that she was facing him, but she kept her eyes steadfastly averted. "I want to help you, Jennifer," he said, his voice soft and low. "You and Tanner have grown to mean a lot to me in the past few days. Please, let me help you."

She gave in and looked into his eyes. What she saw in the green depths was concern and compassion. And something more. She was aware of her own feelings toward him, something more than the usual doctor-patient relationship. He had grown to mean a lot to her, too. For a moment she entertained the idea of just letting herself go, falling into those stalwart arms, letting sturdy, capable Eric deal with all of this for her. But her mind was reeling too hard. Everything was so confusing! So frightening!

She saw Eric start to lower his head and knew he was going to kiss her. Her first impulse was to pull away. This was a complication she didn't need right now. But his eyes were mesmerizing, pulling her into their depths, making her want to feel his arms, his lips, his everything. She closed her eyes, deciding to let it happen, to let herself go.

Then she thought of Tim. *Is he here now? In this very room? Watching?* Her eyes flew open, and she pushed herself back.

At that same moment, Scotch started to whine the same low guttural sound she had emitted a few nights earlier. Jennifer shoved Eric aside and rushed back over to Tanner. Scotch had her head in Tanner's lap, one paw scraping at his knee, her eyes riveted on the boy's face, which had an all-too-familiar distance about it. Jennifer felt fear strike her heart.

"Eric! It's happening again!"

Eric hurried over to the couch and sat down gently next to Tanner. He waved a hand in front of Tanner's face, but the boy seemed totally unaware. "Tanner?" he said quietly. No response.

"Eric, do something!" Jennifer hissed. Her face was frighteningly pale, her eyes wide and colorless.

Eric reached up and placed a hand on either side of Tanner's head, turning the boy's face toward his own. Tanner's head swiveled easily, without resistance, like a ventriloquist's dummy. His eyes remained unfocused, his face wooden.

"Tanner!" Eric said, almost a shout this time.

Scotch whined even louder and tried to crawl up onto Tanner's lap.

Jennifer collapsed into a heap on the floor at Tanner's feet, her hands on his knees, tears streaming down her face. This was more than she could bear! Never had she felt so damned useless! She wanted to protect her son, to help him, but she had no idea where to begin. She buried her face in her hands and sobbed.

As if someone had thrown a switch, Scotch's incessant whining ceased and the dog backed up a step, sat down, and cocked her head at Tanner.

Jennifer's head bolted up, and she examined Tanner's face closely, with an expression of fearful hope. "Tanner?"

"I'm okay, Mom," Tanner said softly. "Dad said to tell you he won't hurt me."

"Oh, God!" Jennifer sobbed. She reached up and hugged her son.

When she released him, Tanner said, "He also said to tell you he likes Eric and that you should trust him."

Jennifer stared slack-jawed and unblinking at first Tanner, then Eric.

Eric smiled sheepishly and shrugged. Tanner grinned widely.

Jennifer sucked in a deep breath, released it slowly through pursed lips, and swiped at her tear-stained face. Then she stood and headed for the kitchen. "I think I need a drink," she said.

*   *   *

"Why don't you and Tanner come and stay at my place tonight," Eric suggested as they all sat around the kitchen table eating the grilled cheese sandwiches Jennifer had fixed. Puttering in the kitchen had always been one of her main modes of distraction. She usually made tomato soup to go with grilled cheese, but today she opted for a Bloody Mary instead. The alcohol burned as it went down, but the warming glow she felt once it hit her bloodstream left her feeling calmer.

"Why?" Jennifer asked. "Do you think we're in danger here?"

"I don't know," Eric said, pulling on his chin thoughtfully. "But we do know that someone has been in here already. Do you want to risk being here the next time someone tries to search the house?"

Jennifer thought about that. "No," she admitted.

"Can Scotch come, too?" Tanner asked, shoving the last piece of his second sandwich into his mouth.

"You bet," Eric said. "I wouldn't go anywhere without her. She seems to be able to sense when you are going into one of your fugue states. She makes a good warning system."

Jennifer looked down at the golden retriever. She was lying beneath Tanner's chair, her eyes moving back and forth from one person to the next. Jennifer smiled at the dog and then tossed her the rest of her sandwich. Her appetite wasn't nearly as good as Tanner's. Scotch got up, scarfed the sandwich down, and then returned to her spot beneath Tanner's chair.

"I don't want to put you out, Eric," Jennifer said. "I can stay at Carny's house for a while."

"Who is Carny?"

"She's my best friend. Has been for years. I wouldn't be here today if it wasn't for her. She lives in the next house over." She gestured in the general direction with a nod.

Eric shook his head. "I would feel better if you were with me," he insisted. "If you've been watched, then they'll know Carny is your friend. It wouldn't take a rocket scientist to figure out where you were."

Tanner giggled at that.

"What about Evan?" Jennifer asked.

Eric's face clouded over and suffused with red. "Do what you want," he said tersely, lowering his head and focusing intently on the crumbs left on his plate.

Jennifer stared at the top of his head and sighed. They sat in silence for a few moments, each dealing with their own brand of ghost. Finally Jennifer asked, "So, what do we do now? I can't hide out for the rest of my life. And how do we know we won't be followed to your house if we're being watched that closely?"

Eric raised his head and leaned across the table eagerly, as if he had been waiting for her to ask just that question. "I have an idea," he said.

Sometime later, Eric was on the phone to the hospital. "I want to admit Tanner Bolton this evening," he said. "Diagnosis—possible brain lesion. Call Radiology and have them set up to do a CT scan. Tonight."

When he was done, he hung up the phone and turned to Jennifer. "Your turn," he said.

Jennifer dialed the number for Evan's home. After listening to the now-familiar message on his answering machine she said, "Evan? This is Jennifer. Tanner is being readmitted to the hospital today, just for some tests. But the doctor said it's important that he be as rested as possible so he's not allowing any visitors. I'll call you in the morning and give you an update." After hanging up, she picked up the phone again and called Evan's office, leaving the same message with his secretary.

"He might be in shortly," the secretary said. "He called a little while ago and said the jury had gone to deliberate. He often waits it out here. Should I have him call you if he shows up in the next few minutes?"

"No," Jennifer said. "We're leaving for the hospital right now. Just tell him I'll catch up with him as soon as I can."

"Okay. Sorry about your son. I hope he'll be okay."

"Thank you, Marilee. I appreciate your concern."

Jennifer hung up the phone. "Okay," she said. She looked around the kitchen as if she had misplaced something. "I guess I'll go and pack some things." She turned and disappeared from the room, leaving Eric and Tanner alone.

"I'm glad you believe me," Tanner said to Eric.

"No problem." Eric gave his shoulder a reassuring squeeze. "One thing I've learned from studying medicine is that there are always things we can't understand. I try to keep an open mind."

"Do you think Mom really believes me?"

"I think she's coming around. Give her time. It's a lot to try and swallow all at once."

"Yeah, I guess it is. I kind of wondered myself in the beginning."

"Wondered about what?"

"If it was really my dad talking to me. For a while I thought maybe it was space aliens trying to take over my mind or something. I saw something like that on TV once."

"I'd say a little less TV might do you some good," Eric said with a smile. "And I wouldn't mention that theory to your mother if I were you. She's freaked-out enough already."

"Yeah," Tanner said. "I guess she is."

Jennifer came back to the kitchen a while later carrying

a large suitcase. "Think this looks like too much for a hospital stay?" she asked Eric, holding it up in front of her with both hands.

"Nah, I've seen some of the local beauty queens check in with three bags that size. If somebody's watching, I don't think it will raise any suspicions. We'll just leave it in the car when we get to the hospital."

"Good." She set the bag down against the wall and shoved her hands in her pockets. "I should call Carny," she said. "She'll worry if she can't get ahold of me."

Eric frowned, hesitating. "Go ahead," he said eventually, "but don't offer anything more than what we agreed on. Okay?"

"I think you're overreacting, Eric. Carny can be trusted. I'd trust her with my life."

"That's exactly what you will be doing," Eric said pointedly. "Yours *and* Tanner's."

Jennifer pouted at him before she picked up the phone to dial Carny's number. The issue was quickly resolved when she got Carny's answering machine. She left the same basic message she had left for Evan. "There. Are you happy now?" she said when she was done and had hung up.

"As a clam." Eric grinned. He pushed away from the table and stood. "Are we ready?"

Jennifer looked around. "I guess so," she said. Her eyes fell on Scotch, who was lying, as usual, at Tanner's feet, her eyes moving back and forth between whoever was talking. "What about the dog?" Jennifer asked. "Won't it look suspicious if we take her with us?"

Eric shrugged. "Who's to say I'm not taking care of her for you while Tanner is in the hospital? Or dropping her off at a kennel? She has to go somewhere."

"I suppose," Jennifer said doubtfully. The whole idea that someone might be watching what they were doing had her nerves on edge. She was trying to picture the scene as someone else might see it, but it was difficult to concentrate.

They headed out to Eric's Ford Explorer, Jennifer fighting the urge to scan the surrounding woods for spying eyes. She vacillated between feeling paranoid and ridiculous one minute, then frightened senseless the next. Eric tossed the suitcase into the back of the car, then stood aside while Scotch jumped in beside it. Tanner buckled himself into the backseat and Jennifer slid into the front next to Eric. It took thirty-five minutes to drive to the hospital and another hour or so to get Tanner registered and settled in his room on the pediatric unit—the very same room he had been in before.

"I'm going to go downstairs to Radiology and check on the CT scan," Eric said, leaning in close to Jennifer's ear and speaking in a near whisper. "Just to make sure they are expecting Tanner. Patients are always delayed, so there should be plenty of time for us to get away before Radiology and the nurses up here get together long enough to figure out that something's wrong."

Jennifer nodded.

"Once I get you two safely settled at my place, I'll call the hospital and tell them you went a little berserk and decided to sign Tanner out AMA. That's means Against Medical Advice."

"Thanks a lot!" Jennifer whispered back. "How come I have to come across as the looney tune?"

Eric smiled and gave her shoulder a little squeeze. "Don't worry. We're not going to lock you away. Not yet anyway."

Jennifer stuck her tongue out at him. Tanner giggled.

"I'll be back shortly," Eric said. Then he kissed Jennifer on the cheek and was gone.

"I think the doc is sweet on you, Mom," Tanner said.

"Yeah, I think you're right," Jennifer said, touching the spot on her cheek.

"I like him," Tanner said.

Jennifer gave his hand a squeeze. "So do I, Tanner. So do I."

A nurse came in, ran Tanner through the usual litany of neuro tests, checked his vital signs, and asked some questions. Then she handed him a pair of pajamas with Snoopy and Woodstock on them and instructed him to change in the bathroom. When the nurse was gone, Jennifer stuffed Tanner's clothes into the oversize purse she had carried in with her.

Sometime later, Eric came in pushing a wheelchair. "Ready?" he asked.

Jennifer nodded, and Tanner climbed out of bed and into the wheelchair. They made their way down the hall to the elevators, Eric joking with an attractive brunette nurse while they waited. Jennifer was both surprised and a bit disgusted with herself to discover that she felt a pang of jealousy.

The elevator took them down to the first floor, where Eric led them down a number of hallways and into a room marked LINEN. When he had closed the door behind them, Jennifer removed the clothes from her purse and handed them to Tanner.

"Here. Change into these. You'll stick out like a sore thumb with those pj's on."

Tanner dutifully ducked behind a row of shelves and emerged moments later wearing the clothes. Jennifer suppressed a smile when she saw how disheveled he looked with his shirt askew, his hair mussed, and his shoes untied.

"Okay," Eric said. "I moved the car around back to the parking lot by the loading dock. Follow me."

After opening the linen room door and scanning the

hallway, Eric motioned for them to follow. The threesome made their way down the hall to another, and down that one toward a large set of double doors. Jennifer was feeling a bit ridiculous about all the cloak-and-dagger stuff, though she could tell Tanner was actually enjoying it, seeing it all as a big adventure. She checked the doorways along the hall as they passed and shuddered when she saw one labeled MORGUE. Like a bucket of ice water in her face, the sign reminded her of just how serious their situation was. Suddenly, all the secrecy didn't seem so silly. Her heart started pounding so hard inside her chest, she was afraid it might burst.

When they finally made it out onto the loading dock, Jennifer breathed a sigh of relief. She glanced at her watch and saw it was close to eight o'clock.

"There's the car," Eric said, pointing toward his Explorer in a near-empty parking lot about one hundred feet away. Jennifer grabbed Tanner's hand and followed Eric down a ramp and up a small incline along a cement wall. Two large Dumpsters were lined up against the wall, and the smell of rotting food (or at least Jennifer hoped it was food—she shuddered to think what else might be in a hospital garbage bin) made her queasy.

Tanner, letting his mother lead him by the hand, tripped over one of his untied shoelaces, almost falling. The motion jerked Jennifer's arm, yanking her back a half step. As she turned to look at Tanner, she felt something whiz by her ear and batted at the air with her hand, thinking it was a fly from one of the trash bins. But then the cement next to her flew apart in a miniature explosion. She stopped and stared at the spot on the wall, her mind struggling to make sense of what she was seeing. Then another part of the wall exploded and panic gripped her heart.

"Someone is shooting at us," Eric said with astonished

disbelief. He stared at the wall a second, dumbfounded. Then he grabbed Jennifer's arm, pushing her ahead of him toward the car. "Run!" he yelled.

If the situation itself wasn't enough to spur Jennifer into action, the urgency in Eric's voice was. She grabbed Tanner's hand in a viselike grip and commanded her feet to fly. She focused her eyes on the car, terror pounding through her veins, expecting any moment to feel the sting of a bullet ripping through her back.

Tanner, unable to meet her frantic pace, stumbled behind her, yanking her shoulder painfully. She gritted her teeth and hung on to his hand, prepared to drag him across the asphalt if she had to. The blacktop exploded off to her left and she veered right, ducking beside a blue Volvo and pulling Tanner down beside her. Eric was right on their heels.

"Why is someone shooting at us?" Jennifer hissed breathlessly, her chest heaving. Her eyes rolled heavenward. "This is so crazy!" Hearing the rising hysteria in her voice, she looked over at Tanner's face, saw the shocked pallor in it, and tried to calm herself down. She had to stay together, for Tanner's sake.

"Run for the car," Eric said, giving her a nudge. "The doors are unlocked. I'll carry Tanner."

Jennifer looked around the end of the Volvo and saw Eric's Explorer across in the next row. It was only about thirty feet away, though under the circumstances, it might as well have been on another continent. Scotch was perched near the back window barking up a storm, her nose fogging and smearing up the glass, the fur on the back of her neck standing up in a huge fluff like an Elizabethan collar. Jennifer bit her lip and cast a frightened glance at Eric.

"Move!" he commanded.

Jennifer sprang from behind the Volvo like a runner

leaving the starting block, not waiting to give herself any more time to weigh the perils of their position. She kept her mind focused on the car, vaguely aware of the sound of Eric's feet pounding behind her. Just when she thought they had it made, she heard a *pop* and then a grunt from behind her. She whirled around to see Eric stumble and fall to the blacktop, pulling Tanner down on top of him.

"No!" she screamed. She dashed over to where Eric lay on the pavement and crouched beside him. Blood was oozing from his right thigh at an alarming rate. Tanner tried to stand up, and Jennifer pulled him back down, shoving him behind her, effectively shielding him with her body in the direction the bullets seemed to be coming from.

"Get to the car," Eric said. He shoved a hand into his pocket and pulled out a set of keys. "Go!"

Jennifer peered out across the darkened parking lot. At this hour there were only a few rows of cars, leaving vast expanses of open lot between the hospital and the small grove of woods that separated the parking lot from the main road. Though Jennifer supposed someone could be kneeling down behind any of the parked cars, her eyes failed to find any evidence of their assailant. The shooter could be anywhere.

"I'm not leaving you here," she argued.

Eric scowled at her, shifted his position painfully, then reached up and grabbed Tanner's arm. "Tanner, run over to the car and stay down alongside of it. Go now!"

Tanner looked at his mother, fear and questioning filling his eyes.

Eric was right. They were too exposed here. But Jennifer couldn't let Tanner run alone. He'd be like a tin duck in a shooting gallery. She grabbed his hand and said, "Let's go, Tanner. Run as fast as you can and keep your head down." She took off running, bent over at an angle, dragging Tanner along beside her, taking care to keep herself between him and the direction of the gunfire. When they reached their goal without incident, she shoved him down alongside the Explorer and said, "Stay here! No matter what! And keep your head down!" With that she turned and ran back to Eric, assuming the same hunched-over position. "Can you get up?" she asked when she was back at his side.

Eric opened his mouth to argue with her, to tell her to go and leave him, but one look at her face told him it would be futile. "I think so," he said finally.

Jennifer helped him struggle to his feet and let him lean on her as they hobbled over to the car. She opened the back door and Scotch tried to come over the back of the seat from the cargo area.

"Scotch! Stay!" she said sternly. The dog obeyed, sitting down immediately, though she had a tensed posture that said she was ready to spring at any moment.

Jennifer helped Eric inch his way across the backseat until he reached the opposite door, taking care to keep his head below the level of the side window. As tall as he was, his legs were still hanging out the door a good foot or more. He grimaced and sucked in a hiss of breath as he bent his injured leg up so that his feet were inside.

Once she had Eric in, Jennifer pushed Tanner down on the floor behind the front seat. "Get down on the floor and stay there!" she instructed him.

When she was sure they were both settled, she closed the back door, opened the front one, reached across the seat, and slid the key into the ignition. She muttered a quick prayer before turning the key and then uttered a second prayer of thanks when the Explorer rumbled to life. She slid the gearshift into reverse and, as the vehicle started to move, quickly maneuvered herself into the driver's seat, trying to keep her head down. With a quick glance around, she cut the wheel hard to the left, shoved the gearshift into drive, and floored the gas pedal. The car lurched forward, the wheels squealing in complaint and the front fender nailing the rear bumper of a nearby Mercedes. She veered through the parking lot and out into a side street. She ran a red light at the corner, cut off an angry driver at the next intersection, and only let up on the gas as they neared the interchange for Interstate 64. Taking the on-ramp, she pulled into traffic and eased the vehicle up to sixty-five, keeping an eye on the rearview mirror to see if she could detect anyone who appeared to be following them.

Half an hour or so later, satisfied that they weren't being pursued, she relaxed a little, flexing her fingers to ease the cramps that had moved in with her death grip on the wheel. An exit for Waynesboro loomed ahead, and, on an impulse, she took it. She avoided the populated areas and instead made a series of turns down rural roads until she came upon a darkened Department of Transportation building. A large parking lot wrapped around the building and a half dozen of the ugly orange trucks with the big black letters—VDOT— on the sides were parked in a row near one corner. Jennifer pulled in around the back of the building and parked close to the wall with the Explorer facing out toward the road in case she needed to make a quick getaway.

"Wait here," she told the two in the backseat. She killed the lights, but left the motor running before climbing out of the car. Scotch, apparently either sensing the urgency of the situation or scared out of her wits, was lying quietly in the cargo area.

Jennifer walked to the edge of the building and peered around the corner, her eyes seeking out any sign of approaching headlights, her ears straining to pick up any sound over the faint thrum of the Explorer's idling engine. Everything was quiet.

She waited.

After ten minutes, she went back to the Explorer and turned off the engine. She opened the back door and helped Tanner out. After stretching, he climbed into the front seat and twisted around so he could see into the back.

"Are you okay?" Jennifer asked Eric.

He nodded weakly. His face was pale and drenched in sweat. The seat beneath his leg was soaked with blood. "Get my medical bag," he said in little more than a whisper. "It's in the back."

Jennifer opened the tailgate, found the bag, gave Scotch a pat on the head and a "Good girl!" before she returned to the backseat and handed the bag to Eric. He rummaged around in it until he found some dressings, a roll of tape, a bottle of peroxide, and a pair of scissors. Jennifer helped him prop himself up so he could look at his leg. He handed her the scissors.

"Cut away the pant leg," he instructed.

Jennifer did as he asked, taking care not to move the leg any more than she had to. When she had the wound exposed, Eric poured some peroxide over his leg, throwing his head back and biting his lip in agony as the stuff foamed into a pink froth. When he could speak again he said, "Clean it off."

Jennifer cleaned around the wound, a deeply furrowed gash that ran across the front of his thigh. It looked as if someone had scooped out the meat of his leg with a sharpened teaspoon. Though the exposed edges oozed a continuous flow of blood, it seemed to be slowing some.

"The heat of the bullet probably cauterized some of the blood vessels," Eric said weakly, echoing her thoughts. He handed Jennifer some Telfa pads, a roll of gauze, and some tape. "Wrap it as tight as you can," he told her.

While Jennifer fixed the dressing, pulling the rolled gauze tightly around the circumference of his thigh to hold the Telfa pads in place, Eric dug around some more in his bag and came up with two bottles of pills. He swallowed two from one, one from the other.

"What are you taking?" she asked as she taped the edge of the gauze in place.

"A painkiller and an antibiotic," he told her.

When she was done, Jennifer climbed into the front seat. Her head fell back against the headrest, its weight seeming too great with the sudden onset of sheer exhaustion that had seized her. "What now?" she said to no one in particular.

"We need to find a safe place to go," Eric said. "Obviously my house is no good. They know you're with me."

"How?" Jennifer asked, turning herself around and resting an arm along the back of the seat. "How did they know we'd be leaving the hospital?"

"I've been thinking about that," Eric said. "The only answer I can come up with is that they must have had your house bugged."

It took a moment for that to sink in. "You mean someone has been listening to everything in my house? Watching me? Listening to me?" Her eyes narrowed to furious slits. "Those bastards!" She spit out the last words, then, remembering Tanner was sitting next to her, wished she could take them back.

"And they're playing for keeps now, Jen. They know what we know. You can't go back there."

"But we don't *know* anything! All we have is a lot of guesses."

"I think it's safe to say that Tanner's grasp of the situation is right on the money," Eric surmised. "Bioceutics had Tim killed. They left you and Tanner alone because they didn't think you had any knowledge of what Tim was working on."

"I didn't. I *don't*."

"And that is what has kept you alive all this time. But now Tanner has information he couldn't know unless Tim told him. And whether or not you believe he is talking to Tim, rest assured Bioceutics believes it."

Jennifer looked at Tanner, barely able to discern his face in the darkness. "They want to kill us," she said simply.

"They do. And they will," Eric said. "Unless we can discover their secret first and expose them. We need some time. Someplace to hide."

Jennifer thought about that for a while. They could travel around, stay in motels under an assumed name. "How much cash do you have on you?" she asked Eric.

"I'm not sure. Fifty, maybe a hundred bucks."

"And I've got forty or so," she said. "That won't get us very far. If we use a credit card, it will leave a trail like bread crumbs. We need to get to a bank so I can pull out some cash."

"Bank transactions can be traced, too," Eric said.

"I know. But we're going to need some money for motels and food and such. Who knows for how long?"

Eric shook his head. "Motels are no good. They need a license plate number and a name. Even if you lie, most of them want a driver's license or something. No, we need to think of something else."

Jennifer stared out into the darkness, listening to the wind soughing in the trees above them. *Where can we go? Where can we hide? Where's the last place anyone would know or think to look?*

The idea came on her in a flash, at first exciting her. Then she dismissed it. *It will never work. It's impossible. And besides, I can't do it.*

Beside her Tanner's hand reached out and found hers. He gripped her hand tight.

"Mom?"

"Yes, Tanner."

"I'm really scared."

She looked over at his face, no more than a pale orb with two hugely round eyes in the center reflecting in the moonlight. She pulled him close and held him, rocking him gently.

"It's going to be all right, Tanner. We'll get through this. You'll see. I know where we can go."

"Where?" came a voice from the backseat.

"Tonight we get a motel room and some sleep. Tomorrow I'm hitting the closest bank for some cash," she said decisively. "And then we're heading north."

9

For the second time in as many nights, the men of MAGI were gathering at the leader's house. The atmosphere tonight was decidedly more strained than it had been the previous evening, and the men hovered near the huge table exchanging whispered murmurs while they waited for Zeus to make his appearance. When he did, an instant hush, laced with an almost-palpable tension, filled the room.

"Take your seats, gentlemen," the leader said gruffly. Dark thunderclouds hovered over his face, making it clear that his mood on this particular night was not one to be trifled with. He yanked his own chair out from the table with great impatience.

As the other chairs quietly scraped and squeaked into place, the men occupying them hung their heads like a group of just-chastised children. A few risked a surreptitious glance at the leader, but most made a serious occupation of studying the creases in their palms or the wood pattern in the tabletop.

"Need I say that I am greatly disappointed with the latest turn of events," the leader said. "Perhaps we were unclear about our mission and intended goals?" His voice was rife with condescension and a few of the heads dropped even lower.

The leader drilled one of the men at the table with his eyes. "What the hell happened, Bartholomew?" he snapped. "Your instructions were to bug the doctor's car and follow them, *not* to shoot at them. I thought I made it perfectly clear that I want the boy alive."

Bartholomew, well tanned from a recent trip to Mexico, blanched so that his skin took on a sickly-looking, yellow pallor. "We were trying to delay them," he half mumbled. "We had a flat tire. They came out before we could get it changed."

The leader's lips pursed into a thin line, the muscles in his cheeks throbbed and twitched. He leaned back in his chair and gazed up at the ceiling. The room remained perfectly still for several moments except for one member's growling stomach.

"Pythias?"

The leader's voice was soft and without menace, yet Pythias jumped anyway. He cleared his throat with a little "ahem," then said, "Yes, sir?" His right eyelid twitched violently.

"Is your part of our plan still on schedule?"

"Yes, sir. Everything is set for tomorrow."

"Good. Hippocrates?"

The man known as Hippocrates lifted his head so fast his neck creaked audibly. "Yes?"

"I want you to use every contact you have along the Eastern seaboard to see if our quarry seeks medical attention anywhere."

"Done."

The leader leaned forward, his arms resting on the table. "Bartholomew, you enlist whatever law enforcement connections you can drum up. I want these people found. Try to do it right this time."

Bartholomew nodded spastically.

"Plato, you monitor the banking networks. They're

probably smart enough not to use credit cards, but watch for it anyway. If they don't use plastic, they'll be in need of money. Watch his accounts as well as hers. If they so much as set foot inside a bank, I want to know it. Understood?"

The man nodded.

"The rest of you utilize whatever means necessary. Check out all family connections, friends, hobbies, any activity that might suggest a destination. That is all."

The leader pushed back his chair and stood. "Do not screw this up again," he added, with a pointed look at Bartholomew. With that final admonition, he strode from the room.

Jennifer pulled into the parking lot of Pleasant Dreams, a small roadside motel located just outside of Orange, Virginia. A garish, red, neon sign announced to all that Pleasant Dreams possessed "cheep" room rates and cable TV. The motel consisted of one long building with ten rooms in the front and another ten in back, painted a color that, beneath the buzzing light of the neon, appeared to be flamingo pink. The office, positioned at one end of the building, had a flip-card sign reading VACANCY hanging in a window made opaque by years' worth of dirt and scratch marks. There were two cars parked in the lot.

After a quick survey of the backseat, Jennifer instructed Eric and Tanner to wait in the car while she went inside to check them in. It didn't take her long to realize that the sight of Eric, with his leg bloodied and swollen and his face pale as the moon's light, might make someone overly curious. As it was, Jennifer felt so nervous, she feared any idiot would be able to see it in her face. She climbed out of the car, easing the door closed, fearful that even that little bit of noise might draw some unwanted attention.

Jennifer opened the office door and winced when the clang of a cowbell overhead announced her presence. In response, a woman who looked to be in her fifties, with a short cap of thick, wiry, gray hair and trifocal glasses balanced precariously on the end of a red, bulbous nose, appeared from behind a curtained doorway. She was a large, fleshy woman, with the hardened look of someone who has seen more than her share of life's cruelties. The smell of stale cigarettes hovered over her like a halo.

"I'd like a room around the back side of the building," Jennifer said. She tried to force herself to meet the woman's gaze, but found the piercing eyes too intimidating and eventually cast her eyes toward the floor.

Without a word, the woman slid a postcard-sized form across the desk top.

Jennifer grabbed a pen that was chained to the counter and proceeded to fill in the blanks, deciding after a moment's hesitation to register them under her own name. She doubted anyone would be able to track them here that quickly. The woman before her didn't look like she would know what a computer was, much less have one on the premises. And besides, she didn't want to try and get around the whole issue of providing some form of identification. As she scribbled in the necessary information, cursing her trembling hands, she was keenly aware of the woman's incessantly probing eyes studying her every move. Jennifer wondered if there was something in her appearance or demeanor that made the woman wary, or if she was just naturally suspicious of anyone who checked in.

When she had completed the form, Jennifer slid it back across the desk. Reluctantly, she raised her eyes and met that austere gaze. A Mexican standoff followed, wherein Jennifer struggled to keep her expression impassive and the woman narrowed her eyes in a steely glint.

After a moment, the woman looked pointedly over Jennifer's shoulder toward the door, where the Explorer sat with the engine still running, then at Jennifer's hands. When she looked back at Jennifer, her eyebrows were raised in a silent question mark.

Jennifer glanced down at her hands and realized with horror that there were traces of dried blood in the folds surrounding her fingernails, apparently a remnant from cleaning Eric's wound. She withdrew her hands and shoved them into her pants' pockets, thinking fast. "Listen, I could really use your help," she said.

The woman cocked her head to one side, her eyes drawn down to narrow slits, waiting.

"I'm trying to hide from my ex-husband," Jennifer said. "He's really crazy! He's already tried to kidnap my son. I took out a restraining order, but it hasn't fazed him in the least."

While the woman continued to stare, Jennifer quickly played back what she'd said and decided it sounded suitably anxious (which wasn't too difficult under the circumstances). She hesitated, chewing her lip and watching the woman's face. Heartened by what she thought was a softening in the woman's icy glare, she plunged on. "I don't know what he'll try next. The man is certifiably nuts! He's even threatened to kill me!"

The woman's eyes widened at that, and Jennifer feared she had gone too far. "I doubt there is any way he could find me here," she added quickly, "but I'd feel a lot safer if my car wasn't in view of the road. My husband has a lot of connections, and I simply can't let him find me."

The woman studied Jennifer silently, seeming to weigh both her words and her situation. Finally, she spoke, the voice surprisingly soft coming from that life-worn face.

"I had me one of them crazy husbands once myself." The corner of her mouth twitched, and Jennifer suspected that was the closest the woman would ever come to a smile. "You can have Room 19. It's around the back. Near the end by the woods." She laid a key on the counter.

Jennifer breathed a sigh of relief and closed her eyes. When she opened them again, she found she was once more the subject of that disconcerting stare. "Thank you," she said, flashing the woman a tentative smile.

It wasn't returned. Not so much as a twitch. "That'll be thirty-five dollars."

Jennifer handed the woman forty dollars in cash. She counted what was left in her wallet and frowned. Six dollars.

The woman handed Jennifer five well-used one-dollar bills for change. "Thanks," Jennifer said, trying another smile. This time the woman acknowledged her with a nod.

Jennifer took the key and left. It wasn't until she was back in the car that she realized the woman had never asked for any identification.

Though the room was very basic and plain, Jennifer was relieved to see it was at least clean. Two double beds occupied most of the space. A cramped bathroom with a shower stall instead of a tub stood at one end of the room; at the other end—near the door and in front of the window—sat a small round table, scarred by cigarette burns and flanked by two mismatched wooden folding chairs. A battered TV, looking a bit incongruous with both a cable box and rabbit ears, sat on the wall at the foot of the two beds, the TV bolted to a stand, the stand bolted to the floor. The decor left something to be desired: the bedspreads were a faded orange-and-yellow floral pattern, the curtains were a brown tweed, the carpet a worn, green shag.

Eric managed to get into the room under his own

power, though he looked as if he might pass out at any moment. With one of his pant legs cut off, and dried blood caking his leg, he looked like a war refugee. At least the pain pills seemed to be working. Maybe, with a little time and some rest, his pallor would improve. Jennifer didn't think he had lost enough blood for it to be life-threatening, though she had to confess she wasn't sure how much was too much. Even a little looked like too much to her.

Tanner didn't look very good either, with big circles under his eyes and a gray cast to his face.

Despite the excitement of the evening's events, or perhaps because of it, they were all exhausted. Tanner climbed onto one of the beds, clothes and all, and drifted off to sleep within minutes. Jennifer collapsed into one of the chairs near the window and watched her son sleep, her limbs so numb and exhausted it left her feeling oddly disembodied.

Eric limped his way into the bathroom carrying his black medical bag, and reappeared some ten minutes later wearing only his boxer shorts and a T-shirt. The blood on his leg had been cleaned off and a new dressing circled his thigh. He lowered himself onto the edge of the other bed, looking wan and thoroughly weary, his injured leg extended out.

He smiled weakly at Jennifer. "Are you okay?" he asked.

"Am *I* okay?" she asked with gentle disbelief. It touched her that he was concerned for her welfare in the midst of his own grievous injuries. "I'm fine. What about you? Are you okay?"

"I'll survive. Or at least I'll survive this," he said, gesturing toward his bandaged leg. "The real question is whether we'll survive Bioceutics." His expression turned grim. "I think we should go for some help, Jen. Maybe we should talk to the police."

Jennifer shook her head. "I don't trust anyone at this point."

"You've been watching too much TV," he teased. "You don't really believe that this is all part of some huge conspiracy, do you?"

"I don't know what to believe, Eric. Besides, what are we going to tell the police? That my son has been communicating with his dead father's ghost? That we know Bioceutics is full of bad people because the ghost says so? They'd lock us up and throw away the keys. Just as soon as they quit laughing. Besides, going to the authorities would only make us easier to find."

"I suppose you're right," he said with a sigh. "I'm just not sure we can handle this on our own."

"Well, we have to. Maybe I *have* watched too many movies-of-the-week, but the fewer people we involve, the better I'll feel. If we're going to assume that Tanner's conversations with Tim are real—not that I'm totally convinced, mind you," she added quickly, holding up one hand. "But if we do accept that assumption, it means that Bioceutics had Tim killed." She leaned forward, rubbing her hands together nervously, her eyes wide and frightened-looking. "I've been thinking about this. Bioceutics is a huge company, Eric. Tim told me that much of their funding comes from the federal government. It concerned him that some of the studies they were working on might not have the most altruistic purposes. He once said there was a fine line between finding a cure for some fatal disease and the latest biological warfare."

Eric frowned. "Are you saying Bioceutics is a front for some sort of secret government or military operation?"

"I don't know," Jennifer sighed. "It does sound a little fantastic when you put it like that. But how can we know?" She reached up and parted the worn curtain, sparing an anxious glance out to the darkened parking lot.

"I'm just not sure I want to trust anyone right now," she said, turning back toward the room. She let the curtain drop back into place and watched as a little puff of dust rolled from the material into the room.

Eric's eyes caught and held hers. "Do you trust me?"

Her lips slid into a gentle smile. "Yes, I do."

"Good." He eased himself back against the pillow, grimacing as he raised his injured leg and gingerly placed it on the bed. "We'll try and sort all this out in the morning. Right now, these pain pills are making me loopy." He punched up the pillow beneath his head and turned onto his side. Jennifer watched him as his eyes slid closed. Within minutes, he, too, was asleep, a gentle snore occasionally sneaking past his lips.

Jennifer rose out of her chair, stepped over Scotch, who had settled herself down in a comma-shaped heap on the floor between the two beds, and slipped in next to Tanner. At first she thought she would leave the room's meager light on, but when she realized it would only serve to make them more visible from the outside, she reached up and turned it off. She thought she'd doze off as quickly as Tanner and Eric had, but her mind kept whirring busily, replaying everything that had happened over the last few days. After tossing and turning for the better part of two hours, she finally got up and settled back into the chair.

It seemed she spent most of her nights like this lately, sitting in a chair next to a window, staring out at the night. As she kept vigil over the darkened parking lot, analyzing the shifting shadows among the trees, she was seized by a feeling of hopelessness. Everything had gone so wrong. And it wasn't over with yet. Someone was probably out there searching for them even now. Would they ever be safe? Just how far did Bioceutics's reach extend? She had no way of knowing, but something in her gut, some instinct—or perhaps even a touch of her own brand of

ESP, she thought wryly—told her that they were in serious trouble. All she wanted was her old life back again. A little normalcy and boredom. But visions of years on the run, marked by a series of temporary way stations where she would always be looking over her shoulder, filled her mind.

Maybe Eric was right. Maybe she was being overly paranoid. But hard as she tried, she couldn't shake off the feeling that they were caught up in something so big, so malicious, so terrifyingly malignant that their chances of surviving it were almost nil. A heavy blanket of despondency wrapped around her, covering her in layers of sadness and despair. She had never felt so lonely in all her life.

She glanced over at Eric and Tanner, envious of their ability to shrug everything off long enough to fall asleep. Then she looked at her watch, twisting her arm in the colorless moonlight until she could see the hands. Two-twenty. She sighed heavily and resumed her parking lot vigil.

Sometime later, Eric was shaking her. "Jen? Wake up."

She shot up in the chair, instantly awake, every nerve on edge, immediately alert.

"Calm down," Eric whispered, placing a gently restraining hand on her shoulder. "I just want to trade places with you. This damned leg is killing me, and I don't want to take another pain pill. They make me too groggy."

"Do you want me to go and get you something else? Some aspirin or something?"

"I already took some. It's not *that* bad. I just can't sleep. Why don't you go and lie down on the bed, and I'll keep an eye out. Okay?"

Jennifer suspected his story about the leg was nothing more than an effort to alleviate any guilt she might feel at having him take over the guard duty. Still, the thought of settling into the bed was irresistible. She stretched her aching back muscles, glanced at her watch, and saw that it was a little after four. "Okay," she said, standing and heading for the bed Eric had just vacated. She eased herself onto the mattress, relishing its soft support, and inhaling the scent that was Eric from the pillow.

"Good night," Eric whispered from the chair.

"Good night."

Jennifer enjoyed a few blessed moments of forgetfulness the next morning as she ascended slowly from the depths of her slumber, feeling the warm caress of the few rays of sunlight that managed to make it past the trees and through the window. The first thing her bleary eyes noticed was the tiny dust fairies dancing in the sunbeam beside the bed. Then she caught the heavenly scent of coffee and stretched languorously, her mouth opening in a wide yawn. She blinked once or twice and then slowly focused in on Tanner's sleeping face on the bed across from her.

"Good morning," said a male voice at her feet.

The sound of Eric's voice brought her abruptly back to the present, and the memories of yesterday, with all their horrifying implications, crashed in on her. With a little groan, she closed her eyes tight, trying to will herself back to sleep, back to a world where everything was right and safe and normal. It didn't work. She gave in and sat up in the bed.

Eric smiled at her from the chair and nodded toward the table. "I went and got some coffee and doughnuts."

She looked over at the table and saw a box of packaged doughnuts, two small bottles of orange juice, and two Styrofoam cups that held, she assumed, coffee. "Where did you get it?" she asked, rubbing her eyes.

"Little place back in Orange."

She registered the fact that Eric was wearing a clean set of clothes: slacks and a green cotton shirt.

Apparently reading her mind, he explained. "I didn't think the locals would appreciate my boxers, so I changed. I always keep a spare set of clothes in the car for those long nights on call."

"You drove?"

Eric nodded.

"How's the leg?"

"Sore, a little stiff, but not unbearable. I managed okay."

"Good." Jennifer climbed out of bed, bypassed the two bottles of juice and the doughnuts, and grabbed one of the cups of coffee. She sipped through the slots in the lid and grimaced as the hot liquid scorched her tongue.

"Careful," Eric warned her belatedly. "The coffee makes up for its taste deficiencies with extremes in temperature."

"So I noticed," she said, scraping her singed tongue over her teeth. She carried the cup back to the bed and sat down. She looked at her watch. Almost seven-thirty. Tanner stirred, turned over, then sat up so suddenly it made Jennifer jump. Hot coffee sloshed out through the slotted lid and onto her hand, adding a burn there to the one on her tongue.

Tanner rubbed his eyes, blinked a few times, looked first at Eric, then his mother, and said, "Oh."

"Yeah, you didn't tell me how scary your mother looks in the morning," Eric teased. "Not a pretty sight to wake up to."

Tanner smiled at that, and though Jennifer knew that had been Eric's goal, she ran a self-conscious hand over her hair, suppressing an urge to run into the bathroom and check out her appearance in the mirror.

"There are some doughnuts and juice over here," Eric told Tanner.

The boy bounced out of bed and skipped across the floor to sit at the table. He attacked his breakfast with abandon, eating three doughnuts and polishing off both bottles of juice.

After tending to their morning ablutions, giving Scotch the rest of the doughnuts and a drink from the bathroom sink, they were on the road by a few minutes after eight—Jennifer driving, Eric in the front seat, Tanner and Scotch in the back. They rode in silence for an hour until Jennifer turned onto Interstate 95 near Fredericksburg, heading north.

"Where are we going?" Eric asked.

"North."

"I can see that," Eric said with gentle sarcasm. "But what is our destination? Or don't you have one?"

"I have one!" Jennifer snapped. "But first we need to get some money. I'm going to stop at a bank in DC, and take out as much as I can."

"Isn't that dangerous? What if the people who are watching have access to computer records of that sort? They'll know we were there."

"That's all they'll know." Jennifer sounded far more confident than she felt. Still unsure of just how far Bioceutics's reach extended, she recognized the possibility that they might have people located in other areas—people who were ready to move on a moment's notice when a bank computer showed activity on her account. She had weighed all these considerations carefully and decided the odds were on their side. Besides, what other choices did they have?

"Where are you planning to go from there?" Eric asked, apparently resigned to the bank stop.

"To my mother's."

"Your mother's? That's crazy! That's the first place someone would look!"

From the backseat Tanner said, "You have a mother?"

Eric turned and looked at Tanner, then stared at Jennifer, his face a mask of confusion.

"Everyone who knows me thinks my mother is dead," Jennifer explained. "I haven't talked to her in years. We had a parting of the ways right before I married Tim, and I cut her out of my life."

"But you know where she is?" Eric asked.

"I know where she was. In Maine."

"What if she's not there anymore?"

Angered by Eric's constant questioning, Jennifer snapped, "Have you got any better ideas?"

Eric took a deep breath. "No. Sorry."

From the back, Tanner asked, "Why don't you talk to your mother?"

"I don't want to go into it, Tanner."

Tanner crossed his arms over his chest and sulked.

Eric opened his mouth to ask another question, thought better of it, and turned to watch the passing scenery.

A few miles outside of Washington, Jennifer got off the interstate and drove around until she found a branch of her bank in a strip mall. She pulled into the parking lot and turned off the Explorer.

"There's a McDonald's over there," Eric pointed out. "I'll go and get us some food while you're in the bank."

"Good idea. Tanner, you go with Eric."

They all climbed out of the car, and Eric and Tanner headed down the sidewalk to McDonald's. Jennifer started to enter the bank, but then turned back to the car and let Scotch out for a few minutes to do her thing. Jennifer told herself it was out of necessity; after all, even the dog had her needs. But a part of her knew she was only stalling, putting off the inevitable. Despite the confidence she had displayed when revealing her plan in the car, her nerves felt as though they were ready to jump out of her skin. She kept glancing over her shoulder anxiously, half-expecting to see someone with a gun trained on her head. After a few moments, she put Scotch back in the car, took a deep breath to lock in her resolve, and entered the bank.

The place was small, but it carried an air of silent importance. Jennifer walked up to an open teller and handed the woman her savings passbook, which she carried in her purse.

"I'd like to withdraw thirty thousand dollars in cash," she said, trying to keep her voice calm so the woman would think she did this every day.

Despite Jennifer's efforts the woman's eyebrows shot up. She took the book, looked at the numbers inside, and said, "That's a lot of money, Ms. uh, Bolton."

Jennifer flashed her best smile of patient tolerance. "I know, but there is this piece of property I just have to have, and I need the money for a down payment before someone else snatches it up." She realized she was mimicking Carny's sultry Southern drawl.

"A cashier's check would be safer," the woman suggested. "It's not a good idea to carry around that much cash."

"I realize that," Jennifer said. "But the man who is selling the property is a rather eccentric old coot, and he simply insists on cash." She rolled her eyes, smiled, and shrugged as if to say "Go figure!"

The woman stared at her, unsmiling. Jennifer licked her lips and swallowed, trying to keep the fear that was making her heart thump like a bass drum from showing on her face.

"I'll need to see some identification," the teller said.

"Of course." Jennifer smiled her best I-do-this-every-day smile and pulled her driver's license from her purse.

The woman studied it, comparing the picture to Jennifer, then laid it on the counter beside the bank book. "Is all of this information current?"

"It is," Jennifer said.

The woman turned to her computer terminal and started typing, while Jennifer concentrated on looking as nonchalant as possible. After what seemed like an eternity, the woman slid Jennifer's license back across the counter. Gathering up the bank book she said, "I need to get this appoved. I'll be right back." Then she disappeared into a nearby office.

The man known to the members of Zeus's group as Plato sat in the den of his spacious hillside home overlooking Lake Anna. The room was hardly typical. One entire wall was filled with television sets, VCRs, radios, and large tape recorders. LCD displays and various lights glowed in shades of red, yellow, green, and blue. All of the TV sets were on, most of them tuned to news channels. Six-inch reels of tape turned intermittently, triggered by activity from whatever source they were monitoring. The tape designated for the Bolton house, which had been activated just one day ago, remained still.

A police scanner sat on a table near a window, its incessant chatter mixing with the subdued volume from the television sets. Three phones, two fax machines, and a trio of computers were positioned along a table that ran most of the length of one wall.

The screen on each computer rapidly flashed through a series of glowing green characters. Earlier, Plato had accessed the main files for TRW, the national credit bureau. Once he had obtained the bank account and credit card numbers for both Jennifer Bolton and Eric Singleton, he had initiated a program that would do a continuous search of the thousands of banking and credit card centers. If any of the programmed numbers showed activity, the computer would let him know.

The program had been running for hours, with no success. Bored, Plato was sitting behind his desk, his feet propped up, reading an article in the latest issue of an underground newsletter entitled *1984*. Named after George Orwell's futuristic book, the newsletter had been started by a group of computer hackers who became concerned that Big Brother was, indeed, watching them. Their recourse, they decided, was to watch Big Brother. The newsletter, which was hand delivered to Plato on a monthly basis, covered all the ins and outs of accessing some of the most powerful data banks in the world.

Plato made his living as an Information Specialist, a title he had coined himself. Basically, he was willing and able to provide any type of information on anyone or anything to whoever was willing to pay for it. His customers to date had included bankers, mortgage brokers, law enforcement agencies, private eyes, even, on occasion, the state and federal government. Though he had a smattering of "legitimate" customers—colleges, think tanks, and even some game shows—the bulk of his business was done for persons whose purposes were not always legal or savory. It mattered none to him, as long as they were willing to meet his price. And so far, there had been no shortage of people willing to pay. The fruits of this little home business had made him a millionaire several times over— and he was only forty-five.

His wife's voice floated into the room, managing to override the cacophony created by the TVs and the police scanner. "Honey? Can you come here a minute? I need your help."

His concentration broken, Plato frowned and lowered the paper he was reading. He rolled his eyes at the ceiling. "Not now, Wendy."

"Please? The Crowns will be here any minute, and I can't reach the buttons on the back of this blouse. You don't want me walking around half-dressed now, do you?"

Actually, he didn't give a damn. But he knew she would continue to pester him if he didn't help her. His office was strictly off-limits, a long-standing policy that irritated Wendy to no end. When her irritation became more than she could bear, she would drum up some stupid excuse to get him to come out. Like now.

Plato slam-dunked the newsletter onto his desk, shoved his chair back, and stomped from the room, grumbling to himself.

Moments after he walked out, one of the computer monitors stopped flickering and a small beep echoed in the den. On the screen, a bank address and phone number were displayed, followed by the name, "Jennifer Bolton," and an account number. The word "Activity" flashed in fluorescent green beside the number.

It seemed like forever that Jennifer stood waiting for the teller to return. Her nerves were frazzled; she felt as if she wanted to scream. Something was very wrong. A tiny alarm inside her brain was sounding, urging her to turn tail and run. Panic bubbled up inside her, and she casually studied the handful of people in the bank, hoping to discern if any of them were showing an undue interest in her. Seeing that nothing looked out of place, she swallowed hard and turned her gaze toward the window, where she saw Tanner and Eric heading back to the car, their arms laden with white paper bags. Though she was relieved to see they had returned safely, she still couldn't shake the feeling of urgency that coursed through her. She sucked in a deep breath and let it out slowly through pursed lips.

Plato returned to his den, locking the door behind him. He scanned the bank of television sets, his attention caught by a report on CNN. He grabbed a remote control, punched in the number of the set, and then increased the volume.

The face of Senator Edward Tranley smiled down at him, highlighted by the ubiquitous flashes of light from surrounding photographers. The senator held a huge pair of scissors in his hands and was about to cut an opening ceremony ribbon. The voice of a woman reporter trailed out from the set.

"Today Senator Edward Tranley is performing the ribbon cutting for his new educational center here in Richmond. The center, designed to provide free occupational training for Virginia's poor, has been completely subsidized by large corporations throughout Virginia. The center is an unheralded victory in Tranley's continued battle to improve the plight of America's poor and minorities."

As the reporter's voice droned on, Plato punched the volume button until the woman's voice could no longer be distinguished from those emanating from the other sets. He shook his head in disgust. As Tranley cut the ribbon, Plato aimed his finger at the screen like a gun and pulled the trigger.

Turning back toward his desk, he scooped up the newsletter and prepared to settle back into his chair. His body froze in a crouched position, halfway to sitting, his eyes focused on one of the computer screens. He dropped the rest of the way into the chair, tossed the paper aside, and quickly snatched up a phone.

* * *

Jennifer was about to succumb to the warning bells inside her head when the woman teller returned carrying a large bundle of cash.

"Here you are, Ms. Bolton. Thirty thousand." The woman painstakingly counted out the money, mostly hundreds and fifties.

Jennifer bit down the urge to tell the woman to hurry— to never mind counting the money, just hand it over—but she knew it might make the woman suspicious. So she bided her time, trying to look complacent and unhurried.

After a heart-stopping eternity, the teller slid the bills into a large manila envelope and handed it over to Jennifer. "You be careful with that," the woman said.

"Don't worry, I will." As Jennifer took the envelope, she heard a phone ring in one of the offices inside the bank. The sound was eerily reminiscent of the alarm that had been steadily ringing inside her head.

"Thank you, and you have a nice day," Jennifer managed to say to the teller. She smiled and turned away, forcing herself to walk, rather than run, outside to the car.

Eric was behind the wheel, Tanner and Scotch were chowing down on burgers and fries in the backseat, and a collection of large paper bags littered the front seat. Jennifer climbed in on the passenger side.

"I thought I'd drive a while," Eric explained. "The leg feels good enough and you look tired."

"Thanks. I am."

"Everything go okay in there?"

Jennifer nodded.

"Ready to hit the road?"

She nodded again.

"Okay, here we go! Eric Andretti at the wheel! Hold on to your hats folks as we take off in the Interstate 500!"

Tanner giggled from the backseat, Scotch barked, Jennifer took a burger from the bag, took one bite, and put it back. Eric pulled out of the parking lot at a snail's pace and said, "You need to eat." His face was pinched with worry.

"I'm not hungry."

"Want me to stop somewhere else?"

"No. Just drive." Jennifer checked the cars around and behind them, still unable to shake off her feeling of alarm. "I'll feel better once we get the hell away from here."

A cream-colored sedan careened into the parking lot that Jennifer and Eric had left just minutes before. A tall, gangly fellow, with long dark hair pulled straight back from his face and gathered into a ponytail, hurried into the bank. Despite the heat, he was wearing a long coat and cotton gloves. He was met just inside the door by a short, redheaded man wearing thick glasses. The red-haired man gestured sideways with his head and then the two of them walked into an office whose door bore a placard reading, "Don Sawyer–President." The bank president shut the door behind them.

"They've already left," Sawyer said. "By the time I got the call, they were pulling out of the lot."

"Goddammit!" The man with the ponytail paced the small room, his feet making no noise as they sunk into the thick carpet. "Were they still in the Explorer?"

Sawyer nodded.

"Which way were they headed?"

"East. Probably toward the interstate."

The ponytailed man snatched the phone up from the desk and punched in a number. After a moment, he said, "They got away. But they're only minutes ahead of us." He listened then, nodding his head occasionally.

Then, "Consider it done." He lowered the phone, punched the set hook button, then dialed in another number.

A female voice on the other end answered, "State Police."

"I need to speak with Ragland."

"Who is calling please?"

"Just tell him it's the Wise Man." The man waited impatiently, stroking his hand over his ponytail and staring out the office window. Sawyer noted that the palm of the glove smoothing the ponytail was stained with oily dirt.

"Ragland here."

"This is the Wise Man. I need an urgent favor. We are on the lookout for a 1993 Ford Explorer, forest green, license plate number PLQ583. Heading is unknown, though they just left the Brookside mall eastbound. Possibly going toward I–95. My guess is northbound. Occupants include a man, mid-thirties, woman, same age, a child, eight years old, and a golden retriever. If you find them, you need to bring them in. We'll take it from there."

"You picked a bad time, Wise Man. We just had a HazMat overturn on I–95 northbound with five other cars involved. If they are headed that way, they won't get far. And someone just held up a bank over in Beltsville. I got a triple homicide at the bank and every available man tied up with either that or the accident."

"Look, Ragland, this is a matter of top priority," ponytail man snapped. "I would suggest you find someone and do it fast." With that, he slammed down the phone.

Sawyer licked his lips and eyed the other man with bright-eyed excitement. "So, you are like an undercover cop or something?" he asked.

"Something like that."

"What did these people do?" The bank president

licked his lips again and rubbed his hands together in anticipation.

"I'm sorry, but that is classified information," the other man answered with great solemnity. "Just be grateful you and your staff were not harmed."

The president's eyes grew wider. "Really?" he said.

Ponytail man nodded. "Please keep this to yourself," he instructed, knowing full well the man would be on the phone as soon as he left the office, sharing the tale of his adventure with his wife and cronies. It didn't matter; anyone trying to follow up on the incident would find a dead-end trail. "It's a matter of utmost national security."

The president nodded eagerly.

"Thank you for your assistance," the man said. Then to himself he added, *you pathetic pig.* He opened the door and left.

Sawyer watched the man leave the bank and climb into his car. Then he scurried back into his office, closed the door, and picked up the phone.

Eric worked his way back toward Interstate 95, then thought better of it and asked Tanner to pull out an atlas stored in a pocket behind one of the seats. Jennifer took the book and opened it to the map for Maryland.

"We should probably avoid the interstates," Eric said, shifting his eyes back and forth between the map and the road.

"How about this Highway 97?" Jennifer suggested, tracking a red line on the map with her finger. "That will take us into Pennsylvania."

Eric nodded his agreement. With the help of an inset map of the DC area, Jennifer directed him toward the highway.

*   *   *

At the state police barracks near Columbia, Maryland, Sergeant Ragland slammed down his own phone and glared at it. "Prick," he muttered. He was fed up with these smart-assed, know-it-alls. Even if the money they paid him was good, it wasn't worth the aggravation. He had enough banked away to retire anyway. Now that his wife was gone and the kids were all married, there was little incentive to stick with these assholes or his job.

He had made his plans long ago: a thirty-foot sloop was waiting for him in the Bahamas and an open-ended plane ticket in his grandfather's name had been purchased months before. His mind made up, he started emptying the drawers in his desk of the few personal belongings it held.

Jennifer continued to watch the surrounding traffic anxiously, studying the face of each driver and paying particular heed to any car that stayed behind them for a length of time. Periodically she had Eric detour down side streets or slow down to be sure that the people behind them went on by.

Tanner got into the action as well, pointing out to his mother anything he thought qualified as a suspicious-looking car or driver. At first Jennifer was concerned about the long-term effects that might have on him, but he seemed to be enjoying himself. She realized that the reality of the situation hadn't struck him. To him, it was all a fun, cops-and-robber adventure on a TV show. *Just as well,* she thought.

She began to relax once they were on Highway 97. The two-lane road was bordered by vast expanses of open land, making any clandestine pursuit of them virtually impossible. Convinced that they were safely away, she let her head fall back against the seat, watching Eric from the corner of her eye. She had been concerned about his ability to drive, both because of his injured leg and the pain pill he had popped back at the bank parking lot. But he seemed to be doing fine.

She shrugged and rolled her neck, grimacing at the ache that tugged between her shoulder blades. Tanner might find all of this a big adventure, but for her, the stress was definitely beginning to wear. Her mind and body both felt drained and exhausted. She afforded herself the luxury of closing her eyes. Just for a few minutes, she told herself.

Within minutes, she was sound asleep.

10

When Jennifer woke, she was startled to see that it was dark outside. "Where are we?" she asked, rubbing her eyes and trying to focus on the countryside.

"In Massachusetts. We just passed Boston. Maine is about an hour and a half from here."

"Lord! I must have been more tired than I realized."

"You were snoozing pretty good," Eric admitted.

"You were snoring, Mom," Tanner said from the backseat, obviously amused.

"No, I wasn't," Jennifer protested.

"You were! Ask Eric!"

Jennifer looked over at Eric. He smiled wickedly and wiggled his eyebrows. "It was a really cute snore," he said.

Jennifer rolled her eyes. "Great," she muttered.

"Feel up to stopping for something to eat?" Eric asked. "It's after eight."

"I am hungry," Jennifer said, hearing her stomach grumble at the mention of food.

"Well, then, that settles it. Although Tanner and I had decided to mutiny if you said no."

"Oh, really?"

"Really."

Eric smiled at her, and Jennifer was struck by how

handsome he looked. She felt a warm rush inside her chest, accompanied by a tiny thrill of hope. Maybe this whole nightmare would go away. If she tried just a little, she could almost imagine this was just a nice vacation away and not a frantic flight for their lives.

She studied Eric's profile as he drove. She liked his face, liked the way his cheek dimpled when he smiled, liked the way his hair hung down over his forehead, liked the way his eyes sparkled when he teased her. Obviously Tanner liked him, too. She thought of Evan, then, and realized that though she liked him well enough, and thought him attractive and strong and independent, there was no real emotion there. The thought of never seeing Evan again didn't bother her much. The thought of never seeing Eric again made panic rise in her throat like bile. Curious. She sighed heavily. *What a lousy time to be falling in love,* she thought.

They polished off two pizzas, filled up the gas tank, and were back on the road inside of an hour with Jennifer driving.

"Where in Maine are we headed?" Eric asked, no longer able to contain his curiosity.

"Portland. Actually, we're going to an island off the coast near Portland."

"An island? As in taking a ferry and all that?"

Jennifer nodded.

Tanner said, "We're taking a fairy? You mean like Tinker Bell?"

Eric choked out a laugh. "No," he said chuckling. "That kind of fairy is f-a-i-r-y. This one is f-e-r-r-y. It's a big boat that carries cars across the water," he explained.

"Cool!" Tanner said. Scotch barked, apparently to confirm Tanner's sentiment.

Eric and Tanner played a game of license plate poker for a while, then Eric went in search of a radio station.

He finally settled on an oldies station, and they drove into downtown Portland to the sound of old Beatles' tunes.

Jennifer pulled into the ferry station a few minutes before eleven. A large schedule board above the ticket office told them they had five minutes before the last trip of the evening. Jennifer borrowed a phone book and, after finding her mother's name listed, bought a ticket for Granite Island.

There were only four other cars in line for the ferry, and theirs was the only one in the lane marked for Granite. Once they were on board, they left Scotch in the car, whining and barking in protest, and went up to the top deck.

The fresh air was a welcome relief after the dark, diesel-scented deck below. With a blast of the horn that made Jennifer jump, the ferry shuddered and got underway amid a cloud of smoke and a whine from the engine.

Jennifer took Tanner's hand and made her way out onto one of two triangular promontories overlooking the end of the boat, their outer edges curved so that they looked like a lobster claw. Though considerably cooler than it had been in Virginia, the night air still carried a hint of warmth. Eric came up and stood close behind Jennifer, the heat from his body radiating cozily against her back. She had an impulse to lean against him, letting his strength and warmth support her, but instead, she gripped the railing with one hand and let her other arm drape across Tanner's shoulders.

The boat chugged past the docks, which Jennifer knew would be bustling with activity by daylight: big steamers being loaded and unloaded, little tugboats maneuvering the bigger ships into place, weathered-looking men on fishing boats operating cranes and forklifts. As they headed out into open sea, a large octagon-shaped structure loomed up off to their left. Jennifer pointed toward it.

"That's Fort Gorges," she explained. "It was built in 1858 and used as a gatepost to ward off incoming ships during the First World War."

Eric and Tanner both peered into the darkness, trying to make some sense of the lightened shadows. As they passed by the fort into more open water, the air grew cooler and the sea choppier. Jennifer spread her feet farther apart to accommodate the motion of the boat, and she felt Eric's hand on her shoulder.

"You don't get seasick, do you?" he asked.

"No, you're safe with me. I've ridden this ferry enough times to know."

"Did you grow up around here?"

"No. I grew up in Virginia Beach. But my parents moved up here when I was in high school. I kind of fell in love with the place and visited as often as I could once I went away to college. Until my father's death."

Tanner, with that damnable curiosity that children possess, asked, "How did your father die? Was he in an accident like Dad? Did somebody kill him?"

Jennifer looked down at Tanner. His face, full of innocence and exhaustion, stared back at her. She reached up and ruffled his hair.

"No, sweetie. My father died from a heart attack."

"What's that?"

Eric chimed in. "That's when your heart gets too sick to keep working. When your heart stops beating, you die."

Tanner chewed on his lip, seeming to digest this bit of information. Then he asked, "Could my heart stop beating?"

"Not for a long, long time," Jennifer said, pulling him in closer. She felt a sudden surge of love for her son, an almost-painful tug at her emotions. Thousands of years' worth of evolutionary maternal instincts welled up in her. She vowed then that no one would harm her child. She would fight to her dying breath to protect him and silently cursed whatever Fates had allowed her son to know so much grief and fear at such a young age.

Eric, sensing her emotional state, snaked his arms around her waist and pulled her and Tanner back against him. Jennifer resisted a little at first, but Eric held on firmly and whispered in her ear.

"You're not alone, Jen. I'm here to help you. We *will* get through this."

She finally let herself lean against him, drawing strength from his strength, feeling her resolve grow, grateful he was with her.

"Thank you," she whispered back.

For a response, she felt the soft warmth of his lips on the back of her head and his arms tightened almost imperceptibly around her waist.

The boat passed between a dozen or so small islands, the full moon illuminating eroded banks with trees growing out from them at impossible angles, looking as if they might topple into the water at any moment.

"Look, Mom!" Tanner said suddenly, nudging Jennifer with an elbow and pointing toward a small outcrop of jagged rocks that created a mini island a hundred feet or so off to their right. Sitting on one of the larger rocks was a pair of sea lions, one almost twice as big as the other. Their fur was sleek and wet-looking, casting off an odd reddish blue tint in the moonlight.

"Those are sea lions," Jennifer explained. "You don't get to see them too often. Every once in a while a couple of them will wander down here from Newfoundland."

"That's really cool!" Tanner said, obviously impressed.

The animals watched them pass with little interest until the larger one, apparently bored with the interruption, closed its eyes and rolled over onto its side. The smaller one maintained a watchful eye until the boat had moved beyond the island and out into another small stretch of open water. The breeze picked up again and Jennifer shivered.

Eventually they were once again shielded by islands on either side, and the ferry docked twice in a period of fifteen minutes. They watched as the other cars on board drove off the boat and down narrow, rickety-looking docks. Within minutes after getting under way, a large, dark shadow loomed up ahead.

"There's Granite Island," Jennifer said, pointing.

The island was considerably larger than the others they had passed, its shore wrapping around for a mile or so in either direction before disappearing around bends in the land.

"We'd best get back to the car," Jennifer said reluctantly. She was thoroughly enjoying this little foray and was loath to have it end. The sentiment was compounded when Eric released his hold on her and stepped back, leaving her back feeling cold and lonely. They made their way to the lower deck and greeted a whining Scotch as they settled back inside the Explorer. Within ten minutes they were on land once again.

Jennifer followed the road toward her mother's house, surprised at how much she remembered. There was really only one main road: a long circuitous route that followed the circumference of the island. She pulled onto a gravel road after a mile or so and bounced down it to a tree-lined lane. This she followed to its end—a clearing nestled in the woods. At its center sat a large, log A-frame, its windows dark and empty-looking.

If it hadn't been for the battered pickup parked nearby, Jennifer might have thought no one was home. She glanced at her watch, saw it was almost one o'clock, and figured her mother was most likely asleep. She turned off the engine and stared out the window, serenaded by the rhythmic tick of the engine as it cooled and the raucous calls of frogs and crickets. Finally she turned to Eric.

"You and Tanner wait here. I want to do this alone."

Eric nodded and leaned over to kiss her cheek. "Holler if you need me."

"Thanks."

She got out and walked around to the front porch. She climbed the three wooden stairs slowly, recalling the time she had sat out here on a late summer's night, discussing her plans for the future with her father. College, teaching, marriage, children—it had all seemed so simple back then. How could she have known what a twisted and hazardous road her life would follow? She was almost glad her father wasn't alive to see what a shambles her life's hopes and dreams had become.

She sucked in a deep breath, bit her lip, and knocked loudly on the door. She waited, her ears tuned to the slightest noise on the other side of the door. After a few minutes, she knocked again. Once she thought she heard footsteps moving inside, but no one came to the door. Her hand was raised, about to knock for a third time, when she heard her mother's voice yell through the door, "Who is it?"

For a fleeting moment Jennifer was tempted to turn and run. Then she realized she had nowhere to run to.

"It's Jennifer, Mom. I need your help. I'm in trouble."

There was a long period of silence and Jennifer worried that her mother might refuse to let her in. Then she heard the lock turn and the door opened. A doughy, round face framed with white hair peered out at her from the dark.

"Jennifer? Is that really you?"

Jennifer recognized the voice, but the face looking out at her was nothing like the one she remembered. Her mother had always been such a beautiful woman, with her peaches-and-cream complexion, the same strawberry blond hair she herself had, and clear, lively blue eyes filled with laughter and love. The woman before her was haggard-looking, with the sickly pallor of a shut-in. Her mother had aged, she realized. And not particularly well. She was besieged by a sudden surge of emotion, a need to cry, and an almost-desperate need to turn back the clock and be a child again, back when life was still innocent and full of love.

"It's me, Mom," she said with a barely controlled voice. "I have my son with me. And a friend."

Her mother stared at her, mouth agape, eyes still half-asleep.

"Please, Mom. I need your help. I'm in trouble."

Her mother cracked the door a bit wider and peered out toward the car. "You have a son?" she asked.

"Yes. His name is Tanner. He's eight, almost nine."

Her mother continued to gape at her for a moment. Then her face split into a smile, and she opened the door wide.

"Bring him in." With that she turned back into the house, leaving the door open behind her.

By the time Jennifer returned, leading Eric, who was carrying their one suitcase, with Tanner and Scotch tailing behind him, the house was brilliantly lit. As they mounted the steps, Scotch, apparently distracted by an enticing sound or smell, detoured off into the surrounding woods, barking excitedly as she bounded away.

Jennifer stepped across the threshold and stopped in the small foyer, scanning the room laid out before her. The foyer opened onto a large great room with a high, beamed ceiling. To the left was a doorway to the kitchen and dining area, to the right, another that led to her parents' bedroom and a guest room. Straight ahead was a stairway that climbed up to the large, closed-in loft area that had been Jennifer's room.

The great room was furnished with old, but comfortable, furniture. A sitting area—composed of a fatly stuffed couch, perpendicularly bordered by two mismatched armchairs, the entire arrangement nestled around an oval braided rug—was situated before a massive stone fireplace that filled most of the front wall of the room. The floors, made of highly polished hardwood, gleamed golden in the soft glow of lamplight.

On the far left wall a stained glass window ran from ceiling to floor, partially obscured by a rolltop desk and chair. Beside the desk sat an antique rocker, its seat shiny and smooth from years of use. Jennifer flashed on a memory of her father sitting at the desk working on his papers, while she sat in the rocker beside him watching multicolored patterns of light dance on the floor as the afternoon sun shone in through the window. The memory filled her with a keen sense of loss, followed by an acute stab of nostalgia. Tears burned at her eyes, and a lump formed in her throat.

Her attention was diverted by her mother's appearance in the doorway leading to the kitchen. Jennifer's expression of wistful reminiscence hardened into one of bitterness as her nostalgic yearnings were swiftly replaced with an all-too-familiar feeling of repugnance. She glared at her mother, feeling all the old animosities return, despising her for what she had done, for all the ruin and destruction she had wrought.

Then, slowly, the hazy veil of Jennifer's rancor lifted and her eyes absorbed the pathetic sight of her mother's aged face and body: the shuffling gait, the worn, terry cloth bathrobe, the thinning white hair with its pink scalp showing through. As suddenly as it had come on, her anger dissipated.

Apparently oblivious to her daughter's mixed emotions, Jennifer's mother approached the threesome and smiled down at Tanner. "So this is my grandson," she said.

Tanner hid behind Eric's legs, peering out over the top of the suitcase with an expression that was a mixture of fear and revulsion. Jennifer saw Tanner's reaction, saw her mother's face fall, and felt a spasm of guilt. She opened her mouth to offer some sort of apology or reassurance, but her mother recovered quickly and shifted her eyes to Eric. "And this is my son-in-law?" she asked with a half smile.

"No, Mother. This is a friend of mine, Eric Singleton. Eric, this is my mother, Jane Harren."

Jane's eyebrows raised in puzzlement, but just for a moment. She extended a hand to Eric and said, "Welcome." Then she cast an inquiring glance at Jennifer, waiting.

Jennifer's first impulse was to resent her mother's prying. What right did the woman have, after all these years, after everything she had done, to know anything about her daughter's life? But then she recalled the dire straits they were in and how badly they needed her mother's hospitality. Who knew how long they would have to stay here? She supposed the woman was entitled to some type of explanation and so decided to oblige her curiosity.

"My husband, Tim—Tanner's father—was killed in a car accident eight years ago," she explained.

"Oh," Jane said clumsily, looking at the floor, her face coloring. "I'm sorry."

An awkward silence followed until Jane raised her eyes to look at Tanner. The boy stepped sideways, further hiding himself behind Eric's legs.

"Tanner," Jane said as if she was tasting the word. "I like that name." She flashed him a smile and then turned away. "You can stay in the loft in your mother's old room," she said over her retreating shoulder. "It's exactly

the same as when she left it." With that, she disappeared
into the kitchen, her gait shuffling, her shoulders hunched.

The words slammed into Jennifer like a knife in her
chest. With sudden clarity, she saw that her mother's pain
had equaled, maybe even surpassed, her own, and the
knowledge filled her with shame. Had she been too unforgiving? Too stubborn? After all, this was the same woman
who had brought her into this world, who had loved her
unfailingly all those years, whose charm and wit had been
an example for Jennifer to model herself after. What had
happened to that woman? Was this pathetic shell of a
human being all that was left?

The sound of Jane's voice hollering from the kitchen
interrupted Jennifer's self-flagellation. "I've put on some
tea," she yelled. "And some hot cocoa for the boy."

A whining and scratching sound erupted behind the
threesome in the foyer, and Tanner left his hiding place
behind Eric's legs long enough to let Scotch in. The dog
darted into the great room and commenced an almost-
frantic, sniffing exploration of its contents.

Jennifer looked up at Eric and said, "Come on. I'll
show you where to put the suitcase." She led Tanner and
Eric down the hallway off to the right. There was a bathroom straight ahead and a bedroom on either side. "You
can set the suitcase in there," Jennifer said, pointing toward
the room on the right. As Eric squeezed past her, she turned
and looked in at what had been her parents' room.

All of the furnishings had been changed. The old
four-poster double bed had been replaced with a twin-
size, its sheets and blankets thrown back from her
mother's hasty exit. Her father's dresser was gone, and
her mother's matching one had been replaced by a small
vanity. Even the curtains were different. The changes
served as a fresh reminder of her father's death, and
Jennifer felt another stab of the old resentment and anger.

In contrast to her parents' room, the guest room hadn't changed: a double bed, an old highboy, a single chair. Then it dawned on Jennifer that with Tanner sleeping in her old twin bed in the loft, it left only this bed for her and Eric. She thought about sleeping with him, not in a sexual sense, but simply sharing the same bed. Though the thought was anything but repulsive, she wasn't sure she was ready for that yet.

Once again seeming to read her mind, Eric said, "I can sleep on the couch."

Jennifer flashed him a grateful smile.

"I don't suppose there's any chance of a shower," he added hopefully.

"Of course. The bathroom is at the end of the hallway. I'll get you some towels." Jennifer led the way, noticing as she did that Eric's limp was more pronounced than it had been earlier. "Is your leg bothering you?" she asked, concern in her voice.

"A bit," Eric admitted. "I need to change the dressing on it and clean it up again."

Tanner stuck close to Jennifer as she took Eric into the bathroom and showed him where the towels and such were. When she had Eric set with everything he needed, she turned and headed out to the kitchen, with Tanner practically clinging to her leg. Scotch joined up with them in the great room, apparently satisfied that there were no threats lurking in the corners.

Jennifer found her mother in the kitchen pouring hot water into four mugs she had set out on the kitchen table.

"Oh, my!" Jane said when she saw Scotch. "A dog, too."

"I hope you don't mind," Jennifer said, feeling like an interloper.

"Of course not!" Jane said with a dismissing wave of her hand. "I love animals! When I was a little girl, we always had a house full of pets. In fact, I had to give up my dog, Max, when I married your father. He was deathly allergic to animals, you know. It nearly broke my heart to give old Max away, though the folks who took him seemed like good, kind people."

This bit of knowledge surprised Jennifer. She never had any idea that her mother loved animals, or that her father was the reason behind the lack of pets while she was growing up. She wondered if her mother had ever resented having to give up her dog. Then she wondered if there were other sacrifices her mother had made over the years, ones Jennifer had not been aware of. She realized just how little she actually knew about her parents' relationship. Maybe she had been too hasty in her judgments.

"Why didn't you get another dog after Daddy died?" Jennifer asked.

"I did," Jane said. "Though not for a few years. At first I didn't want the responsibility of taking care of one. It was hard enough just taking care of myself every day. But then things got pretty lonely around here, so I went over to the mainland, to the pound, and picked up a three-year-old, shepherd-collie mix that was scheduled to be put down the next day." Jane gazed off into space, a gentle smile forming.

"I named him Socks because he had these four white paws." Her smile faded, and she looked back at Jennifer. "He got cancer last year, and I had to have him put to sleep. I decided I had had enough losses for one lifetime and never got another." Tears glistened at the corners of her eyes, and she blinked them away and turned to smile at Tanner. "Do you like hot chocolate?" she asked him.

He didn't answer her right away, but when Jennifer nudged him he managed to mutter an "uh-huh."

"Well, climb right on up here, then," Jane said, patting

one of the chairs at the table. "How about some marshmallows?"

"Okay," Tanner said without prompting. Jennifer
could tell her son was warming up to his grandmother and
had mixed feelings about whether or not that was a good
thing.

"And your mother can sit here next to you," Jane
added, sliding one of the mugs across the table. She
looked at Jennifer and asked, "Where is your friend?"

"He's taking a shower," Jennifer explained. "We're
all a little grungy."

"I see," Jane said, turning to put the teakettle back on
the stove.

Jennifer knew her mother was hoping for more of an
explanation, but she didn't offer any. As she slid into the
chair beside Tanner, she acknowledged to herself that her
behavior was childish and petty, but she couldn't help it.

Jane removed a bag of miniature marshmallows from
the freezer and set it down in front of Tanner. Then she
took the seat across the table from Jennifer, wrapping her
hands around her mug of steaming tea, and sipping it
slowly. Jennifer did the same, and the three of them sat
around the table in awkward silence, sipping at their cups,
trying to avoid eye contact.

It was Jane who finally bridged the gap. "Should I ask
what sort of trouble it is you're in?"

Jennifer sipped at her tea to stall for time. It was
orange-flavored, topped off with a generous dollop of
honey, and felt wonderfully soothing as it went down. She
held the cup beneath her chin, letting the aromatic steam
waft up over her face while she considered her mother's
request. She decided there was little to be gained by hiding the truth and was sure her mother posed no threat to
their safety. So she told the entire story: starting with the
accident eight years ago, then Tanner's recent head injury

and the subsequent strange phenomena, Eric's involvement, and their suspicions about Bioceutics. She ended with the shooting incident at the hospital and their flight to Maine.

Jane gaped at her as the story progressed, ignoring her cup of tea as it cooled on the table.

"That is quite the story," Jane said when Jennifer was finished.

Jennifer could hear the skepticism in her mother's voice and at first it angered her. But then she remembered her own initial reluctance to accept the truth and decided she would try to be more open-minded about her mother's reaction.

"I know it sounds rather farfetched," Jennifer said. "I didn't want to believe any of it myself."

"Are you sure you're interpreting things right?" Jane asked. "Maybe it's not what it seems. Sometimes we can read things into circumstances that aren't necessarily the truth."

For some reason, Jennifer suspected her mother's comment carried some subtle, hidden implications—a double meaning. Was she still talking about their present situation? Or was this last statement some sort of veiled reference to the past? She studied her mother's face, trying to read the impetus behind the words, but the woman's placid expression revealed nothing.

"I wish it weren't true," Jennifer said tiredly. "But I'm afraid it is. Believe me, if I could change the facts and bring back the life I had before all this began, I would."

She realized that her own words also carried a double meaning, making them as applicable to past situations as they were to the present one. These mind games were making her tired and irritable. She looked over at Tanner and saw that both his eyes and his head were growing heavier by the moment.

"I think I need to put this guy to bed," she said, rising from the table, glad for an excuse to get away. She took Tanner by the hand and led him—Scotch, as usual, following close behind—back out to the great room and up to the loft.

At the top of the stairs she stopped a moment, staring at the room that had been hers. As her mother had said, it was exactly as she had left it: her high school banner hung on the wall over the bed, her old stereo was tucked in a corner with an assortment of albums from the late seventies stacked below, her volleyball team trophy gleamed from the dresser, and her ragged, stuffed bear, Dexter, stared back at her from the bed with one glass eye. In the windowsill sat a ceramic unicorn, a gift from Ben Harrington, her first love and the first boy she had ever kissed. A multitude of memories flooded her mind—memories of an easier, more carefree time. For one, fleeting moment she was eighteen again—full of anticipation, planning for her college education and a career in teaching, looking toward a future that stretched endlessly ahead of her. *Odd*, she thought, *how different a path life can follow than what we plan and hope for.*

Feeling Tanner's exhausted body slump heavily against her leg, she shook off her memories and came back to the here and now. She helped Tanner undress, realizing just how tired he was when he didn't protest about his near nakedness as she tucked him into bed in nothing more than his undershorts. Sitting on the edge of the bed beside him, she smoothed his hair back off his face and watched as his eyelids slowly succumbed to the battle to stay open. Something about watching her son's sleeping face always made her painfully aware of how vulnerable and fragile he was. She loved him with a ferocity that surprised her. She knew that if it came down to a choice between her own life and Tanner's, she would gladly give up her own. Was there any other love in the universe as strong or as intense as that of a mother for her child?

The question made Jennifer's thoughts turn to her own mother. She wondered if the same fierce emotion she was feeling now had also consumed her mother when Jennifer was little. If her mother's feelings were even half of what she herself felt, then all the recent years of cold-hearted ostracism had to have been unbearably painful. She tried to imagine how she would feel if Tanner were to suddenly cut her out of his life, refusing all contact. The notion left her feeling shaken and forlorn. Maybe she had been too stubbornly bitter, too unforgiving. Maybe it was time to bury the past.

Scotch leaped onto the bed, allowed Jennifer to pat her on the head, and then snuggled up next to Tanner.

Jennifer couldn't help but smile. "You watch out for him, Scotch," she said, giving the dog a final pat on the head. Then she kissed Tanner on the forehead, and flipped off the light. She started to go back downstairs but remembered something and turned back. She walked over to the closet, opened the door, and flipped on the light, giving the room a faint glow.

When Jennifer came back downstairs, she saw Eric sitting on the couch talking to her mother, who sat in one of the nearby chairs with her feet tucked up beneath her. His hair was dark and damp against the back of his neck, and though he had put his slacks back on, he had forgone the green shirt in favor of the white T-shirt he had worn beneath it. She saw that he had his injured leg stretched out in front of him and was gently massaging the knee.

As she drew closer, she became mesmerized by the way the muscles in his back and shoulders moved beneath the thin white cotton of his shirt as he kneaded his leg. From there, her eyes wandered up to the nape of his neck, saw the way his damp hair curled down almost to his collar, and began to imagine what it would be like to kiss that spot. So caught up was she in her imaginings, that for one brief moment she could actually feel the wet softness of his hair against her lips and smell the fragrance of soap and shampoo mingled with the scent she had come to know was Eric. She felt a delicious tingle deep in her gut, as if her insides had gone all liquid all of a sudden. Then she remembered where she was and the grim facts surrounding their arrival here.

Embarrassed, she shook off the images in her mind, admonishing herself for such flights of fancy. Now was no time for romantic foolishness. The first order of business was to get some rest, then tomorrow they needed to put together some sort of game plan.

As she approached the sitting area she heard Eric say, "Best I can figure, Tim must have made some sort of discovery in whatever it was he was working on. Something big, with far-reaching, maybe even criminal applications. My guess is that he realized what he had and that was what got him killed. It was pure luck that Jennifer and Tanner didn't go with him."

"Any idea what it was he was working on?" Jane asked.

"None," Jennifer answered as she rounded one end of the couch.

Eric turned and looked up at her with a smile. "Tanner asleep?"

She nodded and sat down on the couch next to him. Eager to continue the previous line of discussion, she said, "You know, without knowing what it was that Tim was working on, we don't have a snowball's chance of figuring a way out of all this."

"I'm surprised Tanner doesn't know," Eric puzzled. "If Tim is truly able to communicate with him, why hasn't he told him what this project was about?"

"Maybe he has, and Tanner just doesn't understand it," Jane surmised. "Or maybe Tim's trying to protect him."

Jennifer stared at her mother, amazed at how quickly the woman seemed to accept the fact that Tanner was able to talk with his dead father.

"You may have a point there, Mrs. Harren," Eric said thoughtfully. He cast a questioning look at Jennifer. "Didn't Tanner say Tim mentioned something about some papers that were hidden in the house?"

Jennifer nodded.

"Then maybe he wants us to find the papers."

"That would mean going back to the house," Jennifer said. "That would be suicide."

"Maybe not," Eric said thoughtfully. "Think about it a minute. They know we're onto them, and they should know by now that we've taken flight. Your house is the last place they'd expect us to go. And they've already searched it for themselves."

"Still," Jennifer said, shaking her head, "they'd be bound to have someone watching the place. We can't assume they're stupid."

Eric frowned. "Yeah, you're probably right. Damn! There has to be a way. Let me think about it a while longer." He leaned against the back of the couch and stretched his arms. "In the meantime, my body is screaming for some sleep."

"Mine, too," Jennifer said. "Mother, have you some extra blankets for Eric?"

"Blankets?" Jane looked thoroughly confused.

"So he can sleep here on the couch," Jennifer said.

"Oh. Oh!" Jane looked flustered and got up quickly from her chair. "Blankets. Certainly," she mumbled as she shuffled off down the hall toward the bedrooms.

"I think your mother was expecting us to sleep

together," Eric said, leering at Jennifer. "I think she suspects you are living in sin."

"She should know," Jennifer said bitterly. "She's the expert."

"What?"

"My father left her when he discovered she was having an affair," Jennifer explained, feeling all the old animosity return.

"Oh." Eric pondered this new bit of information. "That explains a lot."

Jane returned with some sheets, a blanket, and a pillow. "Here you are. I hope the couch isn't too uncomfortable."

Eric bounced up and down in his seat. Jennifer suspected he must have taken another one of the pain pills, for the movement didn't seem to bother him in the least.

"Feels like heaven to me," Eric said. "Actually, I'm so tired I think I could sleep on a rock."

"Well, I'm going to go back to bed," Jane said. "I'll see you in the morning. Feel free to help yourself to anything in the kitchen." With that, she shuffled back down the hallway. Seconds later, Jennifer and Eric heard the bedroom door close.

Jennifer rose to head to her own room, and Eric stood up with her, giving her a sly, half smile.

"Since I don't get the delight of sleeping with you, what are the chances of getting a kiss before you go off to bed?" he asked, his eyes gleaming wickedly. His dimple was so deep, Jennifer thought she could lose a finger in it.

She gave him a coy smile. "I suppose it wouldn't hurt."

He removed his glasses, carelessly tossed them onto a nearby chair, and moved a step closer.

As Jennifer gazed up into the green depths of his eyes, he lifted her chin with his hand and lowered his face. Then she closed her eyes, prepared to feel the touch of his mouth on hers. Instead, she felt the soft caress of his lips brush against her forehead. Then he pressed a gentle kiss against each of her eyelids, following that with one on each cheek. This unexpected assault on everything but her lips left Jennifer feeling somehow cheated, and she reached up and wrapped a hand around Eric's head, pulling his lips down to hers.

His kiss was tentative at first, his lips playing lightly over her own, feeling, tasting, exploring. Then his mouth parted slightly, and she felt his tongue dance across her bottom lip.

Jennifer felt herself grow warm beneath his touch, and, despite her exhaustion, her body began to stir. She felt a tingle deep inside and ever so subtly pulled his head closer. Her own lips parted and their tongues explored mutual territory—sliding over lips, teeth, gums—gently at first, then with heated fervor. She felt Eric's arms slide around her waist and pull her even closer to him so that she could feel the hot hardness of him against her belly. She moaned, thrilled at the sensations that coursed through her. Her tongue became more insistent, and she lost herself in the taste of him, all warm and spicy, like the tea.

Eric's mouth left hers and he leaned back, making her moan her displeasure. She opened her eyes and saw his green ones smoldering down at her, taking her in, communicating his need. His breathing was heavy and stertorous; the muscles in his jaw twitched with tension as he waited.

She gave him her answer by arching into him and throwing back her head, exposing the soft white of her throat.

His head dropped and his lips worked their way around and down her neck. It was then that she knew she was powerless to stop him. Not that she wanted to. Her breasts began to tingle, then to ache with the delicious feelings that were coursing through her. She felt his hand snake beneath her shirt, and she grabbed it and urged it toward its mark, needing to feel his touch on her aching breasts. He cupped one breast, flicking his thumb across its nipple, making her moan in ecstasy and arch her back even more, until she was rubbing her groin against the pulsing hardness between them.

His mouth continued its downward journey as the hand beneath her blouse gave up its hold on her breast long enough to reach around behind her and unfasten her bra. Then the hand returned, squeezing around her breast as his mouth moved down to her chest. The hot, wet pull of his mouth on her nipple through the fabric of her shirt was so exquisite, she thought she would die from the sheer pleasure of it. He sucked gently at first, his tongue flicking across the fabric that clung moist and hot against her hardened, aching nipple. Then his tempo quickened, until he was sucking at her breast greedily, like a starving infant. Jennifer held his head against her chest, her head lolling back, the pleasure so intense it was almost painful. Just when she thought she couldn't stand it another minute, he pulled away, leaving her throbbing nipple protruding ridiculously through her shirt. Her head snapped up and her eyes flew open to find his face inches from hers, his green eyes hypnotizing, his lips swollen and red from where they had abused her flesh.

"I want you, Jen," he said hoarsely.

She dropped down onto the couch, lying back against the arm and pulling him down beside her. She watched with hungry anticipation as his hands unbuttoned the front of her blouse, laying aside the edges. Then he slid the loosened bra up toward her neck, exposing her eager breasts to his full view. They heaved with her breathless anticipation, poking up at him, the nipples red and swollen with need. She moaned as his lips once again suckled her, his hands kneading her.

Feeling the delightful quickenings in her body, the liquid heat between her legs, she guided one of his hands toward her pants. Then she found her way inside his shirt, running her palms over the hairless chest, feeling his own nipples harden beneath her touch. She felt his hands undo the button on her pants, felt the zipper slide down, felt the incredible heat of his hand on her mons.

He stood up abruptly, his face a visage of lusty need, and tugged at the waist of her pants. She obliged him by lifting her hips off the couch, and he slid down pants and panties in one smooth move. She wriggled one foot loose but left her pants hanging on the other as she stared trans-fixed at the sight of Eric undoing his own pants. He dropped them to the floor and stepped out of them, his red and swollen penis bobbing.

Jennifer's eyes roved over his body from head to toe, delighting in the half-naked perfection of him, finally set-tling her gaze on his throbbing tumescence. She reached out and wrapped her hand around it, squeezing gently, feeling it pulse against her palm.

Eric closed his eyes and moaned, his head rolling back. His hand came up and wrapped itself over her own, guiding her, showing her how to please him. Jennifer moved her hand with his, sliding up and down his hard-ened member, occasionally rubbing her thumb across the velvety head. When his legs started to tremble, he stopped her and pulled her hand away, kneeling down beside her.

He started to explore again with his tongue, mapping out her breasts, her belly, her thighs. She writhed beneath him, her hands snaking through his hair. When at last he rose up to settle down on top of her, she parted her legs wide for him: ready, wanting, needing.

He entered her hard and fast, and she felt a delicious

shiver course through her entire body like an electrical current. At first she was aware of his injured leg and tried to keep her own frantic movements away from it, fearful of hurting him. But as he continued to plunge into her, she became heedless of anything but the needs of her own body. They moved together, establishing a rhythm, until it was as if they were one creature, totally connected. She felt the sensations that ravaged her body crescendo, and her hands grabbed his buttocks, pulling him even deeper into her, her hips grinding with mindless need against his.

And then Jennifer's world exploded in a fiery display of excruciating pleasure, and, for a moment, she lost touch with the world around her, consumed by the fire within her. She barely heard the sound of Eric's moan above her own, and, as she gradually came back to earth, she felt the liquid heat of his seed spurting inside her.

They lay together in almost-perfect stillness for an interminable time, barely breathing, drained both physically and emotionally. Jennifer was only dimly aware of anything other than the comforting warmth of Eric's body against hers, feeling the rhythmic beat of his heart within his chest and the gentle rise and fall of his shoulders with each breath. She felt as if she was enveloped in a blanket of warmth and security and wanted to let herself be lulled toward sleep.

Then she thought about Tanner or her mother waking up in the morning and coming out to find the two of them entwined together naked on the couch. Reluctantly, she nudged Eric. "I need to get up," she whispered. "I don't want to fall asleep here and have Tanner find us like this in the morning."

Eric propped himself up on his elbows and gazed down at her face. His hair stood up on end from her relentless fingers and his expression was one of satisfied contentment, like a cat that has just had its fill of milk and is now ready to curl up and nap the day away. He reached up with one finger and lazily traced the outline of her lip. Then, with a sigh, he kissed the end of her nose and, with a grunt, stood up.

Jennifer sat up and gathered her clothes together. When she had herself in a state of quasi respectability, she glanced at her watch and groaned when she saw that it was almost three-thirty in the morning. She stood up next to Eric, wrapping her arms around his neck and smiling up at him.

"That was wonderful," she cooed. "I didn't think I had it in me."

Eric gave her a crooked grin. "I assure you, the pleasure was as much mine as yours." He pulled her toward him, wrapping her in his arms, rocking her gently with his body.

She nestled her head against the solid warmth of his chest, hearing the steady thump of his heart, feeling his breath gently stir the hairs on her head. When he finally pulled away, it left her feeling cold and desolate.

"You'd best go to bed," he murmured. "Before I am tempted to try for a second round."

His words stirred her, and for one fleeting moment she played with the thought of pulling him back down onto the couch. But exhaustion won out, and she nodded reluctantly.

"Good night, Jen."

"Good night."

A lifetime of unspoken words passed between them as they gazed into one another's eyes. Jennifer admitted to herself, grudgingly, that she was hopelessly and totally in love with Dr. Eric Singleton. Though the thought was not entirely unpleasant, in view of all that had happened, and was likely to happen, it scared the hell out of her. "Lousy timing," she muttered to herself.

Eric bent down and kissed her lightly on the cheek, then abruptly turned away and picked up the sheets to make up the couch for bed.

Feeling happier, but somehow lonelier than she had in years, Jennifer headed down the hallway to bed.

11

Jennifer slept better than she had in what seemed like
an eternity. It was after ten on Friday morning when her
mind first rose out of a dreamless sleep, the heavenly
aromas of bacon and fresh-brewed coffee coaxing her
into staying awake. Her stomach rumbled noisily, and
she reached down to rub it, the caress of her hand
reminding her of last night when Eric's hands and lips
had tiptoed their way across the same spot. The memory
made her blush, but it also made her shiver with remembered delights. She smiled with lazy contentment and
kicked back the covers, letting the warmth of the morning sun caress her hips where it came in through the window.

She lounged a while, luxuriating in the residual glow
still lingering from Eric's magic touch, feeling a growing
sense of determination. Maybe, just maybe, they could
find a way out of this mess yet. Things didn't seem quite
so hopeless by the light of day. She and Eric together
could do wondrous things! Life could be—no, *would*
be—normal again. It had to be.

Energized by her newfound enthusiasm, she bounced
out of bed and headed for the shower.

Half an hour later, she found Eric, Tanner, and her
mother all seated around the kitchen table enjoying a full

breakfast spread: eggs, toast, pancakes, fruit, orange juice, bacon, and sausages. While Eric looked renewed and refreshed, with his color returned and his hair gleaming wet from a recent shower, Tanner was still in his pajamas, his hair sticking up ridiculously on one side and a tangled mat on the other. Both of them were laughing—raucous, robust laughs that cheered Jennifer's heart and soul. It seemed such a long time since she had last heard her son laugh like that. She saw that the root of all this fun was a sword fight, with forks serving as rapiers, their metallic clinking playing the background tympani for the music that was their laughter.

Jane sat between Eric and Tanner, watching the battle with great amusement while taking care to lean back away from the table in cautious avoidance of the makeshift weaponry. In contrast to her rather washed-out appearance last night, this morning Jane was wearing lipstick and a touch of blush, and her hair was pulled back into a ponytail, with a tiny fringe of bangs hanging down on her forehead. These subtle changes had a startling effect on her overall appearance, taking years off her face and making her more closely resemble the mother Jennifer remembered from so many years ago. In fact, the entire scene was one of such tranquil domesticity that Jennifer felt a yearning ache for years gone by, for a feeling of family again, and for the attentions of a mother she hadn't had for almost a decade.

Jane looked up and saw Jennifer in the doorway. "Good morning!" she greeted cheerfully. "Have a seat and I'll fix you a plate." She jumped up from her seat and headed for the stove as Jennifer made her way to the one empty chair, skirting the swordsmen with caution. "Coffee?" Jane offered.

"Yes, please."

Eric looked over at Jennifer and winked. The distraction cost him the battle as Tanner whacked his fork with a sideways motion and sent it flying across the room.

"Hey!" Eric protested. "No fair! I wasn't paying attention."

Tanner giggled. "You snooze, you lose!" he said, laughing. "Knight Bolton reigns triumphant!" He pumped his fists in the air and whooped.

Jane set a plate brimming with food in front of Jennifer, while Eric cast her a gently scathing glance. "You cost me my kingdom, fair lady," he said grudgingly. "It's a good thing you are a kind and lovely maiden, or I might be tempted to smite you."

Jennifer shook her head in disgust. "Men!" she muttered. Then she dug into her breakfast, surprised at the depth of her hunger. The food tasted wonderful, and she ate heartily, quickly clearing her plate. Even the coffee was perfection, rich in flavor, with a hint of cinnamon. She pushed away her empty plate and leaned back in her chair, sipping the aromatic brew, feeling sated and content. At least for the moment, everything was right and wonderful in the world.

Tanner reached over and grabbed Jennifer's arm, tugging at her sleeve. "Mom! I need to show you my new trick!" he said excitedly.

Jennifer gave him an encouraging smile. "Oh?" On the periphery of her vision, she saw Eric give Tanner a disapproving look and a subtle shake of his head.

"I'm not sure your mother is ready for this, Tanner," Eric warned.

Jennifer's feeling of contentment began to fade. "What?" she asked, looking back and forth from Eric to Tanner with a growing sense of dread. "What is it?"

With a resigned sigh, Eric threw up his hands, shrugged, and said, "Okay, Tanner. Go ahead."

Jennifer nibbled at her lip, feeling decidedly uneasy. She looked at Tanner and waited.

"Watch this," Tanner said with barely contained excitement. He picked up the fork he had been fighting with moments earlier and set it near the edge of the table. Then he stared at it, his hands in his lap, his brow puckered in concentration. His gaze was so intent that Jennifer stared down at the table in bewilderment, perplexed as to what was there that could possibly be deserving of such rapt attention. She saw nothing unusual, just the scraped-clean plates that had held breakfast, some empty juice glasses, and some coffee mugs.

Then she saw the fork move.

At first she thought it was her imagination, or a trick of the light. The movement was so miniscule, her mind instantly doubted what her eyes had seen. Then, as she continued to stare at the fork, it lurched up and off the table, clattering onto the wooden floor.

Jennifer raised her startled eyes to Tanner. "How did you do that?" She bent over and looked beneath the table. "Some trick with your leg?"

"He did it with his mind," Eric said, eyeing her cautiously.

Jennifer's gaze rose slowly, her eyes meeting Eric's, her face disbelieving. "No, he didn't," she said adamantly, her mind refusing to accept what Eric was saying, though something inside her knew it was true.

"I did, Mom!" Tanner insisted. "I can move all kinds of things!" His eyes quickly scanned the room, settling on a spot somewhere over Jennifer's shoulder. "Look at that spatula over there on the counter," he said, pointing.

Reluctantly, feeling as if she were being pulled inexorably to the edge of some precipitous drop, Jennifer slowly swiveled her head around and stared at the spatula. Seconds later, the utensil flew off the countertop, sailing through the air right in front of her eyes. It hit the wall on the other side of the room, leaving a greasy splatter to mark the point of impact, before it dropped to the floor with a rattle.

Jennifer stared at the grease mark on the wall, her mind reeling, her heart pounding. Her breakfast churned inside her stomach, threatening to come back up, and she swallowed hard. Her eyes crawled back to Tanner, her mouth hanging open with shock.

"Cool, huh?" Tanner said, grinning broadly. He leaned back in his chair, his arms folded over his chest, smug pride on his face.

Jennifer pulled her eyes away from her son and gaped instead at Eric, thoroughly dumbfounded. "How?" she managed to mutter.

"Psychokinesis," Eric said. "The ability to move inanimate objects with the mind." He shrugged. "I guess it goes along with his other paranormal abilities, the mind reading and such." He leaned forward, arms resting on the table, his face inches away. "Remember when I was telling you about poltergeists?"

Jennifer slowly became aware that Eric was staring at her mouth. She realized it was agape and shut it abruptly. She made a concerted effort to relax both her face and her mind, not wanting to show how upset she was with Tanner sitting there watching her reaction. Numbly, she nodded at Eric and mumbled, "Vaguely."

"I'll run through it again," Eric said, reaching over and laying a reassuring hand on her arm. "In earlier times, people believed poltergeists were mischievous, and at times malevolent, spirits whose presence was characterized by rapping or knocking sounds, objects flying through the air, and other such strange phenomena. In fact, the word poltergeist comes from two German terms: *poltern*, which means to knock, and *geist*, which means ghost or spirit.

"But a number of modern studies have refuted the

whole idea of ghostly spirits, laying the blame for poltergeist activity at the feet of stressed and frustrated adolescents who are seeking a way of expressing their hostilities and anger without fear of punishment. It is believed by some that the extreme emotional highs brought about by the hormonal surges that accompany puberty, and even prepuberty, allow these children to express themselves through a form of unconscious psychokinesis. In a poltergeist situation the person is unaware of the ability, but in Tanner's case, he is purposely projecting his will, making the objects move."

"Is this related to that needle thing in his head?" Jennifer asked.

"Indirectly," Eric said, nodding. "Assuming the needle has stimulated the gland in the manner we suspect, I think it's the pineal gland itself, rather than the metal, that is causing all of these paranormal abilities to manifest themselves. The metal piece is really incidental."

Jennifer looked over at her mother, who merely shrugged and smiled. Then Jennifer turned toward Tanner. She was relieved to see that none of this appeared to bother him much—in fact, he looked rather pleased with himself. Yet the whole situation struck her as absurdly bizarre, as if she was caught up in some weird television *Twilight Zone*. Doomed to spend eternity in an episode of *Bewitched*. Eric was really Darren, her mother was Endora, and Tanner was . . . Her mind refused to complete the thought.

Realizing how inane her thoughts had become, Jennifer shook herself mentally and made a conscious decision to change the subject.

"Tanner, why don't you go take a shower?" she suggested.

Taking his cue from Jennifer, but seeing the obvious disappointment on Tanner's face, Eric made an attempt to soften the blow. "That's a good idea. And when you get done, you can help us do some brainstorming to figure out where we go from here. Okay?"

Tanner nodded grudgingly, got up from his chair, and scuffed his way out of the kitchen, Scotch, as ever, providing his shadow.

Eric pushed his chair away from the table and stood. "I think I'll take Scotch for a walk," he said, massaging his knee. "My leg gets stiff if I sit still too long. And I think you could use a little time alone to digest all this."

Jennifer nodded dumbly. Eric watched her a moment, concern marking his face. Then, with a sigh, he moved behind her and began to massage her shoulders. "It will be okay, Jen," he said softly. "This behavior of Tanner's is not life-threatening, and, besides, I suspect it is self-limiting."

Jennifer twisted around and looked up at him. "What do you mean?"

Eric shrugged. "Well, understand that this is mostly speculation, but I suspect that the stimulation to Tanner's pineal gland was created by the ionization of that chunk of steel in his head. Without continued exposure to a magnetic source of some sort, the stimulus is gone and the paranormal abilities may eventually subside."

"God, I hope so," Jennifer said. "This stuff is all pretty scary. I don't want my son to grow up as some sort of freak."

"He's not a freak," Eric insisted. "He's just a normal little boy with some extraordinary abilities. He'll be fine. You'll see. And if his abilities never wane, maybe we can get rich letting him pick out numbers for the lottery."

Jennifer knew Eric meant it as a joke, but she failed to see the humor in it at the moment. "Not funny," she said with irritation. She shrugged his hands off her shoulders, stood, and began stacking the dirty dishes on the table. "Why don't you go for that walk with Scotch, and I'll help with the cleanup."

Knowing he had been dismissed, Eric shrugged and left the kitchen, calling to Scotch as he went.

Jennifer carried the dirty dishes from the table to the sink, trying hard to focus on the physical effort involved, concentrating on each step, each movement of muscle, to keep her mind from dwelling on other, more frightening subjects.

"You have a nice family there," Jane said as she rinsed the breakfast plates and stacked them in the dishwasher. "You didn't tell me Eric was a doctor."

"Does it matter?" Jennifer snapped, slamming a frying pan onto the counter.

Jane winced. "No," she answered, her voice sounding injured. She turned back toward the sink, busying herself with the dishes.

Jennifer knew her answer had been unnecessarily curt and instantly wished she could take it back. Her mind searched frantically for a way to apologize, her mouth opening and closing like a beached fish, but everything she came up with sounded trite and insincere. Tension mounted in the ensuing silence, wherein the only noise was the rush of water running in the sink and the occasional clink of dishes. Just when Jennifer thought she could bear it no longer, Jane broke the silence.

"He thinks the world of you, you know."

"Who? Eric?"

"Well, of course Tanner does as well, but yes, Eric."

Jennifer smiled, relieved that the air of affability had been so easily resumed. "I like him a lot, too."

Jane reached over and laid a fragile hand on Jennifer's arm. "I'm glad you're happy, Jennifer. I just wish all this nasty business would go away so you could enjoy what you have."

"Thank you, Mother," Jennifer said, feeling an unexpected rush of affection. She smiled tentatively and laid her own hand atop her mother's. With a sigh, she said, "You and me both."

When all of the dishes were done except the pots and pans, Jennifer, at her mother's insistence, sat down at the table with another cup of coffee while Jane scrubbed at the pans. Jennifer spent the time considering Tanner's newfound abilities, weighing what impact, if any, they might have on his future.

If we have a future, she thought grimly.

The phone rang, and Jennifer saw her mother turn toward the device with a puzzled frown, as if the whole concept of someone calling her was somehow foreign. It got Jennifer to wondering. Did her mother have any sort of social life? Friends? A lover? Or was she as lonely and isolated as Jennifer suspected. There was so little she knew about this woman, the same woman who used to be one of the most important people in her life.

Jane dried her hands on a towel and picked up the phone. "Hello?"

Jennifer tried to act as if she wasn't listening, although she couldn't help but eavesdrop in the small confines of the kitchen.

"Who is this?" Jane asked, her voice tense and edgy.

A feeling of dread settled over Jennifer, and she spun around in her chair in time to see her mother's face blanch.

Jane lowered the phone from her ear and placed a hand over the mouthpiece. "It's someone asking for you," she whispered nervously.

Jennifer felt as if someone had just sucker-punched her in the gut. *How could anyone possibly know to find me here?*

"Someone named Carny," Jane added.

Jennifer's eyes closed with relief. Of course! She had forgotten about Carny, the one person who knew about her mother. She opened her eyes and stood up.

"It's okay, Mother," she said taking the phone. "It's a friend." She placed the phone to her ear. "Carny?"

"Jen! Thank goodness I found you! What the hell is going on? I've been worried sick!"

Carny's voice was frantic and accusing, making Jennifer feel as if she were six years old again. "I'm sorry if I worried you," she said contritely. "I'm fine. Well, not fine exactly, but okay."

"What are you doing up there? I called the hospital to check on Tanner yesterday, and they told me you'd disappeared with him. When there was no answer at your house all day I began to get worried. So I called Evan, but he didn't know where you were either! Jennifer, what in the hell is going on?"

"I said I was sorry," Jennifer repeated, beginning to feel perturbed by this rapid-fire third degree. "I didn't tell anyone where I was going." She paused, taking a deep breath and debating how much to reveal to her friend. Could she trust Carny? The answer was an indisputable yes. But what if the people that were after her and Tanner went after Carny? She could be endangering Carny's life by telling her too much. It was probably better if she were kept in the dark.

"I'm in some trouble and need to hide out for a while. I thought this was the safest place to be. Under the circumstances," she added cryptically.

From the corner of her eye, Jennifer saw Tanner come through the doorway to the kitchen and stop just across the threshold. When she turned to look at him, she saw that he was staring at her with his face full of apprehension. She smiled and winked to reassure him, while Carny continued her near-hysterical interrogation.

"Trouble? What kind of trouble? And what about Evan? He's worried sick! Don't you want me to tell Evan where you are?"

Jennifer thought about Evan, which quickly led to thoughts about last night with Eric. There was no doubt in her mind that she was through with Evan. But she thought that he at least deserved to hear so from her in person.

"No, don't tell Evan where I am. Just tell him I'm okay."

Carny sighed in frustration. "What is going on, Jen?" she asked impatiently. "This is all too weird."

Jennifer never answered. She had glanced over at Tanner again and saw to her horror that his eyes were rolled up and he had that vacant look on his face, the one he got when he was having one of his spells.

"I have to go, Carny," Jennifer said quickly. "I'll explain everything later. Please don't tell anyone where I am," she pleaded. "It's a matter of life and death!"

"But what about . . . "

Jennifer slammed the phone down, never hearing the rest of Carny's question. She rushed over to Tanner, knelt in front of him, and placed her hands gently on his shoulders. "Tanner?" she said softly.

There was no response. Not the slightest acknowledgment he had heard her at all. It was as if his body was just an empty shell and his mind—no, his *soul*—was somewhere else, far, far away. He stood as still and rigid as a statue, his breathing slow and irregular.

Jennifer spoke to her mother over her shoulder. "Mom, go outside and get Eric. Quick!"

Jane hustled out of the room.

Seconds later, Scotch dashed into the kitchen, parked herself at Tanner's feet, and started to whine. A moment after that, Jane and Eric rushed in as well, Jane looking pale and frightened, Eric limping and flushed.

Eric assessed the situation instantly. "Believe it or not," he said breathlessly, "Scotch knew what was happening outside. She started that weird whining sound and hightailed it for the front door just as your mother came out." He stood in front of Tanner and studied his face, then wrapped his fingers around Tanner's wrist, feeling and counting his pulse. "He's okay," Eric said.

As if Tanner heard him, his eyes suddenly shifted and focused in on his mother. He blinked three times rapidly. "Someone is coming," he said calmly. "They know where we are."

Jennifer recoiled as if she had been slapped. An icy finger traced down her spine. "That can't be," she muttered. "They don't know."

"They've always known," Tanner said, his voice a frightening, robotic monotone. "About you." He turned his head, fixing his gaze on Jane.

Jane sucked in her breath and clutched the top of her bathrobe closed.

Eric stood up and steered Tanner by his shoulders, taking charge. "Come on," he said over his shoulder to Jennifer. "Get your stuff together and let's get the hell out of here."

They scrambled to throw their few belongings together while Jane watched, frozen and wide-eyed with fear. When they were at the front door ready to leave, Jane stared at them, her eyes sparkling with unshed tears. "Is there anything I can do?" she asked.

Jennifer looked at her mother and saw fear—fear and a vulnerability that tore at her heart. And there was something else there. Love. Caring. Concern. Hot pressure filled Jennifer's eyes, and she swallowed hard to keep from crying. "Is there somewhere you can go?" Jennifer asked. "It might be dangerous for you here."

Jane shook her head and folded her arms across her chest defiantly. "I'm not leaving here. No one is going to make me leave my home. It's all I have." Her voice was steady and courageous, though Jennifer thought she caught an undertone of resignation as well.

"I'm sorry I dragged you into this mess, Mom."

Jane dismissed her apology with a wave of a hand. "I'll be fine," she said. "I'm glad I could help. If there is anything else I can do, you know where to find me." She gave Jennifer a tentative smile.

Jennifer stared at her mother uncertainly, awash with conflicting emotions, until Eric tugged at her sleeve. "Come on, Jen. We need to get out of here."

The distressed tone of his voice reminded her of the seriousness of their situation. Abruptly, Jennifer bridged the few feet between herself and her mother and drew the woman into her arms, hugging her hard. Then she turned to head out the door.

Eric was loading the suitcase into the back of the Explorer, and Tanner and Scotch had jumped into the backseat, when Jennifer heard the rumble of a car engine coming up the road. The sound paralyzed her with fear and she stood breathless, staring at the turn where the road entered the clearing. Waiting. Frozen in time.

A nondescript, tan sedan rounded the corner in a cloud of dust and screeched to a halt mere feet from the Explorer. Before the vehicle had come to a complete stop, the rear doors flew open and two men hopped out, both of them clad in ill-fitting suits and brandishing guns. One of the men, a burly hulk, looked vaguely familiar, and Jennifer struggled to remember where she might have seen him before. He caught her stare and his face split into a lewdly menacing grin.

With a searing flash of memory it came to her.

A party, some nine years ago, with Tim's coworkers. This man had been there—Tim's lab assistant, or something like that. He had flirted with Jennifer, innocently at first, then becoming obsessive and vulgar as he followed her around the room, occasionally leaning over her shoulder and whispering obscene and disgusting suggestions in her ear. In a final, desperate attempt to evade his relentless pursuit, she had begged Tim to take her home, pleading a vicious headache. The memory of his hot breath in her ear and the crudity of his comments made her shudder. She struggled to recall his name. *Something that starts with a D. Like David or Daniel. But less common than that. What the hell is it?*

"Good to see you again, Ms. Bolton." He practically sneered the word "Ms.," his voice scraping along her spinal cord. He leered at her, his round, bulky face splitting into a grin like a ragged gash, his eyes raping her with a quick assessing glance from head to toe. "Looking good as ever," he said with an approving nod.

Eric sidled over next to Jennifer and laid a protective and possessive arm over her shoulders. "You know this creep?" he asked out the side of his mouth, keeping his eyes on the two men.

Jennifer nodded slowly, her mind reeling with the realization that this man worked for Bioceutics and probably knew about Tim's murder. Had possibly even been involved with it. *What was his name?* Suddenly it seemed a matter of great importance that she remember. Donald? Douglas?

The man waved his gun at Eric. "Move away, Doc," he said.

Eric ignored him, moving even closer to Jennifer.

An evil grin filled the man's face and like a bolt of lightning, the name came to Jennifer—Derrick! Her mouth screwed up with distaste as she remembered his sick and demented behavior. He was obviously a psycho, someone on the edge, no one to be taken lightly. Fearing for Eric's safety if he continued his defiance of the man's instructions, Jennifer turned to tell him he should do what Derrick said—move away from her. But before she could so much as utter a word, she saw a look of shocked surprise cross Eric's face. At the same instant, a red rose blossom erupted on Eric's shoulder. It seemed like an eternity later when she heard the *pop*, and her mind reeled with comprehension. Eric had been shot!

Jennifer screamed.

Eric's knees buckled, and he began a slow and terrifying slide toward the ground. Jennifer grabbed at him, trying to hold him up, grasping desperately at his belt, his arms, his shirt, thinking insanely that if she could just keep him from collapsing, he might be okay. But his relentless slump continued despite her efforts, until he was crumpled on the ground, his hand clutching at the bloody hole in his shirt.

Everything after that seemed to occur in slow motion, like a film clip that was being shown one frame at a time.

Tanner let out a yell from the backseat and scrambled out of the car toward Eric.

Scotch leaped past Tanner and headed for Derrick, her lips drawn back in a snarl, a baneful growl rising in her throat. The dog leaped from the ground barely ten feet from Derrick, her teeth bared and aimed for his throat. Then Jennifer heard the *pop* again and Scotch abruptly dropped from the air like a fly that had been swatted, yelping as her body slammed into the ground.

Tanner screamed—a heartbreaking scream of pure terror and pain.

Eric moaned and fell over into the dirt, his blood seeping into the ground.

From the corner of her eye, Jennifer saw her mother collapse to sit on the stairs, burying her face in her hands.

Scotch managed to right herself and, with one last effort of will, lunged at Derrick again. He hadn't expected

the attack this time, and Jennifer had the brief satisfaction
of seeing Scotch sink her teeth into his leg. Derrick cursed
loudly and, unable to fire the gun in such close quarters
without risking hitting his own foot, he swung the weapon
at the dog's head instead, connecting with a sickening
crunch. Scotch emitted another howl of pain and released
her hold, limping off into the woods, blood staining her
right shoulder, the leg dragging uselessly.

Tanner stood up and yelled. "Sco-o-otch!"

He started to run after her, but Jennifer snatched him
back, pulling him close. "Tanner, no," she said gently.

He struggled against her grip, thrashing his arms
and legs. "Let me go! She's hurt! I gotta help her!
Let—me–GO!"

Jennifer held him with all her might, murmuring in
his ear, trying to calm him, assuring him that Scotch
would be okay, though she didn't believe it for a second.
Tanner continued to fight her, kicking and grunting, until
he almost escaped her grasp. Desperate to stop him,
Jennifer yelled.

"Tanner! NO!"

He froze then, his body stiffened with pent-up
adrenaline. A pathetic whimper passed his lips and he
suddenly collapsed against Jennifer's legs, his body as
limp as a rag doll. Sobs consumed him.

Jennifer felt a white-hot anger boil up inside her. She
lifted her eyes slowly and glared at Derrick with pure
hatred, fighting back an urge to lunge at him herself—
kicking, screaming, and scratching—until she tore him to
shreds with her bare hands! She forced herself to calm
down, letting the anger brace her with a cold composure.

"What do you want?" she asked through gritted
teeth.

"Simple, really," Derrick said mockingly. "We want
you and that wonder-boy son of yours. You're going to

help us find those papers your rocket scientist husband hid."

So there it was. The truth at last. Jennifer felt minimally better now that their foe had been given a face and a purpose. It made them seem less powerful, less omnipotent.

The other man, who had climbed out of the sedan along with Derrick, had been standing off to one side, watching impassively, his gun held down at his side.

Derrick turned to him and said, "You take care of the other two. Leave no witnesses."

It took a moment for the import of those instructions to register in Jennifer's mind. When it did, panic set in and her eyes darted about frantically, urgently seeking an escape, desperate to save her mother and Eric.

Eric! Her mind rebelled at the thought of losing him. It was the horror of Tim all over again. This couldn't be happening! It couldn't!

Derrick waved the gun at her. "Get in the car," he ordered.

There was no way out. She had failed. These sick bastards had won, and now they were all going to die!

With her heart heaving painfully, Jennifer cast a stricken and apologetic look at Eric, her eyes brimming with tears. "I love you," she whispered, her voice hitching.

Eric stared back at her through eyes hazed over with pain, his face a mask of death—pale and grim. His lips moved, but no sound came out. Then his face went slack, his eyes rolled back, and his body collapsed into a limp heap.

Jennifer threw her head back and a guttural, keening wail came out of her throat, echoing off the surrounding trees, sounding like the angry roar of an entrapped animal. "No-o-o-o-o!"

Derrick stalked toward her and struck her across the

face with the back of his hand. It brought her instantly
back to her senses, transposing her anguish into a cold
fury, her rage so complete that she started to lunge for the
monster that was ruining her life, her intent to kill or be
killed.

"Mom?"

Tanner's frightened and quiet voice stopped Jennifer
in her tracks. He looked up at her, his body trembling, his
breath hitching and ragged, his face displaying sheer and
total terror. After a moment's hesitation, she squatted
down and gathered him into her arms, holding his head
against her chest and rocking him as she had when he was
a baby.

Derrick stepped closer and nudged her in the back
with his gun. "Move it!" he growled.

Jennifer glowered up at him, pure venom filling the
air between them.

Eventually, reluctantly, she pulled Tanner to his feet.
"Come on, honey," she urged gently. "It will be all right.
I'll take care of you." She steered him, zombielike,
toward the car and eased him into the backseat, climbing
in beside him. Her arms cradled his head and she continued to rock him gently, murmuring gentle reassurances in
his ear.

Derrick climbed into the passenger side of the front
seat and leered back at her, waving his gun in front of
her face. For one, brief moment, Jennifer entertained the
idea of grabbing it and forcing him to shoot her. She
imagined feeling the quick flash of pain, and thought she
would relish the subsequent blackness and nothingness
of death. It would be a welcome respite from the horrible, searing pain that was this very moment tearing at
her heart, mincing it into tiny pieces. But then Tanner
stirred beside her, his throat uttering a strange, strangled
cry, his face burrowing into her breasts, seeking out her

warmth and protection. And she knew she had to stay alive. For Tanner. As long as these guys wanted the information Tim had hidden, she thought Tanner would be safe. She had to keep her wits about her, remain alert, look for any opportunity for escape. She had to protect her son. Or die trying.

The driver of the car, his hair pulled back into a sleek ponytail, the set of his shoulders rigid, his face invisible to Jennifer, turned the car around and aimed it toward the main road.

Jennifer spared one last glance out the car's window, seeing Eric's inert body where it lay on the ground. Then her eyes raised up and met those of her mother, still sitting on the porch steps. Despite all the years of animosity and the cold hardening of her heart, it was obvious to Jennifer now that her love for her mother had never gone away. All she had managed to do was to bury it beneath her own unforgiving, self-righteous morality. All those years wasted. And now it was too late.

She expected to see fear, or even terror in her mother's face. Yet instead, Jane's lips curled into a resigned but complacent smile. A loving, maternal smile that said, *Don't worry about me. I'm okay. I'm not afraid to die.*

Jennifer stared at that smile until the car turned the bend in the road, obscuring her view behind the trees.

They were turning onto the main road when Jennifer heard the distinctive *pop* sound. Then another. Her heart erupted, and she squeezed her eyes shut, moaning with grief for the loss of her mother and Eric.

Why? her mind screamed. How could any God be so cruel? Eric dead! Her mother dead! Taken away from her by the same cruel twist of fate that took Tim. So many wasted lives! What was it that Tim had uncovered? Was it that important, that significant?

Her eyes turned heavenward, wondering if Tim's spirit was there with them now. She spoke to him in her mind, appealing to him, desperate to understand.

Tell me, Tim! For God's sake, tell me! What have you done?

12

As Brian Wentworth approached the building that housed Dr. Andersen's office, he considered raising the top on his Mercedes convertible. He didn't want to risk being seen and recognized by one of his friends. Not that his friends would have cared. Seeing a shrink was considered by some a symbol of status. But to Brian it was a symbol of weakness and shame, a sign of mental inferiority. And he was definitely not inferior or weak. Just unlucky.

In the end, the warm caress of sun on his face and the cool fingers of breeze ruffling his hair felt too good. So he decided the hell with it.

He had his choice of parking spaces; the lot was virtually empty. Choosing one near the door, he slid the car in so that it overlapped the next space, gunned the engine a few times, and then turned it off. Not for the first time, he wondered why there were never any other patients in Andersen's office when he came for his regularly scheduled appointment every Friday afternoon. He supposed it was the usual deference bestowed on members of his class and wealth. On the one hand, he was grateful for it. The fewer people who saw him here, the better. But it nagged at him nonetheless. The few times he had thought to ask Andersen about it, the man had neatly skirted the issue.

Probably unwilling to admit he's kissing ass, Brian thought. Still, he made a mental note to ask again today.

He glanced at his watch, saw that he was ten minutes early, and leaned his head back, tilting his face toward the warmth of the sun. One more session, he thought. Today was the last. Finally, the end to four months' worth of weekly appointments with the pigheaded shrink. What a waste! If it hadn't been for the fact that he actually enjoyed certain aspects of these silly-assed sessions, he would have quit coming a long time ago. Still, he could have done very nicely, thank you, without it. If only he hadn't made that one, stupid mistake.

It had started when he realized that his family's wealth, combined with his aristocratic, blond good looks, made him a much sought-after commodity with the opposite sex. His first experiences with his newfound power had been heady. That feeling of being in control, of being so superior, was addictive. Unfortunately, it didn't last long. Just long enough to have screwed every last one of the desirables—and a few of the not-so-desirables—more times than he could count. When the thrill started to wear off, he had tried abusive, forced sex, but none of the girls found him repulsive enough to fight. That was when he discovered the downside to all that power and influence: there was no more challenge in it for him. All the girls were too eager, too easy. He was bored.

He supposed it was the oppressive and tiresome weight of that invasive boredom that had led to his current troubles. At first he had sought relief through academic challenges, taking a few college-level courses in computers, math, and science during his junior year. But he managed to maintain straight A's with little effort, no matter how difficult the classes were advertised to be. He knew he was smarter than most people, certainly smarter than the idiots who had the unmitigated gall to think they could teach him something. And though the accolades and praise for his academic achievements assuaged his ego for a while, that eventually wore off, too.

Finding himself with no challenges left, Brian set out to create some.

He started by breaking into the chemistry lab at the high school one night during a basketball game and rigging up a little surprise for the next day. The resulting explosion caused sufficient damage to close the chem lab down for a week and bring a bevy of officials—police, firemen, and arson experts—to the school to investigate. The thrill of being on the edge, of wondering if he would be caught, gave Brian a surge of excitement unlike any he had ever experienced. The officials investigated, interrogated, and intimidated half the student body while Brian sat back and watched, smug and amused. When his own turn at questioning came up, he delighted in playing the role of the frightened, but honorable student who was appalled by such violent and wasteful acts, while in his mind he was laughing at the pathetic efforts of the so-called professionals. Eventually the investigation was dropped, the case unsolved, the "perp," as Brian had overheard an officer refer to him, still at large. He had outsmarted them all.

That made him want to move on to bigger and better things.

Next he broke into the administrative offices and accessed the students' files in the computer system. The self-righteous dumb-asses who ran the school had written down all of the passwords. Though they were hidden, in what Brian was sure they thought were great hiding places, it had taken him less than twenty minutes to find them. Once he was in, he went through and altered a few grades. Mike Collins, a computer geek and the only student to outscore Brian on the algebra tests, got his A's changed to D's. Then Brian went through and pulled up the records of some of his closer friends, and within seconds their grade points were elevated a number or two. Finally, to thank Cathy Pollander for one of the better blow jobs he had ever had, he changed all of her grades to A's.

For the coup de grâce, before exiting out of the system, he attached a virus that froze access to the hard drive and then threatened to eliminate all its data unless the operator could win a slot machine–type casino game.

Not knowing the virus was harmless in reality, the school officials went into a week-long panic, sweating the loss of their data and calling in experts to try and circumvent the virus.

Once again Brian watched from the periphery, aching to tell them it was he who had outsmarted them all, but smart enough to know better. It wasn't until weeks later, when that dweeb Mike Collins complained about his grades, that anyone realized the computer had been accessed by someone inside the school. Thinking they were onto something, the school officials then asked for any students whose grades had been changed to notify the office. But Brian had thought that possibility through as well. All of the other grades he had changed had been elevated rather than dropped, and Brian knew the students he'd made changes on well enough to know they were desperate to improve their grades. Not one of the students came forward.

Once again, Brian had outsmarted them all.

In fact, he might have continued along, creating mayhem on a regular basis, if it hadn't been for that one little slip—a gross error in judgment. It still angered him, though he supposed even he was entitled to an occasional mistake. And his error had not been a tactical one; the job had been carried out as smoothly as all the others. His error had been in wanting to demonstrate his exceptional intelligence, to boast about his abilities. What satisfaction was there in getting away with something if no one knew you were getting away with it?

His only mistake had been in trusting that prick, Danny. The stupid little do-gooder had squealed on him, telling the principal who had killed all the mice in the biology lab, stashing their mutilated bodies in various food items in the cafeteria. Danny had always idolized Brian, and the idolatry went to Brian's head, allowing him to succumb during a moment of weakness. The temptation to show off, to impress the little shit, had proved too great. And now, he was paying the price.

Though Brian had to admit it could have been worse. The school had labeled him a behavior problem and requested a parent conference. They threatened suspension. But once his parents had paid for the damages and then offered a significant donation to the school's budget as an extra incentive, the proposed punishments disappeared.

Except for one. Brian had to see Dr. Andersen for counseling every week until school's end. Brian knew his parents could have made the school waive this requirement as well had they persisted, but the shits had unfortunately decided that it might be a good idea. And so his weekly treks to Dr. Andersen's office had begun.

Determined to make the best of the situation, he had even managed to make a challenge out of them. He knew exactly what the good doctor wanted to hear, knew exactly what behaviors, answers, and comments were desired. During the first weeks of his sessions, Brian manipulated the fat bastard handily, trying to convince the man that he was appropriately remorseful and repentant, and therefore cured of his rebellious behavior.

When that became boring, and with months of therapy still ahead—for the doctor seemed determined to make Brian serve every damned appointment in this ridiculous sentence—Brian started mimicking the symptoms of psychological disorders he uncovered with library research: developing some extra personalities, talking about menacing voices that spoke to him inside his head, and laughing as the doctor scribbled down notes excitedly. Truth be told, Brian began to look forward to his weekly sessions with Dr. Andersen. He rather enjoyed fucking with the old coot's mind. Head games, he'd discovered, could be fun.

Smiling with the memories, Brian raised his head and squinted at his watch. One minute to go. He yanked the keys from the ignition and climbed out of the car by leaping over the door. Before entering the office building, he stopped and dug first one foot, then the other, into the rich red mud of the flower bed that ran along the front of the building. Satisfied that both shoes were thoroughly caked, he strutted into the office, whistling a Pink Floyd song he had heard earlier.

He didn't bother to stop at the receptionist's desk to check in. After nearly four months of visits with Andersen, their pattern was well established. Brian suspected that the arrangement, which eliminated any need for him to wait in the tiny waiting room, was one more example of the special treatment he was entitled to. Someone else might have been impressed, but Brian didn't labor under any false illusions. He knew the red carpet treatment was not so much for him as it was to impress his parents. After all, they were the ones with the deep pockets.

Brian hesitated a moment in the small foyer outside Andersen's office to decide what type of mood he was going to portray today. It was going to be difficult to hide his delight over the fact that today was the last of his sessions. What the hell. Today Brian Wentworth would be . . .

Brian Wentworth. That was certainly good enough for anybody. He started whistling again and strode into the spacious office.

Dr. Andersen smiled to himself when he heard Brian whistling his way into the office. He was glad the boy was in a good mood. Not that it really mattered. His own mood was high enough to carry them both. When he thought about the significance of today's visit, his heart rate sped up with excited anticipation.

It wasn't the first time. Brian had the capacity to trigger that level of excitement each time he came. He was a very special and unique patient. Andersen knew that Brian would undoubtedly agree with that assessment, though the boy thought his popularity was due to his parents' incredible influence and wealth. But Andersen's excitement stemmed solely from the good fortune he'd had in discovering Brian. For Brian was a true sociopath, a human being totally without conscience—a bright, manipulative, amoral little smart-ass. Sociopaths of this caliber were extremely rare.

Brian Wentworth had the capacity to become the Ted Bundy of the nineties: an extremely clever, cold, and calculating mind capable of unconscionable acts of violence. Or a future president of the United States, for not all sociopaths were criminals. In fact, many of the world's leaders, corporate big shots, and well-known entertainers were sociopaths to some degree, using and manipulating anyone they could, coldly and without compunction, in order to facilitate their own meteoric rises.

Regardless of which future Brian might choose, he was the type of patient that could lead to a lifetime of highly acclaimed publications for Andersen, if only he could be treated as just another patient. But Brian had been tapped for The Cause. At times, Andersen resented the fact that he could not cash in on this career-boosting potential, possibly his only shot at worldwide recognition. But Brian Wentworth was precisely what The Cause needed—the right age, the right personality defect, and, more importantly, access to the right social connections.

It was a stroke of pure luck that he came to Andersen when he did. Otherwise, MAGI's Stage Two experiment might still be on hold. So far everything was going along better than expected. Though neither the general public, nor the medical community could ever know it, Brian Wentworth was a huge success, the result of an experiment so advanced, so far-reaching in its implications, so absolutely *brilliant*, that if it were known, it would have preserved a spot in the history books for them all. As it was, Andersen and his cohorts had to settle for a few congratulatory slaps on the back, keeping the news of their staggering success among themselves.

Today was the last day of Brian's required sessions. It was also *the* day.

Andersen had reviewed Brian's chart carefully that morning, to ensure that the documentation offered just enough vague allusions to Brian's personality defect without opening himself up to a malpractice suit for a totally missed diagnosis. He kept another, separate chart locked up in his safe at home, one that read quite differently from the official one. That was the wonderful thing about psychiatry and psychology; as sciences, they were just nebulous enough to leave plenty of room for interpretation among practitioners. There were few clear-cut diagnoses of the kind you had with regular medicine, and no autopsies to second-guess the professionals.

Brian swaggered into the room and dropped onto the couch, using the same insolent, cocky strut he used every time he came in. He immediately lifted his feet up and stretched out to his full length, sliding his filthy shoes along the couch seat.

Dr. Andersen suppressed a grin. Early on in Brian's sessions, he had made a big stink over the boy's habit of putting his feet on the couch. Just as soon as Brian discovered that the habit irritated Andersen, he started doing it with each visit, hoping to take advantage of what he thought was one of the doctor's many idiosyncrasies. In truth, it was a test; Andersen wanted to see just how manipulative and irresponsible the boy really was. Brian had passed with flying colors.

"So how are you today, Brian?" Andersen asked, running his characteristic finger around the inside of his collar.

Brian shrugged and scraped a chunk of mud off one shoe with the other, letting it drop onto the couch. "Fine as ever, I guess," he said with the air of someone who is thoroughly bored. "How about you, Doc? You happy? You get any from the old lady last night?"

Andersen watched Brian, the expression on his face placid and unrevealing. This was a routine game they played, one Andersen referred to in his mind as Shock the Doc. In the past he had alternated his responses between scientific curiosity and deep offense, depending on his mood or on what aspect of Brian's personality he was trying to map on any given day. But today, he had another agenda and chose not to play.

"Carneal," Andersen said slowly. It was his mother's maiden name, a word he could easily remember, and one that Brian was not likely to hear outside the confines of this office. Its effect on Brian was instant and startling.

The boy's cocky and arrogant facade disappeared, his face going slack. His body posture changed, his arms and legs becoming so limp that one arm actually fell over the side of the couch, its hand lying palm up on the floor, with the fingers curled slightly like the edges of a drying leaf. Brian's eyes closed down to tiny slits, so that, for all appearances, it looked as if he was sound asleep.

Andersen smiled. It had taken numerous attempts to hypnotize Brian the first time, long enough in fact that at one point Andersen feared he would never succeed. But then Hippocrates had stepped in and helped out, providing a mild sedative disguised as an antibiotic when Brian came down with a cold a few months ago. With the numbing effects of the medication, Brian had let down his guard just enough to allow Andersen to pull him under. Through hypnotic suggestion, he had created the trigger word so that for future sessions he had only to utter "Carneal," and Brian fell instantly into a trance.

"Brian?"

"Yes?" The word came out slurred and sleepy-sounding.

"Tell me how you feel today."

There were a few moments of silence. Then Brian said, "I *don't* feel today. I haven't felt anything for so long now."

"Does that bother you?"

"Yes."

"What do you want to do about it?"

"I need . . . something. Need . . . do something. Need thrills."

Andersen shifted excitedly in his seat. It was this aspect of Brian's personality that intrigued him the most and that made him perfect for what they needed. The boy's belief in his own superior intelligence and abilities left him seeking new and creative ways to test himself. What Brian Wentworth needed most, like a drug addict needs his fix, was a dose of thrills. Something to get his adrenaline pumping. The boy existed in an almost-constant state of underarousal, a condition that had led to his previous mischievous behavior in an effort to achieve the rush that accompanied both the actual performance of his destructive acts, as well as the subsequent tension as various people attempted to catch him. The problem was, this state of underarousal was very much like a junkie's habit—each time it required more risk, more challenge, and acts of greater immorality in order to achieve the same level of excitement.

In most people, sudden surges of adrenaline generally accompanied fear, so that any real or perceived threats created an uncomfortable state of existence—the oft mentioned "fight or flight" reaction. While small doses of adrenaline could actually enhance the ability to think and respond, the threshold where that response took the opposite turn, making someone essentially useless and disoriented, was relatively low.

In Brian's case, however, the effect was just the opposite. It was the low levels of adrenaline that were uncomfortable. High levels gave him a rewarding rush of euphoria and arousal that were as addictive to his psychological system as heroin was to the physical system.

"Let's talk about that, Brian. About excitement. You have accomplished so much and outsmarted so many people. Where can you go from here? What is there left to do?"

Brian's face was devoid of expression as he considered the doctor's question. "I'm not sure," he said slowly.

"There must be something, Brian. How can you prove that you are smarter than everyone else? More capable than everyone else?"

"Must do something astounding. Attract a lot of attention. Outsmart all the know-it-alls."

"So maybe something that would attract the world's attention? Something that would make the news—be broadcast on television?" Andersen suggested.

"Yes."

"Any ideas?"

"Yes."

"Why don't you tell me what they are?"

"I could kill someone. Someone big. Someone important. But it would have to be perfect." A baleful smile stole across his face. "A perfect murder," he said almost gleefully.

"Do you have anyone in mind?"

"No."

"I know someone who would be ideal, Brian. Someone who is famous now and likely to become even more so in the future."

"Who?"

"Senator Tranley. They say he is going to run for president, and many think he will most likely win."

"Senator Tranley," Brian repeated.

"Did you know Tranley is in favor of initiating a requirement for all boys between the ages of eighteen and twenty-one to go through some type of military training?" This was a total fabrication, but Andersen had discovered during the course of Brian's therapy that the boy had a vehement hatred for the military, thanks to his father's marine background and resultant child-rearing philosophies. Brian loathed everything the military did and stood for, considering them a lower life-form: barbaric, heathen, and stupid.

Brian's brow puckered slightly, and one corner of his mouth twitched violently. "That is insane," he said blandly.

"It is," Andersen agreed. "That alone proves how crazy the man is."

"He should be eliminated."

"Ah, yes. But who? And how? The man is closely guarded. It would take someone truly brilliant just to figure out a way to get by his bodyguard." It was a subtle challenge, and, to Andersen's delight, Brian jumped on the bait.

"I could do it," he said with a satisfied smile.

"How?"

"My parents. Tranley is a friend of theirs, at least as long as they keep contributing money to his pockets. He comes to our house. He's coming tonight."

"Tonight?" Though Andersen had already known this, he sounded surprised.

Brian nodded. "A fund-raiser. It would be easy to kill him while he is there."

"But how could you do it without getting caught? There will be too many people around. You can't commit a perfect murder if you're caught."

Brian's face screwed up with concentration while Andersen bided his time. He really didn't care if the boy was caught. Posthypnotic suggestion would eliminate all memory of this and certain other sessions with Andersen. His only concern was that the plan be foolproof enough to be completed before anyone caught on. But he wanted Brian to believe that the entire idea was his own. And given enough encouragement, Brian was bright enough to come up with something.

"A gun is no good," Brian said thoughtfully. "People would see it."

"True."

"Maybe an explosion of some kind, a bomb in his car."

Andersen said nothing. He just watched and waited.

"No," Brian said finally. "Too risky and too difficult to time." His slack face twitched almost imperceptibly. Andersen wondered if it was a smile.

"How about poison?" Brian asked. "If it was something that could be given on the sly, there would be no way of knowing who did it. There will be so many people around."

"Poison might work," Andersen said carefully, a smile crawling across his face. It was truly a delight to watch the boy's mind work.

"But what poison? It should be something readily available. Easy to get. Maybe something in the house."

"Doesn't your father have a heart problem, Brian?"

"Yes, he does. Do you think some of his medication might do the trick?"

"Possibly. Do you know what he takes?"

"Something called Digoxin, and those little nitro pills you stick under your tongue."

"Ah," Andersen said. "Nitro pills can be very poisonous if you take too many."

"I wonder what they taste like," Brian mused.

"Sort of sweet, like saccharine," Andersen offered, amazed at the way the boy's mind was already sorting out the various ramifications and potential downfalls.

Brian sat in silence for a moment, then said, "I could put them in his coffee. He always has coffee at the end of the night, and he takes it with sugar and milk."

"You could," Andersen agreed.

Brian smiled. "Well then, let the games begin."

Later, after Brian had left the office, Andersen picked up his phone and dialed.

"This is Pythias," he said. "Stage Two is right on schedule. By this time tomorrow, Senator Edward Tranley's only upcoming race will be against the worms waiting to eat his flesh."

13

Jennifer sat in the backseat of the car with Tanner's head nestled against her chest, wondering how she could still be alive when her heart and soul felt so mortally wounded. Her chest heaved with a pain so real, so vivid, it made her wonder if she was having a heart attack. Though she was deathly quiet on the outside, on the inside her soul screamed with agony, begging for another chance, pleading to God, or the Fates, or whoever was in charge of this mess called life, to turn back the clocks and make Eric and her mother alive and whole again.

The ponytailed driver steered the car toward the island's marina, a trip that required less than five minutes. As they pulled into an open parking spot, Derrick turned around and gave Jennifer a threatening look.

"You get out of the car and follow my friend here," he said with a sideways nod of his head. "The kid walks with me. This"—he held the gun aloft—"will be aimed at your son's head. Any funny stuff and your kid's brains will be decorating the dock. Understand?"

Jennifer nodded mechanically.

"Good." A lascivious smile twisted Derrick's face and he shoved the gun into his suit coat pocket. He climbed out of the car and, after a quick assessment of the surrounding area, yanked open the back door and motioned for Jennifer to get out.

Jennifer nudged Tanner, but he didn't move. His face remained buried in her chest, his sobs having dissipated into irregular, rasping breaths. Jennifer placed her hands on his shoulders and gently lifted him away from her. He looked back at her through eyes marred with unbearable pain and despair, making Jennifer's hatred for Derrick grow a hundredfold. She promised herself then and there that she would never rest until she had exacted revenge on the slimy bastard even if he killed her *first*. If Tim could come back from the dead, then so would she! Or if she had to, she would see Derrick in hell. No matter what it took, or how long it took, the son of a bitch would pay!

"Tanner? Honey?" Jennifer had to work to keep her voice calm and composed, when what she wanted to do was scream like a banshee. "Come on, honey. We need to go."

Tanner's face went slack, his eyes empty and vacant, his face totally devoid of expression. "Okay," he said in a tiny, frightening monotone. "If I gotta."

Derrick clamped one hand on Tanner's shoulder and gestured with his head for Jennifer to follow the pony-tailed man. She did as she had been directed, following the other man through the parking lot and down one of the docks toward a small, V-bottom fishing boat with an out-board motor hanging on the back. She resisted the urge to turn around and check on Tanner, some sixth sense telling her that he was shuffling along close behind. She was unwilling to risk rousing Derrick's temper even the slight-est bit, fearful that his viciousness was barely contained as it was. Though she felt sure they wanted Tanner alive—at least for now—the evil gleam in Derrick's eye made any action on her part more of a gamble than she was willing to take, particularly when the stakes were her son's life.

They piled into the boat, Tanner sitting glassy-eyed on the front seat, with Jennifer beside him and Derrick in the seat directly behind. The man with the ponytail yanked the cord on the engine, and it sputtered a moment before roaring to life with a thick cloud of smoke, filling the salt air with gas fumes. Jennifer kept her eyes trained ahead of her as the boat maneuvered away from the dock and slipped out into the main body of water.

The trip took close to half an hour, and by the time they docked again, Jennifer's face felt raw from the wind and the salt spray whipping her hair against her tender skin. Tanner's face was red, too, she saw, but he seemed indifferent of the fact. For the entire trip he had sat stock still, his back curved into a slump, his eyes looking so empty they might as well have been made of glass. His bearing was so frighteningly still, his face so placid, that Jennifer found herself watching his chest just to be sure he was still breathing. His stillness frightened her badly, and she began to wonder if Tanner would ever again be the happy little boy he used to be. Assuming, of course, that they ever got out of this alive.

They were greeted at the dock in Portland by a man who looked too young to be out of high school, much less making a career as a thug. His hair was blond and fine, his cheeks cherubic and tinted a healthy rose color, his eyes round and guileless.

Standing beside him was a slender woman with frizzy red hair that fell just short of her shoulders. She wore sunglasses, so Jennifer couldn't see her eyes, but the pinched set of the pale, thin lips suggested the eyes would be steely and cold. And something about the portion of the face Jennifer could see gave her the creeps. Unlike the men, who were dressed as if they were on their way to a business meeting, the woman was casually dressed in a lavender-colored sweat suit.

No one said a word as they exited the boat and followed the man and woman to a van with tinted side windows. Derrick slid into the backseat, settling in on the driver's side, and then motioning to Jennifer to sit beside him.

Jennifer shuddered as she climbed in, fearing Derrick would continue to make his vapid sexual overtures. Pulling Tanner in beside her, she turned her back on the creep and tried her best to ignore him, though every nerve in her body was keenly aware of his proximity. The blond man slid behind the wheel, and the woman took the passenger seat up front. Apparently ponytail-man was staying behind.

The van pulled out into traffic and threaded its way through downtown Portland along Commercial Street, its occupants tense and quiet. Jennifer was surprised when the driver got on Interstate 95 and headed south. She was sure they intended to take her and Tanner back to Virginia, and she would have thought that flying there would have been a more expedient mode of travel. But then she saw the brilliance in their plan: getting through airport security carrying guns would pose a daunting obstacle. By driving, she and Tanner were kept imprisoned and isolated, away from any thoughts of help or rescue.

Knowing they had a long trip ahead of them, Jennifer huddled over Tanner in a protective shell and closed her eyes. She kept waiting, tensed, for Derrick's encroaching touch, but the most she felt was an occasional brush of his arm against her side when the van swerved through traffic. After a half hour or so she began to relax, whispering a silent prayer of thanks that he was leaving her alone. Perhaps it was the presence of the other woman that kept his behavior in check. Or perhaps his sleazy and disgusting behavior was merely his main means of intimidation—an attempt to rob her of her confidence—and now that he had her as his prisoner he had no further need to use sexual bullying. Whatever the reason, Jennifer counted herself lucky.

Thoughts of Eric invaded her mind, the image of him as he lay on the ground back at the island, his face pale and pained. Then she thought about the night before, of the wondrous sensations and emotions he had tenderly evoked from her. With the thoughts came a pain that ripped through her with such severity, it made her gasp. She felt as if her heart had been torn bleeding and dripping from her chest, like some hapless victim in an ancient Aztec sacrifice. Though she knew the pain was more emotional than physical, the very realness of it scared her, leaving her wondering if it was actually possible to die from a broken heart. In a purely instinctive effort to survive, she made a conscious effort to push the thoughts aside, shoving them down into a tiny, locked room that she envisioned inside her chest, where they could be held and protected until she was able to release them.

Released from the agonizing images of Eric, her mind began replaying the events of the past few days, analyzing them over and over and over again, in an effort to understand how everything had gone so wrong. Was there something she could have done differently? Had she somehow risked both her own and Tanner's lives simply by having the unfortunate timing and judgment of marrying Tim? But that was ridiculous. Without Tim, there would be no Tanner. Maybe she'd erred in giving Tanner that bicycle for his birthday, thereby leading to the accident that had initiated the incredible powers he now seemed to possess.

Maybe they should have gone to the police as Eric suggested. Maybe then Eric and her mother would still be alive, and she and Tanner would be safe and protected.

How on earth had her simple and relatively uncomplicated life become such a frightening and horrifying mess? The questions and self-doubts whirled through her mind until she felt physically and mentally exhausted. Finally, her mind, tired of its incessant circling, simply shut down, leaving her in a state that was somewhere between wakefulness and sleep. She shut out all thoughts, and concentrated instead on the warmth of Tanner's body huddled near her own.

Gradually, she realized that Tanner's breathing had slowed and become more regular. She glanced down at his face and saw with relief that he had fallen asleep. Or at least she hoped it was sleep. She worried that his own mind, after all that had happened, had reached its limit, as had her own, and simply shut down, leaving him in a form of catatonia. She shook the thought off the way Scotch shook off water and told herself that Tanner would be okay. He was a tough, resilient kid. When they got out of this awful mess, he would be just the way he used to be: smiling, playful, devilish, loving. He would be the old Tanner. Right as rain. He *had* to be.

Unable to think or feel anymore, Jennifer dozed off, sleeping fitfully over the next few hours, clinging desperately to the numbness of sleep, so as to block out the frightening world around her.

Eventually, she became aware that the van had stopped. She sat up reluctantly and looked around, feeling Tanner stir to life beside her. At first she was overjoyed to feel her son moving, to see him open his eyes and look around with a normal expression of alertness. But then his eyes widened in terror, and she thought that it would have been better had he stayed asleep—or whatever he was—until they were home. Better to remain oblivious for the entire trip rather than face the cold and terrifying reality of life as it had become.

Jennifer saw that they were parked in front of a Kentucky Fried Chicken, and that the driver and the woman were no longer in the van. Presumably they had gone inside, though the sun reflecting off the building's windows kept her from seeing the interior.

With a jolt, it dawned on her that she was alone in the van with Derrick, and her mind and body became taut with rigid tension. She didn't need to turn around and look to know that he was still seated next to her. The hot brimstone of his breath on her neck was an all-too-close and uncomfortable reminder. It was with the nearest thing to joy she had felt in hours that she saw the driver and the woman exit the restaurant, their arms laden with red-and-white bags.

As the woman handed one of the bags to Derrick, Jennifer saw that her sunglasses were pushed back on top of her head, revealing her eyes. They were puffy-looking and watery, their color a strange, amber shade. And as that feral gaze momentarily fixed on Derrick, Jennifer could see what it was about the woman's face that had bothered her before. It was totally devoid of expression—as rigid and unyielding as stone.

The smells of grease and spice quickly permeated the air, and Jennifer had to fight down a wave of nausea. Tanner sat beside her, his face pale, his eyes wide and blank. When Derrick shoved a box of food at her, Jennifer removed a biscuit and held it in front of Tanner's face.

"Here, honey," she urged gently. "Eat something."

Tanner ignored her, staring straight ahead as if he hadn't heard her. Jennifer tore off a chunk of the biscuit and tried to push it into Tanner's mouth. Though his face was pliant, almost doughy-looking, his lips were set firmly in a grim pose. After the piece of biscuit disintegrated into a pile of crumbs in Tanner's lap, Jennifer gave up and fell back against the seat in frustration.

"*You* eat," Derrick grumbled at her, his mouth filled with a disgusting mass of greasy brown potatoes and gravy. He nudged the box on her lap with one end of a drumstick he held in his hand.

"I'm not hungry."

"Eat anyway."

Jennifer ignored him. She was tired of Derrick's bullying abuse. What was he going to do? Force-feed her?

"Eat, goddammit, or I'll smack the kid around."

His voice sounded almost cheered at the thought, and a jolt of fear ran through Jennifer. Though she doubted Derrick would kill either her or Tanner until they got back to Virginia and found what they were looking for, she had no doubt that the man was capable of inflicting a great deal of pain on either of them. While she felt she could take it—would, in fact, almost welcome it at this point—she shuddered when she envisioned those hamlike fists pummeling Tanner's head.

Shooting Derrick a withering stare, she angrily snatched a piece of chicken from the box and ripped off a bite. Though the spices and grease used to cook the stuff scented the entire inside of the van, in her mouth it tasted like little more than cardboard. She chewed and chewed, wondering what had happened to all of her saliva. When she finally swallowed, the chicken stuck in her throat in a sticky mass. By the time she had finished a piece of chicken and a few spoonfuls of coleslaw, Jennifer's hatred for Derrick had increased to a critical mass, ready to explode and annihilate the man.

By the time the sun set, they were on the Jersey Turnpike. Jennifer had passed the time alternating between imagining all of the tortures she would subject Derrick to if she had the chance and worrying about Tanner's continued unresponsive state. Somewhere near the Cherry Hill exit, her bladder started throbbing painfully, and when she saw a sign for a service area she decided she was going to have to risk Derrick's ire or pee all over the seat.

"Can we stop somewhere?" she asked, startled by the sound of her own voice after the long hours of silence. "I have to pee."

Derrick eyed her suspiciously, weighing her request.

"No problem," he said finally. "But I keep the boy with me, and she goes with you." He nodded toward the red-haired woman, who had yet to utter a single word.

Jennifer nodded her agreement.

"Pull off at the next stop," Derrick instructed the driver.

The blond man acknowledged the directive with a quick glance in the rearview mirror and an almost-imperceptible nod.

Jennifer noticed that Derrick had been careful to avoid addressing either of the other two people in the van by name. In fact, the two men had conversed as little as possible, having exchanged fewer than a half dozen sentences since Portland, and the woman hadn't spoken at all. The thought that this determined effort to keep their identities a secret might mean they intended to eventually release her and Tanner alive gave Jennifer a tiny thrill of hope. If they were going to kill them, why would they care if she knew their names?

The driver pulled off the turnpike at the next service area and parked the van in front of a long building that held a Roy Rogers restaurant, a small convenience store, a vending area, and a service station with six pump islands. The red-haired woman got out and opened the back door. Jennifer climbed past Tanner and meekly followed her inside.

The bathroom was long and narrow, with stalls running down either side. Jennifer chose one of the closer ones, taking care to keep her eyes on the floor to avoid making any eye contact with the other women who were inside. She didn't want to give the red-haired woman any reason to think she was making any attempts, real or imagined, to solicit help. Jennifer feared Derrick's wrath if she were caught, and she suspected his punishment would take the form of some sort of physical abuse against Tanner.

Once Jennifer was enclosed in her stall, the red-haired woman slid into the one beside her. Jennifer stared at the woman's shoes. They were some exotic brand of sneaker, in what looked to be about a size six. The woman was not large, maybe five-four or so, but Jennifer suspected that underneath the shapeless sweat suit, she was all muscle and sinewy strength.

As she sat on the toilet, staring at the scratched-out words of graffiti that had been quickly painted over on the walls, Jennifer dabbled with the idea of trying to write some kind of note, a plea for help, something to alert someone to her situation. But she had nothing to write with, and, even if she did, she suspected the woman would check the stall when she was through. Her suspicions proved right.

Back outside, Jennifer followed the woman back to the van, again taking care to keep her behavior and her facial expression above suspicion. As the woman opened the back door to the van, Jennifer felt her heart skip a beat.

Derrick and Tanner were both gone.

Jennifer whirled around and scanned the busy parking lot, frantically searching for her son. Relief flooded her veins when she saw Derrick coming out the same door she herself had just come through, his hand on Tanner's shoulder, steering him back toward the van. Tanner looked solemn, but otherwise okay.

When Derrick saw the look on Jennifer's face, he

said, "What? You think you're the only one with a bladder?" His eyes raked over her and his face split into a leering grin. "Though I suspect you probably have the prettier bladder between the two of us."

Jennifer flashed him a look of disgust, her mouth curling into a grimace. Her whole body shuddered with distaste.

The smile on Derrick's face faded, and a dark look of challenging menace replaced it. "Fuck with me and I'll rip your bladder out and have a look-see, just to see if I'm right. Now get in the fucking van, Miss Fancy-pants."

Jennifer climbed in, assuming her place in the center again. Derrick pushed Tanner in next to her, then climbed past them both to take his own seat. The woman slid the van door shut, the noise sounding to Jennifer like the closing of a coffin.

The rest of the trip was as deathly silent as the first part. Jennifer was relieved that Tanner had drifted off to sleep shortly after they were back on the road and remained that way for the duration.

It was close to midnight when they finally pulled up in front of Jennifer's house. The place was dark and empty-looking, with an almost-abandoned air about it. Feeling as if she had lost a good friend, it hit Jennifer then that the house no longer held the same magic for her it had before. It had been violated, invaded by these evil people. With sadness, she acknowledged to herself that if they did survive this ordeal, she would have to find somewhere else to live.

Jennifer gently shook Tanner awake and led him out of the van and up to the front door. She hesitated, wondering how they were going to get inside. Her purse, with all her money and her keys, was still in Maine, sitting on the front seat of Eric's Explorer. To her chagrin, Derrick produced a set of keys, selected one, and unlocked the door.

Jennifer steered Tanner toward the stairs but was halted when Derrick clamped a hand down on her shoulder.

"Where in the hell do you think you're going?" he growled.

"I'm taking Tanner up to bed." She shoved his hand off her shoulder like she was batting away a pesky fly.

"No, you're not. The kid has some questions to answer."

Jennifer was incensed. Surely they didn't expect to put Tanner through anything more today! He had had enough. Besides, from the looks of him, they would get little out of him at this point.

"Not tonight," she said firmly. "Look at him! He's exhausted!"

"I don't care."

"Let the kid sleep. We can wait until morning."

It was the first time the woman had spoken, and the rather coarse, rasping sound of her voice startled Jennifer. She watched curiously as Derrick's face flushed a deep red, and his brow drew down with irritation. Then he spun around abruptly and stomped off toward the kitchen.

Jennifer breathed a sigh of relief and bestowed a grateful smile on the woman.

It wasn't returned; the woman stared back at her impassively and said, "Let's go." She led Jennifer and Tanner up the stairs, standing aside at the top to let Jennifer take the lead. As Jennifer flipped on the light in Tanner's room, the woman stood in the doorway, gave the room a quick perusal, and then, apparently satisfied, went back out into the hallway, hovering just beside the door.

Tanner was still half-asleep and functioning drunkenly as Jennifer undressed and tucked him into bed. Once again, she was struck by his lack of protest as he stood before her in nothing but his underpants. Knowing how sensitive he had been about it before, Jennifer felt both alarmed and saddened by his current indifference, worrying that it was an early sign that his personality and spirit were slowly eroding away.

After kissing Tanner on the forehead and smoothing his hair back with her hand, Jennifer decided to go back downstairs, hoping she might yet be able to come up with a plan of some sort now that she was on familiar ground. Besides, she was far too fraught with pent-up tension to be able to sleep. As she left Tanner's room and descended the stairs, the red-haired woman padded softly behind her, like a shadow.

The blond-haired man was nowhere to be seen, but Derrick was sprawled out on the couch, his arms spread along the back, his legs extended in front of him. "Kid all tucked in for beddy-bye?" he sneered.

Though his tone was as full of nasty insolence as ever, Jennifer saw that he darted a surreptitious and wary glance at the red-haired woman as he spoke. It was then that she realized he was afraid of the woman, a rather curious situation considering he had to be at least twice her size. Her confidence bolstered by this knowledge, she decided to ignore his snide comment and walked past him into the kitchen. Her newfound courage was short-lived, however, when Derrick followed her and the woman did not.

Trying studiously to ignore Derrick's ominous presence, Jennifer grabbed the teapot off the stove and went to the sink to fill it. But when she turned back, Derrick was leaning against the front of the stove, his legs crossed, his hands supporting his weight.

"Unh-unh, pretty lady," he said. "No boiling water for you. I bet you would just love to toss a cupful of burning water on my face."

Jennifer glared at him, acknowledging the truth in his statement and even enjoying a brief fantasy of the hideous and painful screams the act would rend from the man. Biting her lip, she turned and set the pot back in the sink. She headed for the refrigerator instead, skirting the table to avoid passing in front of Derrick. She took out a jug of orange juice and then, realizing Derrick was standing right beside the cabinet that held all of the drinking glasses, popped the lid off the jug and lifted it to her lips.

Derrick's eyes followed her every move, that sneering smile ever-present. When she had wet her parched throat, she lowered the bottle and shot a scathing look back at him as she wiped her mouth with the back of her arm.

"Now that the kid's tucked in, what do you say I tuck you in, gorgeous?" Derrick asked in his best sleazy voice.

Jennifer threw him a look of disgust.

"What?" he said, his voice sounding mockingly offended. He slapped an open hand against his chest. "I'm not good enough for you, Miss High and Mighty?"

Jennifer slammed the orange juice down on the table and stormed out of the kitchen, hearing Derrick grunt as he pushed himself away from the stove to follow her. Upon entering the living room, Jennifer was startled to hear the peal of the front doorbell and it stopped her in her tracks. Derrick, apparently intent on his pursuit of her, bumped into her backside, nearly knocking her over.

The red-haired woman rose from her chair and walked quickly to the door. She stood on tiptoe and peeked through the peephole.

Jennifer held her breath, wondering who it might be, fearful that it was Carny. Surely there was no way for Carny to know they were home yet. It was going on one in the morning and unless Carny had ventured through the woods in the middle of the night, there would be no way for her to know there was anyone in the house. The thick grove of trees effectively hid the two houses from view of one another.

The woman reached down, threw back the deadbolt, and opened the door.

Jennifer's heart pounded in her chest and the orange juice she had just swallowed surged up in her throat, the acid taste burningly sour.

On the front porch stood Evan.

He looked over the head of the red-haired woman, saw Jennifer, and smiled. "Jennifer! Darling! Are you okay?" He pushed his way into the house and headed for her, his arms extended to embrace her.

Jennifer took an involuntary step backward and felt the steely cold of Derrick's body at her back. Panic seized her as her mind sought frantically for a way to make Evan stop, to alert him to the danger. But he was coming at her too fast. Unable to think of anything else, she simply held her hand out like a cop stopping traffic and yelled at him.

"Evan, stop! Get out of here! Get help! These people are trying to kill me!"

Evan's face took on a puzzled expression, but his step never wavered. He grabbed her shoulders and pulled her to him, wrapping solid arms around her waist.

Jennifer's mind screamed in frustration. She had little doubt that Derrick would kill Evan the same way he had killed her mother and Eric. Everyone she cared about was ending up dead. She was starting to feel like some human version of the black widow spider. Pushing herself away from Evan, she turned and confronted Derrick.

"Please," she begged. "Don't hurt him, too."

Derrick gave a little snort. "Hurt who? Socrates here? Hey, Reeves. The little lady is trying to protect you," he jabbed in a singsong voice. "Isn't that sweet."

Though Jennifer recognized instantly that something was wrong in what Derrick said, something alarming, it took a few seconds for it to register. Or maybe it registered right away, but her mind simply refused to accept it. Slowly, she turned and looked up at Evan. He smiled at her serenely, and everything became suddenly and sickeningly clear.

"Oh my God!" she mumbled. "You're one of them, aren't you?"

Evan's smile never wavered, nor did he answer her.

The pale fear in Jennifer's face gave way to red anger. "You son of a bitch!" she hissed. "How could you do this? Have you been spying on me all along?"

Evan reached out for her, but Jennifer slapped his hand and sidestepped away from him. "You lowlife worm!" she spat. "To think I trusted you, *slept* with you for Christ's sake!" Behind her she heard Derrick snort with amusement.

Evan tried to look embarrassed but succeeded only in looking stupid. "Now, Jennifer," he said slowly, his voice carrying the husky tones he had used when they were in bed together. "While it's true that our meeting was . . . shall we say, convenient . . . it doesn't mean that my feelings aren't real. I really do care for you."

Jennifer was filled with revulsion and loathing. She felt dirty all of a sudden, as if she had just rolled in something dead and slimy and awful.

"I can't believe how incredibly stupid and gullible I've been!" she said, her voice low. "All this time you people have been watching me, manipulating me, spying on me!"

Feeling thoroughly used and violated, she turned and fled from the room, running up the stairs two at a time, heedless of the fact she was turning her back on them and might feel a bullet crash into her brain at any second.

She ran into Tanner's room and shut the door. The knob had a push-button lock—a flimsy thing she knew could be done in with one swift kick—but she pushed it home anyway in a gesture of defiance. She paced back and forth across the room muttering to herself, her hands wringing together, chastising herself for her stupid naïveté.

Her ears listened for the sounds of pursuit, half-expecting the bedroom door to crash off its hinges at any moment. But when no one came after her, she dropped into the rocking chair by the window, rocking back and forth savagely, trying to come to grips with all the betrayals in her life. How could she have been so stupid! If they gave out an award for moron of the year, she had no doubt she would win, hands down.

She stared out the window at the night sky, at the trees gently swaying in the summer night's breeze, watching the image become blurred as tears filled her eyes. Gradually, her rocking diminished to an almost-indiscernible sway as she hugged her knees to her chest and gave way to the frustrated sobs that boiled up inside her.

She cried until she was spent, drained of all emotion.

14

Senator Edward Tranley dressed for his evening at the Wentworths' with little enthusiasm. He had been feeling under the weather all day and suspected it was due to the exhausting pace of his campaign, though he had heard reports of a nasty flu bug that was making the rounds. Whatever it was, it left him feeling achy and tired, enough so that earlier he entertained the idea of calling the Wentworths with his regrets. But his campaign funds were running dangerously low. An evening with the Wentworths and their very generous, wealthy, and influential friends was an opportunity he could not afford to miss.

When he was finished dressing, he headed downstairs, pausing a moment to scrutinize his appearance in the hall mirror. *Not bad,* he thought. For a once-scraggly street urchin raised in the projects, he was proud of what he had become. Though his face was a bit pugnacious, thanks to a few street battles in his childhood, he was not unattractive. His jaw was square and firm, his eyes a warm brown, his hair black with a sprinkling of silver, his mouth full and quick to smile. He was tall—close to six-foot-three—and his body, which had generally been referred to as skinny when he was younger, now fell more into the category of lean, thanks to a gradual weight gain he had experienced around the time he turned fifty. Age had also lent him an easy grace, eliminating the awkward clumsiness that had accompanied most of his childhood and young adult years.

The suit he was wearing was basic and relatively plain: a dark blue pinstripe he had picked off the rack. Even though he could now afford high-quality, tailored clothes, the frugal lifestyle of his childhood had carried over into his adult life. He discovered long ago that his figure was accommodating to just about any style, and that the right balance of personality and charm could overcome nearly any fashion gaffe. It was ironic, he thought, that his tightfisted spending habits and lack of fashion consciousness were the very things that had appealed to the public, pushing him to the forefront of this campaign.

Satisfied that his appearance was acceptable for tonight's event, he made his way downstairs, where he was joined by his bodyguard, Howard, a hulking and quiet man. Tranley didn't like the idea of having a bodyguard— it seemed too pretentious—and had agreed to it only after his campaign manager had threatened to quit. Despite his initial objections, after a time he had grown accustomed to Howard's ever-present shadow and even came to like the man. Howard was smarter than he looked and came from ordinary, hardworking roots, not unlike the senator himself.

"Are you okay, sir?" Howard asked, concern marking his face. "You look a little peaked."

"Just a touch of the flu, I think," Tranley said, mildly irritated that Howard's comment stripped away some of his confidence. He adjusted his tie self-consciously. "I'm fine."

Tranley led the way outside and climbed into the backseat of the practical and affordable minivan that had become another one of his trademarks. Howard climbed in beside him. The driver, a man hired expressly for this evening, sat patiently behind the wheel, watching in the rearview mirror until he was satisfied that the two men were situated. Then, with a quick nod to Howard, he started the van and drove off.

They arrived at the Wentworths' house a little after nine. After being admitted by the guard at the gate, the van followed a long, curving, uphill drive that led to a sprawling, three-story mansion nestled on a hillside overlooking a private lake. Had it been light out, Tranley would have been able to see the tennis courts off to the right, or the nine-hole golf course on the other side of the lake. As it was, the view was pleasing enough when he noted there were a number of Jaguars, Mercedes, and even a Rolls mixed in with the bevy of cars parked on the lawn beside the huge circular drive, boding a profitable evening. Though Tranley had far more conscience than many politicians, it bothered him not in the least that he was basically begging and prostituting himself for money. Money was what he needed to attain his goal, and once he was there, he was confident his intentions and achievements would be honorable enough and worthy enough to ease any guilt pangs he might have suffered along the way. If you wanted to play the game, you had to abide by the rules.

As he climbed out of the van behind his bodyguard, Tranley looked up at the well-lit house, hearing fragments of cocktail chatter drift out through the open windows. It was a beautiful evening, with a star-studded sky and a gently cooling breeze that had chased away the lingering heat of day.

Once inside, they followed a stony-faced butler through a marbled foyer and into a huge, sunken living room. The room had floor-to-ceiling windows that looked out over the lake and a carpet so thick Tranley felt off-balance as he walked. There were close to fifty people there already, milling about in little groups, most of them wearing a casual version of formal wear, which Tranley suspected was in deference to his own taste in dress. A selection of elaborately crafted hors d'oeuvres was laid out along side bars on the room's periphery and a well-stocked bar covered a third of one wall. There was a minimum of furniture in the room: a few chairs that Tranley thought were probably valuable antiques, a long, curved sectional couch in one corner, and some stools pushed up to the bar. Maids dressed in black-and-white uniforms meandered through the room, freshening drinks, maintaining the mountains of food, and hustling away used plates.

As Tranley made his way into the room, Howard stepped aside and positioned himself a discreet but watchful distance away along one wall, his stolid expression and rigid posture providing a definite disincentive to anyone who might think to engage him in conversation. Despite his daunting demeanor, Howard was actually quite at ease. This was not his first time with this crowd, or at this house. And the senator, though very much in the public eye, was well liked and as yet relatively uncontroversial in his views, making him an unlikely target. His pet causes—help for the poor and the minorities—were hardly the ingredients for an assassination plot.

Tranley mingled with the crowd, making good use of the personal research his aides had done earlier. Prior to any event such as this one, they provided him with index cards filled with tidbits of information about the more influential guests expected to be present. A photographic memory was one of Tranley's biggest assets, and he had spent the few hours before the party memorizing the information on the cards, having discovered long ago that personalizing a conversation went a long way toward making someone feel significantly more supportive and generous.

Brian had seen the senator arrive from his upstairs bedroom window. He waited twenty minutes or so—long enough for the senator to have gone through most of the introductions and greetings—before he headed downstairs to join the party.

As he approached the living room, Brian saw his parents standing in an ever-growing group of people that circled around the senator. His mother was wearing a short, white cocktail dress, her pale blond hair pulled severely back, her reddened lips smiling and moving animatedly as she introduced the senator to some of the guests. Brian thought his mother's appearance fit the nickname he had for her perfectly—the Ice Maiden.

His father, on the other hand, was a picture of warmth and congeniality, his hands constantly touching the arms of his guests, his smile broad and filled with perfectly shaped and gleaming teeth, his graying hair slightly mussed, as if he had just come in from a hard game of tennis.

Brian knew it was nothing but a facade. His father was one of the original phonies, but his friends, and even the senator, all seemed to fall for it. Brian supposed that having unlimited wealth and power went a long way toward explaining his father's seemingly endless popularity.

As he entered the living room, Brian glanced along the wall and found, as he had expected, the senator's ugly and impersonal bodyguard at his usual post. The man spared him a cursory glance and just as quickly dismissed him, turning back toward the main part of the room to observe the goings-on.

Brian grinned to himself at the man's ignorance and stupidity. It was a mistake to dismiss Brian Wentworth so easily. He grabbed a soft drink from one of the maids and then positioned himself near a small cluster of people a few feet from the larger group surrounding the senator. He concentrated on feigning great interest in the conversation going on around him, while watching the senator from the corner of his eye, careful to keep the loathing and disgust he felt from showing on his face. He was well practiced at playing the role of the well-behaved and charming son.

As he watched, Brian kept one hand in his jacket pocket, his fingers rubbing incessantly over the tiny brown bottle stashed within. He had removed the bottle from his father's bathroom cabinet just before coming downstairs, knowing from an earlier scouting mission that the bottle contained thirty or so of the tiny white pills. Despite Brian's outward appearance of attentiveness, in his mind he was reviewing the steps he had so carefully planned, rehearsing every move over and over and over again.

Around eleven, the maids set up the silver coffee service along one of the side bars. Brian knew from past experience that this was a carefully timed signal to the guests to begin winding things down. He had been wandering in and out of the living room for the past hour, trying to look appropriately bored and put-upon by the fact that his parents expected him to hang out with this group in the first place. It was the attitude he knew his parents expected, and it was imperative, on tonight of all nights, that his behavior be as normal as possible.

His heart began to pound with anticipation when he saw the senator eye the coffee and begin working his way toward the table. Though the man was only a few feet from the side bar, it took him nearly fifteen minutes to get there, his efforts impeded by a continuous stream of people buttonholing him at each lull in the conversation.

Eventually, the senator reached his goal and, after

excusing himself momentarily from a monkey-faced woman wearing close to a ton of gaudy jewelry, he poured himself a cup of coffee, adding two lumps of sugar and a dollop of cream.

Once Brian saw that the senator had his coffee cup in hand and was already conversing with the latest person vying for his attention, he put his plan into action, slowly working his way across the room toward the side bar.

When he saw Howard the goon from the corner of his eye, an impulse struck him. He turned toward the man and said, "I'm going for a piece of cake. Want one?"

"No, thank you," Howard said, actually managing to smile.

Brian shrugged and continued on his journey, his feet shuffling, his head down, still playing the part of the teenager who wished himself anywhere but here. Though his posture may have appeared distracted and casual, his every move was carefully calculated.

As he passed by the senator, Brian faked a stumble and bumped into the man's arm. The hot coffee sloshed out of Tranley's cup, splattering on both Brian's shirt and the senator's hand. Tranley sucked in his breath, dropped the cup, and started shaking his hand in the air in an effort to ease the pain from the scalding liquid. Brian's chest was also burned, but by this time his mind had so completely blocked out everything but the plan, he was impervious to the pain.

Brian's mother, who was standing in the small group surrounding the senator, squealed and stepped back. Howard hurried over to the senator's side, anxious to see if the man was all right. Within seconds, two of the uniformed maids were there as well, each carrying a wet bar towel. One of the maids handed her towel to the senator, while the other bent down to soak up the spilled coffee.

Brian stood in the middle of all this, his shirt stained an ugly brown, his face looking appropriately abashed.

"I—I'm sorry, Senator," he stammered. "I wasn't watching where I was going." He looked down at the floor in embarrassment.

The senator wrapped his scalded hand in the proffered towel and smiled affably. "Don't worry about it," he said. "Accidents happen. No harm done."

"Oh, Senator!" Brian's mother squealed. "Are you okay? Did you burn yourself?" She stepped forward and took the senator's hand, peeling away the dampened bar towel like the layers on an artichoke. "Oh, my!" she said when she had the reddened skin exposed.

"Best get some ice on it," someone suggested.

Tranley pulled his hand back and waved the people away. "Really, it's nothing," he insisted. "Very minor. Nothing to get excited about."

Howard, assured his boss was not seriously injured, headed back to his spot along the wall.

Finding himself quickly closed out of the circle that tightened in on the senator, Brian turned toward the side bar and picked up a clean coffee cup and saucer. His thumb and finger loosened the lid on the bottle in his pocket. He glanced over his shoulder one last time. Convinced that no one was paying him the slightest attention, he carefully removed the bottle and poured a small pile of the tiny pills into the bottom of the coffee cup. Then he slipped the bottle back into his pocket and reached toward the elaborate silver urn to fill the cup with hot coffee. Though he knew the senator generally took two lumps of sugar, he dropped in only one, knowing that the saccharine taste of the pills would more than compensate for the missing sugar. Then he added some cream and stirred the concoction a moment before turning back to the crowd.

"Excuse me, Senator," he said, trying to make his voice sound meek and embarrassed. He squeezed his way through the crowd that had fenced Tranley in. Once inside the sacred circle he offered up the coffee cup. "I really do apologize for my klutzy behavior." He smiled his best aw–shucks smile, one he had practiced hundreds of times. "A peace offering."

"Thank you, son," the senator said graciously, taking the cup. "That is very thoughtful of you."

"It was the least I could do, after burning your hand and all."

"And what about you?" the senator frowned, seeming to notice for the first time that the front of Brian's shirt was stained with the spilled coffee. "Did you get burned?"

Brian's mother fluttered toward him. "Oh, Brian! Did you?"

"It wasn't bad," Brian said with practiced awkwardness.

"Well, you should run upstairs and change," his mother said, shooing him away with her hand like he was some pesky fly. "You look a sight!"

That's typical, Brian thought bitterly. His mother was far more concerned over his appearance than the fact that he might have been burned. "I guess I should," he said sweetly, his voice revealing no trace of the malice in his thoughts. With a slight nod of his head, he said, "If you will all excuse me."

He removed himself from the room and made his way upstairs, stopping at the top to hang out over the banister and listen. He imagined in his mind what would happen to the senator once the nitroglycerin kicked in. The book he had read in the library this afternoon was very specific.

First the drug would relax all of the smooth muscles in his body, including the blood vessels, causing a rapid drop in the resistance normally maintained by the circulatory system as blood is pumped through. An odd sensation of heat would then spread down from his face to his torso, then into his arms and legs, a result of the tiny capillaries near the surface of his skin dilating and filling with hot blood. His blood pressure would drop precipitously as the lax circulatory system struggled to function, causing beads of clammy perspiration to pop out on his face and chest. The surge of blood through the enlarged arteries in his brain would make his head start to pound with an intolerable force, as if a tiny army of men armed with hammers were trying to knock their way out of his skull. Within seconds, every blood vessel in the senator's body would be so relaxed, they would have all the resistance of a wet paper sack. His heart would pound furiously in an effort to get more blood out to the oxygen-starved organs, while his lips and hands turned a deathly shade of purple. In less than a minute, the senator's entire circulatory system would collapse, causing an almost-instantaneous death.

Back in the living room, while Brian was doing his mental assessment of the senator's demise, Tranley ran a shaking finger along the inside of his collar and loosened his tie a bit. Beads of sweat popped out on his forehead and he felt as if all the blood in his body had suddenly dropped into his feet.

"I don't feel too well," he muttered to no one in particular, though a redheaded woman in front of him was carrying on about something. He wiped the back of his hand across his brow. "If you will excuse me."

He turned to leave, but paused when he felt a rush of light-headedness. The room started to heave as if an earthquake were rocking its foundation. He tried to lift his leg to take a step, but it seemed to be made of lead, refusing to budge. His hands went numb and it took every ounce of concentration he had to maintain his grip on his coffee cup. Aware that everyone in the room was watching him curiously, he spotted a nearby chair and aimed for it, making one final, desperate effort to get his legs moving.

He never made his goal. Without so much as a single step, the senator collapsed onto the floor.

From his spot at the top of the stairs, Brian heard someone scream, "Call an ambulance!" followed by the frantic sounds of commotion: people running, furniture being pushed aside, instructions being yelled out. He smiled to himself and left his post to walk down the hall and into his parents' bedroom. From there he entered the adjoining bathroom and, after carefully wiping the outside of the tiny brown bottle in his pocket, placed it back on the shelf in the medicine cabinet. Any fingerprints in the bathroom itself, he knew, would be eliminated by the housekeeper's daily efforts. Feeling smug and quite pleased with himself, he made his way to his own room and prepared himself for bed.

15

The house was deathly quiet, making Jennifer wonder what the people downstairs were doing. Were they all still there? Were they asleep? Or were Evan and Derrick sharing a good laugh over her trusting foolishness?

In the stillness she could hear the faint song of chattering cicadas serenading the full moon. She sat motionless in the rocking chair, gazing out the window at the top of the small roof over the back porch, mesmerized by the moon's light reflecting off the particles in the tiles like a hundred tiny diamonds.

And then it hit her.

She waited another twenty minutes, barely breathing, her ears alert for the tiniest noise. Everything below was so quiet she could hear the occasional faint ticking sounds of the house settling. Finally, she unfolded herself from the chair, tiptoed over to Tanner's bed, and sat down beside him. She bent down and whispered in his ear.

"Tanner?"

His eyes fluttered open and he jolted upright, his eyes looking around the room fearfully. Quickly, Jennifer placed two fingers over his lips and tapped her own mouth with the finger of her other hand. To her relief, Tanner's wide-eyed expression relaxed, and he nodded his understanding.

When she was sure he would stay quiet she leaned over and whispered in his ear again.

"We're going to make a run for it, Tanner. Out the window and down the tree. Like you did last summer. Remember?"

Tanner's eyes shone bright in the moonlit room. He screwed his forehead up in thought, then nodded almost imperceptibly.

Jennifer stood up, gathered pants, shirt, and a pair of shoes, and handed them to him.

"Dress as quietly as you can," she whispered.

Tanner obediently took the clothes and pulled them on, taking care to move as little as possible. When he was done Jennifer motioned him over to the window.

After undoing the lock, she slowly nudged the bottom sash up. It gave with a tiny creak, and she froze for one heart-stopping moment, listening for a sign that someone below had heard it. When no one came crashing through the door, she slid the window up the rest of the way. Then she stood and stared at the screen, muttering an oath under her breath.

Tanner tiptoed over to his dresser, carefully opened the top drawer, and reached inside. Then he came back to the window and handed her a Swiss Army knife. It had been a gift from Evan last Christmas, one they had fought over as Jennifer felt it was too dangerous for a young boy. Now, she smiled grimly at the irony. She opened the blade and carefully sliced through the fiberglass mesh, pausing occasionally to see if the faint ripping sound was arousing any attention from below. When she had an opening big enough for them to squeeze through she motioned Tanner out. She watched, holding her breath as he sat on the sill, then twisted around, easing himself over until he was hanging by his hands. He dropped the few inches to the roof with the stealth and quiet of a cat.

Jennifer followed suit, trying to control her jangled nerves and cursing her unsteady arms and legs, fearful she would slip and make too much noise.

She took Tanner's hand, and, together, they crept to the roof's edge near an old oak tree that grew a few feet from the porch. A branch hung about five feet above the roof's corner, and, without waiting for Jennifer to tell him, Tanner jumped up and grabbed it, inching his hands along its length until his feet touched another branch below. Then he quickly scrambled his way down to the lowest branch and, with a short swing, dropped to the ground.

Jennifer followed, grimacing when the branch swayed noisily under her heavier weight. Within seconds, she, too, was on the ground. She grabbed Tanner's hand and ran.

As they scurried their way along the path to Carny's house, Jennifer prayed Carny would be home. The woman was always disappearing for days on end, particularly during the summer break from school, on what Carny called mini vacations. Jennifer suspected there was a man involved with each of these vacations and had often wondered if Carny wasn't involved with a married man, a liaison she had to keep secret. Jennifer had been tempted to ask on many an occasion, as she watched Carny find and then dispose of boyfriends as if they were last year's clothes. But so far she had managed to restrain herself, feeling that Carny would reveal the details of her love life when she was ready.

When they reached the clearing on the other side of the woods, Jennifer was relieved to see Carny's car parked in its usual spot beside the house. She led Tanner around to the back door, tested the knob, and, finding it locked, went over and removed a key from beneath the ivy planter. She opened the door and dragged Tanner inside, locking up again behind her.

They tiptoed through the darkened house and up the stairs to Carny's bedroom. Jennifer motioned for Tanner to stay in the doorway as she made her way over to Carny's bed. She could hear her friend's faint snore as she reached down to nudge her awake.

"Carny?"

Carny's eyes flew open, and she sat straight up in bed with such suddenness Jennifer swore under her breath.

"Christ! You scared the hell out of me!" Carny hissed when she saw who it was.

"Sorry," Jennifer half whispered. "It's just me."

Carny blinked and tried to run her fingers through her hair, which stood out from her head like a knotted halo. Her hands were shaking slightly, and Jennifer could see a throbbing pulse in her neck by the moonlight that shone in through the window.

"Shit, Jen! I thought you were a burglar or rapist or something. What in the hell is going on?"

"I need your help. Someone is trying to kill us!"

"What are you talking about?" Carny asked impatiently. "I thought you were in Maine. What is going on?"

"I can explain later. Right now I need you to help me and Tanner get away from here."

Now that her eyes were awake and had adjusted to the moonlit darkness, Carny could see Tanner's outline in the doorway. She threw back her blanket, sat on the edge of the bed, and flipped on the lamp on the bedside stand.

Jennifer promptly reached over and turned it back off. "I'm afraid someone will see it," she whispered. "There's enough moonlight to see by."

"This is too weird, Jen."

"Please, Carny," Jennifer begged. "I don't know where else to go."

"Why not go to the police? I can call them right

now." Carny reached for the phone on the nightstand, but Jennifer stopped her by grabbing her hand.

"No! I don't trust them. I don't trust anybody. Please! We have to hurry. Once they discover we're gone from the house, it won't take them long to make their way over here. If they knew about my mother, they sure as hell know about you."

"They who?" Carny asked with a hint of irritation.

"Bioceutics. They want some papers or something that Tim had. Some project he was working on. Carny, they killed Tim!"

Carny stood up and grabbed Jennifer by the shoulders. "Okay, let's just calm down. You're getting hysterical here. Look, I don't know what's going on, but I think it's pushed you over the edge. You and I both know Tim died in a car accident."

"It was no accident! They planned it. Tanner and I were supposed to die, too."

Carny cocked her head to one side and studied Jennifer's face. "How do you know this?" she asked.

"Tim," Jennifer said. Then she bit her lip, wishing she could yank the word back. She was having enough trouble convincing Carny without mentioning that Tanner had been communicating with his long-dead father. "Look, Carny, you just have to trust me on this. We have to get away from here now! Your life is in danger, too. They've already killed my mother and Eric!"

Carny's face took on a troubled expression for the first time. "Your mother is dead?"

Jennifer swallowed hard and nodded. "They found us in Maine and brought me and Tanner back here. They shot Eric and my mother."

Carny studied Jennifer a few moments longer and then said, "You're serious, aren't you?"

"Of course I am! Do you think I'd joke about something like this?"

Carny studied Jennifer's face another few seconds before seeming to come to a decision. She went to her dresser and took out some clothes.

"The car keys are next to my purse on top of the microwave. You take Tanner out to the car, and I'll be right behind you."

"Thank you, Carny," Jennifer said, the relief apparent in her voice. She turned and left the room, taking Tanner with her. After grabbing Carny's oversize purse and the car keys from off the microwave, Jennifer led Tanner out to the car. After settling Tanner into the backseat, she slid into the front and waited, quiet but alert, scanning the surrounding area. When Carny finally came out and slipped in behind the wheel, Jennifer breathed a quiet sigh of relief and handed Carny the keys.

"Keep the headlights off until we reach the main highway," Jennifer said. "I don't want to alert anyone."

Carny nodded silently. She slid the keys home and turned them, both women grimacing and casting an anxious look around when the engine started up. Though the car was well tuned and relatively new, the quiet purr of the engine sounded like a lion's roar. It was at least fifteen minutes later, when they were headed west along Interstate 64 with no sign of any headlights tagging along close behind, before Jennifer began to relax.

"So, you want to tell me what's been going on?" Carny asked, breaking the shroud of silence that had lain over them since they left the house. "Or do I have to stay in the dark?"

Jennifer filled her in—starting with Tanner's odd behavior after the bike accident, Eric's speculations about Tanner's apparent powers, their flight to Maine after the shooting incident at the hospital, and the trip back to

Virginia, including the crushing discovery that Evan had betrayed her.

"I should have known they would know about my mother," Jennifer said, her voice laced with remorse. "My stupidity cost her and Eric their lives." She cast a glance over her shoulder at Tanner, relieved to see that he was curled up in the corner, thumb planted in his mouth, apparently asleep.

"And I can't believe I fell for Evan's slick and sleazy moves," she said with disgust. She punched her thigh. "Damn! How could I have been so stupid!"

"Don't be too hard on yourself," Carny said. "Let's face it, no one in their wildest dreams would have believed all this conspiracy crap about Bioceutics. Not to mention this thing about Tanner talking to Tim's ghost." Carny shook her head. "I have to tell you, Jen, I'm having a hard time with some of this myself. It sounds like the plot to a bad movie."

"I know," Jennifer said. "It does sound crazy. Believe me, I didn't exactly become an instant convert myself. If it hadn't been for Eric . . ." Her voice trailed off, the mention of Eric making her throat tighten up.

Carny glanced over at her. "You really fell for him, didn't you?"

Jennifer nodded, unable to speak. For a moment, she indulged herself, letting in the memories of Eric, trying to recall those moments—frozen in time and memory like a still photograph—that were marked with tenderness and affection. But the anguish and pain came back as well, and when it became unbearable she forced the memories back into that special locked room she kept inside, holding them safe until she could take them out and examine them without feeling as if everything in her life was torn asunder. She made a determined effort to focus on the here and now. She gazed out the window of the car at the passing scenery, seeing the farmhouses scattered along the surrounding hillocks, yearning for the cozy security and mundane lives of those sleeping inside.

"I don't know where to go," she said to Carny. "I'm afraid that no matter where I am, Bioceutics will find me."

"Well, I do have an idea," Carny said. "There's this guy I dated for a few months last fall who has a cabin in the mountains, near Afton. The relationship didn't last, but we parted friends. And I happen to know two very important facts about the guy—other than the fact that he had the best pair of buns I've seen in years."

Jennifer laughed. "And what is that, I shudder to ask?"

"One, the guy only uses the cabin twice a year, once in the fall and again between Christmas and New Year's. And the second," she said gloatingly, "is where he keeps the key."

"You mean he leaves it there?"

Carny nodded smugly. "Yep! You know what a nosy bitch I can be. I spied on him one morning when he didn't know it and saw him check to be sure it was still there."

Jennifer shook her head in amazement. "You are something," she said with a half grin. "I guess this guy's cabin is as good a place as any. But how do we know it will be safe?"

"Why wouldn't it be? Even if these people at Bioceutics know about me, they aren't likely to know about every guy I dated. Besides, I wasn't with the guy all that long, and I haven't seen him since last fall." She shrugged. "It's the best I can think of on the spur of the moment."

Jennifer sighed. "I guess you're right. Besides, I don't know where else we can go. I left all my cash and credit cards in Maine, and anyway, I'd be willing to bet they'll be watching the banks and such." She felt the overwhelming frustration, which seemed as inevitable to her current lifestyle as breathing, threaten to take over.

Desperate to distract her mind from its frightening train of thought, Jennifer reached over and flipped on the radio to break the silence. It was tuned to an easy listening station and the melodic tones of Whitney Houston filled the air. Jennifer stared out the side window and watched the road roll by, focusing on the hypnotic effect of the white line along the side of the road in an effort to lull her mind. She was yanked back to the present when the DJ interrupted with a late-breaking news story.

"Senator Edward Tranley, who was rushed to the UVA Emergency Room earlier this evening, after collapsing at a fund-raising party at the home of wealthy grocery store magnate Miles Wentworth, is reported to be improving. Sources state that Senator Tranley's collapse was from a combination of the flu and exhaustion from his intensive campaign efforts. Senator Tranley is reported in stable condition, and is being treated for dehydration and some minor burns suffered when a cup of coffee he was holding at the time of his collapse spilled on his chest and abdomen. Doctors anticipate the senator will be released within the next day or so. In other news . . . "

Jennifer reached over and turned the radio down to a faint murmur. "Thank goodness he's okay," she said. "It's no wonder he collapsed from exhaustion with the pace he's been keeping lately."

Carny glanced over at her. "You look a little exhausted yourself," she observed.

Jennifer shrugged. "I am." She gazed out the window, staring at the white line again, her mind racing. "They're not going to stop until Tanner and I are both dead," she said, her voice heavy with fatalism.

Carny gazed back at her, chewing on her lower lip.

"Don't you have any idea what it was Tim was working on?" she asked.

Jennifer shook her head. "All I know is that it was something to do with genetic engineering. But beyond that . . ." She held her hands palm up and then let them drop into her lap. "If only he had told Tanner what it was."

"Are you sure he didn't?"

"Pretty sure. Tanner would have said something."

"Unless Tim tried, and it was just too technical for Tanner to understand," Carny suggested.

"I don't know," Jennifer said, her voice laced with frustration. "All Tanner has said so far is that Tim hid some papers somewhere in the house. If that's true, I wish I knew where the hell they were. Maybe if I knew what this was all about, I'd know where to go from here."

Carny's brow drew down thoughtfully. "If Tim really did tell Tanner he hid these papers, why didn't he tell him where?" she asked.

"I don't know," Jennifer said with annoyance. She buried her face in her hands for a moment, then ran her hands through her hair. "I'm not convinced there *are* any papers. I've been living in that house for eight years now, and I never found anything that sounds like these papers. And the people from Bioceutics have searched, too. If they were there, I think someone would have found them by now."

"Maybe you're overlooking something," Carny persisted. "Think back. When Tanner was having these spells, did he say or do anything that might give you a clue?"

Though she thought it was a waste of time, Jennifer obliged by thinking back over the past few days, replaying them scene by scene in her mind for the umpteen millionth time. Finally, she shook her head.

"There's nothing. All Tanner knew from Tim was that Bioceutics had him killed and that he supposedly hid some important papers. All the rest of Tanner's little episodes were mind-reading stuff, like knowing that Eric had been adopted, and that the phone was about to ring . . . things like that. He even told Evan he would lose this case he's working on."

"He did lose," Carny told her.

Jennifer barked a short laugh. "Well, he sure had Evan pegged right," she said disgustedly. "A loser all around."

Carny shot a sidelong glance at Jennifer. "Doesn't it freak you out a little that Tim's ghost might be hanging around somewhere?" she asked with a little shiver. "I mean, it isn't every day that your long-dead husband comes back to speak to his son. Have you ever felt him? Or seen him? Anything like that?"

"Not really," Jennifer said, trying to recall the times Tanner had gone into one of his fugue states. "Though I must admit Tanner's behavior is a little creepy at times. He gets this faraway, blank look on his face, almost as if his soul or spirit or whatever has left his body. He seems totally oblivious to his surroundings. One time, he even wandered off. I found him sitting in the middle of the basement with all the lights off . . . ."

Jennifer froze. Then she turned and grabbed Carny's arm so abruptly it made the car swerve. "Carny! I think I know where the papers are hidden! We have to go back!"

Carny gaped at Jennifer as if she had just seen her head pop off and spin around. "Go back? Are you crazy? I thought you said these people are trying to kill you!"

"They are!" Jennifer said with such enthusiasm that Carny began to wonder if her friend had finally gone over the edge. "The only reason we're not dead already is because they haven't found those papers. They think

Tanner knows where they are. If they find them before we do, Tanner and I are history."

"And you think you know where they are?" Carny's voice was rife with criticism.

"Yes! They're in the basement! It all makes sense now! Why didn't I see it before?" Jennifer slapped her forehead with an open palm. She stared at Carny with eyes that were wide and a little too bright. "That's why Tanner was in the basement that one time. Tim led him down there! The papers are hidden somewhere in the basement!"

Carny eased the car onto the shoulder and shifted it into park, letting it idle. She turned toward Jennifer, one arm resting on the back of the seat. "Okay," she said. "Suppose you're right. Suppose the papers are hidden in the basement. How do you propose to get them? There's no way you can get into the house without them knowing."

"I don't know, Carny. But I'll find a way. I have to. I know every nook and cranny of that house. If those papers do exist, I'll find them. It's the only hope I have left."

"They'll kill you," Carny argued.

"I'll find a way," Jennifer insisted stubbornly. "Turn around."

Carny placed a hand on her friend's shoulder. "Jennifer, you're not thinking clearly. What about Tanner?" she asked, gesturing toward his sleeping form in the backseat. "Are you going to risk his life, too?"

Jennifer considered that a moment. "I'll have to hide him somewhere," she said thoughtfully. She snapped her fingers. "I can leave him with you at the cabin! That way he'll be safe. I'll go back by myself."

"And what if you don't come back?"

Jennifer swallowed hard. The excitement in her eyes dulled noticeably, and her face became grimly serious. "If I don't come back, then you have to promise me you'll look out for him." Despite the bravado of her words, Jennifer felt tears burn at the edges of her eyes.

Carny turned back and grabbed the steering wheel with both hands, flexing her fingers around its rim. "You're crazy," she said slowly. "We're going to the cabin, like we planned. This asinine idea of yours will never work."

"I suppose you're right," Jennifer sighed, her tears welling even higher. When they finally leaked their way down her cheeks, Jennifer swiped at them irritably. As Carny glanced over her shoulder and eased back onto the interstate, Jennifer reached over and opened Carny's purse. "Got a tissue in here?" she asked, peering into the oversize bag. She shoved aside the leather wallet that lay on top and froze when her eyes fixed on the item beneath it.

"Jennifer, no!"

Jennifer heard Carny's frantic words, and some distant part of her mind knew that her sanity was dependent on following that command. Yet despite the warning bells, her hands closed on the item and slowly withdrew it from the bag. Holding it in front of her, Jennifer felt her stomach fall to her feet. She glanced up and studied Carny's face in the eerie greenish glow from the dashboard.

Carny cast her a quick, sideways glance.

"Carny?" Jennifer's voice came out as a whimper. She felt as if she was hanging on to the end of a rope, dangling over a precipitous drop, the rope slowly slipping through her hands. "Carny?" she repeated.

Carny squeezed her eyes shut a moment, then turned to look at Jennifer. "I'm sorry, Jen," she whispered.

Jennifer fell back against the seat, her mind reeling. The frizzy, red-haired wig slipped from her hands, falling onto the floor at her feet. Then her mind snapped shut, closing out all thought, refusing to confront the reality that was smacking her in the face. Her eyes stared out the windshield, seeing nothing. She was dimly aware that her ears popped to compensate for the rising altitude in the road as they climbed up the side of the mountain. She barely felt the odd, empty thud in her chest as her heart skipped a beat. Then the last of the rope that was her life line slipped through her hands, and she felt herself falling, falling, falling . . .

And then she felt nothing.

16

When she came to, Jennifer knew she was sitting in Carny's car and could tell that it wasn't moving, but that was all she knew. She felt funny—fuzzy-headed and disoriented—and she struggled to remember where she was and how she had come to be there. She squinted and sat up, looking around her at the thick copse of trees that surrounded the small clearing where the car was parked.

The sun was up, its golden light filtering through the trees, leaving dapples of light and shadow on the ground, the car windows, and the seat. Directly ahead, Jennifer saw a small log cabin nestled among the trees—a boxy-looking structure with a steeply slanting roof, a stone chimney climbing up one side, and a small porch at the front. A strong scent of pine permeated the interior of the car, and through the inch or so opening in her window she could hear the early morning lilt of animal chatter and birdsong. For one brief second, the idyllic surroundings had Jennifer wanting to lean her head back and close her eyes, letting the scents and sounds drown out everything else in her mind. But then her memory returned in a sudden, searing flash.

Tanner!

She whirled around to look in the backseat and uttered a tiny moan. There was no one there. She was alone in the car. Tanner was gone. Carny was gone. Her whole life was gone.

A squeaking sound brought her head back to face forward, and she saw the door to the cabin open. Jennifer watched as Carny stepped out onto the small wooden porch, pausing to look around before she came down the three stairs, heading for the car. With a chill, Jennifer saw that there was a pistol tucked into the waist of Carny's jeans.

The sight of the gun did her in. She fell back against the seat, uttering a strangled cry of defeat. There was no point in fighting anymore. Carny's betrayal—the one person in her life she was sure she could trust—had undermined the last vestiges of her will to fight. Carny—her friend, her confidante, her *sister*—was going to kill her. Not that it mattered anymore. For all intents and purposes, she was dead already.

Eric's words came back to haunt her; he had been right all along. She had trusted Carny with their lives, and now they would all pay for it. Eric already had. And thanks to her blindingly stupid trust, Carny had an idea where the papers were hidden, so there was no further need to keep herself or Tanner alive.

Carny opened the car door. "Oh, good," she said. "I was just going to try and bring you around." She stepped back. "Let's go inside."

"Where's Tanner?" Jennifer's voice, though filled with resignation, still dripped with venom. "What have you done to Tanner?"

Carny frowned at her, her brow puckered. "Come on, Jen. Inside."

With the best expression of disgust and hatred she could summon, Jennifer climbed out of the car. She glared at Carny, wanting to say something—something burning, something scathing, something to let her know just how deeply wounded she was—but her mind and tongue failed her. Lowering her head, she walked toward the cabin, hearing Carny's footsteps behind her, wondering if the pistol was still tucked in her jeans, or if it was, at this very moment, aimed at the back of her head. What was it like to die? Would it be painful? Peaceful?

Then she wondered if Tanner was still alive. If not, she prayed that his end had been painless. If she found out otherwise, she vowed she would go down fighting, ripping Carny's face off even as she gasped her last breath.

She mounted the cabin steps feeling as if her legs were weighted down with lead boots, and opened the door. She stepped into a darkened room and, unable to see after the bright light from outside, stopped a moment to let her eyes adjust.

A small voice came out of the dark in front of her. "Mom?"

Tanner! Tanner was still alive!

She called out to him, heard the sound of his feet as he ran toward her, saw a dim shadow, and held out her arms. He plunged into them, hugging her tightly. She held him as close as she could, breathing in the scent of his hair, relishing the warmth of his breath on her neck. Her arms enveloped him, wanting to pull him even closer, to absorb him through her skin. She held him tightly and cried, the tears dribbling down her cheeks and off her chin into Tanner's hair.

As her eyes gradually adjusted to the dimly lit interior she blinked to clear the tears away and realized there was another person standing a few feet away. Her brief sense of relief was instantly vanquished. Reluctantly, and with menace in her eyes, she looked up, knowing in her heart that she would be facing Derrick once again. So convinced was she that Derrick's simpering and sadistic face would be staring back at her, she actually saw, in her mind's eye, his vapid, leering grin. Then the image shifted, and Jennifer's mouth fell open.

"Eric?" She blinked again, harder, convinced that her overwrought mind was conjuring up imaginary images in an effort to avoid reality.

He grinned stupidly at her, wagging a couple of fingers in a wave.

"Are you alive?" Jennifer asked haltingly. For one brief moment she thought that maybe Tanner's powers had grown to the extent that he was able to bring the dead back to life, not just communicate with them.

"Last time I checked," Eric said. "Though a bit the worse for wear." He came toward her, and Jennifer released Tanner and threw herself into Eric's arms, half-expecting his image to dissolve right before her eyes. Instead, she felt the very real, very solid warmth of him.

"Oh, Eric! You're real! You're alive!" Her arms wrapped tight around him, fearful that if she didn't hang on tight enough, he might slip away. In response, she heard Eric draw in a sharp, hissing breath.

"Ouch! Careful there!" he said, twisting back away from her.

Belatedly, Jennifer felt the bulk of a large bandage beneath his shirt, one that wrapped around his left shoulder and chest. She stepped back and looked at him, still not trusting her eyes. Maybe her mind had finally cracked. Maybe this was nothing more than a hallucination. Or maybe she was dead already. Reunited in the afterlife with Tanner and Eric.

"I don't understand," she said slowly, afraid to believe what her eyes were seeing.

"Maybe I can help clarify things for you," Carny said from behind her.

Jennifer had been so stunned to see Eric alive, she had momentarily forgotten all about Carny. She turned and gaped at her.

"I know you feel as if I have betrayed you, Jennifer," Carny said. "But in reality all I have done is deceive you a little. And that was out of necessity."

"Carny's a spy, Mom!" Tanner said excitedly. "Like James Bond! Except she's a girl," he added with some disappointment.

"A spy?" Jennifer repeated. The room was beginning to spin, and her knees started to wobble.

Eric grabbed her arm and said, "I think you'd better sit down before you fall." He led her to a nearby couch and gently pushed her down onto it, settling in next to her and draping his good arm across her shoulders. Tanner climbed up on her other side and nestled his head against her arm.

Jennifer's mind was reeling with a zillion questions. Hard as she tried, she could make no sense out of all this.

Carny sat in a chair across from the couch and leaned forward, resting her arms on her knees. "Perhaps it will help if I start at the beginning," she said.

Jennifer nodded dumbly, her mind too bewildered to do much else.

"It started back when Tim first went to work for Bioceutics. He was assigned, as you said, to the genetic engineering section. He was working on some gene-splicing experiments when he accidentally made a remarkable discovery. Actually, two remarkable discoveries. One, was a technique for mutating certain genes through a process that uses injectable nucleotides."

"What's a nuclear tide?" Tanner asked.

Carny laughed. "It's nuc-le-o-tide. They're nitrogenous bases that link up with one end of the deoxyribose."

Eric was nodding his head, but Tanner and Jennifer merely looked puzzled.

"Anyway," Carny continued, "there are only four types of nucleotides." She ticked them off on her fingers. "Adenine and guanine, which always pair up together, and thymine and cytosine, which also have to pair up together. Having these nucleotides pair up properly is requisite to the double helix formation in DNA, and to the replication process." She paused a moment to see if her audience was following her lecture. When they asked no questions, she continued.

"Tim discovered a synthetic nucleotide that, when injected with an appropriate marker, can bond in place of one of the four naturally occurring nucleotides, thereby altering the DNA structure."

"And producing a mutation," Eric said.

"Exactly!" Carny bestowed a proud smile on Eric, one that Jennifer recognized as her standard teacher's smile, the one she kept in reserve for her prize students. Except Carny wasn't really a teacher after all. Was she?

Carny continued her explanation. "The problem with Tim's discovery was that it only worked on certain genes, as others had a tendency to be less stable. Still, it was a remarkable find as it had far-reaching implications for the treatment of certain medical conditions.

"The second discovery Tim made was that one of the genes, one that was particularly susceptible to this mutative process, was the gene involved with the regulation of serotonin."

"What's that?" Tanner asked.

Carny smiled at him. "Patience, my boy. I'm getting to that. Serotonin is a hormone and neurotransmitter that acts as sort of an aggression regulator. Tim did some experiments with mice and monkeys, adjusting their level of serotonin and observing what, if any, effect it had on their behavior. What he found was that the animals with particularly low levels of serotonin had a tendency to become extremely violent. In fact, the monkeys with the lowest serotonin levels would, when provoked, attack and kill the other monkeys in their group, including their own families. This finding was rather startling, as monkeys are notoriously social animals, with a keen sense of family."

Jennifer held up a hand and gave a quick shake of her head. "Slow down. Let me see if I'm following all this. Tim found a way to alter the genetic code for the regulation of this serotonin. Correct?"

Carny nodded.

"And he also discovered that if this serotonin gets too low, it can lead to extreme aggression and violence?"

Again, Carny nodded. "And to make matters worse, he also discovered that when a low serotonin level is combined with a high noradrenaline level"— she paused and looked at Tanner—"noradrenaline is another hormone. One that helps prepare the body to react to danger."

"Fight or flight," Jennifer said. Carny nodded. Tanner looked at his mother like he was really impressed.

"Anyway, the combination of low serotonin and high noradrenaline is like throwing a lit match on a puddle of gasoline. Behavior becomes explosive, with frequent episodes of impulsive violence. Just as scary is the combination of low serotonin and low noradrenaline. When the noradrenaline levels drop low enough, it causes a state of underarousal. This combination made the monkeys seek out violent behavior in an effort to produce a high of sorts—a more predatory, cold-blooded violence that occurred without provocation."

"That's all very interesting, Carny," Jennifer said. "But what does it have to do with us?"

"I think I'm beginning to see the light," Eric said slowly. "And I don't like what I'm seeing."

"It's not a pretty picture," Carny agreed. "Tim began to get suspicious when Peter McClary became extremely interested in the experiments."

"Peter McClary!" Jennifer said. "Tim's boss?"

Carny nodded.

Jennifer turned to Eric. "McClary is the one who insisted Tim take a vacation. He even offered us the use of his cabin in West Virginia."

Carny went on, her voice more subdued than before. "It seems that McClary arranged to have Tim demonstrate one of his monkey experiments to a group of people he invited to the lab late one night. Tim thought it was an odd request, particularly when he viewed it in conjunction with McClary's unusual interest in the whole experiment. So, as a precaution, he hid a tape recorder in the lab. The demonstration went off without a hitch, the injected monkey killing and maiming its partners. The invited guests were not only not appalled by the demonstration, they became very excited.

"That alone was enough to worry Tim, but then he was asked to leave the lab while McClary and his guests hung back. Tim obliged, but later went back and listened to the tape he had hidden. What he heard sickened him.

"He realized that the group was a secret and subversive organization of neo-Nazi types—bigots of the worst kind. Their goal was to eliminate all of the undesirables: minorities, poor people, cripples, and such. Much like Hitler's regime during the Second World War. They saw Tim's experiment as the perfect vehicle for achieving this goal. They felt that with the ever-increasing rate of violent crime in our country, an additional escalation would be seen as nothing more than a normal continuation of this trend. With the use of Tim's injectable nucleotide, they hoped to genetically mutate as many of these undesirables as they could, thereby achieving two purposes. One, the undesirables would exercise their violent tendencies among themselves, thereby eliminating many of them. A sort of self-inflicted genocide. Second, the resultant social chaos would make it easy for the group to step in and seize control of the government.

"They also discussed the possibility of combining mind-altering therapies with the more cold-blooded, pre-meditated violence recipe to create an army of cruel and merciless assassins.

"As if hearing all of that wasn't frightening enough, Tim became even more disturbed when he realized that he recognized many of the people in the group: high-level, well-positioned, and well-respected members of the community, such as lawyers, doctors, policemen, and politicians."

Hearing that, Jennifer realized that her initial impulse not to involve the police was probably a wise one.

"Anyway, Tim became concerned and placed a call to the FBI."

"Tim called the FBI?" Jennifer said, askance.

Carny nodded. "Anonymously, of course. He tipped off the person on the phone that something illegal and immoral might be going on at Bioceutics, though he wasn't specific. We were able to trace the call to Bioceutics and figure out that it was Tim who placed it. We did a little investigating, discovered McClary's little elitist group, but no illegal activity. They were a bit zealous in their beliefs, but had yet to act on any of them.

"So then we started looking into Tim's research. We

discovered the main gist of his experiments, but the impact of it all eluded us at first. No one was able to put two and two together. In fact, we were about to dismiss the whole thing as nothing more than another subversive group we would need to monitor, when Tim was killed in that car accident. We thought that was a little too much coincidence and investigated. Sure enough, we discovered that the accident was no accident."

"Then Bioceutics did have Tim killed," Jennifer said.

Carny nodded soberly. "Yes, they did. We found a remote control explosive device that had been planted on your car's brakes and tires, and another one on the steering and brake lines of the gas truck you hit. The weather obliged some by providing the rain-slicked roads. It took some clever timing on their part, but they pulled it off."

"See, I told you, Mom," Tanner piped up.

"I know, honey." She ruffled his hair. "I'm sorry I didn't believe you." She looked at Carny. "What I don't understand is why? Why kill Tim?"

"Apparently he was asking too many questions, getting too curious. Obviously he knew something was going on, or he wouldn't have stashed the evidence he had."

"Evidence? Of what?" This was from Eric.

"Well, the tape, of course. But Tim also had the forethought to hide some of his notes regarding the process involved in his experiment. We think he either approached McClary with his suspicions and told him about the incriminating tape, or perhaps the group invited him into their fold and Tim refused. Whatever the scenario, Tim had become a definite liability in their eyes and had to be eliminated."

Carny paused and everyone in the room stared off in silence, absorbing the implications of Carny's revelations. It was Eric who spoke first.

"So they planned to have these undesirables, as they called them, eliminate themselves, and at the same time to develop a team of genetically and psychologically altered assassins to eliminate others."

Carny nodded. "Except Tim second-guessed them."

"So they didn't do it?" Jennifer asked hopefully.

"We think they have now," Carny said. "It took them eight years of trial and error, but I believe they have finally discovered the missing link they needed."

"Then what do they want with us?" Jennifer asked.

"Well, there is still the tape. We have no actual proof of what is going on. That tape, and any other evidence Tim might have stashed, has the potential to blow their whole scheme. I firmly believe that you and Tanner were meant to die in the same accident that took Tim's life. As soon as we discovered that the accident had been arranged, we started watching you closely, in case they tried for a second time. But when McClary couldn't find the evidence Tim had hidden, I think they decided it might be wiser to let you live, in hopes that you would eventually lead them to the tape."

"My God!" Jennifer said, falling back against the couch.

"How did you get involved with all this, Carny?" Eric asked.

"I was a plant put in place way back when Tim first made his phone call. I was supposed to take a job as a teacher, and make some noises about how irritated I was with the so-called undesirables. Jennifer, do you remember Paul Jensen?"

"The vice principal?"

Carny nodded. "We discovered he was a member of McClary's little group. So after saying all the right things in front of Jensen, I was eventually invited in. Though only on a limited, need-to-know basis. Jensen assigned me to you, to see what information I could find out about Tim. They didn't tell me why at first, although I, of course, already knew. It was perfect, really. It gave me an opportunity to keep tabs on the group and what they were doing as well as to befriend you, giving me an inside line to Tim." Carny gave Jennifer a pained look. "I'm sorry I didn't know about their plans to kill Tim. If I had, I would have tried to save him."

"So you are like a double agent," Tanner said, obviously impressed.

Carny smiled at him. "Yeah, I guess I am."

Jennifer said, "You mean McClary and his group think you're one of them?"

"They do. Why do you think they made it so easy for you to get away from the house?"

Jennifer's face screwed up in puzzlement. Looking back on it, she realized that their escape had been ridiculously easy, considering everything else the group had managed to do. "I get it," she said slowly. "They were banking on my friendship with you, figuring you're the first person I'd run to. And if I *did* know where the papers and the tape were hidden, I would confide in you. They let us escape on purpose."

"Exactly."

Jennifer's eyes took on a haunted, wild look. "Then they know we are here," she said with panic edging her voice. She started to stand.

Carny raised her hand up, palm outward. "No, they don't. Relax. They trust me enough at this point that they let me take you off, thinking you might suspect something if you thought we were being followed. They have no knowledge of this place, which, by the way, is government owned. Their main purpose in keeping me on the payroll all these years was as a sort of insurance policy, just in case you ever did find the papers. They figured you would confide in me before anyone else."

"But I don't know where they are," Jennifer protested. "I mean, I have a general idea now, but back then I didn't even have that."

"I think they realized that. But they didn't know if the evidence might someday turn up. Actually, they've paid little attention to you until recently. When they found out what was going on with Tanner—these conversations he was supposedly having with Tim—things got a little frantic. And though they still believed you knew nothing about the tape or the papers, Tanner was apparently convincing enough to make them worry. I think some of the things they overheard had them pretty concerned."

"So they did have the house bugged," Eric said.

Carny nodded. "I'm not sure how they became alerted to what was going on with Tanner, but something tipped them off, and they started eavesdropping on you just a few days ago."

"That explains what happened at the hospital," Eric said, looking over at Jennifer.

"That little incident went all wrong," Carny said. "Though they may well have meant to kill you, Eric, their main intent was to kidnap Jennifer and Tanner. They wanted them alive."

Jennifer's mind flashed back on the incident, and the terror she had felt at the time washed over her again. She shivered. "I thought you were dead," she said to Eric. "How did you get away from that thug up in Maine?"

Carny answered her. "That thug happens to be one of our people. Another plant. He's been with the group for three years now. Fortunately, the bullet Eric took in his shoulder didn't hit anything vital. We flew him down here last evening."

"What about my mother?"

"Safe and sound at a safe house in Canada," Carny told her. "Along with Butterscotch."

"Scotch is okay?" Jennifer said wide-eyed.

"Well, she took a bullet in her leg that required some surgery, but, except for a limp, she's progressing nicely," Carny told her with a smile.

"She came back from the woods right after you left," Eric explained. "It was all we could do to keep her from eating the agent that was left behind," he said with a chuckle.

"Oh. Thank goodness!" Jennifer's face split into a huge grin. "And to think I thought it was all over." She turned and cast an apologetic look at Carny. "I thought you were really one of them, Carny. I thought you were going to kill me, for heaven's sake!"

"I won't hold it against you. Under the circumstances . . ." She shrugged and grinned back.

Jennifer shook her head in amazement, recalling the empty terror she had felt when she found the frizzy red wig in Carny's purse. "That disguise you came up with was pretty good," she said.

"It's amazing what you can do with a wig, some contacts, and a little latex," Carny said with a shrug. "Actually, the group wasn't sure I could pull it off. They thought you'd recognize me."

"I didn't have a clue," Jennifer said. Her face drew into a puzzled frown. "But you called me at my mother's. How did you get to Maine so quickly?"

"You just assumed I was calling from Virginia," Carny explained. "In actuality, I was on a cellular phone, calling you from Portland. I convinced them to take me along, telling them you would be easier to handle if I was there. But that was only if the original plan failed, if you recognized me or something else went wrong."

"But how did you know where to find me?"

Carny shrugged. "It wasn't hard to figure out. I knew about your mother and figured you'd think that was a safe hideaway. When I discovered that McClary's group also knew about her, I knew I had to get involved somehow. I had a couple of agents posted at the ferry landing. They called me as soon as you showed up."

Jennifer again shook her head in amazement. "Eight years? You've been following this case, acting like a spy, for eight years?"

Carny smiled and shrugged. "Sort of. But very part-time, from the periphery. Since I managed to get the group to trust me to some extent, I've continued to be available to them over the years, figuring it would allow me to monitor their activities. It certainly paid off when they started showing a keen interest in you again. Over the years we've had a couple of agents who managed to infiltrate the group to some degree. We felt they bore watching, though until recently, we thought they were nothing more than another subversive group with high aspirations and few actual accomplishments. To be honest, we'd begun to doubt that Tim ever hid any evidence. If he had, we would have found it by now. Either us or McClary. Both Tim's lab and your house were thoroughly searched back when you were in the hospital after the accident. Without that evidence, or any real proof of illegal activity, all we've been able to do is watch. But I knew something was up with the group here lately. There's been a certain level of excitement and activity at McClary's house that led me to believe they had not only discovered the missing data from Tim's experiments, but were actually using it. Then when Tanner here started coming up with information he had no way of knowing, it got the group interested in you again."

Carny flashed Jennifer a weak smile. "I wish you had told me what was really going on with Tanner," she said. "It would have saved us a lot of trouble."

Jennifer recalled her decision to keep Tanner's odd declarations about Tim to herself, back when she believed they were nothing more than delusions. "I'm sorry. I honestly thought Tanner was suffering from some sort of mental or emotional problems along with his physical ones. Besides, how was I supposed to know you were spying on me?" she asked, her voice carrying a hint of betrayal.

"I wasn't, really. At least not for many years. Although that was the impression I wanted McClary's group to have. My friendship with you was the edge I needed for them to keep me involved. But our friendship, while admittedly convenient, was just that—a friendship. During the years I've been monitoring McClary's group, I've continued to work for the Bureau on other cases. You know all those mini vacations I take all the time?"

Jennifer nodded, recalling her suspicions that Carny was involved with a married man.

"Well, most of those were training or debriefing sessions, or other cases I was called in on. The teacher cover has served me well, giving me the scheduling flexibility I need. And the reason I've been able to pull it off is that my background really is in mathematics. My specialty is code breaking."

"Cool!" Tanner said.

Carny smiled warmly at the boy. "To be honest with you, you were one of the more enjoyable assignments I've had." Her gaze grew serious as it shifted to Jennifer. "I may have deceived you about some things, Jennifer, but not our friendship."

Jennifer studied the other woman's face and saw the

sincerity there. She was relieved to know that her trust in Carny had not been totally misplaced, though she was still struggling with all the deception and betrayal that had occurred.

"So now what?" Jennifer asked.

"Now," Carny said, getting up from her chair, "we need to find the evidence that Tim stashed before McClary's group gets their hands on it. As I mentioned, my involvement with the group has been relatively limited. They allowed me to know what their purpose is and what they were after from you, but my exposure to the actual group members has been restricted to a mere few— and I suspect most of them are fairly low on the food chain. We still have very little knowledge of the people involved at the top. We have long suspected that McClary is the ringleader, and that he maintains a database of some sort. But he is a very rich and powerful man, with a house that is guarded better than Fort Knox. We'd love to search the place, but so far we've had no legal reason to solicit a search warrant. And our attempts to bug his house have been unsuccessful. We've watched it, of course, but he entertains quite frequently, and we have no way of knowing which of the people who come and go are members of this group and which ones are simply guests. I've had my suspicions about Evan for some time, but I never had any proof. Until now."

"Evan?" Eric asked, looking back and forth from Carny to Jennifer. "What are you talking about?"

"It seems that Evan is one of them," Jennifer said with contempt, her shock over that discovery now fully replaced by anger over the way she had been used.

"Bastard!" Eric spat out. "I knew there was something about him I didn't like." Then with a lopsided grin he added, "Besides the obvious, of course."

"Anyway," Carny went on, "most of the people you've

had contact with, Jennifer, are nothing more than hired help. People who do the group's dirty work for money. We need some hard evidence of who the real power people are."

"Dr. Singleton is doing something," Tanner said.

Everyone turned and stared at him. Eric leaned back so suddenly it was as if he'd been slapped.

"I mean Eric's dad," Tanner added. "That day in the doctor's office when he told that guy he gave him a vitamin shot. He was lying. I could hear what he was thinking. I just didn't know what it all meant."

"Shit!" Eric said, running a hand through his hair. "Of course! It makes sense when I think about it. The old man always was rather intolerant of certain types of people. Not to their faces, of course. But I can remember many a night at the dinner table when he would carry on about the poor white trash, or the kikes, or the niggers. It drove my mother crazy when she was alive."

"And," Carny added, "he's in a perfect setup to administer this stuff. It would also explain how the group got wind of what was going on with Tanner."

Eric sat in crushed silence, staring at the floor, shaking his head.

Jennifer reached over and laid a hand on his shoulder. "I'm sorry, Eric," she said.

"Don't be," he said brusquely. "I never liked the old bastard anyway." With that, he got up and headed outside.

Jennifer frowned after him, chewing on the inside of her cheek.

"He'll be okay," Carny said. "He just needs a little time."

Jennifer looked over at her. "Time is something we don't have much of," she said. "Where do we go from here?"

Carny walked over to the couch to take the spot Eric had just vacated. "I have a plan," she said.

17

"Are you sure about this, Carny?" Jennifer asked from the backseat of Carny's car, where she sat beside Tanner. Eric was in the front seat, Carny behind the wheel. They were driving down the road that led to Carny's house, the headlights slicing into the darkness, creating an army of marching shadows along the trees that lined the drive. "I don't like the idea of involving Tanner. Are you sure he'll be safe?"

"Believe me, they're not going to do anything to harm Tanner until they get the information they need. He's the only link they have right now to the missing data and the information about their group. They know they have to get to that information before anyone else, and if that means using Tanner's abilities, they'll do it. And besides, I won't let anything happen to him." She reassuringly patted the gun she had snugged in a shoulder holster.

Jennifer had one, too—a .38 caliber semiautomatic that Carny had taken great pains to familiarize her with. She and Eric had undergone two intense hours with Carny back at the cabin, practicing loading, firing, and marksmanship. Though the deadly steel felt less foreign now than the first time she held it, Jennifer still didn't like the thing. It weighed cold and heavy and ominous where it was tucked inside the back of her jeans. A long shirt hid it from view, but Jennifer was still very much aware of its presence. Had it not been for her fear for Tanner's safety, and the fact that Eric's injured arm severely hampered his shooting ability, she wasn't sure she would have let Carny talk her into carrying the thing.

"Still . . ." Jennifer frowned. "Maybe we should call in some reinforcements. What about your people at the FBI?"

"Until we know for sure that we have enough evidence to put these bastards away, they're not going to want to tip their hand. We've got to find that tape and those papers."

"I don't know, Carny," Jennifer said, shaking her head. Back at the cabin, in the light of the day, the idea had seemed perfectly logical and sensible. But now, under the dark shroud of night, with Tanner about to be parted from her, the whole thing seemed far too dangerous.

"Do you have a better idea?" Carny asked.

Jennifer had to admit she did not.

Carny pulled up in front of her house and turned the car off. "You and Eric go on," she instructed. "I'll wait about ten minutes before I call them."

Jennifer swallowed down the panic that rose in her throat when she thought about letting Tanner out of her sight. She turned to him and pulled him into her arms, hugging him fiercely.

"You be careful, okay?" she said, choking back tears.

"Don't worry, Mom. Carny and I can handle this. I can be a good secret agent."

His hair was tousled, his eyes luminous with excitement, his cheeks flushed with anticipation. Jennifer knew he had no real concept of just how grave and dangerous their situation was. To him it was nothing more than a form of play, albeit a little more exciting than his usual. Just another James Bond movie. She started to caution him, to make him aware of the danger, but then thought better of it. Perhaps it was better to leave him imbued with that childish bravado rather than frightening him. She released him from her arms reluctantly and, with one last, longing look, climbed out of the car along with Eric.

Carny pulled a lever that popped the lid on the trunk. Eric stepped to the back of the car, removed a tire iron and a torn flannel rag, and then, with as little noise as possible, gently lowered the trunk lid back into place until he heard it catch. Wielding the tire iron like a sword with his good arm, he swished it through the air a few times, grinning at Jennifer. "After you, my lady," he said, giving her a little bow.

Jennifer rolled her eyes. Eric was no more serious about this than Tanner. *Boys will be boys,* she thought with a sigh, and, as Carny led Tanner into the house, Jennifer and Eric quietly slipped off into the surrounding trees.

They made their way along the trail until they reached the edge of the woods. There they crouched behind some bushes and peered out across the clearing toward Jennifer's house.

There were three cars parked out front besides Jennifer's: one was the van they had traveled in from Maine, one was Evan's Porsche. The third car was a cherry red, early model Volkswagen Beetle with a license plate that read, OLYMPUS. The house was ablaze with light, every window glowing warmly with mocking invitation. Jennifer felt anger rise up in her at the thought that these people had commandeered her house and invaded her private domain for their own perverted use.

Eric glanced at his watch. "They should be leaving any moment now," he whispered.

They waited.

Jennifer could hear the swish, swish of her heart pounding in her ears. The bulk of the gun bit into her hip as she squatted. One of her legs began to cramp, and a squadron of mosquitoes descended upon them, biting at every available patch of skin. Afraid to slap at them because it might make too much noise, Jennifer brushed at them instead, cursing under her breath and grimacing each time she felt one of the tiny bodies smear beneath her hand.

She shifted her position to ease the ache in her leg and sighed quietly. *Where are they? Why aren't they coming out? Something must have gone wrong.* Just as she was about to tap Eric on his shoulder and suggest they turn back, the front door to the house opened. Instinctively, Jennifer ducked behind her bush, peeking out between the branches.

"It's show time," Eric whispered in her ear.

They watched as Evan, Derrick, and another man exited the house. The third man, who looked to be in his mid-thirties, was dressed in a pair of jeans that had obviously seen better days, and a faded blue T-shirt. His hair was close-cropped and blond, his facial expression grim. He strode purposefully to the Volkswagen and slid in behind the wheel.

"That's McClary!" Jennifer hissed as she recognized him.

She glared at the man she had once thought a friend. Tim's murderer. For a brief moment she entertained the idea of running out of the woods, pulling the gun from her waist, and blowing the murderous bastard away right there. The impulse both surprised and shocked her, and she swallowed hard to get a grip on her emotions.

Derrick and Evan climbed into the van. Then they followed McClary's red Volkswagen down the driveway, spitting up a small cloud of dust behind them.

Jennifer and Eric watched the fading red glow of the taillights until they disappeared. Then they left the safety of the woods and ran across the lawn to the house.

Carny knelt down in front of Tanner as he stood in the middle of her living room. "Do you know what to do?"

Tanner nodded, his eyes big and wild-looking.

"Are you afraid?"

"A little," Tanner admitted.

"Good," Carny said, ruffling his hair. "A little fear helps to keep your senses sharpened."

They heard the sound of a car outside, and Carny stood up abruptly. She nervously smoothed her hair with her hands, then gave one final pat to the gun hidden beneath her shirt.

"They're here," she said to Tanner. "Go and sit on the couch."

Tanner did as he was instructed, his rigid steps and wide-eyed expression broadcasting his fear. Carny was actually glad to see it. She needed him to look frightened; it would make things more believable. Tanner sat on the edge of the couch and folded his hands in his lap, staring at the front door.

Carny greeted the threesome at the door.

"I still don't understand why you didn't just bring him to the other house," McClary grumbled, gesturing toward Tanner.

"You'll understand in a moment," Carny said, shutting the door and walking to the center of the living room.

McClary sat in one of the chairs, while Derrick leaned against a nearby wall, chewing a toothpick that rolled from one side of his mouth to the other. Evan walked over and sat on the couch next to Tanner.

"Hey, Tan," Evan said. "You doing all right, son?"

Tanner turned and glared at him with such menace that Evan leaned back away from him, his face looking wounded.

"I'm sorry Tanner's mother can't be here to enjoy this little show," Carny said. "All her doubts about her son's abilities would have been erased once and for all." She shrugged and smiled evilly. "But, she just got out of hand."

"What did you do with the body?" McClary asked her.

"Don't worry," Carny said. "I dropped it into a ravine up in the mountains. By the time anyone finds it, if they ever do, the bugs and animals should have picked her bones clean."

Tanner turned and gaped at Carny. Her voice sounded so convincingly chilling, he found himself starting to believe that Carny was one of the bad guys and that his mother was really dead. Tears blossomed in his eyes.

McClary saw the glistening wetness and nodded approvingly.

"Now," Carny said with great drama, "if you will all remain quiet while I turn down the lights, Tanner is going to get in touch with his father."

She looked around at the group, a smile of smug satisfaction on her face. McClary shifted nervously in his seat, Derrick plucked the toothpick from his mouth and pushed himself away from the wall, looking tensed and ready to spring. Carny went around the room, dimming one of the lamps and turning off the others, casting the room in a kaleidoscope of shadows. Then she took a candle off the mantel and lit it, making the shadows dance. Cupping her hand around the flame, she walked across the room and took a seat on the couch next to Tanner, on the side opposite Evan.

"Tanner?" she said softly.

Tanner looked up at her, his face glowing strangely white in the dimmed light.

"I want you to look at this flame."

Tanner obliged, his eyes shifting toward the candle and taking on a dreamy look.

"Look at the flame and let your mind relax," Carny urged softly. "Empty all thoughts from your head and think about the colors in the flame. See the yellow? See the blue? The flame is warming you, making you feel good all over."

Evan, who had been staring at the flame as Carny talked, blinked suddenly and looked away, giving his head a little shake.

"Look at the flame, Tanner," Carny cooed.

She smiled inwardly as Tanner's lids drooped and his face went slack. The kid was good.

"That's good. Now, I want you to think about your father. Imagine that your father is inside the flame all warm and cozy. He is reaching out to you. He wants to talk to you."

Carny grew quiet a moment, continuing to hold the candle in front of Tanner's face, waving it ever so slightly from side to side. From the corner of her eye she saw Derrick shift his position nervously and look around the darkened room. She had to suppress a smile. Despite her nervousness, she was actually enjoying this little performance.

"Hi, Dad."

Tanner's voice made everyone in the room start,

including Carny. There was a ghostly quality to his tone that raised goose bumps on her arms.

"I need your help," Tanner said.

McClary leaned forward anxiously from his chair.

Eric and Jennifer bypassed the front door and silently circled the house. They hugged the walls, feeling the stored heat of the day radiating out from the bricks. Eric paused at each of the ground floor windows to look inside.

"Looks like it's all clear," he announced when they were back at the front porch.

"Okay," she said. "Here goes nothing." She took the lead, walking to the back of the house. She stopped and pointed to a small window that sat at ground level. "That's it," she said.

Eric removed the piece of flannel material from his pocket and wrapped it around one end of the tire iron. When he was done, he looked at Jennifer, raising his brows in question.

She gave him a nod.

He knelt, took a deep breath, reared back with the tire iron, and swung it at the window.

The iron bounced off the glass, and, even with the muffling effect of the flannel, the sound was glaringly loud. Jennifer looked around anxiously. She heard a sharp intake of breath from Eric that made her nerves jump. But when she swung her eyes toward him, she saw him reach up and massage his injured shoulder. She grimaced as she realized the pain that must have shot through his shoulder from the jarring impact.

"Are you okay?" she whispered.

Eric nodded. "I'll be all right."

He stayed still a moment, waiting for the pain to

subside. Then he took a deep breath, gritted his teeth, and made another swing at the window. This time he was successful, and they both exhaled a breath of relief in conjunction with the satisfactory tinkle of breaking glass. Eric dropped the tire iron and reached over to gingerly remove the glass shards that clung to the frame. When it was clean, he thrust his feet through the opening, twisted around, and dropped himself into the basement.

"Okay," he said in a quiet voice from inside. "Jennifer Bolton, come o-o-on down!"

Jennifer followed him through the window into the dark, dank-smelling basement. Once she had her feet firmly on the floor she turned toward the main part of the room and squinted, trying to make some sense out of the gray-black shadows. She heard a faint scratching sound—more of a scurrying sound actually—and shuddered as her mind tried to envision how large a bug it would take to make that much noise. Suddenly her body seemed alive with faint crawling sensations, and she brushed frantically at her arms and legs, finding nothing. Which was just as well. If her hand came into contact with something crawling and hairy, she knew she'd never be able to contain the scream that was housed just at the back of her throat.

"This way," she said when she thought she had her bearings, leading Eric by the hand toward the base of the steps. She moved ahead cautiously, taking tiny steps and sweeping her free arm in front of her until she felt the edge of the aluminum shelves and saw the dim whiteness of the washer and dryer. Then, feeling more confident of the layout, she lengthened her steps, only to bang her shin painfully on the stairs as she overestimated the distance.

"Damn!" she hissed, rubbing her leg.

Eric eased her aside. "You stay here," he said. "I'll get the light."

Jennifer heard him climb the creaking wooden stairs, saw his shadow as it obliterated the fine line of light that was leaking beneath the basement door, then jumped as the whole room was suddenly filled with blinding light. She blinked as her eyes adjusted, and though the presence of the light was reassuring, it also left her feeling strangely exposed and vulnerable. She hugged herself and looked about the room nervously.

Eric came back down the stairs and stood next to her. "Well, where do we start?" he asked.

"When I found Tanner, he was in the furnace room over there," Jennifer said pointing.

Eric led the way, turning on the overhead light once he was in the room. Jennifer grabbed two flashlights off a shelf and followed, handing one to Eric. Once inside the tiny room, she gave it a quick once-over, hoping for a flash of enlightenment. Instead, all she got for her efforts was a glimpse of a centipede as it darted under the edge of the water heater.

"Well, I guess we should start looking," Eric said.

"You take the water heater," Jennifer said quickly, shivering and swiping at another imaginary crawling sensation on her arm. She pushed the lawn chair, in which Tanner had been sitting the day she found him, to one side. "I'll look around the furnace."

She examined the exterior of the furnace, shining the flashlight along the side next to the wall, behind it, and then reluctantly, beneath it. All she found were cobwebs and dust balls.

Next she examined the furnace itself. She pulled out the filter tray, found it matted with dust and dog hair, and shoved it back into place. Then she examined the ribbed air flow outlet tube that led from the top of the furnace into a hole in the ceiling. She poked at the tube with the flashlight to see if something might have been stashed inside. There was nothing.

"Any luck?" Eric asked her.

"No. You?"

"Nada. I checked the generator, too," he said.

Jennifer bit her lip with frustration. "We've got to find it!" she said. She thought hard. "Maybe it was just a coincidence that Tanner was sitting in this room," she conjectured. "Maybe the tape is hidden out in the main room somewhere."

"I don't have much faith in coincidence," Eric said. "Stop a minute and think back to the day you found Tanner in here. What did he do? What did he say?"

Jennifer chewed her lip and thought back. "He was sitting here," she said, pointing to the lawn chair. "Except it was facing the furnace." She grabbed the lawn chair and put it back in its original position. Then she closed her eyes, remembering back, reliving the moment of dread when she had seen that vacant look on Tanner's face.

"I knelt to talk to him," she said, her eyes still closed, her mind envisioning the scene. "He was mumbling, babbling something about killing. 'Stop the killing,' I think it was." She stopped a moment, trembling as she recalled the effect those words had had on her. Then, after a deep breath, she continued.

"Then he said something about water. 'It's in the water' or something like that." Jennifer's eyes flew open suddenly. "Of course," she said slowly, staring at Eric. "It's in the water!"

Eric stared back at her, puzzled.

"Don't you see?" she said, her voice tingling with excitement. She didn't wait for Eric to answer. "At first I thought Tanner was just babbling nonsense! Then, when I started to think he was actually talking to Tim, I thought he was just repeating what Tim was telling him, that Bioceutics was killing people by putting something in the water."

Her face broke into a satisfied grin. "But it wasn't anything from Bioceutics that was in the water, it was the tape. The *tape* is in the water! Tim must have hidden it inside the water heater!"

Eric's face lit up with dawning comprehension. He walked over to the water heater and examined the outside closely. Then he turned back and planted a quick kiss on Jennifer's cheek. "Wait here," he said.

He disappeared into the main part of the cellar, reappearing a moment later carrying a variety of tools. He tried three different wrenches before he found one to fit the bolts that held the water heater lid in place.

"Here we go," he said. And he went to work on the first one.

Carny was amazed at Tanner's ability to act. His entire body had gone slack, and somehow he had managed to give his eyes an empty, almost-soulless, look. "Tanner," she said quietly, "can you ask your father where the papers and the tape are?"

McClary leaned even farther forward, so that only a few inches of his butt were left on the chair. His eyes were glued to Tanner's face.

Tanner said nothing.

"Tanner?" Carny tried again, beginning to feel nervous. What was the child doing? Was he too frightened to remember what they had practiced?

"I understand," Tanner mumbled. His eyes were directed at Carny, yet she had the distinct impression he was not looking *at* her, but through her. She resisted an impulse to look over her shoulder. "Dad says something is wrong," Tanner went on.

Carny frowned. That wasn't what they had rehearsed. Tanner was supposed to say the papers were hidden in the basement—in *Carny's* basement. She tried to redirect him.

"Can your dad tell you where the papers are, Tanner?"

Tanner's face remained blank, but his voice took on a new edge. "Mom is in trouble!" he said. "There's someone going to our house!"

Carny felt all the blood drain out of her face.

"What the hell?" McClary muttered. He stood up and crossed the room, fixing his scowl on Carny. "What the hell is the brat talking about? I thought you said his mother was dead!" he thundered.

"She is!" Carny argued. "I don't know what he's talking about."

"Carny! Hurry!" Tanner said, his voice growing more urgent. "We've got to help Mom!"

"Tanner!" Carny nearly shouted. "What are you talking about?" She swung a frantic look at McClary. "I don't know what's wrong with him. He must be having a delusion about his mother." She turned back to Tanner. "Tanner! Can you hear me?"

Tanner's face suddenly changed, losing its nonexpressive visage. He blinked, shuddered, and looked around him at all the faces in the room before focusing on Carny. His shoulders slumped, and sadness filled his eyes. "I messed up, didn't I?" he said pensively.

Carny thought hard and fast, seeking a way to salvage the situation. But her mind came up empty.

"It's okay, Tanner," she said resignedly. She reached out and caressed the side of his face with her left hand while reaching inside her shirt with the other.

"You bitch!" McClary said coldly. "You lying, sneaking bitch!"

Carny saw McClary reach for his gun, just as she felt her hand wrap around her own. In her peripheral vision she saw Derrick step forward and knew her chances of beating them both to the draw were slim. With one hand she shoved Tanner hard, pushing him onto the floor. With the other she pulled out her gun and fired. Her shot went wide, exploding in a rain of plaster in the wall behind McClary.

Unfortunately, McClary's aim was better. Carny felt the bullet slam into her chest, felt an oddly hot sensation, followed by a frighteningly cold one. The room wavered and dimmed.

Then she felt nothing more.

After turning off the main water line and flipping open the pressure release valve, Eric loosened the fittings around the pipes running into the top of the water heater and pried the lid off, exposing a layer of brownish pink insulation material. He swept the stuff aside, revealing a six-inch-square panel that was bolted to the top of the heater.

Grabbing a wrench, he applied it to the first of the four bolts, his arm muscles straining as he gradually increased the pressure. Beads of sweat popped out on his forehead and he shifted the weight of his body, trying to gain additional leverage. His face turned red, his knuckles shone white. After a moment he paused, took a few panting breaths, then tried again, putting all his strength into the effort. Still the thing refused to budge. He finally gave up, dropping the wrench to his side and letting out a sigh of exasperation.

"Here," Jennifer said, holding out her hand. "Give me the wrench."

Eric turned his head and looked at her, his face both amused and skeptical. Jennifer stared back, eyebrows raised, wiggling the fingers of her outstretched hand in a give-it-to-me gesture. With a shrug, Eric handed her the wrench and stepped aside. Jennifer gripped the handle tightly, reared back, and swung it at the bolt. The clang of metal on metal reverberated through the basement. She repeated the process a few times, then handed the wrench back to Eric. "Here," she said. "Try it again."

Throwing every muscle he had into it, Eric blew out a breath of relief as the bolt groaned and finally gave way.

Jennifer smiled up at him. "It just needed a woman's touch."

"Right," Eric said, rolling his eyes. "Remind me never to piss you off. The way you attacked that thing is scary!"

Jennifer's grin broadened.

The remaining bolts proved to be equally stubborn, but they eventually loosened up. "Last one," Eric said, unscrewing the final bolt. "There!" He dropped the bolt to the floor and picked up a screwdriver. Jennifer watched as he worked it under the lip of the panel to pry it loose. The piece popped off with relative ease, and Eric laid it to one side as he stood on tiptoe to peer inside the heater. Steam wafted up and out, surrounding his head in a ghostly bonnet.

"Hand me a flashlight," he said, holding out a hand. Jennifer handed it to him ,and he shined it into the heater.

"Bingo!" he said.

"What?" Jennifer asked, chewing on the side of her thumb. "What is it?"

"Some sort of bottle." Eric dropped back onto his heels and glanced around the room. "I need a towel or something to grab this with. It's too hot for bare hands."

Jennifer disappeared into the main room of the cellar, returning a moment later with a worn, stained towel. Eric held the cloth in one hand, and with the other he fished around in the hot water with the wrench, levering the bottle against the top of the heater until he could grab it with the towel. When he finally managed to snag it, he held his treasure aloft, his face splitting into a triumphant grin.

The outside of the bottle was spotted with lime deposits, but the glass was still clear enough for them to see a roll of papers tucked inside. The lid of the bottle had been screwed on and sealed with some type of hard plastic, making it airtight. Eric set the bottle on its side on the floor and covered it with the towel. Grabbing the wrench, he smashed it down on top of it, shattering the glass. Using the towel to brush aside the jagged shards, he gingerly lifted out the papers. As he unrolled them, Jennifer saw page after page of handwritten notes.

"That's Tim's writing!" she said, recognizing the angular scrawl immediately.

As Eric unrolled the final bit, a tiny cassette tape fell out.

"We did it!" Jennifer squealed. "We found it!" She reached over and hugged Eric.

"And I do appreciate your efforts," said a male voice behind them.

Jennifer let go of Eric and whirled around to find Peter McClary standing in the doorway, a gun in his hands pointed directly at their heads. Beside him stood the young blond-haired man that had driven the van back from Maine. He had a firm grip on the collar of Tanner's shirt with one hand; the other held a gun to Tanner's temple.

"Good work, Smithson," McClary said over his shoulder to the blond man.

"I might have missed them if it hadn't been for that banging noise," Smithson said.

"It's a good thing you decided to come back here when you did. Otherwise their little trick might have worked." McClary held a hand out toward Eric, his face splitting into a triumphant grin. "I'll take those papers now, if you don't mind."

Eric handed over the papers and the tape.

McClary stuffed the tape into his jacket pocket and then glanced at the papers. Nodding his satisfaction, he rolled them back up and stuffed them in his pocket as well.

"Nice work," he said with a nasty grin. "Your efforts will do much for our cause." He turned and looked over his shoulder. "Derrick, I know you want to take care of Mrs. Bolton personally. She's all yours."

Derrick stepped past McClary into the tiny room, grabbed Jennifer by her collar, and hauled her to her feet. Jennifer swung at him, her fist colliding with his shoulder. Derrick laughed and slapped her face.

Eric started to lunge at him but froze when he saw McClary's gun swing back toward his head.

Jennifer scanned the group, rubbing the side of her face. "Where's Carny?" she asked, her voice filled with dread.

"Your friend is dead," McClary said. "As you will be soon."

Derrick jerked Jennifer's arm painfully and dragged her past the other two men into the main portion of the cellar. As she went by Tanner, Jennifer reached out to touch his face, her hand caressing his cheek. Tears bloomed in her eyes. "I'm so sorry, Tan," she muttered.

"How touching," McClary sneered. "Get her the hell out of here."

Derrick yanked on her arm again and Jennifer howled. Derrick shoved her toward the stairs.

"Be sure and stash the body somewhere it can't be found if you mark her up too bad," McClary added.

"You bastard!" Eric hissed.

McClary stepped forward and swung the gun up against the side of Eric's face, knocking him onto his side on the floor. "Shut the fuck up!" McClary yelled.

Tanner, still in the grip of the blond man, glared at McClary, his face filled with dark rage. Then, curiously, his face relaxed so that it looked almost serene. His eyes slowly slid closed.

Derrick was at the base of the stairs, shoving Jennifer upward, when a can of paint flew off one of the shelves near the wall and smashed into his head.

"What the hell!" Derrick muttered, massaging his head.

Jennifer had seen the can come off the shelf, and she stood staring at Derrick, then at the can, her eyes wide with amazement.

McClary had turned, too, his expression equally astonished.

Jennifer looked back at Tanner and saw that his face bore that horrifying blank expression; his eyes were closed, his mouth slack. Then his lips started to move, creating a hushed, whispering noise. As the sound grew louder, all heads turned in Tanner's direction, staring. Eventually, Jennifer was able to make out distinct words issuing from her son's mouth.

"Help me, Dad," he was saying. "Help me." He hissed the words over and over again.

An odd metallic bang sounded from behind Jennifer, followed by a loud scraping noise. She turned and saw that the washing machine was rocking from side to side, walking its way across the floor the way it did when the load became unbalanced. The lid started banging up and down, adding to the cacophony.

"What the hell?" McClary muttered. He turned and looked at Tanner. "It's the kid!" he yelled. "He's doing that weird shit with his mind!" He stepped forward and slapped his hand hard across Tanner's face.

Tanner's eyes flew open and narrowed down to a steely glint. His brow furrowed; his fists clenched. Then his eyes rolled up into his head so that only the whites showed.

And all hell broke loose.

The temperature in the room grew noticeably colder, as if a frigid blast of arctic wind had blown through the cellar. The air was instantly filled with flying objects: hammers, saws, screwdrivers, paint cans, magazines, and nails—all of them undulating in midair like some macabre dance parody. For a moment they seemed to be hurtling about randomly; then they gathered together, forming two miniature cyclones of paraphernalia. One of the cyclones centered itself around McClary, the other around Smithson. Across the room, a carton of laundry detergent flung itself from a shelf and started spinning wildly, its contents spewing through the air. Distracted by the movement, Derrick glanced toward the box and the soap flew into his face, coating his hair, filling his mouth, and covering his eyes. He swore loudly, swiping at his face, trying to wipe the grainy stuff away.

The cyclones wobbled and spun. Smithson ducked as a hammer whizzed by his head, then groaned as a screwdriver hit home, burying itself up to the hilt in his shoulder.

McClary spun wildly, his eyes wide, swinging the gun back and forth as the air around him filled with spiraling items. Nails pummeled his neck and shoulders. A large carton of books slid across the floor, and the books started shooting out the top, battering him from all angles. He swatted at them, grunting as they pummeled him from head to toe.

There was a loud groan of straining metal followed by a popping noise. Eric came charging out of the furnace room, ducking between McClary and Smithson, and grabbing Tanner's arm as he ran by. Dodging the storm of books that filled the air, he headed for the shelves near the washer, hauling Tanner along beside him. From the furnace room, a fountain of hot water spewed out from the water heater onto the floor, the spreading puddle oozing its way into the main portion of the cellar. The air in the room continued to grow colder.

Seeing that Derrick was still preoccupied with trying to wipe away the detergent that burned his eyes, Jennifer ducked past him, heading toward Eric and Tanner.

Eric yelled at her. "Jennifer! The gun!"

In her terror, she had forgotten about the gun that was still tucked inside the waistband of her jeans. She reached back beneath her shirt and grabbed it, flipping off the safety catch. Derrick, his eyes cleared enough to see that she had moved away from him, bellowed and charged at her.

"Jennifer! Watch out!" Eric yelled.

Jennifer spun around, holding the gun with both hands and aiming it at Derrick. Her finger tightened on the trigger. For one brief second she hesitated, keenly aware that she was about to shoot another human being, possibly kill him. Then she remembered Derrick's leering grin at the house in Maine, remembered Tanner's frightening withdrawal, remembered her vow of revenge. Her eyes narrowed in anger, and, with Derrick only a few feet away, she pulled the trigger.

The gun spit, jolting her arms painfully. The impact of the shot forced Derrick back against the stair railing and he gazed down at his chest in disbelief. Then his eyes slid upward, meeting Jennifer's. At the sight of the raw anger she saw reflected in those eyes, Jennifer took an involuntary step back. Her arms began to shake, but she held the gun steady, still aimed at Derrick, prepared to shoot again. She held her breath, watching, waiting. When she saw the anger in Derrick's eyes fade into a blank glaze, she finally let her breath out. Derrick's own breath eased out in a mirroring response as he slid to the floor.

Lowering the gun, Jennifer looked back toward Eric. The temperature in the room had continued to drop, and the hot water spewing from the furnace room was creating a thickening fog that swirled through the air. Peering through the haze, Jennifer could barely see Tanner standing beside Eric, his eyes still rolled back, his fists balled up, his brow furrowed in concentration. She turned her eyes toward Eric and saw his gaze suddenly shift to a spot behind her. When she saw his eyes grow wide and his mouth open to warn her, she whirled around.

Smithson was coming at her amid a hail of books, clothing, wrenches, nails, and cans. She swung the gun toward him and fired. His step faltered slightly and a momentary expression of surprise crossed his face. Then he lunged toward her again.

At first she thought she must have missed him. Then she saw the blood staining his belly. She raised the gun higher and pulled the trigger again. Smithson stopped so suddenly it appeared as if he had run into an invisible wall. A small red dot appeared on his forehead before his eyes rolled back and he collapsed into a heap on the floor.

Jennifer felt something slam into her arm and thought that some of the flying debris must have hit her. Then she felt a searing hot pain shoot up to her shoulder, numbing her arm. Her hand lost all feeling and the gun slipped from her fingers, landing with a loud thud on the floor. She blinked, staring in confusion at her arm, seeing the small hole in the sleeve of her shirt, watching the blood flow out and over the material, dripping onto the floor. It was a moment before she realized she'd been shot.

She looked over at McClary, who was now at the center of a huge tornado of flying debris, ducking and batting at the items as they battered him. From the midst of this storm he was sporadically firing his gun in Jennifer's general direction. A handsaw flew into his face, opening his cheek down to the bone, and he screamed and flailed his arms. He fired the gun again and Jennifer heard the bullet whiz past her head. Quickly, she dropped to her knees on the floor.

McClary slipped in the puddle of water that was forming at his feet, falling onto one knee and struggling to regain his footing. The gun fired, this time hitting the washing machine with a loud clang. Eric tried to pull Tanner down to the floor but he stood rigid, refusing to bend, his eyes open now and fixed on McClary.

Jennifer spared a quick glance at her son and, once she was sure he was unhurt, turned back toward McClary. The steaming fog continued to fill the frigid air. Tendrils of it were being spun like cotton candy into the tornado of debris, sucked into the whirling mass. The air above McClary crackled as if a miniature lightning storm hovered over his head. The whirling mass of fog and debris surrounded him—circling, twirling, closing in—wrapping him in a cocoon of cold white fury. McClary ducked and dodged, bellowing like some crazed and wounded animal. Then he fixed his gaze on Jennifer and raised his gun, the muzzle pointed straight at her face.

Frantically, she tried to scoot out of his line of fire,

but the numbness in her arm seemed to have spread to her legs. All she managed to do was collapse onto her side, feeling the gun she had dropped earlier bite into her ribs. She struggled to make her injured arm work, trying to get at the weapon, but it was no use. Her whole body felt paralyzed, whether from fear or some grievous injury, she didn't know. Unable to move, she lay helpless on the floor, knowing she was going to die. She saw McClary smile at her—an evil, humorless smile—and she closed her eyes, waiting for the final bullet.

Instead of a bullet piercing her flesh, a heart-stopping scream pierced the air. Jennifer opened her eyes and saw McClary huddled on the floor, a pair of hedge clippers buried almost to the handles in the center of his chest. His blood-slicked hands tried desperately to pull the shears out, but the cyclone of debris circling around him kept pummeling him, hampering his efforts. As Jennifer watched, horrified, a screwdriver drove itself into McClary's throat, a hacksaw sliced into his arm. Then a heavy mallet smashed into the side of his head.

McClary opened his mouth to scream again, but instead of sound, all that came out was a rolling string of blood. With a final, astonished look at Jennifer, he slumped the rest of the way to the floor, lying in the puddle of steaming water that was now stained red with his blood.

As if someone had thrown a switch, all the items flying through the air dropped to the floor, filling the room with clangs, bangs, thumps, and thuds, burying McClary in a small pile of tools, books, and clothing. The room grew suddenly, and eerily, quiet.

Jennifer squeezed her eyes shut.

"Are you okay?" Eric's voice was close to her ear.

She felt his arm slide around her shoulders, and he pulled her up against him.

"Mom?"

Jennifer opened her eyes and saw Tanner standing beside her, his face full of fright and concern. She held her good arm out to him and he squatted beside her, his arms snaking around her neck, his head nestling beside her own. His body trembled, and she could feel the rapid flutter of his heart beneath his shirt.

"Are you okay, Tanner?" she asked.

She felt his head nod.

"Did you do all that?" she asked. "The books and . . . stuff?"

"Dad helped me." His voice sounded so childlike it was hard for Jennifer to believe he had just wrought such havoc. "They killed Carny and Evan," he added with a sob.

"Evan, too?"

"He . . . he tried to help me after they killed Carny." Tanner released his hold on his mother's neck and wiped a sleeve across his nose. "He was yelling at that man." Tanner pointed toward McClary's body. "Evan was mad because that other man told him he wouldn't hurt me or you. Evan tried to take me out of the house, and they shot him."

Jennifer listened, stunned. Maybe she had been a little too harsh in her judgment of Evan. Maybe he had genuinely cared for her and Tanner after all.

Eric gently nudged Jennifer and stood up. "We need to get you some help for that wound," he said, holding a hand down to her. "Can you stand?"

"I'll try."

Eric's sturdy arm snaked around her waist, supporting her. She managed to stand, but the room wavered frighteningly.

"You can do it, Mom," Tanner said beside her.

The sound of her son's voice, his faith in her abilities, seemed to lend her strength. After a moment, the room stopped spinning and her legs felt almost normal. Leaning some of her weight on Eric, she shuffled toward the stairs.

There they paused when they realized that Tanner was still standing where they had left him, his head cocked to one side, as if he was listening for something.

"Are you coming, Tanner?" Eric asked.

Tanner straightened his head and looked toward his mother and Eric. Then he shrugged and headed toward the steps.

"Yeah," he said. "If I gotta."

EPILOGUE

Jennifer stood in the middle of Eric's bedroom looking around with an expression of weary sadness. With the bed stripped, the closets bare, and the pictures off the wall, the room had an empty, hollow feel, not too unlike the way Jennifer herself had felt so many times during the past five weeks.

She and Tanner had been staying here ever since that awful night in the basement, as neither of them had any desire to go back to their own house. The memories were too vivid, too painful. And even if they had wanted to go back, the authorities had cordoned the place off, along with Carny's house.

She had attended Carny's funeral, but not Evan's. With Carny's death, she felt as if she had lost a member of her family. Though she was still struggling to come to grips with Carny's double life, in her heart she knew Carny's friendship and love had been genuine. She missed her sorely.

Not so, Evan. Though it appeared that their initial meeting and his subsequent pursuit of her had been purely coincidental, she still couldn't believe that his attraction to her had been based solely on affection. She had forgiven him much in light of his attempts to save Tanner in the end, but couldn't quite bring herself to attend his funeral. His betrayal and her own gullibility still weighed too heavily.

Hearing a car pull up outside, Jennifer walked over and looked out the window. She watched Eric climb out of the Explorer, noting that his face looked drawn and tired. The past few weeks had been particularly hard on him. The tape and papers Tim had hidden revealed the names of the men in McClary's group—among them, Eric's father. A search of McClary's house had yielded a list of names in a computer database that included members of other groups like McClary's, as well as some very interesting video footage of the secret group meetings that had taken place.

When the elder Dr. Singleton's involvement became known, Eric closed down the office and helped the authorities search through all the patient files, trying to uncover which patients had been injected with the altering nucleotide. At first they were unable to find anything. Then Eric discovered a safe hidden beneath the carpet in his father's office that contained copies of certain patients' charts, with the experimental information included. Though it appeared that only two or three people had actually been injected, there were numerous others marked as future targets, most of them members of minority groups: homosexuals, African-Americans, Asians, Jews, and what Eric's father had labeled poor white trash. The ramifications of what might have been, had the group not been stopped, was mind-boggling.

As if discovering the horrible deeds of his father wasn't traumatic enough, Eric himself had come under suspicion for a while. It had taken weeks before the authorities became convinced he wasn't involved. He, Jennifer, and Tanner had all been subjected to endless days of intense questioning, marked by raised brows and obvious skepticism when they tried to explain how Tanner's special abilities had helped them uncover the plot. In light of the rampant disbelief, Jennifer and Eric

decided it would be unwise to mention Tim's involvement, and had carefully coached Tanner accordingly.
They felt it would be better to let the authorities think it
was Tanner's mental abilities alone that had provided all
the information. If they were having trouble believing in
ESP, they certainly weren't going to buy into the idea of a
ghost too readily. And, Jennifer and Eric reasoned, it
would only add to the already-frantic sensationalism that
surrounded the case.

Though they were eventually absolved of all blame,
people still looked at them strangely, the public's opinions inflamed by all the publicity. Despite the authorities'
efforts to keep the whole thing under wraps—particularly
when they found out how prominent some of the members
of the group were—the media had managed to root out
most of the story. It had taken weeks for the hordes of
reporters and cameras finally to abandon their posts outside Eric's office and house, frustrated by his and
Jennifer's refusal to talk with them. Though even now an
occasional reporter with high ambitions could be found
lurking about or trying to reach them by phone. It became
apparent to Jennifer and Eric early on that they would
have to leave the area if they ever hoped to escape their
newfound notoriety.

It was Jennifer's mother who offered the solution.
Having found a male friend in Canada while she was hiding, she had decided to stay in Montreal. She offered the
house on Granite Island to Jennifer. After some hesitation
and a number of long, cleansing talks with her mother on
the phone, Jennifer finally accepted. She had put her
father's ghost to rest along with Tim's. Feeling as if her
life was being managed by some fateful higher power,
Jennifer took it as a good omen when they heard that the
doctor on Granite Island was looking to retire. Eric had
flown up to interview for the position and was hired on the

spot. That eliminated any final doubts she may have had. It was the first thing in her life to go right in what seemed like forever.

She moved away from the window and closed the suitcase that lay on the bed. Picking it up, she winced as her injured arm complained.

Eric was coming through the door as she reached the bottom of the stairs. From the living room she could hear the sounds of Scotch and Tanner wrestling on the living room floor. The sound of Tanner's laughter was like sweet music to her ears, for she had feared she might never hear it again. How he had managed to come through it all with his personality intact was a puzzle. Jennifer thanked God every day for keeping a protective hand over her son.

There had been a period of time, in the weeks immediately following that fateful night, when she had reason to worry. Tanner's behavior was withdrawn and sullen, his previous zest for life seeming to have vanished.

It was Eric who finally sat Tanner down for a talk, trying to determine exactly what was bothering him. Jennifer suspected it was all the emotional trauma of being held at gunpoint, having their lives threatened, fearing Eric was dead, and watching Carny and Evan die. It turned out she was wrong. With the amazing resiliency that children seem to possess, Tanner had put all that behind him, chalking it up to nothing more than a wondrous and exciting adventure.

While the memories of that week (had it really been only a week?) were still very much in the forefront of Tanner's thoughts, the depression he was experiencing was related solely to Tim. Tanner could no longer hear his father's voice, and he missed him.

Eric had handled the situation with an understanding and sensitivity that made Jennifer's love for him grow tenfold.

"I think your Dad has moved on to a better place," Eric had told him. "He was here because he had some unfinished business. Now that he knows you and your mom are safe, and the bad guys have been stopped, he has no need to be here."

"But I miss him," Tanner said, tears welling up in his eyes.

"Of course you do," Eric said. "I am sure he misses you, too. But just because he can't talk with you anymore, don't think he isn't still up there somewhere, watching over you. Your father obviously loved you very much. And someday, many, many years from now, when you go to heaven, I'll bet your father will be there waiting for you."

Tanner looked up at him, his eyes glistening. "Really?"

"I'm sure of it," Eric said. "And in the meantime, your father is probably enjoying himself in the very best part of heaven. Because your father was a hero, and heroes get special treatment."

Tanner nodded thoughtfully. "Yeah, he was a hero, wasn't he?"

"You bet. And so were you. That's how I know you will both be together in hero heaven some day."

After that, Tanner's mood had slowly improved. Though he still demonstrated an ability to read minds from time to time—picking up on an occasional thought—there were no more of the fugue states. And, as Eric had predicted, most of his other paranormal powers seemed to have abated. Jennifer began to see hope for a normal life looming on the horizon.

Yet, despite her hopes for the future, she still felt as if a heavy blanket of depression was draped around her shoulders. Her heart ached daily—for Tim, for Carny, for all the families whose lives had been ruined—even for

Eric. While going through the office files secreted in the hidden safe, Eric had uncovered the information about Barry Hanover. Watching his father's very public arrest had been hard enough, but when Eric realized the full extent of his father's evil, the burden of it weighed so heavily on him that he actually walked stooped over for days afterward. Though Jennifer tried hard to ease Eric's guilt, it was difficult. The faces of the six Hanover children still haunted her, as well.

When the authorities told Jennifer about Dr. Andersen's involvement, she was stunned. Though she had to admit she hadn't particularly liked the man, she never suspected he was so truly evil and misguided. Her shock only deepened when she heard about the safe they found in Andersen's home, which contained the second, "real," file on Brian Wentworth and details of the plot against Senator Tranley. It was this revelation that had so fired-up the public. When they learned how close the much beloved political figure had come to being murdered, they were outraged.

As each day revealed more of the various groups' members and activities, Jennifer became more and more sickened. Already, the list of those involved was staggering: people in high positions of authority, well-respected members of communities—even members of the military and the government. The only good news was that, as far as anyone could tell, the groups were still relatively small. Nonetheless, Jennifer couldn't help but wonder if they had merely scratched the surface of this bunch of zealots. On more than one night she was haunted by nightmares of the people whose names were not discovered. She would awaken in a cold sweat, wondering if they were still out there, plotting and planning a new form of their perverted brand of "housecleaning."

She was glad they were leaving Virginia. An isolated

island off the coast of Maine sounded like just the type of secure seclusion they needed right now. Granite Island, with its tiny population, seemed an unlikely target for a plot of this magnitude.

Jennifer set down the suitcase she was carrying and massaged the ache in her arm.

Eric smiled at her, but it was a wan and weary smile. He reached out and pulled her into his arms, holding her in a fierce grip as if he feared she might disappear if he let go.

"Are you ready to go?" he asked, his breath warm as a summer's breeze against her hair.

He released her, and she stood back, looking up into those green eyes. "Are you?"

He nodded, then looked around the house, his face a mask of sadness. "It won't be easy to put all this behind us," he said.

"I know. But as long as I have you and Tanner, I know I'll be okay."

He smiled at her again, and this time the smile held a glimmer of hope. His eyes held more than that.

"Well, you've got me, whether you want me or not," he said.

She gave him a crooked grin. "I want you," she whispered.

At that his eyes grew sultry, and Jennifer's heart quickened as she saw the passion in their green depths.

Eric sighed heavily. "We best get on the road," he said. "Before I'm tempted to delay things." His eyebrows wiggled suggestively.

Jennifer lifted her lips toward his, intending to give him a quick kiss, but his arms grabbed her waist and pulled her to him when she would have stepped back, his lips crushing her own.

"Geez, don't you guys ever stop?"

Jennifer pulled away reluctantly and turned to see Tanner standing in the foyer watching them. Scotch sat beside him, her tail wagging furiously, her tongue lolling.

"Does it bother you?" she asked.

Tanner cocked his head to one side and studied them a moment. Then he smiled. "No, not really," he said.

"Good thing," Eric said. "Because I'm not about to stop. Had you said yes, I would have had to tickle you within an inch of your life." He lunged at Tanner.

Scotch barked and jumped up at Eric. Tanner squealed with delight and ran outside, with Eric and Scotch both in close pursuit.

Wearing a smile of contentment, Jennifer picked up the suitcase and headed out the door.